PRAISE FOR M

'Just brilliant, Mark Edwards re___ __ __ _cague of his own'

—Lisa Jewell

'Heart-in-mouth stuff, with a twist I didn't see coming. Edwards is at the top of his game'

—Erin Kelly, for *Keep Her Secret*

'I was hooked by this clever, fast-paced and addictive thriller . . . I loved it'

—Claire Douglas, for *Keep Her Secret*

'Like a Reacher, but with a hero like the rest of us'

—Linwood Barclay, for *No Place to Run*

'*No Place to Run* is another cracker from Mark Edwards'

—Elly Griffiths

'The perfect thriller to pack in your suitcase this summer . . . A high-tension, exhilarating read'

— *Heat* Book of the Week, for *Keep Her Secret*

'My head is spinning from all the twists!'

—Katherine Faulkner, for *Keep Her Secret*

'An almost unbearably suspenseful thrill ride . . . Edwards never lets up on the throttle . . .'

—Lisa Unger, for *Keep Her Secret*

'The King of Thrillers does it again with *Keep Her Secret* – dark, twisty and full of OMFG moments'

—Susi Holliday

THE
DARKEST
WATER

ALSO BY MARK EDWARDS

With Louise Voss

Forward Slash

Killing Cupid

Catch Your Death

All Fall Down

From the Cradle

The Blissfully Dead

THE
DARKEST
WATER

MARK
EDWARDS

THOMAS & MERCER

This is a work of fiction. Names, characters, organizations, places, events, and incidents are either products of the author's imagination or are used fictitiously. Any resemblance to actual persons, living or dead, or actual events is purely coincidental.

Text copyright © 2024 by Mark Edwards
All rights reserved.

No part of this book may be reproduced, or stored in a retrieval system, or transmitted in any form or by any means, electronic, mechanical, photocopying, recording, or otherwise, without express written permission of the publisher.

Published by Thomas & Mercer, Seattle

www.apub.com

Amazon, the Amazon logo, and Thomas & Mercer are trademarks of Amazon.com, Inc., or its affiliates.

ISBN-13: 9781662508943
eISBN: 9781662508950

Cover design by Dan Mogford
Cover image: ©Serge75, Kamenetskiy Konstanting / Shutterstock;
©Tim Robinson / ArcAngel

Printed in the United States of America

For Sebastian, who made my life brighter while I was writing this book

PROLOGUE

There was something on the tideline. A dark shape in the dawn gloom, bigger than the usual flotsam the waves brought in. Harry squinted, wondering if it might be a grey seal that had somehow made its way here from the nature reserve to the south. He rubbed at his eyes, frustrated. Was the twenty-twenty vision he'd always been so proud of fading at last?

He knew he needed to go and take a closer look, but all his instincts were telling him to turn and head in the other direction. The cafe in the village would be opening in a minute, and Brenda made the best bacon and eggs in Cumbria. It was cold out here, even if it was, according to the calendar, the first day of spring. The sky was pale cobalt, the moon still visible, a thin disc shimmering behind clouds so thin they appeared two-dimensional. Last night, when he'd taken his evening walk, the sky had appeared to crack open, pink and orange spilling through the gap in the heavens, and he'd thought to himself *shepherd's delight*. Today was going to be a beautiful day. But not yet.

Not with that shape on the tideline.

Harry forced himself to make his way down the beach. One step, then another, telling himself to get this over with. The sky brightened a little as he trudged across the hard, damp sand, and in the distance, across the water, the coastline of the Isle of

Man loomed out of the darkness. Behind him were sand dunes and, further back, the silhouette of the nuclear power station. He could hear the gulls waking up, that coastal dawn chorus that had soundtracked his entire life.

As he got closer to the sea, the sand got darker and damper. He was almost at the tideline now, and he could see the object more clearly. It was round, the size of a football, definitely not a seal. He smiled with relief, kidding himself that it was just a ball some kid had left behind.

Except it wasn't quite ball-shaped either, was it.

He ached to go straight to Brenda's cafe. *English breakfast, please, Brenda, and a mug of tea, you know how I like it. No sugar, I'm sweet enough.* He'd go home with a full belly and put the telly on, his favourite quiz show, reruns of *Miss Marple*, then a wander down to the general store to pick up a pint of milk. Maybe he'd call his daughter or have a little flutter on the horses. An ordinary day in his ordinary life.

But that ordinary day was already ruined, he knew, and his legs wouldn't do what his brain was telling them. They kept walking towards the object, until he knew exactly what he was looking at.

He stared at it.

And the object – the head of a man, mouth wide open in a silent scream – stared back.

PART ONE

1

The front door of the coffee shop opened, and Calvin Matheson looked up from his spot behind the counter and said, 'Oh. It's you.'

'Lovely to see you too, husband.' Vicky came over and gave Calvin a quick kiss on the lips.

'I didn't mean it like that. It's just . . .'

'He thought you were a customer,' said Tara, the coffee shop's sole employee, who was sitting at one of the empty tables. 'Our first of the day.'

Calvin sighed and went over to the espresso machine. He'd bought it second-hand at auction. Some other coffee shop had gone bust and all their stuff had ended up going under the hammer. If things didn't pick up here very soon, this machine would be going back to the auction house so yet another would-be entrepreneur could give it a go.

'Cappuccino?' he asked.

He set about making his wife's drink, enjoying the ritual, the heat of the steam as it hissed at him. It was a beautiful machine, all gleaming chrome, imported from Italy. He sprinkled powdered chocolate on top of the foam and set the cup before her.

'There you go. Made with love.'

'Shame it hasn't got any alcohol in it.'

'Bad morning?'

'The usual. Someone found a litter of kittens in an alleyway round the back of the Co-op. Five of them, dumped there, barely alive. The vet's taking a look at them now.'

Vicky managed the local animal shelter, taking in and attempting to rehome stray or unwanted cats and dogs. She had already told Calvin she couldn't stay long, because she had a new volunteer starting today.

'People,' said Calvin.

'Yeah. People.'

'We need a few more of them to come in here,' said Tara, who was half-listening while scrolling through her phone.

Tara was twenty-three, almost half Calvin and Vicky's age. A digital native, she likely couldn't remember a world without social media. No, of course she couldn't. Watching her thumb bob and thrust, Calvin wondered if she'd be able to survive if TikTok and Instagram and Twitter disappeared.

He sat beside Vicky at the counter, watching her sip her cappuccino. Today was officially the first day of spring. The tourists, if they ever came, wouldn't start arriving until Easter, a few weeks away. He wondered if they would find their way to the end of the High Street where Therapy was located.

'I walked up the road earlier,' he said. 'Peggy's was packed out, as always.'

'My mum goes there,' said Tara.

Calvin made a despairing gesture. 'See? I can't even get my one staff member's mother to come here. What hope do I have?'

'She *is* extremely tight,' Tara said. 'It's their bottomless cups of tea. Maybe we should start doing that.'

As she spoke, she didn't look up from her phone. Her thumb was permanently in motion.

'Maybe we do need to cut our prices,' Vicky said.

'But I'm barely making a profit on each sale now. Maybe I should give up and go work at Peggy's,' he said.

'There's no need to snap.'

'Sorry.' He took a deep breath. Located the flame of anger and poured cool water on it. 'It's just . . .'

Vicky kept assuring him that she didn't care about the money she'd invested, that it was his happiness she cared about, and he believed her – to an extent, anyway. But he didn't want to let her down. He didn't want to let *himself* down. Looking around at the empty tables, seeing all the cakes and pastries and biscuits that were going to end up in the bin, he felt a flutter of panic in his stomach, replacing the anger.

What was he going to do?

Because if business didn't pick up rapidly, this dream was going to be over before it had begun.

ϖ

The first time Vicky had tasted Calvin's lemon drizzle cake, she'd told him he should be famous. At the very least he should be working for himself, not in a hotel kitchen. It was her who had encouraged him to open his own bakery-slash-coffee-shop. It was her who had put all her savings into it, not only telling but showing him she believed in him. She'd told him she'd remortgage the house – which had originally been hers before he moved in – if she had to.

When she'd first suggested it, he'd been reluctant. He'd had his own place once before, when he was in his late twenties. He'd used all the money he'd inherited when his parents died to open a restaurant in Carlisle. It had been far tougher than he'd expected and he'd lost everything.

'I understand,' Vicky had said. 'But this time will be different. You should concentrate on baked goods. Cakes, bread, all the stuff

7

you're best at. And instead of a city like Carlisle, you should do it here in Elderbridge.' That was her hometown, in the west of the county, about forty miles from where Calvin had grown up. Elderbridge wasn't one of the Lake District's tourist hotspots like Windermere or Keswick, and it wasn't close to any of the most popular lakes. No poet had immortalised this place by wandering lonely as a cloud here. It was off the well-beaten track: a quiet, sleepy town where very little ever happened.

'But it's up-and-coming,' Vicky had insisted. 'Go and search on Airbnb. Last year there were about three properties here. Now there are twenty.' She'd deepened her voice to a movie-trailer growl. '*This summer* – the tourists are coming, and they want cake . . .'

'Won't they all go to Peggy's?'

That was the village's existing bakery, a big place that was part of a chain. Everyone went there, even though the coffee was mediocre and none of the baked goods were made on the premises. It was overpriced and underwhelming, but it was safe and they did buy-one-get-one-free deals for pensioners.

'Not if there's somewhere better.' Vicky had put her arms around him and was looking up at him, her body pressed against his. 'Don't you want a challenge? Don't you want to be your own boss?'

He did. Of course he did. And with Vicky's faith, and money – topped up with a business loan – he had gone for it. They'd opened in February, deciding that would give Calvin time to get into the rhythm of it before the fabled tourists arrived at Easter. Their first task had been to lure locals. Calvin made a single hire, Tara, who lived just down the street from his new premises, and came up with the name Therapy, because he believed cakes and coffee were a form of medicine that could make anyone feel better.

But now, a month after opening, the initial flurry of interest from locals had fallen away – they'd gone back to Peggy's – and

Therapy was failing. Their bank account was emptying. And Calvin was starting to wonder how long it would be before he had to get a job, his heart broken and dreams shattered.

ϖ

He was shaken from his panic by the sound of Tara laughing.

'What is it?' He heard the irritation in his voice but couldn't stop it.

Tara placed her phone face down on the table. 'Nothing.'

'Come on, tell me. What's so hilarious about this situation?'

'I was just watching a funny video.'

'Let's have a look,' said Vicky, giving Calvin a glance that said *cool it* before going over to sit beside Tara, who showed her the phone screen. Calvin could hear a song he didn't recognise, a female rapper, and a man shouting over the top of it.

'Oh, I've seen this one,' Vicky said, but she laughed anyway. Then she grew serious, turning her attention back to Calvin. 'Hey, perhaps this is what you should do. Promote this place on social media.'

Tara nodded. 'I've been trying to tell him that. Did you hear about that chip shop in the Midlands that went viral after these kids started posting about it?'

'"Went viral",' Calvin said. 'What does that even mean?'

Tara and Vicky exchanged a look. 'You know Calvin's allergic to social media,' Vicky said. 'The very idea's enough to give him a rash. He's not even on Facebook.'

'I know. It's mental. I thought all old people were on Facebook.'

'Oi!'

Tara's grin was mischievous. 'My gran's addicted to it. She spends half her life copying and pasting inspirational quotes and

9

sending them to everyone she's ever met. I don't get why Calvin's such a refusenik.'

'It's because I don't feel any need to share what I had for dinner or to argue with strangers about politics.'

Tara rolled her eyes. 'That's such a clichéd response.'

'He's a private person,' said Vicky.

'That's right. I don't want—'

'What?' asked Tara. 'Old girlfriends looking you up?'

'Something like that.'

'I don't really want your exes sliding into your DMs either – but I do think it's a good idea,' said Vicky. She looked around the empty shop and Calvin felt a tug in his stomach. He hated for her to think of him as a failure.

'Yeah,' said Tara. 'You need to put yourself out there more. I mean, you know you're not my type, Calvin, but you're a good-looking guy. It's the beard and the blue eyes. My mum told me she wouldn't kick you out of bed, anyway.'

'But she still goes to Peggy's?'

Vicky put her hand on his shoulder. 'She's right, you know. We *should* be using your smouldering looks to bring in the punters. Maybe some pictures of you in the kitchen with your shirt off.'

'I am not doing that!'

Both Vicky and Tara exploded with laughter.

Vicky wiped her eyes. 'Teasing you is too easy. But this *is* a good idea. Social media, I mean. If we can come up with the right content.'

'Like what?'

The two women exchanged a look. There it was. He'd exposed a chink in his armour. Lowered his resistance an inch. And in that moment he knew he wouldn't be able to put the barriers back up.

'We can help you,' Vicky said. 'I can set up the accounts for you, show you how it works. It'll be fun.'

'Can't you just do it *all* for me?'

'Nope, sorry. Stuff like this – it needs the personal touch. It has to be authentic. You're the creative here. It needs to be you.'

'It needs to be *real*,' said Tara.

Vicky had her phone out and was flicking through a load of video clips. He didn't even know what the platform was called but it looked hellish to him. An endless parade of young people showing off. She stopped on a clip of a woman, dressed in chef's whites, prancing around a kitchen.

'I am *not* dancing,' he said.

Vicky and Tara, who had come over to look, laughed again.

'I need to get going,' Vicky said. 'My new volunteer is going to be wondering where I am. But this is going to be fun.'

2

'Oh we do like to be beside the seaside,' muttered DI Imogen Evans as she made her way down the beach towards the tent. Inside the tent was a body. Or presumably a body. So far, all anyone had seen was the head.

The local constabulary had already secured the area, although the poles that held up the crime scene tape kept blowing over in the wind that came in off the sea. More successful was the tarpaulin walkway that had been stretched out across the pebbles. It was impressively efficient, especially from a force that rarely had to deal with such incidents.

'Why do I feel like I'm walking the gangplank?' Imogen asked herself as she negotiated the wooden walkway that led towards the plastic tent. 'Also, why am I talking to myself?'

This was something she'd recently found herself doing more and more. It was, she had decided, a result of having too much to worry about. The constant battle between her work and home lives. Imogen's partner, Ben – a freelance copywriter – was supposed to do the bulk of the childcare. Imogen was the main breadwinner and worked much longer hours than Ben. But that mental load, the one that had started with Ava's birth four years ago, was hard to, well, *off* load.

It was challenging enough when the incidents she had to deal with were minor drug busts and traffic altercations. She hadn't had to deal with a murder since she'd moved to the Lake District and the small town of Elderbridge. It was a few years, in fact, since she'd dealt with a homicide. The last body had been that of Lucy Newton's doomed 'assistant', left behind when the serial killer escaped from custody. Before that there had been another multiple murderer, the Shropshire Viper, who had terrorised the county he was named for. It was rare for any British cop to encounter one serial killer in their career, let alone two. Imogen had spent the last few years hoping bad things didn't really come in threes. 'Please let this be a freak accident,' she said as she reached the far end of the tarpaulin, which was being held in place with rocks. A CSI met her outside the tent and handed her a set of protective gear, which she donned before going inside, where she found another crime scene investigator and a uniformed officer, a man in his twenties. The still air, which had already turned fetid, made her want to go back out into the wind. It was silent in here. Dominated by the object on the ground. The head.

She crouched in front of it, getting her first look at the victim's face. He had a beard that had gone grey either side of his chin. His hair had also been going grey and was thin on top. Hazel eyes. Full lips. Late fifties, she guessed.

She couldn't help but picture him trying to suck in a final breath as the waves washed over him. The sand looked like it had been packed tight around his neck, loosened a little by the tide rolling in and out and, presumably, by the man trying to move his head. Had he screamed? Cried for help? Or had he accepted his fate, knowing no one would hear him out here? Maybe, if he was lucky, he had been unconscious. Drugged, perhaps. Knocked out.

She would have to wait for the pathologist's report.

'Detective Inspector Evans?'

She got to her feet and found herself facing the uniformed officer. He was about twenty-seven, she guessed, with sandy hair and an earnest face.

'Steve Milner,' he said, introducing himself. There was a keenness in his voice that told her how thrilled he was by what might turn out to be his first big case. 'I was first on the scene?'

'I don't know, were you?'

'I . . . What?'

'I'm just teasing you, constable,' she said. 'You did that thing? Where you end a sentence with a question mark?'

'Did I?'

His cheeks had gone pink and she had to fight the urge to ruffle his hair.

'Come on, let's get out of here.' She was eager to get away from the stuffy atmosphere inside the tent. To get away from the buried man.

PC Steve Milner followed her as she headed back up the walkway to the foot of the sand dunes. It was a nice day apart from the wind, a flotilla of photogenic clouds stretching over the sea. Drigg was a few miles west of Elderbridge, its main feature being the vast beach with its sand dunes and views of the Irish Sea. There, in the distance, was the Isle of Man, a place Imogen had never visited. Turning towards the dunes, she saw the hazy silhouette of Sellafield, the nuclear power station. Perfectly safe, everyone said, but whenever she went near it she felt the urge to ask someone to check her over with a Geiger counter.

'So, are you a local lad, Steve?'

'I am. Born and bred around here.' He said it with pride, gesturing in the vague direction of the power station. 'I live a few miles up the road. That's how come I was first on the scene. You transferred from Shropshire, right?'

Of course he would know who she was. Everybody did. Her reputation and fame as the cop who had put the Viper behind bars preceded her everywhere she went. Not only was the case itself well known by everyone in the UK, having appeared on newspaper front pages for months, but there had also been a TV dramatisation of the story – a rather sensationalist one, as if the story of the serial killer who had wanted his victims to die with smiles on their faces wasn't sensational enough. The Viper had been played by Sean Bean – talk about an upgrade from the real thing – while Imogen had been played by an actress who didn't look anything like her. The actress wasn't even a natural redhead!

More detrimentally, the adaptation had brought enough attention to make her and Ben – played in the series by another *Game of Thrones* alumnus – feel the need to leave Shropshire. Imogen had wanted to go back to London, believing she would be anonymous in the big city, but she had started her career with the Met and had left under a cloud, swearing she would never go back there. Besides, London property prices were *ridiculous*. When a job had come up with Cumbria Police, she and Ben had decided the Lake District would be a great place to raise a child. It was quiet and beautiful and just the right side of boring.

Also, she was even less likely to encounter another serial killer here.

'Yes, Shropshire, that's right,' she said, not wishing to linger on the subject of her past. 'Do you know who the victim is? Do you recognise him?'

'No. I've never seen him before.'

'And we haven't identified him yet?'

'Actually, we have. Or rather, we know where he lives. The man who found him, Harry Walsh, told us he lives in Drigg.' That was the tiny village nearby. 'He gave us the address but we haven't matched it with a name yet. I was waiting for you.'

She looked down towards the tent that covered the victim, and tried to imagine what it must have felt like to stumble upon such a horrific find.

'Let me guess – Harry Walsh was walking his dog.' She could imagine the animal barking like crazy when it found the poor buried sod.

But Steve surprised her by saying, 'No, he just comes to the beach every morning for his constitutional, as he put it. Every evening too. Been doing the same for fifty years, since he was a kid.'

'He lives close by?'

A nod. 'Ten minutes' walk in that direction.'

'Excellent. Let's go and have a chat.'

'Now?'

'Yep. Witnesses have a habit of forgetting stuff. We need to get Mr Walsh's statement before all the little details leak out of his ears and float away into the ether.' She frowned. 'I think there's a mixed metaphor in there somewhere.'

Steve stared at her.

'What are you waiting for?' Imogen said. 'Lead the way.'

She followed Steve up the path through the dunes and towards the village. As they walked, she called her commanding officer at the station in Penrith and gave him an update. He advised her that a team would be arriving at the beach very soon to remove the body. The CSIs had already started combing the beach for evidence.

'Feel free to commandeer any of the local uniforms,' she was told.

When they reached Drigg, Imogen paused to look around. Ahead of her was a small train station, and beyond that, a cluster of houses: sturdy semi-detacheds and bungalows, all built to withstand the sea air.

'There's not much here,' Steve said. 'I think the population is about four hundred. There's the church. A village hall. A single shop. There are a few bed and breakfasts and a growing number of Airbnbs dotted around the outskirts and this train station – but, well, that's about it.'

'It's like the edge of the world,' she said, regarding the bleak landscape. There was a nature reserve to the west. A few low agricultural buildings. The ever-present power station. And, on the horizon, the great expanse of the beach and the Irish Sea beyond.

'Yeah. Awesome, isn't it?' It was hard, even for someone like Imogen, who had been born with *cynic* tattooed on her soul, not to warm to Steve's puppyish enthusiasm. 'I live in the next village over. Seascale.' He pointed to the north.

'Even closer to the power station?'

'It's perfectly safe.'

'I guess a lot of people round here work there?'

'That's right. My dad works there, in fact. And no, he is nothing like Homer Simpson, before you ask.'

'He's more like Mr Burns?'

Steve blanched, and she immediately felt bad. Poor guy probably heard that joke all the time, and Imogen hated being unoriginal with her wit.

'Sorry,' she said.

He shrugged. 'It's all good. Right, Harry Walsh's place is just along here.'

They turned off the main road on to a side street. Harry's place, a pebble-dashed semi that an estate agent would describe as 'needing modernisation', was halfway along. Imogen knocked and Harry came to the door straight away.

He reminded Imogen of one of those dogs. The ones with sad faces. Basset hounds. He was bald on top but with long hair at

17

the back that hung over his shoulders, resembling dog ears, but it was the pink, rheumy eyes that cemented the canine resemblance.

'Morning, sir,' she said, introducing herself. 'Could we have a chat?'

He gestured for them to follow him into a small living room that smelled of Vicks VapoRub. He slumped on to a sofa where a fat tabby cat snoozed. It opened one eye to regard the visitors before going back to sleep. Imogen brushed crumbs from an armchair before sitting down. Steve pulled up a wooden chair.

'Oh, it was horrible, horrible,' Harry said, launching straight into it, clearly distressed by what he'd found.

'I can imagine,' Imogen said gently. 'It must have been a terrible shock.'

With her coaxing, he went through exactly what had happened that morning. His feelings. The almost-otherworldly sense of foreboding that had vibrated through his bones upon his approach. She glanced up at Steve. The young officer had seemed remarkably unaffected by the sight of the head when they were inside the tent, but, hearing Harry describe finding it, he had begun to go a little green around the gills.

Imogen let Harry finish, then said, 'I'm told you recognised the man you found.'

'That's right. I mean, I don't know his name but I've seen him around. Down on the beach and in the village. Quiet sort of chap. Not keen in engaging in small talk, you know? I tried to have a chat with him once, to get him to sign my petition about keeping dogs off the beach, but he wasn't interested.'

'You don't like dogs?' Steve asked.

Harry stretched out a hand to stroke his sleeping cat. 'I don't mind them. I just don't want their shit all over my beach.'

'Fair enough,' Imogen said. 'Could you tell us where the man you found lived?'

'Of course. I'll show you.'

He took them outside and pointed along the street. 'See there, past the last house? There's a footpath that leads into the woods. Follow that path and you'll come to a small house. There's only one, so you can't miss it.'

Of course, Imogen thought. The victim lived alone in some creepy woods.

This case had her name written all over it.

3

The house was, as Harry had promised, easy to find, although it was more of a bungalow than a house, a one-storey wooden building that looked like it could be easily blown down by a big bad wolf.

The rear of the property was crowded by trees. At the front was a small garden, and the whole thing was surrounded by a fence with a gate that was falling off its hinges. There was a sign that read *PRIVATE PROPERTY KEEP OUT*. Imogen felt a shudder go through her. This place was just like the house where the Viper had lived.

'Are you okay?' Steve asked.

'Oh, someone just walked over my grave, that's all.'

Not knowing if the victim lived alone – though this place seemed the exact opposite of a lively family home – Imogen rang the doorbell and waited. There was no reply. The proper procedure would be to call the station and get a locksmith to come along and open the property. But Imogen was impatient to know who their victim was. She felt around in some stone plant pots on the front porch, hoping to find a key. Nothing. There was no key under the doormat either. With no plausible reason for kicking down the door, she was about to give up and contact the station when Steve called to her from around the building.

'The side door's open,' he said when she got there.

'That's handy.'

He hesitated. 'Should we go in?'

'I think that would be the right thing to do. We need to ensure no one else is in danger, don't we?'

Steve – looking a little dubious, bless him – went through the door into a kitchen. Imogen followed.

It was cold in there. The sun barely reached into the property, and Imogen could imagine that it stayed cool even in the height of summer. The kitchen was neat and clean, with a few pots and pans stacked up by the sink. A metal rack contained over a dozen tins of beans and soup. She checked the floor for signs of a dog or cat bowl, but there was nothing.

'Try not to touch anything,' she said to Steve. 'The murderer might have been here, so we're going to have to get the CSIs in once they've finished on the beach. We're just looking for something that tells us the victim's name, okay?'

The obvious place was inside the front door. Hopefully there would be a letter lying on the inside doormat with the occupant's name on it. But there was nothing. There wasn't any post on the sideboard either, and she hadn't spotted any in the kitchen.

'Look at these,' Steve said from behind her.

The paintings that hung on the walls of the hallway were clearly all by the same artist, and they were grotesque. One of them showed weeping men and women being herded by demons through a gate, presumably into Hell. Another showed a naked man sitting in what appeared to be a prison cell, crying tears of blood. A third picture was of a child, sitting on a bed. A demon with a twisted, sneering face sat beside the child, its arm over her shoulder.

'I don't know much about art,' Imogen said, 'but these are bloody horrible.'

Using her sleeve to cover her hand so she didn't leave finger-prints, Imogen opened the nearest door to reveal a bedroom. She went inside. There was a double bed, unmade, and more of the worrisome paintings on the wall, all by the same hand.

She checked the pillows. Although it was a double bed, with two pillows beside each other, only one of the pillows was dented and there were several grey hairs on the pillowcase, matching the hairs she'd seen on the man on the beach.

The man without a name.

'I wonder . . .' she said. She peered closer at a painting that showed another scene from Hell, wondering how anyone could go to sleep with this in their bedroom. But she was looking for a signature, and there it was, pleasingly legible: *LEO JAMES*. She checked the other paintings and the same signature was on them too.

'I think I have our victim's name,' she said as she went back into the kitchen, where Steve was searching the surfaces and shelves for paperwork.

She saw movement out of the corner of her eye.

There was someone outside.

Imogen didn't hesitate. She dashed out through the side door. 'Hey!'

Someone was running down the lane that led away from the house, moving fast. Almost immediately, they vanished into the trees to the left – but not before Imogen was able to make out, from their body shape, that it was a young woman. She had been moving so fast that Imogen wasn't sure, but she thought she was slim, with long hair, brown or black.

'Hello?' Imogen called out again, giving chase. She entered the trees at the same spot where the woman had disappeared from view, then stood still for a moment, listening. Apart from birdsong, there was silence. She made her way into the trees a little further but there was no sign of the woman.

Imogen walked back to Steve, who had come outside and was standing by the gate.

'She's vanished,' she said.

Steve went back inside and Imogen stood for a moment, catching her breath. In the last ten minutes she had felt something stir in her that had lain dormant for a long time. A tingling that she hadn't felt since she'd been on the trail of the Viper. A lot had changed in that time. She'd moved in with the man she loved. Had a baby. Come to live here in the Lakes. And during those years she had never admitted to herself that she missed that feeling of excitement – and its close relative, danger. Only now, as the sensation spread through her body, could she acknowledge it.

There was something exciting and dangerous going on here. And it felt good.

4

'So, how many hits have I had?'

It was Monday evening. As soon as Calvin and Vicky had got home, Vicky had helped him set up his account and, together, they'd made his first-ever social media post: a one-minute video in which he gave tips for making the perfect brownies. Vicky had edited the video on her phone, added all the hashtags, and shown him how to post it. That was two hours ago.

'I think most of the views so far have been you watching it yourself,' Vicky said. They were on the sofa now. The TV was on in the background but neither of them were paying any attention to it.

'I've only watched it . . . twenty times?'

'Hello, my name's Calvin and I just hate looking at pictures of myself.'

In the video, for which he'd trimmed his beard and put on a clean T-shirt that showed off the muscular arms that Vicky said were his best feature, Calvin talked to the camera while beating together the ingredients in a bowl. It had, to his great surprise, been fun. He'd been worried Vicky would make him shoot loads of takes but she said it was better if it looked natural and not overly slick.

'So far, you've got ten followers, which isn't bad for two hours, but we need to get more content up there.' A pause. 'Are you sure you don't want to dance around the kitchen?'

He grinned. 'I'll dance around the kitchen with you. I'm just not going to let you film it.'

'Spoilsport.'

Calvin scrolled through the app Vicky had installed on his phone, watching other people's baking videos. While he did this, her phone pinged repeatedly, the sound of new messages arriving.

'What are *you* doing?' he asked her, and their cat – a huge, fluffy tabby called Jarvis – looked up from the armchair opposite as if Calvin had spoken to him. Jarvis was a rescue that Vicky had adopted after being unable to find him a home, a scruffy former street cat with torn ears and enormous paws. For the first few months they'd had him he'd refused to come out from behind the sofa, hissing at them if they tried to touch him. Instead of the litter tray, he had used their bathtub. But over the next few months, with almost constant TLC and patience, he had come to tolerate them. Now, it was almost as if he liked them. And he no longer used the bath as his toilet.

'Hmm?' She was halfway through typing a message.

'Are you texting your secret boyfriend again?'

She didn't laugh like she usually did. 'It's the street WhatsApp group.' Calvin didn't use WhatsApp and wouldn't have been in the group anyway. As far as he could tell, it was mostly people trying to organise petitions or arguments about parking.

'What's happening? Not another planning permission scandal?'

'We're talking about that guy who was found on the beach.'

'What guy?'

She put her phone down. 'You live in a world of your own, don't you? Someone was found on Drigg Beach this morning. He'd been buried up to his neck in the sand, and left to drown as the tide came in.'

Calvin's good mood instantly disappeared. 'You're joking.'

'You really think I'd make up a joke about something like that? I'm just shocked you haven't heard about it. It's all anyone's talking about.'

'It was . . . a murder? Not a prank gone wrong?' It was a seaside trope. The dad buried by his kids in the sand.

'Definitely not a prank. Apparently, Drigg Beach has been crawling with police all day. Sharon at number twenty knows someone who works at the police station. She said they're treating it as a murder. Buried and deliberately left on the tideline so the water would . . . Are you okay? You've gone white.'

'I'm fine. I just . . . Do they know who the guy was?'

'No. Some hermit who lived in the woods nearby, apparently. The police haven't released any details yet but they're saying that cop who was in that TV show is the SIO.'

Calvin gave her a blank look. He never watched police dramas or read crime novels.

'Senior investigating officer. Are you sure you're all right? It's not . . . the thing that usually triggers you.'

He wanted this conversation to end. 'It's a horrible image, that's all. An awful way to die.'

'Yeah, and it happened a few miles from here. There's someone out there, maybe someone who lives here in Elderbridge, who did it. Which is why the WhatsApp group is going crazy.'

'Can we change the subject?' Calvin asked.

'What, back to you and your social media efforts?'

Were they going to have an argument? He was about to remind her that it had been her and Tara's idea when she said, 'I'm sorry. I think this murder thing is getting to me. You're right. We should change the subject.'

Calvin racked his brain for something that wasn't related to death or social media. 'How was your new volunteer?'

'Oh, she seems great! Louise, her name is. She's about our age and is obsessed with cats. She was wearing a sweatshirt with a picture of her first "baby" on it.'

'The baby being a kitten?'

'Yep. A cute little ragdoll. Anyway, when I brought in the box of kittens from the alley she was great. Fed them all and got them settled in, then went round and introduced herself to all the other cats and dogs. "Hello, I'm Louise and I'm delighted to meet you."'

'Oh dear.'

'I think she's going to be great.' Vicky yawned. 'I'm exhausted. Are you coming to bed?'

He was tempted. He was tired too. But he also knew that if he went to bed now, after the discussion about the man on the beach, his dreams would be awash with dark water; the tide lapping over that poor soul on the beach, stealing his last breaths, choking his screams.

He suppressed a shudder. 'I'm going to stay up for a while, do some more research.'

'You mean you're going to scroll through social media?'

'Vicky,' he said, 'it was your idea. I won't be long.'

She kissed him and, with a little roll of the eyes, went to bed. Two hours later, when his eyes were sore from staring at his screen – but he'd managed to erase the image of the guy on the beach – he followed her.

5

Imogen parked in front of the bungalow, having driven up a lane that was so narrow that branches had scraped her windows on both sides. This road didn't have potholes – it *was* a pothole. If she'd still had her Pagoda, the beloved vintage Mercedes she'd reluctantly sold when she was pregnant – trading it in for this sensible and extremely boring Ford Focus – she would have parked on the outskirts of the woods and walked.

She stood by the front gate, hand resting on the *Keep Out* sign. In the twenty-four hours since his body had been dug out of the hole in which he'd been buried, Leo James's place had already been combed through for foreign DNA, and Imogen had been informed that the CSIs had found a number of long dark-brown hairs which had been sent off for analysis. Imogen suspected these hairs belonged to the girl who had given her the slip yesterday. Unfortunately, unless this girl was in the DNA database, the hairs wouldn't lead the police to her.

They had no idea who she was. Nor did they have any idea who Leo James – whose DNA had also been sent off to the lab – was. Because, according to official records, Leo James didn't exist. The police only knew his name because, along with the signed paintings, they'd found some diaries in which he'd written his name repeatedly, like a child practising their signature. Sadly, these diaries contained nothing more than lists of tasks: buy oil, fix gate, put down rat poison. There were no letters, no bank statements or bills. Leo James appeared to live completely off-grid. He had his own electric generator, heated his house using oil, and had access to a well for water along with a cesspit. There was a greenhouse behind the bungalow in which he grew vegetables, and he'd kept chickens in the garden, which had been taken away by the RSPCA for rehoming.

There were signs that he wasn't *wholly* self-sufficient: boxes of cereal and tins of beans in the kitchen, plus bottles of wine and cider. He had toilet paper and soap. The guy who ran the village shop confirmed that Leo, who rarely spoke, had shopped there once a week, always paying with cash. A Land Registry search told them that the bungalow was in the name of a woman named Irene Jacobson, who had died in 2003 with no family. Was she Leo's mother? If so, there was no record of his birth, and Steve had been all around Drigg talking to the older residents. They all swore that Irene had had no kids – not that they knew of, anyway. And if she was his mother, why did he have a different surname? None of the villagers knew Leo. Like Harry, they'd all seen him around, but hardly anyone had spoken to him. The pub landlady had never seen him. The postman said he rarely delivered anything to the house in the woods; certainly nothing that wasn't junk mail.

Imogen had been assigned some bizarre cases in her time. But this was the first time she'd had to investigate the murder of a ghost.

Instead of going into the bungalow, she walked down the path to the woods the young woman had vanished into. She stepped through the trees into the shade and ducked beneath a low-hanging branch before pushing through the foliage and following the path the girl had taken.

The trees were only just beginning to turn green again after a winter that seemed to have lasted forever. Stinging nettles attempted to penetrate her clothes and mud squelched beneath her trainers. As she made her way through the woods, she thought back to that morning's team meeting, at the station in Elderbridge.

'We don't have the full pathologist's report yet,' Imogen had said to the room. 'But the early indications, from water in his lungs, are that he drowned.'

'No shit,' one of the older cops mumbled.

Imogen fixed him with a stare, and held it as she went on.

'When we dug him out we found that his fists were clenched and there were abrasions on his neck from where he had repeatedly turned his head from side to side against the sand. This leads us to believe he was conscious at least some of the time he was buried, although we don't know if he was awake when he went into the hole. Nor do we know if he walked to this grave or was carried, although my guess is he was forced to walk. Possibly to even dig the hole himself.'

Another of the cops, a woman at the back of the room, spoke up. 'It must have taken ages to dig one deep enough for a man to stand in.'

'He was kneeling. And the sand on the tideline was damp, so it wouldn't have been that difficult.'

'Ah. Got it.'

Imogen pointed to a chart on the screen behind her.

'These are the tidal times for this month. As you can see, high tide was at three seventeen on Monday morning. Mr James was buried just inside the tideline. The sea would have lapped over his head numerous times before completely covering him. He would have known what was happening to him.'

She let that sink in. The room was silent.

'The nature of this murder tells us two things. Firstly, the perpetrator is familiar with this beach and the timings of the tide. Perhaps he – or she, of course – looked up the information online.

But my guess is that they used their own knowledge. Secondly – well, you tell them what we think, Steve.'

The young constable turned to his new colleagues. Because he'd been first on the scene, and had been involved in the initial investigation of Leo's house, Imogen had drafted Steve into her team. He had been as thrilled as she'd expected. This was all new to him. Exciting.

Steve cleared his throat. 'The nature of the murder, the sadistic nature of it, knowing the fear and panic the victim must have felt . . .'

Imogen had to force herself to picture the horror of it. Leo must have yelled or screamed between waves. He must have clung to the hope that someone would hear him and come. Had the murderer stood there watching the whole time? She had a feeling he – because it was almost always a he, wasn't it – would have. That he would have wanted to ensure no miracle escape occurred. Or perhaps he'd stood there because he enjoyed watching Leo die.

Steve was still talking, the room enrapt. 'We think this tells us that whoever did this to Leo James hated him. They wanted him to die in the worst way possible.'

This line echoed in Imogen's head long after the meeting ended. Here in the woods, the vegetation was growing thicker and Imogen was starting to think she was going to have to give up, turn back and go home, when she suddenly reached a mesh fence.

Through the fence: a graveyard, and a church.

Of course. The woods had led her to St Bartholomew's, the village church here in Drigg. A little way along the fence, there was a gap where it had come away from a post. She pushed her way through into the cemetery and was immediately caught by a gust of wind that bit through her jacket like the breath of the dead.

'Get a grip, Evans,' she said, talking to herself again.

31

She walked up to the church, but was disappointed to find the doors locked. She turned and looked around the yard. She couldn't see any other gaps in the fence. If the girl she'd seen outside Leo's place had followed the same path and slipped through the same gap, she'd have had to exit through the main gate. Disappointingly, Imogen couldn't see any CCTV here.

Beyond the gate there was a large, attractive house that overlooked the churchyard. The vicarage. Or was it called a rectory? She wasn't sure.

Hoping the vicar, or his wife if he had one, might have seen something yesterday afternoon, she walked up to the front door and knocked.

There was no reply.

She tried again, but was met with nothing but silence. She would have to come back another time, or send Steve. Or perhaps this was a wild goose chase. The young woman might simply have been a rubbernecker, a local who'd heard about the murder and come to gawp at the victim's house. Everything Imogen had learned about Leo James so far told her he'd kept himself to himself. He was that most old-fashioned of things: a hermit.

She headed back towards the fence and the woods. But as she walked through the graveyard she felt a prickle on the back of her neck.

She turned and saw a figure in the window of the vicarage. A man watching her. He was too far away for her to make him out clearly but he had blond hair and was tall and skinny.

He saw her looking and slipped away, into the shadows.

She was about to return to the house and knock until this person answered the door when her phone beeped. It was a message from Steve. The pathologist was ready to see her.

6

It was Wednesday morning, and Calvin was driving Vicky to work because her car had gone in to be serviced.

She scrolled through her phone the whole way. When she gasped, he thought she must be reading about the murder, which in the two days since the body had been found had not only consumed her WhatsApp group but the entire community. It was all anyone wanted to talk about. Who was the victim? Where had he come from? Who had done it? *Were they going to do it again?* The beach was still closed and the police had been going door to door in Drigg looking for witnesses, and Calvin found it hard to believe that someone could commit such a gruesome crime in this quiet place without being seen, so after she gasped he expected Vicky to tell him the police had arrested someone, or that someone in her group had come up with a new theory. But instead she laughed and said, 'This is amazing.'

'What is?'

'Have you checked your app this morning? Looked at the numbers?'

'I barely had time to clean my teeth. What is it?' Excitement flared. 'Have we gone viral?'

'Talk about beginner's luck. I think you might be about to.'

Yesterday, Tara had taken a box full of cakes to the retirement home where her gran lived, and recorded the residents' reactions as they'd tried them. 'Cute old people,' she'd said. 'Kids on social media love them.' Calvin had been sceptical. Did anyone really want to watch a bunch of octogenarians munching cake?

When he'd gone to bed last night, a few hours after Vicky had edited the videos Tara had made at the retirement home and posted them online, they'd had a couple of hundred views. That, he'd thought, was impressive, but now? Had they got more?

'How many?' he asked.

'Five thousand so far. But it's increasing fast. You're getting loads of comments too. It's the Maud video that's doing it.'

Maud was an eighty-eight-year-old woman with an infectious, naughty smile. In the ten-second post, Maud took a big bite of Calvin's chocolate cake, groaned with pleasure and exclaimed, 'Mmm, better than sex.'

Vicky began to read out some of the comments. *I'll have what she's having! Maud slays for real! You go girl!*

'Watch this,' Vicky said, tilting the phone in his direction when they were waiting at a red light. She refreshed her screen. The view count bumped up from seven to eight thousand.

'Well. This social media lark is easy,' Calvin said as the light turned green.

Vicky slapped him with the back of her hand. 'It's actually that you're a jammy sod. But let's not get overexcited. These things can fizzle out pretty quickly. Remember that video I posted of the kitten with a Poirot moustache?'

'I loved that kitten. What was his name?'

'Purr-oh. I thought he was going to go viral, but for some reason the algorithm killed the post and it sank without trace.'

'A crime. You should have asked Purr-oh to investigate.'

They pulled up outside the shelter, which was a little way down a country lane on the outskirts of the village, next to a housing estate. Calvin could hear dogs barking from beyond the fence. As always when he visited, he was glad he didn't live around here.

Vicky handed Calvin her phone and he scrolled through the comments. The hashtags #bemoremaud and #betterthansex were appearing in lots of them. At least, he thought they were called hashtags. He didn't understand half the comments, with all the slang and in-jokes that only young people would get. *Better than sex I'M SCREAMING* with a grinning-skull emoji, and *She tells no lies.* But it was clear that they found Maud highly amusing. Tara had been right. The Gen Zers who used this app loved 'cute' elderly people.

'Is it the algorithm making this happen?' he asked.

'I don't know. Maybe some big account shared it. I'm not really sure how it works, to be honest.' Vicky took the phone back. 'The best thing is that your follower count is ticking up and people are checking out your other posts too.'

'And users can see this is connected to an actual real-world coffee shop? They can easily find out where it is?'

'Yes, don't worry. It's all there in your profile.'

Needing to use the loo, he accompanied Vicky into the shelter's reception, a prefab building at the front of the property. He used the facilities, and when he came out he found Vicky showing the Maud video to Louise, the new volunteer. Vicky introduced her to Calvin, and Louise said a friendly hi before returning to the phone.

'Go Maud,' said Louise with a laugh. She was wearing a sweatshirt featuring a feline silhouette with the words *In case of an emotional breakdown, place cat here.*

'We need to get some more videos up,' Vicky said. 'Keep it going.'

Calvin made a suggestion. 'Perhaps we could bring some cake here, film the dogs tucking in.'

'Cake is bad for dogs,' Louise said with a frown.

'I was only joking.'

'I really don't think it's something to joke about.' She glared at him like he was the type of person who would dump a box of puppies on the side of a motorway.

Behind Louise, Vicky wagged a finger at him and he tried to suppress a laugh.

As he drove back to the village, Calvin tried to enjoy the view and stop wondering if the coffee shop would be full, the Maud video having brought in dozens of curious customers, desperate to have what Maud had. He found himself drifting into a pleasant fantasy in which the cash register didn't stop ringing, customers wept as they were told everything had sold out, and camera crews turned up to interview him about being an internet sensation.

By the time he got to the centre of Elderbridge, his pulse was racing. He parked and hurried down the high street – past Peggy's, which was busy as always, then round the bend so he could see Therapy. There were no queues out the door. He knew it had been a silly fantasy. But the video had twenty thousand views now. Surely a few of them had come from local people, and some of them might have ventured down to check out this new cafe.

He pushed open the front door – and promptly and fully deflated. There were two tables occupied. The same as the day before.

So much for the viral effect.

ꞷ

A few more customers came in during the morning. None of them had seen the videos and they looked blank when Tara asked them about social media. One woman said a friend of hers had told her to check this place out. Another couple told Calvin they were staying at an Airbnb nearby. Perhaps they weren't going to need to go viral. If the tourists were beginning to arrive and word of mouth was spreading, which was what he'd always hoped for, maybe that would be enough.

But during a break after lunch he checked his stats again. They were still ticking up steadily. Fifty thousand views of the Maud clip. And Therapy had a thousand followers now.

Before closing the app he noticed something he hadn't looked at before. His inbox. There were over a dozen messages in there. He thumbed through the list quickly. They were all from strangers, mostly women but a couple of men, and almost all of them were a single line, saying things like *Your cakes look awesome* or *Hope I get to visit your place some day!* There were a couple saying Maud was clearly an actress – *She's a FAKE!!* – but for the most part the messages were positive.

He was about to close his inbox when he noticed that one of the messages was from a local woman who called herself BlondieMel. It was also the only message that used full sentences, capital letters and proper grammar. Her avatar was a picture of a cake: a blondie, in fact. He guessed, without really giving it much thought, that her username was a play on both her hair colour and her favourite type of cake.

> *Just watched your videos. Hilarious! I live just across Foxton Water and wasn't aware that your coffee shop had even opened. As a keen baker myself I will definitely have to come and check it out. Best of luck to you. Mel. PS Maud is a star. Hope I'm like that when I'm old, LOL.*

Okay, so she had *almost* used proper grammar. Encouraged by this message from a local, and not wanting to lose a potential customer, he fired back a reply.

Thanks Mel! Hope to see you at Therapy soon. And yes, Maud is amazing. Best wishes, Calvin (proprietor and head baker).

The coffee shop had gone quiet again. Calvin put his phone back in his pocket but, as the afternoon went on, he had to resist the urge to take it out again. He'd read all about this: how addictive social media was, how users became dependent on that little shot of dopamine that came with new comments and views and messages. He wanted to see if anyone had left a comment or messaged him to say they were on their way, hopefully bringing a dozen wealthy and hungry friends with them.

He knew this was stupid. He knew he was showing the first signs of addiction. But none of that mattered. He was simply unable to fight the impulse to check, so he got his phone out again.

There were numerous new comments but they were mostly of the *Maud yasss slay queen* variety – what the heck did that mean? – and were posted by kids many miles away. But he noticed he had a new message.

BlondieMel had replied to his reply.

I will definitely come and sample those delicious-looking cakes. Has the viral attention been good for business? I hope so!

He immediately typed out a response. As someone who mostly used his phone to make phone calls and check the football scores, he wasn't the fastest typist and it took him a couple of minutes to write.

Sadly it hasn't resulted in the crazy rush I was hoping for. But please tell all your friends to come down and try our wares. Thanks again for the good wishes.

He was about to sign off when he heard Tara say, 'Calvin.'

'Hmm?'

'Stop staring at your phone and look out the front window.'

He did as she said.

'Am I hallucinating?' he asked.

'If you are, it must be one of those group hallucinations, because I'm seeing it too.'

There were about a dozen teenagers heading for the front door, phones in hand. He saw some of them posing outside, talking to their phones as they took selfies with the Therapy sign behind them, or perhaps they were making short videos. The first of them came in, followed by the rest. Within minutes, almost all the tables were full and the place buzzed with noise and life. This was how he'd always imagined it.

'They must have just got out of school,' Tara said.

Calvin didn't have time to speculate. There were orders to take, drinks to prepare. Fifteen minutes later, a load more customers turned up: mostly parents with kids in tow.

'Someone sent me a link to your video with the old lady and I've been spreading the word around the school gates,' said one of the mums as she ordered two brownies. 'I didn't even realise this place was here.'

'I don't think anyone did.'

He messaged Vicky telling her a miracle had happened. Tears pricked the backs of his eyes as he sent it. Could this be it? Could his fortunes finally be turning around? On a high, he made a short video showing the packed-out coffee shop, scanning the crowd so he'd have something new to post on social media. A message of thanks. As he saved it, he realised he hadn't sent the reply to BlondieMel.

He deleted the rather negative message he'd been planning to send and wrote: *It's been phenomenal. You should get down here before everything sells out, and tell all your friends!* x

She must have been on the app at that moment because her response came back immediately.

Great news! And I will! x

A kiss? It was only when he read her reply that he realised that, in his enthusiasm, he'd put a kiss at the end of his own message.

Oh well. What did it matter? He put his phone away and, in the rush to serve his new customers, forgot all about it.

7

'I don't bloody believe it.'

'Hello, Imogen.'

Karen Lamb stepped out of the shadows like Hannibal Lecter approaching the front window of his cell. Imogen was momentarily speechless.

'Small world,' Karen said, a smile twitching at the corners of her mouth. Her eyes took in Imogen's body, head to toe then back again, and, as always when she encountered Karen, Imogen was sure the pathologist was imagining her on the slab, picturing using her scalpel to slice Imogen open before lovingly removing her organs one by one.

She was going to put it in her will: that whatever happened to her, under no circumstances should Karen Lamb be allowed near her corpse.

'What are you doing here?' Imogen asked – 'here' being the pathology department at Furness Hospital, a short drive from the place where Leo James had died; a short distance for his body, which was laid out ready for the autopsy, to have travelled. 'In Cumbria, I mean.'

'Same as you, I imagine,' Karen replied. 'An opportunity arose and I decided it was time for a change of scenery. Somewhere I could indulge my passion for open-water swimming.'

'Bit cold for that still, isn't it?'

'Oh no.' Karen's eyes shone. 'Winter swimming is the best. When you feel your body temperature drop to the point where everything is in danger of shutting down. It's exhilarating. You should come with me sometime.'

'Over my dead body.'

Karen raised an eyebrow but didn't say anything else. Her famous silence, which Imogen eventually felt compelled to break. What were the odds? Karen in Cumbria too. Still, she guessed there were a limited number of opportunities for senior pathologists in England, and Cumbria wasn't that far from Shropshire.

'You didn't need to wait for me, you know, before starting the autopsy. I only need to know the results.'

'Wait in my office, then. But it would be your loss.'

It was a challenge she couldn't resist.

'Let's just get on with it.'

Another little smile. 'Excellent. Scrubs and masks are over there.'

Imogen donned the protective gear and went over to stand on the opposite side of Leo's body. Up to this point, she had only seen him from the neck up. He was long and scrawny, skin stretched tight over his ribs. No tattoos or piercings, but scars criss-crossed his arms.

Karen saw her notice them. 'Looks like a possible history of self-harming.' She looked closer. 'Though these scars are all old, so I'd say it's something from the past.' She lifted one of his arms to examine the wrist. 'Hmm.'

Imogen saw it too. Thin dark lines on the flesh. 'Bruising?'

'Yes. It looks very much like his wrists were secured with cable ties. See where the plastic dug into the skin? The ties were removed before he went into the hole, but I'd say only just before.'

Karen carried on with the external examination. In the background, on the radio, Tears for Fears were singing 'Mad World'. Great, Imogen thought. Now she would forever associate that song with Leo James's cadaver.

'He appears to have been in good health, externally at least. No injuries. No sign of a fight or of physical harm, apart from where his wrists were secured. Some mild abrasions on his knees from where he knelt in the hole. Lots of sand beneath his nails and some in his ears. There are marks on his palms too, which indicate he dug the hole himself.'

Had been forced to dig it, Imogen assumed.

'Let's see how healthy Mr James was on the *inside*.'

Karen opened Leo James up. She confirmed that he had indeed been healthy. A former smoker who had quit. Some light damage to the liver but no sign that he was a heavy drinker. His stomach was empty, indicating he hadn't eaten in the hours leading up to his death. Was that because he'd been tied up? Held prisoner? How long had he been with his murderer before they'd walked him across the sand?

'Seawater in his lungs, which confirms he drowned.' She shook her head. 'The way he died reminds me of this horror movie I watched back in the eighties. Wotsisname was in it. What was it called?'

'I don't do horror movies. I really don't need any more nightmare fuel.'

'Hmm. It will come to me.' She paused for a second then shook her head again. 'We'll have to wait for the toxicology results to see if he was taking or given any drugs, but there's no sign that he was.'

'If he was on medication,' Imogen said, 'he didn't get it from a doctor. He wasn't registered with a GP.'

'Interesting. And I'm not a dentist but, looking at his teeth, I'd say it's been a long time since he had any dental treatment. A couple of his back teeth are broken and I imagine they must have caused him some pain.'

Imogen explained how Leo had lived completely off-grid. 'It's only been forty-eight hours but so far we can't find any dental records that match him. We've fast-tracked his DNA sample too and he's not in the database. We have absolutely no idea who he is. I don't even know how old he is.'

'I'd guess he's in his mid-forties. My estimation would be forty-five, but he could be five years older or younger than that.'

Imogen was shocked. 'I thought he was about sixty.'

Karen's smile was thin. 'It's the beard and the weathered skin. He looks like he spent a lot of time outdoors, in the sun and the wind. But his internal organs tell a different story.'

'I don't think it was just the weather that aged him. His art indicates he was a tortured soul,' Imogen said. 'It was all scenes from Hell. Suffering and misery.'

When the autopsy was finished, Karen said, 'We can release his body now, so a funeral can go ahead.'

'Okay. I'll inform the council.'

'Oh, yes. No next of kin, of course.'

'Nope.'

Karen busied herself putting Leo's organs back inside him. 'An intriguing fellow,' she said.

Imogen turned away, not wanting to watch this part. She'd seen enough already; was already going to have bad dreams tonight.

'Have you ever seen or heard of this method of murder before?' Imogen asked.

'I haven't. It does seem like a risky way to kill someone. Elaborate and slow.'

'But why?'

Karen shrugged. 'Perhaps the murderer was trying to extract information. Told him they'd only free him before the tide came in if he spilled. It's either that or someone really hated him and wanted to hurt him.'

'That's what we think. That it must have been personal. But what kind of information might he have had? And who would a hermit have beef with?'

Karen had finished. She put a sheet over Leo's body and took her gloves off, washing her hands in the metal sink in the corner, her back to Imogen.

'That's your job, detective, not mine. But I'm presuming everyone here is going to be expecting great things of you. The famous serial killer catcher.'

She patted Imogen's arm.

'Forty-eight hours already and no leads?' Karen's smile was fake; a glint of glee in her dark eyes. 'Perhaps I'll see you in the next place you end up fleeing to.'

8

Calvin couldn't remember the last time he'd been this happily exhausted. Therapy had been so busy that they'd stayed open for an extra hour and sold out of everything. Now he was sitting on the sofa with his phone, too full of adrenaline to go to bed, even though he and Tara would need to get up before dawn and go straight into work. He had plans to pull out some of his secret-weapon recipes, the luxury cupcakes and sublime banana bread he'd been holding back. Some of his recipes really *were* better than sex.

He picked up his phone, seeing that he had more messages to reply to. There was one from the local paper, asking him if he'd be happy to give an interview for a piece about the new coffee shop in Elderbridge, something he'd been trying to get them to do since he'd opened.

'Guess what?' he said to Vicky as she entered the room carrying two cups of tea. He showed her the message from the journalist.

'Fame at last,' Vicky said.

'It's all down to you. If you hadn't come up with the idea . . .'

She was modest as always. 'I think it was Tara.'

'But you encouraged me. You edited the videos.'

'Yeah. I guess I *am* the world's best wife.'

Vicky had some work admin to catch up on, so she opened her laptop and got on with it while Calvin returned to his phone, which had never seen so much action. He went through all the comments on his posts, liking them and responding to questions.

He was shocked when Vicky stood up and said, 'Right. I'm going to have a bath, then bed.'

'Already?'

'Calvin, it's eleven.'

He couldn't believe it. Two hours had passed without him even noticing, so absorbed had he been in the world on his smartphone.

He was still wide awake, so he went to the kitchen and opened a beer. He knew drinking alcohol to aid sleep was never a good idea – it was the slipperiest of slippery slopes – but he needed to do something to stop himself feeling so hyper.

He took his beer and phone with him into the bedroom. Vicky was in the en-suite bathroom, soaking in the tub. He sat on the bed. Jarvis was already there, at the bottom corner on Vicky's side, where he always slept.

Calvin's eyes fell on the wedding photo that sat on the dresser. They'd married at the register office in Elderbridge, and nearly everyone there had been a friend of Vicky's. Calvin's only guests had been a couple of friends from the catering college where he'd learned his trade, along with an aunt, an uncle and a pair of cousins. Both his parents were dead and he wasn't in touch with anyone he'd grown up with, even though Reyton, his home town, was only forty miles away from where he and Vicky lived now. Vicky had spread the word among her friends, instructing them not to ask Calvin why he had so few guests. *He's a very private person*, she'd told them. But only she knew the roots of his solitude lay in what had happened to Freya, his sister. And even she didn't know the whole story.

Nobody knew the whole story. Except for the people who had been there, of course.

In his wedding speech, Calvin had joked that when he and Vicky met he was like one of Vicky's stray cats, in need of rescuing. He had been semi-homeless, sleeping on the couch of a colleague at the hotel where he was working, heavily in debt, earning a pittance and not knowing how to get out of the bad place he was in.

'Luckily,' he'd said in his speech, 'unlike all the other poor toms she looks after, she didn't make me get my balls chopped off.'

It had taken Calvin a long time to get Vicky's whole back story – which, in the end, she had told matter-of-factly. She was the only child of a single mother who had been diagnosed with multiple sclerosis when Vicky was eleven. She had spent her teenage years and much of her twenties as her mother's carer. After that, she'd trained as a social worker but hadn't enjoyed it, so had moved into animal welfare. She'd worked as an RSPCA inspector for years, leaving and setting up Elderbridge Cat and Dog Rescue shortly before she met Calvin.

'I'm marrying an actual saint,' he had said, raising a toast to his new bride.

He lay back on the bed with his phone, listening to Jarvis purr. He closed his eyes for a moment, thinking he might drift off, but he felt his phone and social media app calling to him.

The views and comments were still increasing. He went through them, painstakingly liking the comments and replying to those that asked questions. There were more messages too, most of them short and sweet, not requiring anything more than a thanks, though some of them asked if he could share recipes or answer their baking questions. He spent some time replying to them.

Then he spotted another message from BlondieMel.

Hi Calvin – I popped in to Therapy this afternoon! Wow, what an amazing place, and it was so cool to see it so busy. You were rushed off your feet so I didn't feel I could say hello. I tried the orange and ginger cake and it was sublime! Good coffee too!

I'm only an amateur baker, and nowhere near as talented as you. I used to work in a cafe. I mostly did waitressing but I was itching to show them what I could do in the kitchen, LOL.

Anyway, congrats on your success and your amazing cakes. Have you thought about publishing a recipe book? Or maybe sharing some of them online? Whatever, I'll be back!

Mel x

He was thinking about how to reply when Vicky came into the room, wrapped in two towels – one around her body, the other on her hair.

'You going to sleep in your clothes?' she said.

'Hmm?'

He was concentrating on the screen, hardly listening.

'Don't worry. Just . . . I need to dry my hair before I get into bed.'

She sat at her dresser and turned the dryer on. Calvin went back to his phone. He needed to reply to Mel. She was a new, paying customer; it would be rude to ignore her. He was just too tired to think of anything witty or clever.

He saw Vicky looking at him in the mirror. She switched off the dryer for a second. 'Why don't you put the phone down and go to sleep?'

'I will.'

He took his phone into the bathroom and held it while he was cleaning his teeth, tapping out a quick holding reply to Mel: *Thanks for coming in! Will reply properly tomorrow.*

He hesitated, then decided not to add a kiss. He hit send.

Calvin peed, then, before leaving the bathroom, felt compelled to check his messages one more time.

She had already replied.

Don't worry, I know how busy you are. Night night Calvin. Don't let the bedbugs bite xx

He stared at the message through half-closed eyes. Was that a bit overfamiliar? The message and the double kiss?

So exhausted he could hardly think straight, he sent back a quick reply.

Goodnight.

He hesitated, then added a kiss.

9

The reporter, a dark-haired woman called Elissa who used a wheel-chair, arrived at ten the following morning, accompanied by a photographer. Elissa interviewed Calvin while her colleague took lots of photos of him, Tara, and the cakes and muffins and bread that filled the display cabinets. In some of the photographs, Calvin leaned back against the espresso machine, his apron tied around his waist, feeling a little dishevelled from rushing around since arriving here at five.

'Nice to be able to cover something upbeat,' Elissa said when they'd finished. 'Instead of bodies on beaches.'

'You cover crime as well?'

'Oh, it's a tiny paper. One minute it's a sponsored run or a dog with a musical talent, the next it's a horrible murder.' She paused. 'Except, in the twenty years I've worked here we've only had one horrible murder – this one.'

Calvin had been so absorbed in his own business the last twenty-four hours that he hadn't even thought about the murder. He'd heard the beach was open again but that was about it.

'Do they know the victim's name yet?' he asked.

'Leo James. A hermit, by all accounts.' She dropped her voice to a whisper and her eyes shifted left and right. 'I'm wondering if he was in witness protection or something. Like, in hiding? And maybe his past caught up with him. This is lovely coffee, by the way.'

'So you think it's an isolated incident? Not, I don't know, a serial killer?'

She almost spat her coffee into her lap. 'A serial killer? Around here? Unless they follow Detective Evans around, I think we're fine.'

'Well, I guess that's a relief. Maybe you should put that on the front page. "Not a serial killer." Try to calm people down.'

'What, and kill our sales? This is keeping us afloat! Anyway, I'd better let you go. You've got a lot of customers waiting.'

He followed her gaze towards the queue. Today's clientele wasn't mostly teenagers who'd found Maud 'cute'. It was a regular mix of people: pensioners, parents with babies and toddlers, business people having meetings. There was even a guy in the corner with a laptop, perhaps working on the Great British Novel. This was all Calvin had ever wanted. His own place, happy customers, the till ringing, a well-fed and caffeinated crowd. He felt something inside him unknotting. A tension he had hardly been aware of.

All his adult life, he had been wary of happiness. Rejected it, pushed it away, telling himself he didn't deserve it. Even on his wedding day he had looked at himself in the mirror and felt a spasm of guilt and self-loathing. Perhaps the guy on the beach, if the journalist's theory was correct, had spent his life looking over his shoulder, wondering if he could allow himself to be happy. Calvin was like that too. When Therapy had appeared to be failing, he'd told himself it was no more than he deserved.

But maybe now, just maybe, it was time to let the light in. To stop torturing himself.

Time to be happy.

ω

He sat opposite Vicky in the Royal Oak, their local pub, which was within walking distance of their house. Half his pint had already gone and Vicky was on her second glass of wine. She was telling him about some altercation she'd had that afternoon with a man who said the shelter had stolen his cat, which had been found in a terrible state in someone's garden, starving and flea-ridden. A neighbour must have told the man where his cat had been taken, and he'd turned up demanding its return, 'screaming and effing and blinding, making threats. He was threatening to smash the place up if we didn't "return his property". I thought Louise was going to punch him. I had to step between them. Then Louise told him if he didn't leave she'd set a Doberman on him. She seemed deadly serious. In fact, her exact words were: "If you don't piss off right now I'm going to introduce the insanely vicious Doberman we rescued yesterday to your meat and two veg."'

'Blimey. And that worked?'

'I've never seen a man run with his legs crossed before.'

They finished their drinks and Calvin went up to the crowded bar. A large group had just come in and none of them seemed to know what they wanted.

Realising he'd be waiting a while, Calvin didn't even attempt to resist the itch. He got his phone out.

There was another message from BlondieMel.

> *Hi Calvin. I decided to be brave and post a pic of my own ginger and orange cake along with the recipe. I have a secret ingredient too which gives it the X factor. But I decided against including that because, well, it's secret!!*

This was followed by a laughing-face emoji.

> *Here's the link! Hope you had another great day, Mel x.*

He clicked the link. The cake she'd posted a photo of did look good.

What's the secret ingredient? he wrote back. *Come on you can tell me.* He added a winking emoji.

'What can I get you?'

He had been so absorbed in the world of his phone that he'd forgotten he was standing at the bar. He ordered the drinks and a couple of bags of crisps and went back to Vicky.

'Is this dinner?'

He tore the bags open. 'I'm starving. Been too busy serving people to eat anything all day.'

She reached across and squeezed his wrist. 'It's brilliant. I knew you'd turn things around.' She paused. 'What were you doing on your phone? At the bar?'

'Huh? Oh, just, you know. Checking the dreaded app.'

A sigh. 'I feel like the drug dealer who gave you your first hit.'

'Yep, it's all your fault.' He popped a crisp in his mouth. Salt and vinegar. His favourite. 'I need you to help me come up with some more content ideas.'

'Sure. Not right now, though, okay? My brain is too tired.'

They chatted for a while longer and got more drinks. Then Vicky got up to go to the ladies. He watched her go, admiring the slink of her hips as she walked, then found himself tuning in to the conversation at the next table.

'Can you imagine what it must have been like? If he was conscious?'

'I heard they found him with his mouth open, like he'd died screaming.'

Calvin couldn't bear it. The image of the man drowning, water filling his lungs, was too much. He didn't want to hear or think about it. He needed to distract himself, and there it was – his phone, in his hand, and he was opening the app and checking his messages.

> *The secret ingredient? I could tell you but then I'd have to kill you, LOL*

Smiling, he fired back a reply.

> *Whatever. I don't really care . . . Go on – tell me, tell me!*

She sent back the laughter emoji followed by the person putting a finger to their lips. Then another message arrived.

> *It's great that you've been so busy and it isn't even tourist season yet. You'll probably have to hire someone else. X*

He had already thought about this and was considering taking on a temp or two for the summer.

> *Maybe! But my number two, Tara, has been doing a great job. She's a star.*

> *That's great. I was just thinking—*

He didn't get to finish reading the sentence, as his phone was plucked from his grasp. He swivelled round, shocked.

It was Vicky, standing behind him, studying the screen of his phone.

'What are you doing?' he said.

She didn't remove her eyes from the screen, but flicked at it with her index finger. 'Who's BlondieMel?'

His immediate response was to feel guilty. But this was rapidly followed by defensiveness. Mel wasn't some random woman he was messaging behind his wife's back. This was business. Customer service.

'She messaged me to say she liked my videos.'

'Yeah, I can see. And you wrote back. Numerous times. With kisses!'

'I only put a kiss on a message once, which I did automatically without thinking.'

'Um, twice actually.'

'Really? I must have done that when I'd had a drink.'

'Oh, right. So you're getting drunk and sending flirty messages.'

'Vicky, sweetheart . . .'

She held up her palm. 'Wait. I haven't finished reading all these exchanges.'

His guts flipped over several times as he watched her scroll. Had he sent flirty messages? Made some stupid joke that could be taken the wrong way?

'Is she the only one?' Vicky said after a minute. She was back in her seat opposite him now. 'Let's see.' She poked at the screen, obviously going back to look at his inbox. 'Hmm, looks like it. The only lengthy correspondence, anyway. I'm not sure if that's good or bad.'

'I was just being polite,' he protested. 'I read it's what you're meant to do if you want to build an audience. Respond to all your followers.'

'Yeah, a brief thanks. A like. You're not supposed to become their bloody pen pal.' She shook her head. 'And you're definitely not supposed to flirt with them.'

'But I don't think I was flirting.'

She put on a deep voice, in a warped impersonation of him. *'The secret ingredient? Go on, tell me, tell me. Kiss.'*

'I was just being friendly. People put kisses on their messages all the time. It doesn't mean anything.'

Vicky was putting her coat on, not looking at him. 'Let's go home.'

She walked towards the door before he could stop her, and Calvin had no choice but to follow. Vicky was already halfway across the car park, her long legs carrying her at top speed towards home. Calvin had to jog to catch up, falling into step beside her.

'Vicky, sweetheart, I promise. I was being courteous. That's all.'

'So you would have had the same conversation if it was with a man?'

'Yes, of course.'

'Really? With kisses?'

He opened his mouth to repeat his answer, then thought, *Would I?* He definitely would have responded to BlondieMel if she had been male, but would he have engaged in a protracted conversation? He didn't know. But he definitely wouldn't have put kisses at the end of his replies.

'Anyway, BlondieMel might *be* a man,' Vicky said.

She had finally slowed down so they were walking at a more reasonable pace. The moon was out and the sky was clear, dotted with bright stars. This was one of the wonderful things about living here: the vastness of the night sky, the lack of light pollution. It was the kind of night that would perfectly frame a romantic stroll home. But not tonight.

'A man? What are you talking about?'

She made an exasperated noise. 'I forget how naive you are sometimes. Have you never heard of catfishing?'

'I've heard of it,' he said, in a tone that suggested he didn't actually know what it was. He had a vague idea. There'd been a film, hadn't there? A TV series? He knew it had nothing to do with marine life, anyway.

'For all you know, BlondieMel could be some big hairy bloke still living in his parents' basement. Has it not entered your brain that Mel is also a man's name? Ever heard of Mel Gibson? Mel Brooks? Or it could be an elaborate scam. Someone playing a long game with the eventual goal of asking you to lend them some money, or invest in their business – or, I don't know, help their sick mother.'

'Where on earth are you getting this from?'

'Calvin, it happens all the time! The internet is crawling with scammers and frauds and people pretending to be someone they're not. Did you not think it weird that your new pen pal doesn't have a profile photo of herself – or *him*self? I had a quick scroll through BlondieMel's posts and there isn't a single personal photo. They've only done half a dozen posts. Five nature shots and a cake. They really could be anyone.'

She handed his phone back to him. She had Mel's profile page open. Vicky was right: there were some posts about trees and lakes, accompanied by snippets of poems that Calvin half-recognised. Wordsworth? Then there was the recent orange and ginger cake. The one with the secret ingredient. The video clip included a point-of-view shot of someone, presumably Mel, folding the mixture in the bowl.

He showed it to Vicky. 'Those are a woman's hands.'

'Hmm. Probably. Unless Mel is a teenage boy.'

'What?'

He snatched the phone back and stared at Mel's profile. It gave so little away that it could have been generated by AI, or a corporation tasked with coming up with the most vanilla social media profile ever.

'The point is,' Vicky said, her tone softer now, 'Mel could be anyone, any gender, any age. Maybe they're exactly who they say they are, not that they've said very much that's personal.'

She took his hand.

'I know you weren't trying to flirt with her. Or encourage her. I know you're not intending to run off with the first person you meet online. I just want you to be careful, that's all. Don't encourage this person. And don't spend so much time replying to their messages, or anyone else's. You're way too busy and it's really annoying to be in a room with someone who's not *actually* in the room because they're too busy chatting with other people on their phone. Do you understand?'

'I do.' He sighed. 'I never wanted to join social media in the first place. Maybe I should quit, delete the account. I'm sure our new customers will keep coming back.'

'You don't need to overreact. You're good at it!'

'Tara and you are good at it. I've hardly done anything.'

'Maybe. But the account's doing well. It's definitely helped business. You don't need to spend so much time on it, that's all. And you don't need to respond to everyone who creeps into your DMs.'

They had reached their house.

'So,' he said after they went inside, 'what am I supposed to do when Mel messages me again? Ghost her? Is that what it's called?'

'No. Give the message a like and send back a quick thanks or "sorry, super busy". Leave longer and longer gaps between replies. She'll be fine. She'll move on to someone else. That's what these people do.' She put her arms around him. 'I love you, you idiot. But, hopefully, to BlondieMel you're just a passing fad.'

10

Calvin knew something was wrong as soon as he turned on to the street and saw the door of Therapy standing wide open.

It was Friday morning, just after five, the sun still to rise, street lamps splashing orange sodium light on to the pavement. Calvin had been deep in thought, coffee tumbler in hand. He still felt a little contrite after his conversation with Vicky last night. So far this morning, he hadn't checked his phone once.

Then he saw the open door. Surely he and Tara hadn't forgotten to lock up yesterday? He broke into a jog and, reaching the door, peered inside. The lights were off and it was darker inside the cafe than it was out in the open. Dark and silent. It struck him that if there was someone here, he wouldn't be able to see them. It would be easy for them to crouch beneath a table or behind the counter.

'Hello?' he said.

Nothing.

Might his assistant have arrived here before him and left the door open to let some air in?

'Tara?' He realised he was whispering and, feeling ridiculous, pulled himself up to his full height. More loudly he called, 'Tara?'

'I'm here.'

She sounded weak. In pain. He hurried through the cafe, following her voice, and found her lying at the bottom of the stairs that led up to the office. She was on her back, in the dark, blinking up at him as if she'd just woken up.

'Tara?'

She tried to sit up, then cried out. 'Ah, fuck.'

He quickly got down into a crouching position beside her. 'What is it? What happened?'

She groaned and he finally had the sense to get up and turn the lights on before returning to his spot beside her on the ground.

'It's my wrist,' she said through gritted teeth. 'It really hurts. I think it might be broken.'

Calvin looked at it and winced. It was already starting to swell.

'What happened?' He looked up the staircase. 'Did you fall?'

Her jaw was clenching and unclenching from the pain. A broken wrist. Was that bad enough to call an ambulance? He didn't think so. But he needed to get her to the hospital. Where was the closest one? He was so busy thinking through the logistics that he didn't take in what Tara said next for a couple of seconds.

'What?' he asked.

'I said, there was someone here. In the office.'

'Here?' He got to his feet, bracing himself. What could he use as a weapon?

'Relax. They've gone now. I thought . . .' She panted from the pain, and he wanted to tell her to save her energy. 'I thought I'd get here early, make a start, and as soon as I came in I heard someone upstairs. So I went to take a look.'

'Oh, Tara.'

'I know, I'm an idiot.' She hissed the last word, tears in her eyes. 'I need painkillers. I can't move it at all.' She swallowed. 'I went up the stairs, thinking it was probably you. When I reached the top of the stairs they came rushing out and barged straight into me. Knocked me down the whole flight.'

'Did you see their face?'

'No. I hardly saw them at all. They came out of the office so fast that all I saw was a blur. I think they were wearing a hoodie. White skin. I think. But I honestly couldn't even tell you if it was a man or a woman. I mean, I presume it was a bloke but it wasn't like he needed to use much strength to make me fall. I was right there on the top step. Oh God, I need to see a doctor.'

He helped her up, taking care not to touch her injured wrist, which she gripped with her other hand.

'Can you walk?'

'Yeah. I feel like I've been hit by a truck but my legs are still working.' Again the pain made her eyes fill with tears. 'I'm sorry, Calvin. I think I'm going to have to take the day off.'

He laughed.

On the drive to the hospital, Calvin called Tara's girlfriend, Alex, who was already in her car and on the way to A&E before he'd even hung up.

'I'm going to have to get back to the cafe,' he said once Alex had arrived and they were settled in the waiting room. 'I really can't afford to stay shut for the whole day. Unless . . . you want me to stay here with you?'

Tara shook her head. 'No, you go. There's nothing you can do, is there?'

Back at the coffee shop, he went straight up to the office. He had called the police from the hospital. The person he'd spoken to said they would send someone round to take a look. 'Is anything missing?' they'd asked.

Was there? He checked around the office now. There wasn't much here to take. Receipts, delivery slips, messy piles of paper-work that needed sorting out because admin wasn't one of Calvin's strengths. But nothing worth stealing. He used his own laptop, which he took home every night, and they didn't keep any cash on the premises. There was nothing here worth stealing, but a burglar wouldn't know that.

Before heading down to the kitchen to start work, he pulled out his phone so he could text Vicky and let her know what had happened. She texted back straight away.

> *Oh no! Poor Tara! How did the burglar get in? Have they done any damage?*

Calvin had already checked the front door. It wasn't damaged and there were no smashed windows or any other signs that someone had broken in. Could they really have forgotten to lock the door last night? He couldn't remember locking it but that didn't mean anything. He couldn't remember half the things he did on any given day.

As he went to put his phone away, it flashed: another message from a new fan. He read and 'liked' it, then found himself navigating to his last message exchange with Mel.

Could BlondieMel really be a catfish? It was strange that she hadn't posted any pictures of herself, but then there were lots of social media users, he had discovered, who either hardly posted at all or only put up pictures and videos of animals or nature or food, or who only shared memes and jokes. Tara had told him a lot of these accounts were bots, but from the tone of her messages he was convinced Mel was not only a real human but a woman.

He also knew Vicky had been right when she'd advised him to stop corresponding with Mel. In the aftermath of that argument in the pub he had spent some time examining why he had felt the need to do it. Was it politeness? Good customer service? Or something else? Was he desperate for friends? It was true that he had always found it hard to get close to people. It had been a pattern in his life since that awful summer when Freya had died. When he did make friends or formed relationships – including with Vicky – it was because the other person pushed him into it and didn't give him the option to withdraw.

Chatting with Mel had been a little like that, and even though he didn't actually know her, or what she looked like, or anything about her at all to be honest – she liked cakes, that was about it – breaking contact with her did feel a little like the flames of new friendship had been snuffed out before they could start to burn. It was crazy, but he found himself mourning what might have been. A new friend. When was the last time he had made one of them? He couldn't actually remember.

He got up and headed to the kitchen. Maybe he could draw a positive from this experience. After nearly thirty years of closing himself off, perhaps he was finally ready to start making friends again.

But it was something he could focus on when he wasn't as busy. Right now, he had a business to run.

ༀ

Tara popped in on the way home from the hospital. Her left arm was in a sling and her expression immediately told him what he'd feared.

'The good news: they gave me some excellent codeine. The bad: my wrist is indeed broken,' she said. 'The nurse said I'm going to be out of action for six to eight weeks.'

He groaned.

'I'm sorry.'

'Please, Tara, you have nothing to apologise for. I'll still pay you.'

'Maybe I could come in, work the till. Entertain the customers with my banter.'

But that wasn't what he needed her for. He needed someone to help prepare the food, serve customers and clear tables. He needed her with two working arms.

Perhaps reading his mind, she said, 'I could do the social media stuff. I can use my phone okay.'

'Yes. That's a good idea. You could take the whole thing over. Replying to messages. Everything.'

This was the silver lining. With Tara running the social accounts, he wouldn't need to look at them anymore. Wouldn't need to answer messages.

'There's a user on there called BlondieMel,' he said with a grimace. 'She's a bit over-friendly and I might have encouraged her.'

'Oh yeah?'

He cringed. 'I think it's best to ignore her, or restrict replies to a word or two.'

Tara sounded amused. 'Got a stalker, have you? That didn't take long.'

'I don't think she's a stalker exactly.'

'Just be thankful you're not a woman. You should see the stuff that fills our inboxes.' It was her turn to grimace. 'Did the police talk to you? About the break-in, I mean.'

'No, not yet. I called the station again. I get the impression all the police around here are too busy trying to find the person who buried that guy on the beach to deal with any other crimes.'

Tara shivered. 'They still don't have any idea who he is or who did it?'

'No. They're bloody useless.' His low opinion of the police had been formed when he was a teenager, after what had happened with Freya. As far as he could see, anyone could get away with anything in this country. 'Even that supercop, the one they've brought in, doesn't seem to be making any difference.'

Tara sighed, then took her phone out of her pocket. She was right-handed; it was fortunate she had broken her left wrist. 'You're going to need to recruit someone to cover for me, aren't you? Want me to put it on the socials? *Help needed. Must be awesome but not as awesome as Tara.*'

'Nobody could be.'

She pulled a face. 'Please. But leave it with me. We'll get you someone new in a jiffy. I'll do it now.'

Calvin also put a card in the window.

'Old-school,' said Tara.

'That's how I roll.'

Tara went home, leaving him on his own. As the morning progressed, Therapy got increasingly busy. Apparently the coffee machine at Peggy's had broken down, so all their customers had trooped down the road to Calvin's. He couldn't keep up. Everything was selling out, there were tables where people had been waiting for twenty minutes, and they were all eyeballing him, huffing and making passive-aggressive comments.

He was on the verge of telling everyone they could eat for free if they were happy to help themselves – or maybe he should close up for the day and go curl up in a dark corner – when a woman walked up to the counter and said, 'Calvin?'

He was in the middle of trying to fulfil an order. He gawped at her, confused, his brain trying to process three hundred things at once.

'I'm here about the job?'

He looked her up and down. She was in her late thirties, he guessed, with ash-blonde hair tied back in a ponytail, dressed in jeans and a sweater. Petite, with small hands and fine bones. She wore black-framed glasses perched on a button nose, and a silver pendant on a slim chain around her neck. The pendant was in the shape of a turtle.

'Are you okay?' she asked, with a high-pitched nervous laugh.

'Sorry.' Had he been in a trance? 'I'm a little bit busy, as you can see.'

They both looked around the coffee shop. It seemed like everyone was gazing towards Calvin, wondering where their order was. He half expected them to break out into a chorus of 'Why are we waiting?'

His attention returned to the woman. She looked sane. Normal.

'So you're interested in the job?'

'Very much so.'

'Do you have experience of working in a place like this?'

She nodded. 'I worked in one of the busiest cafes in Dublin for two years.'

'Do you know how to work an espresso machine like this one?'

She tilted her head and studied the machine for a moment. 'Easy. I can bake too. I mean, I'm not as skilled or experienced as you, but I know the basics and I'm a quick learner.'

Out of the corner of his eye he could see a man waving a ten-pound note at him, trying to get his attention.

'Can you be available to work from seven till five? We're open seven days a week but—'

She didn't let him finish. 'Absolutely.'

'Do you have any criminal convictions I should know about?'

'Absolutely *not*.'

He nodded. 'Final question: can you start now?'

She smiled. 'Just tell me what you need me to do first.'

He handed her an apron which bore the Therapy coffee cup logo and pushed the tray containing two cups and three slices of cake towards her. 'Put this apron on and take this order to table three. That one.' He pointed.

'No problem.'

As she put the apron on, he said, 'Oh. I forgot to ask your name.'

She tied the apron string behind her back. 'Actually, we've been chatting online.' She stuck out a hand for him to shake. 'I'm Mel.'

11

It was a beautiful morning for a cremation, Imogen thought as she took her seat beside Steve. Beyond the windows the sky was a perfect blue, the sun throwing warm light through the glass, illuminating the dust that hung in the air. At least, she hoped it was dust, and not the remains of the last person who'd been cremated here.

Sometimes she cursed her own imagination.

There were only five of them here: Imogen, PC Steve Milner, a woman with curly grey hair who had introduced herself as the celebrant – the person who officiated the cremation – and then, on the other side of the aisle, a man in a dog collar – presumably the local vicar – and a young guy with sandy-blond hair. Imogen didn't recognise him, though from the expression on his face Steve clearly did, and this recognition appeared to be mutual. Steve was not in his usual uniform but rather a cheap black suit. It made him look even younger, like a sixth-former who'd been dressed by his mum.

This was what would once have been called a pauper's funeral. Paid for by the local authority. The cheapest coffin on the market. No friends. No relatives.

Imogen faced forward, listening to the celebrant – who had very little to work with – before watching the curtains close to conceal the coffin.

She wondered if somewhere out there, Leo James had people who loved him. A mother and father. Siblings. People who would never know what had become of him.

Maybe, in this instance, that was for the best.

The service ended and they made their way towards the exit, the reverend and the young man he was with heading out first. Imogen held Steve back.

'Is that the local vicar?' she asked.

'Yes. Reverend Delaney.'

'Do you know who that young guy is?'

The set of Steve's mouth told her he wasn't a big fan of Delaney's companion.

'That's DJ O'Connor. I think the D stands for Derek. Derek John, as I recall.'

'Who is he?'

'Local small-time drug dealer. A nasty piece of work. He spent a few months in detention when he was fifteen, sixteen, for selling cannabis. That would have been five years ago.'

'What's so nasty about him?'

'He's a violent thug. There was a guy who DJ accused of looking at his girlfriend. A tourist. DJ beat him pretty badly, broke his jaw. He's always in fights and I'm pretty sure he's still dealing. Unfortunately we haven't been able to pin anything on him that sticks.'

'So what's he doing with the vicar?'

They stepped out into the sunshine. Delaney and DJ were standing on the path that led to the car park. The younger man had a cigarette in his hand and appeared to be asking if it was okay to smoke it here. The vicar waved a hand towards the gate and DJ skulked away, the bottoms of his suit trousers scuffing the paving stones, and he sparked up his cigarette as he got to the exit.

Imogen and Steve approached Delaney, and Imogen introduced herself. 'I visited your church the other day. St Bart's.'

'Oh, really?' He seemed delighted, and Imogen felt a flush of embarrassment.

'Not to, uh, worship. I was looking for someone.'

'Oh?'

'You know Mr James's house is very close to the church? The other side of the woods?'

'That's why I'm here.'

'You knew him?'

Delaney smiled. 'I did, yes. He came into the church a few times. Not during my service – I got the impression he didn't like crowds – but when there was no one else around. I found him in the pews, sitting quietly. Praying.'

'Did you have a conversation with him?'

'I had several, detective.'

'May I ask what they were about?'

Delaney hesitated. 'In my line of work, we have to keep confidences, even of those who are no longer with us.'

That was frustrating, but Imogen decided to come back to it. Right now, before DJ returned from smoking his cigarette, she had another question for the vicar.

'What are you doing with DJ O'Connor?'

There was that smile again. So calm and serene. She imagined it would be difficult to have a good argument with Delaney. He was the kind of person who would drive her crazy by refusing to take part in a shouting match.

'He's been helping me out at the rectory. Working as an odd-job man, tending the gardens, doing repairs, that kind of thing. It's all part of my mission, detective. Bring in members of my flock who might benefit from guidance.'

'And how did you know DJ needed guidance?'

'Oh, I know a lost soul when I see one.'

'Was Leo a lost soul?' Steve asked.

'He was haunted, certainly.'

DJ was walking towards them now, having finished his cigarette. Imogen noted that he didn't flick it away but extinguished it beneath his sole then popped the butt back in the box. Very civic-minded of him. And as he walked towards them, it struck her. It was DJ she had seen in the vicarage on Tuesday, watching her through the window.

Was DJ a likely suspect for the murder of Leo James? Surely he couldn't be assumed *not* to be. But right now, when she had no other suspects at all – apart from the elusive young woman in the woods – Imogen knew she needed to be careful. It was too easy to clutch at straws, to construct a false narrative. There was no evidence whatsoever connecting DJ and Leo. The only connection between them was geography. Oh, and now DJ was at Leo's funeral – but would anyone attending the cremation of a man they'd murdered look so utterly bored?

DJ nodded at Steve. 'All right?' He turned his attention to Imogen. 'Oh, it's you.'

'Detective Inspector Imogen Evans.'

'Yeah. I've seen you on telly. You're famous.'

'I hear you're well known around these parts too.'

He shrugged. 'I'm a changed man now, thanks to the reverend here.'

'Oh yes? Found God, have you?'

'Actually, He found me.'

There was the trace of a smirk on his lips, like he was clearly taking the piss. She glanced at Delaney and saw that he was annoyed by DJ's tone. So he wasn't completely taken in by him.

'I'd like to ask you—'

She didn't finish the question. Out of the corner of her eye she saw there was someone watching them from the other side of the memorial garden, half concealed behind a skinny tree. It was a young woman. Imogen was certain it was the woman from the woods.

The moment the woman realised Imogen had clocked her, she turned and ran.

'Go that way!' Imogen urged Steve, motioning to the left. The memorial garden was surrounded by a tall hedge and there was only one exit, the gate DJ had gone through to smoke, but the woman had panicked and headed in the other direction, threading her way between the shrubbery, towards the rear of the garden. There was a raised area, ringed by a low wall, with a single tree at its centre, surrounded by plaques bearing the names of people who had been cremated here. The woman ran straight towards it, checking over her shoulder, eyes widening when she saw Imogen gaining on her.

Now that she'd had a good look at the woman ahead of her, Imogen could see she was barely an adult. Eighteen or nineteen, she guessed. Fast and fit. In an open area she would have easily outrun Imogen.

Steve, though, was just as quick as the girl – but not quite as agile. He reached her and tried to grab hold of her. She swerved, eluding his grip, and he stumbled over a rock as she sprinted towards the exit.

But she had to get past Imogen first.

'Stop!' Imogen commanded. 'We just want to talk to you.'

The girl stopped, panic on her face. She looked over her shoulder at Steve and, all of a sudden, gave up. Her shoulders slumped and she sank to the ground, crumpling on to her haunches.

Imogen approached her slowly, as if she were trying to catch an animal that might take flight again if spooked.

The girl took something out of her pocket. For a horrible moment Imogen thought it might be a knife and she froze. But it was an asthma inhaler. The girl took a puff and looked up at Imogen.

'It wasn't me,' she said.

Imogen and Steve, who was behind the girl blocking any escape attempt, exchanged a glance. 'What wasn't you?' Imogen asked.

'Leo.' The girl's breathing was sharp and ragged. 'It wasn't me who killed him.'

12

The girl was called Billie Whitehead and she was nineteen years old. That was a relief, because if she'd been younger they'd have had to find an appropriate adult to sit in, which was always a pain. Unfortunately, the bout of asthma she'd suffered in the memorial garden meant she needed to be checked over by a doctor before Imogen could interview her. That took two hours, the doctor finally giving the all-clear at quarter past one. It was Friday, four days into the case, and here – at last – was their first potential witness. Imogen couldn't afford for anything to go wrong here.

Imogen and Steve sat opposite Billie in the interview room. She'd already given them her personal details and address, explaining that she lived with her parents in Drigg. Looking at the map, Imogen saw their house was a ten-minute walk from Leo James's place.

'Billie, this is to remind you that you're not under arrest. We want to ask you some questions, that's all.'

'Yeah.' Billie sipped from the can of Diet Coke they'd given her.

'Firstly, do you know who murdered Leo James?'

'What? No, of course I don't.' She sounded genuinely shocked by the question.

'What was your relationship with him?'

Billie pulled a face like she'd found a slug in her can of drink. She was pretty, with clear skin and big eyes like a manga character, although there were dark shadows beneath them. 'I didn't have a *relationship* with him. He was well old.'

'I didn't necessarily mean a romantic relationship with him. But can you tell me what you were doing outside his house on Monday twentieth of March, and again at his funeral today?'

'I went because I felt sad for him. He didn't have any friends and I didn't like the idea of him being burned up with no one there to say goodbye. I mean, no one who knew him.'

'But you didn't come into the service.'

'Yeah. Because you were there. I thought it might just be the vicar or whatever.'

'Reverend Delaney. Do you know him?'

'Nah. Well, I mean, I've seen him around. I . . .' She seemed to want to say something else but stopped herself.

Imogen waited, and when it became clear Billie wasn't going to expand, she said, 'So you stayed outside because you didn't want us, the police, to see you?'

'Yeah.'

'And why did you run?' Steve asked.

'Because I didn't want to have to tell you my whole life story, like I'm doing now.' She sat back, apparently pleased with herself for coming up with this line.

Imogen smiled sweetly. 'Let's go back to Monday and address that part of my question. Why were you at Mr James's house?'

Billie took another sip of Coke, clearly doing this to give herself time to think.

'Come on, Billie,' Imogen said, wanting to snatch the can away. 'Answer the question.'

She huffed. 'I was there to get my camera.'

'Your camera?'

'Yeah.' There was a long pause, during which she was obviously weighing up how much to tell them. 'I promised him I wouldn't tell anyone. He was, like, super private.'

A camera had been found among Leo's possessions. An early digital camera, probably dating from the late nineties. When they'd checked the SD card, all they'd found were photos of the beach.

'I understand your desire to respect his wish for privacy, Billie. But Leo isn't around anymore. And you want us to catch the person responsible for his death, don't you?'

'Yeah, course.' Another groan, followed by a resigned sigh. 'He was teaching me photography. He was really good at it, and I asked him if he could show me how he did it. He didn't want to but I pestered and nagged him until he gave in. He's been giving me lessons for ages.'

'What kind of photography?' Imogen asked, bracing herself. Were there other types of photos out there, beyond the kind some reclusive middle-aged man might want to take of a nineteen-year-old girl?

'Nature. The beach. The sea. The woods. Animals and birds and all that.'

'He didn't . . . take photos of you?'

'What, nudes? You've all got dirty minds, haven't you. He likes women his own age. I know that for a fact.'

'How do you know?'

Billie shifted awkwardly in her seat, glancing at the door. 'I just do.'

'How?'

'Just things he said, all right?'

She was clearly hiding something, and Imogen made a note on her pad. Had Billie seen him with a woman? She decided to move on. Antagonising Billie, trying to push too far, would only be counterproductive. 'Can you go back and explain how you and Mr James met? How you knew each other?'

'I saw him on the beach, taking photos, and asked him if I could take a look. He was taking pictures of these birds. Sandpipers. Cute. He didn't want to show me at first, but I went on until he gave in. Then I asked him if he could teach me. He said no but, well, I followed him home, knocked on his door. Kept going back until he gave in.'

'You wanted to learn photography that badly? And he was that good?'

Billie shrugged. 'I was bored. And I knew it would piss off my mum if she knew I was hanging out with . . . this older guy.'

'You want to piss your mum off?'

Billie narrowed her eyes. 'She deserves it.'

That felt like a distraction. Imogen needed to stick to the subject of Leo James.

'All right, so you pestered him until he agreed to tutor you?'

'Yeah. It wasn't easy. I think, in the end, he was lonely, you know? He wanted someone to talk to, even if it was a nineteen-year-old girl. He told me I reminded him of a girl he'd known a long time ago. An old girlfriend or something. Then he gave me his old camera. Said it was fine to take pics on a phone, like him, but if I really wanted to learn—'

'Wait. You said on a phone *like him*.'

'Yeah. You've got good hearing.'

Imogen ignored the sarcasm. They'd been unable to find any record of Leo having a phone. There was certainly no contract registered to his address, or even a bank account he could use to pay for it. 'He had a smartphone?'

'Yeah, an old iPhone. But it didn't have a SIM card in it. He just used it on Wi-Fi.'

They hadn't found this phone among Leo's possessions. Nor had there been broadband at his house.

'Where did he use Wi-Fi?'

Billie shrugged. 'There's loads of free Wi-Fi around. The cafe in the village. The petrol station. The shop.'

'Did he get rid of this phone while you knew him?' Imogen asked.

'Nah. He had it the last time I saw him.'

'Which was?'

'Saturday.' Six days ago. Two days before they found his body. Did that mean the killer had taken the phone? Was it important? Could there be something on there the murderer wanted to erase?

'These photos,' Imogen said. 'The ones Leo was taking. What did he do with them?'

'Nothing at first. Not until I persuaded him to get an Instagram account.'

Imogen was stunned. She exchanged a look with Steve, who seemed equally shocked. 'He was on Instagram?'

'Yeah. I said it was a massive shame for him not to share his photos. I showed him how to set up an account and upload pictures, use hashtags, all that stuff. He got quite into it. He did it totally anonymously so no one knew who he was, but he had a couple of hundred followers.'

Imogen took out her own phone. She had a private Instagram account that she used to share family photos with her own relatives and friends, only accepting follower requests from people she knew in real life. Ben was the same. There were too many Shropshire Viper fans out there for her to risk doing otherwise.

'What was his username?' Steve asked.

'I can't remember.'

Imogen tutted. 'Come on, Billie.'

A huff. 'All right, it was Sandpiperphotos. One word. Lame, but it's what he came up with.'

Steve searched on his phone and showed Billie. 'Am I spelling it correctly?'

'Yeah, but that's what I was about to tell you. It's been deleted.'

'When did that happen?'

'Last Monday.'

The day Leo's body was found.

'Did you save any of the photos?' Steve asked. 'Or, even better, a list of his followers?'

'Why would I do that?'

Imogen sighed and drummed her fingers on the table, trying to work out if and how Leo having an Instagram account was significant.

'Are we nearly done?' Billie asked.

'Almost. Just a few more questions. One, why did you run on Monday, when you saw me?'

'I thought you might try to blame me. Think I was involved. And I didn't want my parents to know I was friends with someone much older. Someone who'd just been murdered.'

'Hold on. This was only a couple of hours after he was found. How did you know what had happened?'

Billie appeared confused for a moment. Or was it fearful? Then she pulled a scornful face and said, 'God, everyone in the village was talking about it by then. It was already all over TikTok.'

Of course.

'Final question: can you think of anyone who might have done this? Someone Leo had a falling-out with?'

Billie shook her head.

'Did he seem worried about anything in the days before he died?'

'I don't know. He always seemed worried.'

'Did he? What about?'

'That's what he was like. He was always going on about Hell and punishment and consequences.'

'Like in his paintings.'

'Yeah, exactly. Though he told me he'd stopped painting a while ago. That the photos were all he needed.'

Imogen mulled this over. The paintings were, literally, hellish. If he'd been taking photos of the beach, that hardly seemed the same. Perhaps she needed to see the photos to understand; if, indeed, there was anything to understand.

'He used to read me these long poems. I think they were poems, anyway. All this stuff about the circles of Hell. I didn't really understand much of it, to be honest.'

'Dante's *Inferno*?' Imogen asked. She knew a single line from it: *Abandon hope all ye who enter here.*

'Yeah. That was the one. The thing is, even though he was always going on about Hell, it wasn't fire he was afraid of. It was water. Rivers, lakes, the sea. It terrified him. I asked him why he lived so close to the sea and he told me it was so he would never forget.'

'Never forget what?'

Another shrug. 'He clammed up. He never told me anything about his past. All he ever told me was that he came from Cumbria. The other side.' She waved an arm. 'East.'

Imogen wrote that down. She was trying to think if there was anything else she could ask this young woman.

Again, Billie spoke unprompted.

'When I heard he was dead, my first thought was that he must have done it himself,' she said.

Imogen looked at her.

'I know it's impossible – he couldn't have buried himself – but you know what?' Her words made goosebumps ripple across Imogen's flesh. They were so bleak. As dark as Leo's paintings. 'I bet he wasn't sorry to go. I bet as the tide came in and the water covered his head, he was glad to be put out of his misery.'

13

'You did *what?*'

He had known Vicky would be like this. Had braced himself for it on the drive home.

'I didn't know it was her, BlondieMel, when I offered her the job.'

'I know that – but you could have *un*-offered it to her the moment she told you.'

He had found Vicky in the back garden when he got home, weeding and generally tidying the beds around the edges of the lawn. After a long winter of neglect, the whole space badly required some TLC – including the back wall, which was in danger of crumbling, and the shed, which was starting to resemble a serial killer's lair. Vicky was kneeling in the dirt, gardening gloves on, cheeks flushed pink from the exertion.

She got up, taking her gloves off.

'I was desperate, Vicky. You should have seen it in there. I was on the verge of crawling into the broom cupboard and having a breakdown.'

'I'm going to *lock* you in the bloody broom cupboard. I cannot believe you hired her.'

He shook his head. 'She's nice. She's not a catfish. She only started today but she made the whole place run as smooth as . . .' He tried to think of something. 'A smoothie? She's good with the customers, didn't make any mistakes, sorted out the horrific back-log of orders in no time. And she knows something about baking too, so she can help me out in the kitchen.'

'She sounds too good to be true to me.'

He put his hands on Vicky's shoulders. 'Right now, I'd say she's a godsend.'

Vicky broke away. 'Where does she live?'

'Just across Foxton Water.'

'And how old is she?'

'I don't know. Thirty-eight, thirty-nine?'

Vicky frowned. 'Is she from around here originally?'

'I don't think so. She mentioned something about working in Dublin, but she doesn't sound Irish.'

'You didn't ask to see her CV?'

'No. I told you, I had to hire her on the spot. She offered to put one together and send it to me but I don't really see the point. It's a temporary job in a coffee shop. She's not going to make off with all our riches. And I've spent the day with her. Like I said, she's nice. And I don't fancy her.'

This was true. He didn't find her attractive in the slightest.

But saying that, he quickly discovered, was not the smartest thing he'd ever done.

Vicky put her hands on her hips. 'Why did you feel the need to say that? Did I mention that you might fancy her?'

'I just thought . . .'

'What? That I'm some green-eyed horror who can't bear the idea of, *gasp*, her husband working with a woman?'

'No.' He wished he could rewind time and retract his words. 'Of course not. But you weren't keen on me messaging her. That was . . .' He had strayed into dangerous territory and didn't know how to get back.

'That was what?'

'You gave me sensible advice. You were right. I was spending too much time replying to her messages and she could have been anyone. But now we know she isn't a hairy-arsed bloke squatting in his basement. She's a blonde woman called Mel.'

'Oh, so she is blonde?'

'And I'm not going to spend any more time on social media now because Tara's going to do it. That's good news, isn't it?'

'Stop trying to change the subject.'

'I'm not!'

Vicky sighed. 'Look, I'm pleased you've found someone to help you so quickly. I know what a nightmare it would be if Louise broke an arm and I had no one to help me with the animals. It just seems weird that this woman you were chatting to online turned up as soon as you advertised the job, and you actually gave it to her!'

'Is it weird, though? She follows me, so she would have seen the post about the job. She lives locally, which is what originally got her interested in my social media account, and she's into baking – the other thing that attracted her to my account.'

'Not you?'

'Huh?'

'It wasn't you, Calvin Matheson, that attracted her? That made her apply for the job?'

'No! She certainly hasn't given off those vibes at all.' He was starting to feel irritated now. He hadn't done anything wrong. As far as he was concerned, he'd acted swiftly to deal with a problem. That was it.

He went on. 'Listen. I haven't given her a contract. It's all very casual. If she does *one* weird thing, I will tell her it's not working out. But I honestly think it's going to be fine. And it's only for eight weeks, until Tara comes back.'

'Hmm.'

'Come on.' Calvin grabbed hold of her and pulled her into a hug. 'I love you.'

Vicky tried half-heartedly to wriggle out of his embrace, turning her cheek away from his kiss. 'I love you too, idiot that I am.'

'I also think—'

She broke fully away from the hug and pointed a finger. 'If you say you think it's cool that I'm jealous, I will hit you over the head with that spade.'

He laughed.

'What were you going to say?' she asked.

'Oh, nothing.' He smiled his most innocent smile. 'Absolutely nothing.'

ϖ

Calvin went into work at five the following morning and found Mel waiting outside beneath the street light.

'Reporting for duty, sir,' she said with a salute. 'Declaring war on hunger, going into battle against empty bellies.' She winced. 'Oh God, was that totally cringe? Are you going to fire me already? I'm just overexcited, that's all. It's so nice . . .'

She trailed off.

'What?'

'It's embarrassing. It's just . . . It's been a while since I had a job. It's great to have something to get out of bed for.'

He wasn't sure how to respond to that, but he also knew he didn't want Mel to get too attached to this job.

'I did mention this is a temporary position, didn't I? Just until Tara is able to work again.'

'Oh yes, of course.'

He paused, sure she was going to say something else, but she remained quiet, an inscrutable expression on her face.

'All right,' he said at last. 'Come on, let's get started. We've got a lot to get ready.'

Inside, Mel put her apron on. As she tied it, he noticed that today's pendant was a silver butterfly. Seeing him looking, she said, 'I have a whole collection. Different animals. People always buy me them as gifts.'

Had she thought he'd been looking at her chest? He made sure he kept his gaze fixed on her head as he got her started on croissants. He had prepared the dough the previous day, then left it in the fridge overnight. He showed her how to cut the dough into triangles before gently rolling it into its croissant shape, glazing each one with beaten egg, then putting them into one of the three ovens.

She picked it up quickly. He was impressed.

'Have you made croissants before?' he asked a little later, when they had been removed from the oven and were cooling down.

'No. I've warmed up those ready-made croissants you get in tubes from the supermarket, but that's it.'

'Well, you're a natural.' He bit into one of the still-warm croissants. It was perfect. Soft and chewy but with just the right amount of flakiness. 'Are you *sure* you haven't done this before?'

'Scout's honour.'

Next he showed her how he made the brownies that had quickly become one of their most popular items. As he put them in the oven, Mel had a look on her face like there was something she badly wanted to say. Something she couldn't get out. 'Calvin—'

She was interrupted by a banging at the front door. 'Hold that thought,' he said, and went to investigate.

It was a PCSO, a police community support officer. She introduced herself as Becky Green.

Calvin heard himself saying, 'They didn't think it was important enough to send a real police officer?'

Becky bristled. 'I'm perfectly capable of doing the initial report on this, sir.'

'All right. I apologise.' He gestured for her to follow him up to the office, where she made notes in a small pad.

'Was there any sign of forced entry?' Becky asked.

'No, none.'

'And who has keys?'

'Just me and my assistant, Tara. Oh, and my wife has a spare set.'

'Anything missing?'

'Not that I can see. I don't really leave anything valuable here.' He explained that it was mostly paperwork. 'It's all in disarray and needs organising.'

Becky gestured at a messy pile of paperwork. 'Are these bank statements? You need to be careful. Identity theft is a big issue. If your bank and card details were here, somebody might be able to clone a card or get access to your account. You didn't have any passwords or PIN numbers written down, did you?'

He had no idea. 'I don't think so.'

Becky gave him a patronising smile. 'It's worth changing your passwords, maybe get new cards, just in case. Keep an eye on your accounts for any unusual activity.'

He groaned. He didn't have time in his life for all this admin.

'Have there been any other break-ins around here?' he asked.

'Not recently, no.' She did a final circuit of the coffee shop, making more notes. 'I'd get a proper security system put in if I were you. An alarm. CCTV.'

It was something he'd been meaning to do since day one. But it was another annoying admin task, plus he hadn't been able to afford it.

'I definitely will.'

As he was showing the PCSO to the door, Mel came out of the kitchen. Becky did a double take. 'Oh. You work here?'

Mel folded her arms. 'I do.'

'I hired Mel after Tara was injured when she disturbed the burglar,' Calvin explained.

'Yes, I spoke to Tara earlier. Shame she didn't see his face.' Becky sighed, as if this was all Calvin's fault for not having a sufficient security system, and as if Tara was an idiot for not getting a good look at the intruder. Calvin took several deep breaths to prevent himself from telling this PCSO exactly what he thought of her.

'I can't stand that woman,' said Mel, after Becky Green left.

'You know her?'

'Yeah. Well, I've encountered her. These kids have been harassing me. Hanging around by the lake, doing drugs, making loads of noise. They start fires too. The first time they did it after I moved in last year, I went down there to ask them to go somewhere else and, well, they told me to eff off. Since then, they shout stuff at me as I go past, call me a bitch. Horrible stuff. Worse than all that, they sneak around my house at night, tapping on the windows, whispering through the letterbox. Trying to scare me.'

'Mel, that's awful. And the police sent that PCSO out?'

'Yeah, and she said they can't do anything. The kids – I call them that but at least one of them is in his twenties – they deny everything, of course, and there's no evidence. I must admit I lost my temper with Becky bloody Green. Accused her of not being a real cop, of playing dress-up.'

Calvin, who had done something similar when the PCSO turned up, winced.

'It's just . . .' Mel's voice cracked and her eyes filled with tears. She sucked in a breath and flapped a hand in front of her face.

'It's okay,' he said.

'I'm sorry. It upsets me, that's all. They're horrible – especially the ringleader, the older one. He's this little twat called DJ. There's something wrong with him, in his head, you know? The way he looks at me, it's like . . .'

'What?'

'Like he's got no soul. His eyes are black, with nothing behind them.'

Calvin opened his mouth, unsure how to respond, and that was when the smell hit him. Something was burning.

He rushed into the kitchen, followed by Mel, and headed straight to the nearest oven. He opened the door and was hit by a blast of smoke. The brownies.

Grabbing a cloth, he pulled the tray out and set it down on the stovetop, stepping back from the swirling smoke, rushing over to open the window.

'I'm so sorry,' Mel said.

'It's fine. These things happen. We'll make another batch.'

Mel headed to the big walk-in fridge to fetch more ingredients.

'Isn't it time to open up?' said another voice.

He turned. It was Vicky, waving her hand in front of her face. 'What happened here?'

'Some brownies got over-browned,' he replied. 'How come you're here?'

But Vicky didn't appear to be listening. She was staring towards the walk-in fridge and Mel, who was busy gathering flour and eggs and hadn't seen Vicky come in.

'Vicky?' Calvin said.

'What? Oh. I was hungry. I had an appointment in the village.' That usually meant she was visiting a prospective adopter and checking out their home, making sure it was suitable for a dog or cat. She dropped her voice to a whisper. 'Is that Mel?'

'It is.'

'I need to talk to you.'

Vicky gestured for him to follow her out of the kitchen.

'What is it?' He didn't want to seem impatient but there had already been so many disruptions this morning, and customers were about to start arriving.

Vicky hissed at him: 'I recognise her. Your new woman.'

'What?'

'Mel.' She grabbed his forearm. 'I *know* her.'

14

Vicky led Calvin further away from the kitchen. 'She came into the shelter a couple of days ago.'

'To do what?'

'She said she was looking to adopt a cat.'

'Is that it? I thought you said you know her. But what you actually mean is that she came into the shelter looking for a pet. I don't understand how that's any kind of big deal.'

'You don't think it seems like a big coincidence?'

'Um, not really, no. Don't you have people come in every day looking for a cat?'

'Yes, of course we do. But you can't tell me it's not weird that this woman came in the same week she was striking up a relationship with my husband on his new social media account.'

He processed this. 'It's a coincidence, that's all.'

'Really? It seems like a big one to me. Do you know what I think? I think she came into the shelter to check out the competition.'

'You're not serious.'

'Oh, I'm very serious.'

He couldn't believe this. 'Vicky, this is insane.'

'I am not insane.'

'I didn't say *you* were insane. I was talking about the situation. And the fact that you're putting two and two together and getting one million.'

Vicky looked towards the kitchen, where, presumably, Mel was preparing the next batch of brownies. Calvin didn't want to be having this conversation with Vicky. Customers would be showing up any minute and he needed to get the food out, warm up the coffee machine.

'Can we talk about this later?' he said.

But Vicky wanted to talk about it now. 'Have you heard of parasocial relationships?'

'Vicky, I need to get on . . .'

'A parasocial relationship is when someone feels like they know someone they see online or on TV. It might be something harmless like someone becoming really invested in, I don't know, the life of a soap opera character. Or it can be much more serious, like when someone starts to believe they and a pop star are meant to be together.'

'Like in that Eminem song.'

'Yeah, exactly. I mean, that's an extreme case. It might just be some teen girl crying over Harry Styles posters or whatever.'

'Wait. You think Mel might be experiencing one of these para . . . things with me? I'm not a celebrity.'

'That doesn't matter. I think when Mel saw your videos, saw that you're into baking and realised you live locally, it sparked something in her. This feeling that she had a connection to you. It probably took quite a lot of courage for her to send you that first message. But when you wrote back it was like chucking petrol on the flames.'

He raked his hands through his hair. 'Vicky, I think you're overreacting massively. She has shown no sign whatsoever of being attracted to me. She doesn't flirt. She never touches me or stands close to me when we're talking. I never catch her looking at me. She doesn't bloody play with her hair when we're interacting. She doesn't fancy me!'

Vicky was quiet for a moment, absorbing this. 'You're not very good at telling when women fancy you. It took you ages to get the hint with me.'

'That's only because I couldn't believe someone as gorgeous as you could like someone like me.'

She rolled her eyes.

'Also,' he said, 'how would Mel know that my wife ran the shelter? There's no link between us on our social media. You haven't been mentioned on the Therapy account.'

'I don't know.'

'It's just a coincidence, Vicky.' He paused. 'Did she take a cat?'

'No. She said she was going to come back, but she never did.'

'Possibly because she started working here and has been busy.'

Vicky looked towards the kitchen again. 'There's something off about her. All my instincts are buzzing.'

'You've only met her once, and I'm presuming you only talked about cats?'

'I don't need to spend more time with her to know she's bad news. I can tell from her messages. She's . . . damaged. And we know what you're like with damaged women.'

He stared at her.

'I'm just saying, you have a history of it. Trying to help damaged women. Because—'

'Because of what happened to Freya.' This was something he and Vicky had talked about before. Vicky had gently put forward the suggestion that, because he believed he had failed to save his sister, he kept trying to redeem himself by helping other troubled women. It had led to one of their biggest-ever arguments. He rejected what he thought of as pop psychology. Though he was also aware that Freya was a subject he couldn't go near without, as everyone said these days, being 'triggered'.

'Don't get angry,' Vicky said.

'I'm not angry.'

'Calvin, you've gone red. Take a deep breath.'

He did, and he took a moment before speaking again. 'I think you're wrong about Mel. I wouldn't have been able to cope without her yesterday or this morning, preparing all the food.'

'Oh yeah. What did you call her? A *godsend*.'

'Are you trying to make me lose my temper?' He was talking through clenched teeth now and he could actually feel his blood getting hotter. 'I can't talk about this anymore. I need to open up.'

'Calvin?'

Both he and Vicky looked in the direction of Mel's voice. She had come out of the kitchen. Had she overheard? He went cold to think that she might have.

'Should I start to bring out the croissants and the other pastries?'

'Yes please.' He gave Vicky a meaningful look. 'I'll help.'

Mel hesitated and Vicky took the opportunity to jump in. 'Hi Mel. I'm Vicky. Calvin's wife. We've met before.'

Mel looked blank.

'At the animal shelter.'

'Oh! Yes, of course. I, um, I've been intending to come back, but now I've got this job here and—'

Vicky cut her off. 'Don't worry, it happens all the time. But maybe once Tara returns to work and you're back at home during the day . . .'

Mel stared at her. 'Yes. I guess.'

Vicky turned back to Calvin with a broad smile on her face that only he could tell was fake. 'I think I'm going to skip breakfast and head back. Louise will be wondering where I am.'

She pecked him on the lips and headed towards the door, where several customers were waiting to be let in. Turning back, she said, 'Nice to see you again, Mel.'

Calvin followed her out, letting the customers in and telling them he'd be with them in a moment. He didn't feel that they'd resolved their conversation and didn't want to let Vicky go with any bad feeling hanging between them. 'Wait.'

She stopped.

'Are we okay?'

Her eyes darted through the window towards Mel, who was seating the customers, and she sighed. 'Yes, we're okay. I do trust *you*, you know.'

'But not her?'

Vicky was silent for a moment. Eventually, she said, 'Just . . . keep an eye on her.'

'Yes. All right.'

Vicky took one last look at the coffee shop; at Mel, heading behind the counter to make coffee. 'Because if you don't, I will.'

15

All day, the coffee shop was busier than he had ever imagined possible. A constant stream of customers. Full tables. The cash register ringing and the card machine beeping. By four thirty they had sold out of everything, and Calvin had to put a sign on the door that said *Sorry – drinks only*. Then he called a local temp agency and told them he urgently needed help. There was no way he and Mel could cope on their own much longer if things stayed like this.

It was a wonderful problem to have.

After closing, he collapsed at the closest table, so exhausted he couldn't stand, but so full of adrenaline his legs still twitched, his knee bouncing up and down. Mel sat opposite him.

'I'm glad everyone's gone,' she said. 'I was starting to think if I hear about that murder one more time . . .'

'You're not a true-crime fan?'

She looked appalled. 'Not when it's this close to home. I only live a couple of miles from the beach where they found him.'

'Did you know him?'

'The victim?' She shook her head firmly. 'Never even seen him. But I hate the weird pleasure people seem to get from it. Like it's another piece of juicy gossip. Even if he deserved to die, it's still horrible.'

Calvin furrowed his brow. 'What makes you say that? That he might have deserved it?'

'What? Did I say that? Oh. It's just . . . well, it seems like some sort of revenge killing, doesn't it? That's what they said in the paper, anyway. If somebody wanted him to suffer that badly, he must have wronged someone, don't you think?'

'Or there's a crazed psychopath on the loose.'

'Please. Calvin.'

He groped for a way to change the subject, settling on, 'Well . . . it's been quite a week.'

He could hardly believe that just five days ago the coffee shop had been dead. A day after that, Tara had posted the Maud video. Mel had started messaging him, then Tara had got injured and Mel had turned up to answer his job ad. Now, business was booming. Everything had changed in such a short space of time.

There was no denying it: Mel had been a star again today. Tireless and efficient; organised and brimming with positive energy. There had been a moment during the morning, when every seat in Therapy was occupied and the orders were coming thick and fast, when he'd marvelled at how in sync the two of them were, like dancing partners in perfect harmony, knowing exactly where they needed to be and what to do next. He could feel the energy of the busy coffee shop pulsing through him, and looking at Mel – a relaxed smile on her face as she carried another tray of cakes and coffee to a group of satisfied customers – he could tell she felt it too. They had caught each other's eye and smiled. He didn't want to be disloyal to Tara, but he wondered if she would have been able to cope with this rush.

'I just have to say, Mel . . . Thank you so much. You've saved me. I don't know what I would have done without you.'

She stared at the tabletop, too embarrassed by his praise to maintain eye contact.

'It must be amazing seeing the place so busy,' she said.

'It is. Such a relief too. Vicky invested a lot of her savings when I opened this place, and if it carries on like this we'll earn all that back sooner than I ever thought possible.' He stretched his arms out. 'I'm shattered. And we have to do it all again tomorrow. It's going to be hectic.'

'At least we'll have the new temps.'

'Not yet. They can't start till Tuesday.'

'We'll cope,' Mel said with a smile. 'Just the two of us.'

He was hardly listening. 'I'd be tempted to ask Vicky to come in and help, but she's going away.'

Mel double-blinked. 'Oh, really?'

'Yeah. It was her Christmas present. A night at this spa hotel. She's been putting it off for ages because she's always so busy, but she arranged it a couple of weeks back, before we got busy here. The only night they could do was tomorrow. A Sunday night, which is annoying.'

'She's going on her own?'

'Well, I can't get away, for obvious reasons. But it's cool. She deserves a treat. A day without worrying about stray cats and homeless dogs.'

Mel's gaze returned to the table surface. 'I feel terrible about not taking a cat. I could tell Vicky was annoyed about it.'

'She wasn't at all.' He hoped the lie wasn't evident in his voice. 'She understands.'

'Are you sure?'

'It's fine, honestly.' *Actually, Vicky thinks you're a weirdo and doesn't like you working here.* Desperate to change the subject, he said, 'I'd better get going. I promised Vicky I'd take her out to dinner tonight.'

'Well, please apologise to her again from me. I don't want her to dislike me.'

'She doesn't.' He touched her lightly on the shoulder. 'It's all good, Mel. Don't worry.'

He hurried out, trying not to think about the way she'd reacted to his touch. She'd drawn in a sharp breath and the skin around her throat had flushed pink. That wasn't good, was it? Maybe, he told himself, she just wasn't used to physical contact. It didn't mean anything.

He looked back over his shoulder. Mel was staring into space, stock-still, as if his touch had frozen her to the spot.

ϖ

The restaurant, which was on the other side of Elderbridge, specialised in seafood and was excellent. It was cosy and warm, and in the candlelight, at the end of what had been one of the busiest but most rewarding weeks of his life, Vicky looked more beautiful than ever.

He'd treated them to an expensive bottle of Sancerre and was a little tipsy. He was glad they'd left the car at home and come by taxi. For the first time in ages, he was feeling flush.

He raised his glass. 'To us. And success. And my gorgeous wife.'

'You're drunk.'

'Only a little. I'm always telling you how gorgeous you are, aren't I?'

They sat in companionable silence for a minute. This was one of the best things about their marriage. They didn't feel the need to fill every quiet moment with conversation.

'About earlier,' Vicky said. 'I've been thinking about it. About Mel, I mean. Maybe I overreacted.'

'Really? I mean, yeah, I think you did overreact. I'm just surprised you've changed your mind.'

'Oh, I haven't changed my mind. I still think there's something not quite right about the way she bombarded you with messages and then turned up looking for a job. But I've decided she's probably harmless.'

He laughed. 'I guess that's something.'

'I mean, this isn't *Fatal Attraction*, is it? I'm fairly confident you're not going to screw her in the sink while opera blares in the background, and she's not going to turn up at our house looking for a bunny to boil.'

'I can assure you I am definitely not going to screw anyone in any sinks.' He pushed away the memory of how Mel had flushed earlier when he'd touched her shoulder. He had already convinced himself it was nothing. It had been hot in the coffee shop. She'd probably already been flushed and he hadn't noticed. 'I've been thinking about it too, and I disagree there's anything suspicious about her turning up looking for a job.' Was he trying to persuade himself? He kept going. 'I mean, we set out to attract people to the coffee shop. Mel was one of the people we attracted. Because she's local she reached out directly to me, that's all. And then, purely coincidentally, she saw we had a job going; a job she's qualified for. That's it.'

'Hmm.'

'She's also extremely good at it. Today was absolute madness – so busy it could have been completely overwhelming – and Mel was amazing. An absolute star.'

'So you keep saying,' Vicky muttered. 'It sounds like you won't want Tara to come back at this rate.'

'If trade remains this good I'll need both of them.' He reached across and took her hand. 'Honestly, Vicky, everything is good. I want you to go away tomorrow knowing you have nothing to worry about.'

ϖ

The taxi dropped them in front of their house, which was a small detached place at the end of a cul-de-sac. A little further along was a wood that was popular with dog walkers, the path eventually leading to a school and its playing fields. It was a nice place to live but a little boring. In the taxi home, Vicky had read out a few of the latest messages in the neighbourhood WhatsApp group.

> *My friend with the contact at the station reckons the victim was in witness protection and the person they were hiding from finally found them.*

> *I haven't been able to go to the beach since it happened.*

> *This red-haired cop, Imogen Evans. Seems like it was a fluke that she caught that serial killer.*

> *Yeah, the police are hopeless.*

'I think you'd fit right in with this group.'

'I'm sick and tired of hearing about this drowned guy.' He realised he was echoing Mel from earlier but it was true. Every time he heard it mentioned he pictured it. Sightless eyes. A slack mouth. Skin turning blue. It was too awful.

He paid and tipped the driver, giving twice as much as he usually would.

'More wine or shall I put the kettle on?' Vicky asked as they went into the kitchen. 'I think I—' She stopped. 'Someone's been in here.'

The way she said it sent a chill rippling across Calvin's flesh. 'What do you mean?'

'Can't you feel it?'

'No.' He stood there, completely still, trying to feel whatever it was Vicky was feeling.

She walked around the kitchen, then into the hallway. 'It's the atmosphere. I know you probably think I'm crazy but . . .' Her voice dropped to a whisper, as if something awful had just occurred to her. 'What if they're still here?'

She was so convincing. Suddenly, he too believed there had been someone in the house. Someone who was likely to still be here.

Calvin led her back into the kitchen. 'Wait here,' he said in a low voice.

He withdrew a butcher's knife from the block.

'What the hell?'

His voice dropped to a whisper. 'If there is someone here . . .'

'What, you're going to stab them?'

He ignored her and stalked from the room. This was his house. It was his job to protect it.

He checked the utility room and the garage. Both empty. There were no signs of a break-in and nothing appeared to have been disturbed. The living room was empty too and, he was sure, just as they'd left it.

Satisfied there was no one hiding on the ground floor, he went up the stairs, slowly, clutching the knife tightly, afraid that someone might rush at him like they had Tara.

He reached the landing and checked the nearest door, the bathroom. Empty. Same with the spare room. That left the bedroom, the door of which was shut. It wasn't a door they customarily closed.

He took a deep breath and pushed the door open, holding up the knife.

A shape flew at him out of the darkness and he jumped backwards.

The shape meowed.

'Oh my God. Jarvis!'

The cat strutted around the landing, tail high, eyes narrowed like he was pissed off. Calvin put the knife down, scooped the cat up and carried him back down to the kitchen.

'It's all clear. Flipping heck, Jarvis nearly gave me a heart attack, though. He was trapped in our bedroom.'

He expected Vicky to laugh with relief. Instead, she said, 'What? I didn't do that.'

'Not deliberately, I'm sure.'

The cat was up on the counter now, pestering them for food. Calvin squeezed some out of a pouch and set it on the floor. Jarvis turned his nose up at it and left the room.

'I'm *certain* I didn't shut our bedroom door,' Vicky said.

'Really? You'd remember?'

Now she looked unsure.

He put his arms around her. 'It's completely normal to close or open doors without remembering.'

'Maybe for you.' But she still looked doubtful.

'For everyone.'

'Why would either of us close that door?'

She rubbed her arms and went to the front window to look out at the dark street and the woods beyond. Calvin knew what she was thinking: how easy it would be for someone to slip in and out.

He poured Vicky a glass of wine and stood beside her, facing the shadows outside. 'No one's been in here,' he said.

She took a sip of wine and said, 'Actually, I don't want this. I'm going to bed. I haven't even packed yet and need to get up early. Are you coming?'

He hesitated. He was wired now and the mood had been ruined. 'I'm going to stay up for a bit and watch telly.'

'Okay, fine. Make sure you lock the front door properly when you come to bed, okay?' She spoke quietly but clearly. 'Because I'm certain I didn't shut the cat in our bedroom.'

16

Monday morning. Imogen pulled up outside St Bartholomew's and took a moment to enjoy the view: the steeple stretching up to the powder-blue sky, daffodils blooming around the edges of the churchyard. Getting out of the car, she could hear birds calling to each other in the treetops. It was so peaceful. She was tempted to sit on the closest bench for a while and enjoy a few minutes of tranquillity, something she hadn't experienced since . . . Actually, she couldn't even remember the last time she'd had a moment of peace. Sometime before she became a mother.

She knocked on the vicarage door and was greeted by Reverend Delaney.

'Detective.' He sounded delighted to see her. 'I was just head-ing over to the church. Follow me?'

He strolled past her without waiting for a response, and she had to break into a jog to keep up. Moments later they were inside the church, and she was following him down the aisle, between the pews. It had that particular musty smell that threw her back to her childhood, when her parents had sent her to Sunday School for a brief period – probably to get her out of the house so they could have some time on their own. Like most people she knew, she only went to churches for christenings, weddings and funerals. She and Ben hadn't even got married in one; they'd had their ceremony in a register office in Telford. Delaney appeared to be doing a sweep of the church, looking for stray Bibles and hymn sheets, which he gathered from the pews as he went.

'There was supposed to be a wedding this afternoon,' he said. 'But I've just had a call from a very upset father of the bride.'

'Don't tell me the groom's got cold feet?'

'No. The bride. She's done a moonlight flit, left a note saying sorry but she needs to go and find herself.'

'Good luck to her. I can barely find clean clothes in the morning, let alone myself.'

The vicar smiled politely.

'I was hoping to speak to DJ.'

'Oh. He doesn't live here, you know. He'll be at home. Do you have his address?'

She did. And she'd known DJ didn't live here. She'd actually wanted a word with the vicar, after the interview with Billie, about a couple of subjects.

First, as it happened: DJ himself.

'How did you meet DJ?' Imogen asked. 'You said he was a lost soul but I'm wondering what brought him into contact with you.'

'A lost soul. Hmm. Perhaps "lost sheep" would be a less grand description. Certainly a young man who could benefit from some guidance.'

'Which is what you've been giving him? Spiritual guidance?'

Delaney smiled. 'I think you've got the wrong end of the stick, detective. DJ works for me as an odd-job man and occasional driver. This isn't some form of indentured servitude. He's not paid with prayers. I employ him. I put an advert up in the shop in the village and DJ applied. I hired him because he told me he was handy and that he needed the money. I suppose I also saw that, by employing him, I could offer him some guidance.'

'But is he a Christian?'

'You'd have to ask him that.'

'I will.' A pause. 'Did it not bother you that he has a criminal record?'

'Have you ever heard of forgiveness?'

She nodded. 'I've *heard* of it.'

'Oh, detective.' Delaney was clearly saddened by Imogen's lack of faith in humanity.

Imogen went on. 'Was DJ with you the evening of Sunday nineteenth?'

'The night of the murder, you mean? Actually, he was. We had a baptism that afternoon, and in the evening I asked him to stay and carry out some repairs in the church toilets. We've had an ongoing issue with the plumbing, an unfortunate series of leaks, and we've had some complaints.' He wrinkled his nose.

'I suppose that's a great alibi,' Imogen said. 'The local vicar.'

'Well, yes. Unless, of course, I'm the murderer. That would be quite Agatha Christie-esque, wouldn't it?' He wiggled his eyebrows, as if this idea rather appealed to him.

'So DJ was here all evening?'

'Yes. It was more troublesome than I anticipated, so he was working until around ten. I paid him double, of course. Which is still less than the cost of a qualified plumber. Sadly a critical concern, funds as low as they are.'

Could DJ have gone out after helping the vicar fix his loo to murder Leo? It seemed highly unlikely, given the elaborate, time-consuming mechanics of the crime, but Imogen's experience had taught her that the unlikely was far from impossible.

'Can I ask you about Leo James too? You said he used to come to the church.'

'And I told you that any conversations I had with him are confidential.'

'Between you, him and God?'

'Exactly.'

'But surely you want his murderer caught?'

Delaney didn't say anything.

'From speaking with Billie Whitehead—'

'That's the girl who was at the cremation?'

Imogen indicated yes. 'It seems clear to me that Leo was tormented by something. He appeared to have a keen interest in Dante.'

Delaney grimaced. 'Too rich for my Church of England tastes.'

Imogen ploughed on. She could feel herself straying into territory she didn't quite understand and wanted to keep it as simple as possible. 'His paintings back this up. Lots of images of souls being tormented in Hell. I know little about theology, reverend, but I understand guilt. If someone fears going to Hell, would that not be because he believed himself to be a sinner?'

'We are all sinners, detective.'

She looked him in the eye. 'Did he come here because he was looking to be absolved of his sins? To be granted the forgiveness you mentioned?'

'I'm sorry. But I can't tell you that.'

'I think he did. And I think that's why he cut himself off from society, erased all links with his past. He was trying to get away from something he'd done. Something he thought would send him to Hell.'

She tried to seek out the truth in Delaney's face. Leo must have spoken to him; perhaps told him what he was hiding from. Perhaps even who he was hiding from. But, maddeningly, the vicar was a closed book.

ϖ

Drigg Beach caravan park was only a stone's throw away, on the other side of Drigg, but by the time she got there the sun had gone behind a bank of cloud that showed no sign of shifting. She parked in the lane outside the main gates and looked at the power station in the distance, imagining she could sense its nuclear hum.

The ground beneath her feet was sandy, the beach a five-minute walk from here across a gently sloping field. If the hushed church grounds were peaceful, the quietness of this place was desolate, like she'd been pitched to the edge of the world. She guessed it would be livelier during the imminent tourist season, but today – as more black clouds gathered overhead – it seemed like the ideal venue for the holiday from hell.

Imogen made her way past several rundown caravans. Most of them appeared to be empty, likely only used for vacations, but according to her new colleagues several of the caravans were permanent homes, some of them owned by their occupants, some of them rented out.

Imogen had spoken to DJ's former probation officer earlier, who had told her DJ had inherited the caravan from his grandmother, who had raised him after his mother 'buggered off' when DJ was barely out of nappies. The grandmother had died while DJ was in prison and he'd moved straight into the caravan when he got out. It was located at the end of a row of static caravans towards the rear west corner of the park, and was about seven metres long, with a small outside area with a plastic table and chairs. An ashtray on the table contained what looked like roaches from spliffs.

Imogen looked through the window and DJ stared back out at her from a sofa on which he was sitting, holding the controller of a games console. He didn't seem that surprised to see her.

'Let me guess,' he said after opening the door to her. 'You've got no suspects for this weird burial murder so you've decided to come sniffing around here.'

Sadly, he wasn't that far off the truth.

'Can I come in?' Imogen asked.

'Yeah. Wipe your feet.'

She wasn't sure if he was joking but she did it anyway, stamping her trainers on the doormat, watching sand puff around her ankles. DJ went back to the sofa where the PlayStation controller lay. On the screen, some kind of hideous post-apocalyptic creature stood with its back to the camera, the action paused.

'*The Last of Us*?' Imogen asked.

'Yeah.' He sounded surprised. 'You a gamer?'

'No, but my husband is watching the TV show and keeps telling me about it. It's not my thing. I'm not a big fan of zombies.'

'They're not *zombies*. They're infected. That's a clicker.'

'I stand corrected.' A little dog emerged from behind the curtains at the far end of the room and trotted up to them. A French bulldog. It allowed Imogen to scratch its ears. 'Cute dog.'

'Her name's Cop Killer.'

Imogen blinked at him.

'Just kidding. She's actually called Lola. What do you want, Detective Evans? If you want to interview me about that bloke's death, shouldn't we be at the station?'

'I'm just here for a little chat.'

'Huh.'

'I was wondering if you could talk me through your movements on the evening of March nineteenth. That's last Sunday.'

'I know when it was. I was at St Bart's for the whole bloody evening, fixing the bog.'

'Are you a trained plumber?'

DJ spluttered with laughter. 'I watched a video on YouTube that showed me what to do. Although the whole system needs replacing. The pipes—'

She held up her palm to forestall a diatribe against the church's plumbing. 'And what time did you finish that?'

He appeared to think about it. 'Around ten, I guess.'

That matched what Delaney had told her.

'Did you walk home?'

'Yeah.'

'You came straight here? What route did you take?'

The dog sat there panting, staring up at DJ. She was, Imogen realised, quite old, going grey around the ears, her legs stiff. DJ lifted Lola up and put her on his lap, stroking her gently. He didn't look like such a bad lad now, though she had encountered plenty of criminals who were kind to animals and cruel to their fellow humans.

'I walked through the village. Nowhere near that dead bloke's house or the beach.'

'Did anyone see you?'

He made an exasperated noise. 'I thought this was a friendly chat. No, nobody saw me. It was late. Dark and cold. I came back here, had a couple of beers to wind down, played some *Last of Us*.'

'Did you know Leo James?'

'I saw him at the church a couple of times, talking to the reverend. Never spoke to him myself.'

'What about Billie Whitehead?'

'That girl at the crematorium? Not really. I've seen her around, though, of course. She would have been a year or two below me at school and I've seen her at the pub and stuff.' He continued to stroke the dog, not making eye contact. 'What was she doing there? Don't tell me she was shagging him. Not that I'd be surprised.'

'Why do you say that?'

'I dunno. Just . . . He looked like a creep and I've heard she likes older men.'

'Really?' Was this just scurrilous village gossip?

'Yeah, she's got a rep. Did you ask her about him?'

'Yes, I did.'

'And she denied shagging him?' He frowned.

'You seem strangely interested.'

'Do I? We're all interested in other people's sex lives, aren't we? And I don't like to think of a young hottie like her screwing an old goat like him. I remember when he came to see the vicar, thinking he had that paedo vibe.'

'"Paedo vibe"?'

'Yeah. Well, maybe not an actual paedophile. But a bloke who likes them young. Some old paedo who lives in the woods waiting for Little Red Riding Hood to stumble past.'

She stared at him.

'And maybe Red Riding Hood's dad or brother or uncle found out what the Big Bad Perv was up to and decided to deal with him. Or maybe she's got another admirer. The jealous type. Maybe another old guy in his forties. Now, are we done?' He nodded at his paused game. 'I really want to kill this fucking clicker.'

Imogen left the caravan, hugging herself against the cold.

It had been a useful chat for unexpected reasons. Because that could be Leo James's secret, couldn't it? The thing he was tortured by guilt over; the reason he thought he might be headed to Hell to be tormented by demons. An attraction to young girls. Okay, Billie was an adult, but barely. Could all this stuff about Leo teaching her

113

photography be a lie? Had she been sleeping with him? She was so young, and he was not only more than twenty years her senior, but he looked even older. It happened, though, didn't it? It happened all the time. Just like people got upset and jealous all the time. After money, so-called love was the number-one motive for murder.

Imogen headed back to her car, knowing exactly who she needed to talk to next.

17

They closed at five thirty on Monday afternoon, having sold out of everything again. It had been insane all day.

'I wonder if I'll ever get a day off,' Calvin said after locking the door.

'The temps start tomorrow, don't they?' Mel said.

'Yes. Thank God.'

They set about cleaning up. Calvin was tired to his bones, and all he wanted to do was go home and collapse on the sofa. Vicky was due home from her spa trip around eight, but he planned to go to bed early and catch up on some sleep before another five o'clock start the following morning.

'Right,' he said, when the cleaning was finally finished. 'I'll see you in the morning.'

'Yes. I'll—'

To his great surprise, she burst into tears.

He sprang from his seat.

'Mel?' He hovered in front of her, unsure what to do. Should he put his arm around her? In the end, he kept his distance. She had her head down, sniffing and swiping at her eyes. 'What's the matter? Was it something I said?'

More sniffing.

'Mel? Talk to me.'

'I'm so sorry.' Her voice was thick with tears. 'It's nothing you've done. It's . . .' She shook her head. 'Something else.'

'What?' He spoke gently, trying to coax it out of her.

'No, you're my boss. You shouldn't need to get involved.'

'Come on,' he said. 'Come and sit down.' He led her to the closest table. 'Tell me what's happening. Is it . . . a boyfriend?' He felt horribly awkward asking.

'I don't have a boyfriend. I'm single, Calvin. It's nothing like that. I wish I *did* have one.'

She seemed determined for this to sink in.

'Are you sure it's not something I said or did? Have I been working you too hard?'

'Oh God, no. You haven't done anything wrong. You're perfect. The perfect boss, I mean.'

He laughed awkwardly. 'I guess I am pretty amazing.'

She didn't laugh. Instead, she glanced up at him through her eyelashes, Princess Diana style, before returning her gaze to the floor. 'You are.'

He was beginning to feel embarrassed now. Uncomfortable. He remembered the way she'd flushed on Saturday when he'd touched her shoulder. There hadn't been any signs since then that she liked him, which had allowed him to relax. But now, all these compliments. He looked at her, waiting for her to tell him what was wrong, half-hoping she wouldn't.

'I don't . . . I don't want to go home.'

'Why? What's going on, Mel?'

There was a long pause; so long he thought she'd gone into a trance. He was about to prompt her when she said, 'Do you remember I told you about those yobs who've been harassing me? And the police refusing to do anything about it?'

'I do.' It came back to him clearly. The way she'd described the ringleader having black eyes, as if he had no soul. The image had stayed with him. 'DJ, was it?'

'You remember.' She sounded amazed.

'Miracles do happen. But what about him? What has he done?'

There was a long pause before she was able to speak. 'Do you remember I told you they were creeping around my house at night, tapping on the windows, trying to scare me? Pointing and laughing at me when I went past them. Making rude gestures. All the stuff the police said they couldn't do anything about.'

'I remember.'

'It's got worse. Last night when I got home they were hanging around like they always do, but they'd started a fire down by the lake. This is about a hundred yards from my front door. Whenever they do this the smoke blows towards my house so I can't have the windows open. Plus they were making a racket. They had one of their cars parked there with all the doors open, the stereo pumping out some godawful noise. That terrible droning music they all listen to these days. And they were yelling and being lewd and smoking weed, which also stinks.'

'I get the picture.'

'Honestly, I believe in live-and-let-live, but as soon as I got out of the car the bonfire smoke blew into my face and this so-called music was going *boom boom boom*, and one of the girls said something and they all laughed – and I know it was directed at me because I could see them looking over. And DJ made a horrible hand gesture which got the others shrieking with laughter. I was tired and grumpy after a long day here so I marched over to them.'

'I don't blame you.' He could imagine how she must have felt at the end of her tether. It took courage to confront a rowdy gang of teenagers. 'But I'm guessing it didn't go well?'

She sighed. 'You could say that. The moment I started trying to talk, they all just laughed and started chanting at me, drowning me out. Then one of the girls said to DJ, "She wants you," and that made them all erupt with laughter again, and DJ looked me up and down – this amused sneer on his face – and said, "Nah, she's butters, mate." And then they all started clapping and chanting "Butters, butters."'

'"Butters"?'

'Yeah. It means ugly.'

Calvin could feel the anger stirring in his belly, like long-dead embers that had come back to life, glowing orange. No amount of breathing would stop this, because Mel was describing exactly the kind of person he hated, doing exactly the kind of thing that prodded the sore spot inside him. Stupid, cruel, entitled young men, not caring how much hurt they caused.

'It got worse,' Mel said. 'After they'd stopped laughing and chanting, I yelled at him. At DJ. I told him *he* was the ugly one, that I hoped he caught himself on fire and that I wouldn't piss on him to save him.' She put her face in her hands. 'Oh God, I can't believe I said that.'

'What was his reaction?'

'He got up and walked over to me. I was trembling. Like this.' She held out a hand to show him. 'He's tall and he loomed over me. And he said, "Say anything like that to me again, bitch, and I'll drown you in this fucking lake."'

'Oh my God.'

'You should have seen his face. He meant it, Calvin. He's evil. Even his friends looked shocked, like it wasn't a game anymore.'

'Did you call the police?'

'No. I told you, they never do anything. And now I'm scared. What if he's there, waiting for me?' She hugged herself. 'I don't want to go home.'

Calvin didn't hesitate. 'I'll come with you.'

'I can't ask you to do that.'

'I'm not taking no for an answer. I'm sure they were empty threats. But if they're there, I'll have a word with them, show them you've got friends who aren't going to let them get away with it.'

'I'm so grateful,' Mel said. 'I can't believe you're willing to do this for me.'

Calvin waved a hand. 'Oh, it's nothing. What else are friends for?'

She gathered up her belongings and he watched her for a minute, thinking ahead. He was alarmed to find that part of him relished the prospect of a confrontation, that his blood was heating up.

He knew what Vicky would say. That this was him trying to be a knight in shining armour. That, when it came to women who were in trouble, he had a saviour complex. And he had allowed her to diagnose him, hadn't he? Let her think she knew why he was like this.

It was all because of what had happened to Freya.

The thing was, Vicky was right.

But she didn't know everything. And if he had anything to do with it, she never would.

18

August 1995

It was one of the hottest days on record. Calvin had been half-listening to Radio 1 all afternoon, lying in a shady spot in the garden, devouring a novel called *The Secret History*, which he had started reading in an attempt to impress a girl. The girl was called Camilla, which was also the name of a character in the book. Calvin had fancied her all through sixth form, only gathering the courage to strike up a conversation with her in the final weeks of school, just before they took their A levels. As he read he made mental notes, and tried to memorise quotes that he could repeat to the real Camilla – a willowy redhead who smoked Marlboro Lights like it was her religion – the next time he saw her.

In the background, the sounds of Blur and Edwyn Collins and Seal drifted across the garden. *Newsbeat* came on and the newsreader announced that the temperature had peaked at over 35 degrees Celsius in some parts of the country. Here, in the small town of Reyton, on the eastern edge of Cumbria, in the shadow of the Pennines, it was 'only' 33.

In the distance, Calvin could hear a lawnmower buzzing. Children in a house down the street playing in a paddling pool. A dog barking incessantly.

Among the muted babble, he heard voices coming from the house. Freya, his seventeen-year-old sister, one year younger than Calvin, was home.

She'd just finished the lower sixth, and she was, Calvin was certain, his parents' favourite. While he'd drifted through school doing just well enough, Freya had got ten A-grade GCSEs. She was pretty too – with a smattering of freckles across her nose and a smile that had been perfected by years of wearing braces – but without being conceited about it.

She was changing, though. Their parents hadn't noticed yet. But Calvin had.

'Hey, Freya!' he called from his position on the lawn beneath the tree. 'Freya!'

She poked her head out through the patio doors.

'Can you bring me a can of Coke from the fridge?'

'Get it yourself!'

Groaning, he hauled himself up and made his way across a patch of scorched grass to the patio, dodging a fat bumblebee, drunk on sunshine, that wobbled into his path.

Freya was in the kitchen with her best friend, Emily. They were both seated at the dining table, eating strawberries from a large bowl. Calvin went to the fridge and took out a Coke. It was icy, beaded with condensation, and he held it against his forehead.

'*Scorchio*,' he said, quoting a character from a sketch show.

'I'm dying,' said Freya.

Emily fanned herself with a takeaway menu. 'I think I'm already dead.'

'Is that mine?' Calvin asked, noticing that his sister was wearing a Boo Radleys T-shirt. Definitely *his* T-shirt. He'd bought it when he'd seen them supporting Blur at Mile End Stadium back in June.

'I didn't think you'd mind. It's shrunk in the wash anyway.'

He was going to protest, but realised he didn't really mind.

'We should start getting ready,' Freya said to her friend, changing the subject.

'What for?' Calvin asked.

'There's a band playing at the Cricketers tonight.' That was the pub in the village. 'We're going to see them.'

'Who?'

'They're called Duchess. They're local.'

'In other words, they're bound to be shit.'

'Actually, they're all right,' Emily said. 'And the singer's *gorgeous*.'

'Do you want to come?' Freya asked. 'Or are you too busy being a grumpy twat?'

He laughed. The pub would be like the inside of an oven, full of sweaty bodies, and the band would undoubtedly be terrible. The beer garden would be packed out with old people.

'I saw Camilla today,' Freya said while he was still thinking. 'She asked me if I was your sister.'

'What? Really? What did you say? You'd better not have said anything embarrassing.'

'What, like telling her you still sleep with a teddy bear?'

Emily sniggered.

'I don't! I'm going to kill—'

'Jesus, take a chill pill. I didn't tell her anything that would put her off you. But I did find out she's going to be at the Cricketers tonight.'

ᛒ

Calvin didn't *only* go to the pub because there was a chance of bumping into the girl he fancied. He went because, although Freya was the golden child, the clever, pretty one, she also had a habit of getting herself into scrapes. And Calvin, as her older brother, saw it as his role to look out for her.

It had started when they were very small. He was the one who had to keep an eye on her when their parents were busy; the one who had to prevent her from eating Lego or putting the kitten down the toilet; the one who went running for help when she stuck a frozen pea up her nose or stood on a wasps' nest. Years later, when she started secondary school and he was in the second year, there had been an incident with a group of bullies – these girls who had decided they didn't like Freya. Calvin had noticed how unhappy his sister had become, her reluctance to go to school, her new habit of chewing her fingernails. She had started wetting the bed too.

She'd insisted everything was okay – until one day, after school, he'd found her surrounded by the group of girls, led by a third-year called Rose who was a notorious horror. They had Freya up against the wall, five or six of them, snarling insults and threats. Calvin, who was younger and physically smaller than Rose, said, 'Hey!' His voice was in the middle of breaking and it had come out as a squeak which made the bullies guffaw. But he didn't care. He squared up to Rose and the others, warning them that if they didn't leave his sister alone, he would kill them.

After that, they moved on to some other poor girl. But Freya was freed from their attentions.

Over the following years, there had been other incidents. More bullies. An aunt who came round their house occasionally and who'd picked on Freya, criticising the way she spoke, the things she ate, until Calvin told her to leave Freya alone. He knew eventually Freya would have to fight her own battles, but for now, why not look after her when she needed it? She had always seemed to appreciate it.

In the past, anyway. Recently, she had stayed away from him at school and kept to herself at home. When he'd overheard her

123

complaining to Emily about how her boss at her Saturday job was treating her unfairly, and he'd tried to offer advice, she'd told him to butt out. He'd hardly seen her all summer – which was why he was surprised that she'd encouraged him to come to the pub.

Until he got there and, out in the beer garden – which was just as busy as he'd feared, with seemingly everyone in the village crowding the trestle tables – she asked him to buy her and Emily a couple of bottles of Hooch, an alcoholic lemonade.

'Can't you buy them yourselves?'

'No. That barmaid knows we're only seventeen.'

'Is that the real reason you asked me to come?'

'Please, Cal,' Freya said. 'I promise to tell Camilla that you don't have any gross habits.'

'In other words,' added Emily, 'she's prepared to lie.'

'Haha. Very funny.'

But he went to the bar and bought their alcopops, along with a pint of lager for himself. It was relatively cool and quiet inside the pub, the hot weather having drawn everyone outside. He could see the band's equipment on the little stage in the corner, but there was no sign of them.

There was no sign of Freya or Emily either, when he went back into the beer garden. Annoyed, he lingered by the steps that led into the pub for a minute, then went looking for them.

He found them over in the corner, by the hedge, sitting on the grass with a group of blokes – and a few young women – who appeared to be in their early twenties.

Calvin paused for a moment to take in the scene. Freya was sitting cross-legged on the ground, listening to a guy with a shaggy mod haircut and round John Lennon glasses who was clearly trying to look like Liam Gallagher. The guy was talking animatedly and Freya was leaning forward, listening intently.

She was smoking a cigarette. Calvin was shocked. He'd never seen her smoke before.

He approached her and handed her the bottle of Hooch. Emily took her drink too, before turning back to talk to another member of this group – a tall, skinny guy with vivid ginger hair who was wearing a heavy army coat, on to which he had pinned several large home-made badges which bore slogans like *EAT THE RICH* and *I BELIEVE IN NIHILISM*. Calvin rolled his eyes at the guy's dedication to his message: *I'm so cool that even a heatwave can't make me take my coat off*. Skulking behind him, clutching a bottle of red wine, was a skinny young woman with pillar-box-red hair, wearing a Suede T-shirt, fishnet tights and huge Doc Marten boots that came up to her knees. She looked way too edgy to be in the beer garden of this Lake District pub. Calvin imagined she yearned to be in Camden, drinking with Blur.

This had to be the band.

'Who's this?' the guy Freya was talking to, the Liam Gallagher wannabe, asked.

'This is my brother, Calvin,' she replied in a bored tone. She tapped ash from her cigarette and took a drag, sending out a plume into the still air. 'Calvin, this is Milo.'

'Nice one,' said Milo. 'Family's what it's all about, yeah?'

Calvin tried not to laugh. Milo might have looked like the singer in a working-class band from Manchester, but he sounded like a minor royal. A posh kid playing at being common. Despite the sweltering temperature he too was wearing a coat: a blue parka, complete with furry hood.

'You're the singer with Duchess?' Calvin asked.

'Guilty as charged,' said Milo. He pointed his own cigarette towards the ginger bloke wearing the army coat, and the woman in the massive Doc Martens. 'That's my brother, Simeon, and Piper, my big sister. Aka my rhythm section.'

'They're a family band,' said Freya. 'Like Oasis.'

'One day,' Milo said, 'we'll be ten times bigger than them.'

Calvin looked at Freya, expecting to see amusement on her face, but she was gazing at Milo like she actually believed him. Oh God . . . She really liked this idiot.

'Camilla just arrived,' Freya said, nodding towards the pub garden entrance, and Calvin turned to look.

'That your bird?' Milo asked. 'She's well fit.'

Calvin cringed – who said 'bird'? – and Freya frowned.

'Not as fit as you, though,' Milo told her.

Couldn't Freya see this guy was full of crap? Calvin had to get away, and not just because he wanted to talk to Camilla.

'Looking forward to your set,' he said, then nodded at Freya. 'Don't leave without me, okay? I'll walk you home.'

She glared at him. 'I'm not a baby.'

'Yeah, big bruv,' said Milo. 'She's a grown woman.'

Rather than tell the singer that, actually, she had only just turned seventeen – realising that it would make him look like a hypocrite for buying her alcohol – he walked away.

As he made his way over to Camilla, he bumped into his best friend, James, who he had known since they were at infant school. James was dark-haired, tall and skinny, a ball of nervous energy who lived on a diet of Coca-Cola and hamburgers but who never gained weight. He lived in a tiny house and was the best in their class at drawing, as well as having a talent for finding copies of *Playboy* in the woods.

James asked Calvin if he wanted a drink, then went to the bar, leaving Calvin with Camilla, who gave him a big hug. She was sweaty but smelled great, and he had to step away quickly to prevent his body from rudely announcing how pleased he was to see her.

'I love that book you recommended,' he said. '*The Secret History*.'

'Cool. I knew you would.'

James reappeared with drinks. The three of them chatted, and Calvin noticed that Camilla kept playing with her hair, which was, apparently, a good sign. He forgot all about Freya and her new wannabe rock-star friend, until James said, 'Who's that bloke Freya's talking to?'

Camilla grimaced. 'Oh God, not Milo.'

'You know him?' Calvin asked, surprised.

'Yeah. Him and Simeon and Piper. The Stewart siblings. They all went to Bramblesham.'

That was the expensive private school on the outskirts of the village.

'Milo is the youngest. He's three years older than us. The other two, Simeon and Piper, are twins. My mum did some gardening for them one summer and took me with her to their house. It's a flipping mansion.'

'Really?'

'Yeah. Well, maybe that's a slight exaggeration, but it's like this huge house and it's absolutely stuffed full of all this mad shit. Taxidermied animals and Persian carpets and grand pianos and millions of ancient books. These posh little dogs running around everywhere, shitting on the expensive rugs. They've even got a swimming pool. Apparently, their mum is the daughter of some famous writer who left her the house and tons of money. I didn't know it at the time, but later my mum told me the house smelled of weed – and dog shit – and that both Mr and Mrs Stewart are hippies who let their kids do whatever they like.'

'Rich hippies,' said James.

'Yeah. I've also heard that Milo is a total slut. Shags everything that moves. That's definitely his main motivation for starting this band.'

Calvin looked over and saw that both Milo and Freya were on their feet now. She was standing very close to him, laughing at something he was saying.

'He sounds like a twat,' James said with a frown.

'He's worse than that. He's bad news,' Camilla said. 'Very bad news.'

19

Vicky drove through Elderbridge, knuckles white on the wheel. She couldn't wait to get home. She was going to have a long soak in the bath, open a bottle of wine and surprise Calvin. He wasn't expecting her home till eight and it was only half six.

She was looking forward to seeing his look of happy surprise.

There had been moments during her time at the spa when she'd begun to wonder if she was losing her marbles. It was a horrible feeling, like an itch deep in her brain. The spa was supposed to make her feel better, relaxed. Unwound. Instead, having time to relax and free up space in her always-busy mind had done nothing but allow all the bad, paranoid thoughts to rush in.

It had started well, though.

When she'd reached the spa, she'd gone straight to the pool and swum twenty lengths before going into the steam room. After that, she'd gone for a back and shoulder massage. A young woman with strong hands had instructed her to lie on her front on the massage table, and complimented her on her skin before getting to work.

Ten minutes in, the masseuse had paused and said, 'Are you okay? This is supposed to be relaxing but your muscles appear to be getting tenser.'

'I'm fine,' Vicky had said. 'Please, carry on.'

But the truth was, she wasn't fine.

It had started on Saturday night, when they'd got home and she'd become convinced someone had been in the house. She was sure she hadn't shut Jarvis in the bedroom. She never closed doors behind her when she was at home. There was no need unless it was freezing and she was trying to keep the heat inside a room. Even then, she usually forgot. She had been, as her mum always said, born in a barn.

But she had scoured the house then and there had been no sign that anything was missing. No sign of forced entry either. You couldn't call the police because your bedroom door was shut, could you?

She was also convinced Jarvis wouldn't have done it. He had been known to pull doors open by hooking his paw around them. But why would he *close* a door? She just couldn't picture him doing it.

Calvin had kept telling her she must have shut it and forgotten. She'd wanted to believe him. She had gone away vowing to put it behind her.

But lying there on the massage table, feeling herself relax as the young woman attempted to work the tension out of her shoulders and the knots from her spine, she'd thought: *What if it was him?*

What if it was Calvin who'd been in the house and shut Jarvis in their bedroom?

What if he'd gone home between closing the cafe and picking her up and taking her to the restaurant? Gone home with someone else.

Taken another woman into their home. *Into their bedroom.*

And now he was gaslighting her.

Her mind kept going back to the conversation she'd had with Louise on Saturday afternoon after leaving the coffee shop and coming back to work.

'You won't believe this,' Vicky had said. 'This Mel woman. The one who was sending all those messages to Calvin.'

'The one he's given a job to?'

'Yes.' When she'd first told Louise, she'd said it like it was all a big joke. Like, *you won't guess what my daft husband has done.* They'd laughed good-naturedly about it. Now it didn't seem so funny, and Vicky needed someone to talk to. 'Guess what? She's been here, looking for a cat. And now she's changed her mind, if she was ever really interested in the first place.'

Louise had been halfway through an inventory, totting up how much food they had left. She paused to give Vicky her full attention. 'You're joking.'

'I wish I was. You weren't here when she came in. I think you were collecting that poodle. But she strolled in here saying she wanted to adopt a cat. Don't you think it's weird? Suspicious?'

She was looking for Louise to tell her she was being silly. Overreacting. But instead Louise said, 'It's totally suspicious. Like, well, she came here to take a look at the competition.'

That was precisely Vicky's fear.

'What does she look like?' Louise asked.

'Mousy. Petite. She's not Calvin's type.'

'Hmm,' Louise said.

'What?'

There was a long delay. 'I don't want to worry you, but she sounds like one of *them.* An internet shopper.'

Vicky had never heard this phrase before.

'The kind of person who sees something she wants online and thinks she can have it. Everything is just a click away. Put it in your basket and you're done.'

'Are you making all this up?' Vicky asked.

'No. There was an article. Plus it happened to a friend of mine. She was happily married, thought her husband would never look at another woman, good sex life and all that. And then he met this other woman online, in some forum, and they started messaging

131

back and forth. Then the woman suggested they meet and he agreed because, well, he didn't want to hurt her feelings.'

That was exactly what Calvin was like. Afraid of hurting people's feelings. Women's feelings, anyway.

Louise went on: 'She'd been going through a tough time, she said. Next thing my friend knew, he was moving in with her.' She shook her head. 'With men, novelty always wins. Novelty and flattery. They want shiny toys and someone to boost their ego.'

Louise had gone back to counting trays of dog food. 'That's why I stick with cats. I mean, yeah, they'll go to whoever's going to feed them the tastiest treats as well, just like men. But at least you can lock the cat flap and keep them indoors. You can't lock a man up, unfortunately.'

ω

At the spa, Vicky had forced herself to push the paranoia away and enjoy the rest of the massage. She just about managed it, until later, when she woke up in the middle of the night and it all came flooding back. An image of a naked Calvin, in their bed with Mel. And Louise's voice, telling her men liked *novelty* and *flattery*.

She sat up. It was 3 a.m., the worst possible time to have such thoughts. The time when the rational mind was at its weakest, and all the dark emotions and crazy twists of logic rushed in to take good sense's place.

This was completely out of character for her. She wasn't a jealous person, had never acted like this before, certainly not with Calvin. Back when she was a teenager she'd had a boyfriend who'd messed her around and cheated on her, and she'd been justifiably jealous then. But she'd emerged from that toxic relationship vowing she would never allow herself to be treated like that again. That she would only be with someone who respected her. Someone she could trust.

She had never had any doubts that Calvin loved her. She'd never caught him flirting with another woman and he had never shown any sign that he was bored in their marriage. On top of that, she didn't really think Mel was his type. Most of his exes – not that there had been many – had been curvy, like Vicky. His celebrity crushes were quirky, alternative types who made Calvin laugh. Mel was nothing like that. As far as Vicky could tell from their two brief encounters, Mel was far from a great wit, and her looks and personality were hardly quirky.

There was something about her, though . . . something that set all Vicky's warning bells off, as if she were a grazing animal who had detected a predator lurking nearby. It seemed ridiculous when Mel appeared so ordinary on the surface, but if the internet age had taught its citizens anything it was that predators came in many forms, and most of them wouldn't show their teeth until the last second. An 'internet shopper', Louise had said. It sounded like something a journalist had made up. But it also rang true. It was a step up from the parasocial relationship, which was almost wholly one-sided. Vicky knew people who spent hours every week scouring property websites, fantasising about the homes they wanted to live in. She even had one or two friends who had ended up living in those dream homes. Maybe Mel was like that, but instead of targeting her dream home she had targeted her dream man.

So, at three in the morning, Vicky picked up her phone and tried to find out what she could about Mel.

It wasn't easy. Mel's social feed was one of the least interesting Vicky had ever seen. The latest photo was of the counter at Therapy, and the display case where the cakes were kept.

Am now working at the best cafe in the Lakes! read the caption. *Got the best boss too. Come along and try his delicious creations!*

There it was. Flattery. It was how she had started her relationship with Calvin, by sliding into his DMs and praising him, even though he hadn't even made the video that had got him all that attention. Vicky wondered if Mel kept the compliments flowing when she and Calvin were at work.

Praise, however, wasn't the most effective weapon if you wanted to get Calvin to notice you. There was another that was far more powerful.

This was what Vicky worried about most. If Mel was clever, if she was able to figure Calvin out, she would discover his Achilles heel.

All Mel needed to do was act like she needed rescuing.

Vicky was aware of several women Calvin had done the old 'knight in shining armour' thing for in his life. First, there was Wendy, who he'd worked with at the hotel. When her landlord started harassing her, Calvin had gone round for a word. Then there was Kareena, a young woman who used to live on their road, whose boss was a bully. Calvin had helped her find a new job. Finally, there had been Jenny, an old friend of Vicky's, who had confessed to Calvin at their wedding that her husband often got violent. Calvin had found a shelter for her to go to and driven her to the police station to report him. Jenny was divorced now, and happy, and told everyone that Calvin was an angel.

It had only come out later, when Vicky and Calvin had been married for a year, why he was like this. It was because of his sister, and her death. Vicky had noticed that all the women Calvin felt the urge to help were the victims, in one way or another, of horrible men.

Hating herself a little, Vicky next logged in to the Therapy account. She wanted to see if there were any further message exchanges between Calvin and BlondieMel. There weren't. *But*, whispered the voice of paranoia, which sounded very much like

Louise, *why would there need to be?* They could say anything they wanted to in person. When they were alone in the cafe.

Or, she thought – paranoia dragging her back to that closed bedroom door – alone at Calvin and Vicky's house.

She finally forced herself to put down the phone at six. Watched the sun come up then went out for a run around the grounds of the spa. Out in the fresh air, she was able to talk some sense into herself. Calvin loved her. Calvin wouldn't be interested in Mel no matter how much she flattered him, how novel she was, and although he had a need to help women in distress he'd never dated any of them, as far as Vicky knew.

On top of that, she reminded herself she had no evidence he'd been in their house with Mel. Maybe the cat *had* bashed into the door and closed it. Maybe a draft had blown the door shut. Maybe Calvin had popped home for some other reason he didn't want her to know about – a surprise he had planned for her, perhaps.

By the time she got back to her room and into the shower, she'd put the hours of madness behind her. She went back to bed, intending to lose herself in her novel. Almost instantly, she fell asleep, not waking up till lunchtime.

ϖ

Vicky had listened to the radio all the way home, a station that played greatest hits, mostly from the eighties and nineties. She sang along loudly to The Cure and The Waterboys. Singing was cathartic. It got the endorphins flowing. Perhaps, instead of a spa, next time she'd book herself into a karaoke booth for the weekend.

'The Whole of the Moon' ended and the news came on.

'Police in Cumbria have appealed again for witnesses following the murder of Drigg resident Leo James, who was found buried on the beach close to where he lived.'

Then that cop came on, the one with all the red hair. Vicky had watched the dramatisation of that serial killer case she'd been involved in.

'We are looking for anyone who might have had contact with Leo, including on social media, in the weeks leading up to his death, as well as anyone who knew him at any point in the past. A sketch of Leo James can be found on the Cumbria Police website. We are hoping someone will come forward who will be able to tell us more about him and his life.'

A sketch? Did that mean they didn't have any photos of him? It was bizarre, and it sounded like the police investigation had stalled.

Vicky parked in the driveway and went inside, eager to get a hug from her husband. But the house was empty, apart from Jarvis, who ran up to her making that lovely chirruping noise that she liked so much. She picked him up and kissed him on his head, carrying him towards the kitchen to feed him.

As she was about to enter the kitchen, she looked up at the doorframe. There it was: the security camera she'd put there yesterday before leaving for the spa, the one she'd ordered when she'd gone to bed on Saturday night. The camera was tiny and discreet; unlikely to be spotted by an intruder.

Or a cheating husband, said the little voice.

She was confident Calvin would never notice it. There were cobwebs that had been up there for two years.

The camera connected to an app, which she had downloaded to her computer. Putting the camera up, she had sworn to herself she would only leave it there for a couple of weeks. Just until she was sure that everything was fine. She had deliberately installed the app on her computer and not her phone so she wouldn't be able to spend her time at the spa checking it obsessively.

It was quarter to seven. Calvin ought to be home by now. Where was he? She guessed he was still at work – *with Mel?* – or had popped into the supermarket on the way back. Maybe he'd decided to nip into the pub. She almost phoned or texted him to let him know she was home early, but no, she wanted him to be surprised when he walked through the door. She thought she might take him straight to bed.

But first, she needed a bath.

She went into their bedroom, because she always preferred to use the bath in their en-suite even though the water pressure was terrible and the tub always took ages to fill. While she waited she went back into the bedroom, thinking she should start unpacking, shaking her head slightly at how Calvin had left the bed unmade.

Unable to bear seeing the quilt like that, crooked and hanging off the edge of the mattress, she grabbed the edge of the duvet and lifted it so she could straighten it out – and something caught her eye. In fact, for a moment she couldn't believe she was seeing it. She thought she must be hallucinating. Perhaps she was back in her hotel room at 3 a.m. and was imagining this.

But no. The object that had been hidden beneath the duvet, on Vicky's side of the bed, was real.

She picked it up. It was a pendant on a fine chain, the clasp broken as if someone had pulled at it and snapped it. The pendant was made of silver and was in the shape of a bee, wings outstretched, stripes across its back.

A woman's pendant.

But not Vicky's.

20

Calvin followed Mel's Land Rover on to country roads that hugged the edge of the lake. She indicated then turned right on to a lane that was crowded by shrubbery on either side, and only wide enough for a single vehicle. Calvin didn't think he had ever been out here before, this hamlet on the other side of Foxton Water from Elderbridge. Drigg, where that guy had been found buried and drowned, was close to here, on the coast.

They reached the end of the lane, which opened out into a clearing, and suddenly they were right beside the lake, shrubbery giving way to reveal the great expanse of water. The road continued alongside the lake and, to the right of that, stretching down to the water, was a beach, if that was the correct word. The ground looked rough and was dotted with rocks and boulders. Somewhere a little further along this beach, smoke rose into the air.

A bonfire. Opposite where this fire burned, Calvin saw several cottages. Mel indicated again and turned left, pulling up outside the middle dwelling. Calvin parked behind her and took a moment to get his bearings. The cottages were on the western edge of the lake, with Elderbridge on the other side. Sellafield was to the north, and Drigg Beach, where Leo James had been buried, a stone's throw to the west. Between here and Drigg was the caravan park where, according to Mel, this DJ character lived.

Getting out, he was immediately hit by the smell of smoke, which was blowing straight towards them from the beach. It made his eyes sting. On top of that, he could hear the thud of music and the sounds of laughter.

'I take it that's them,' he said to Mel as she got out of her car. 'DJ and his friends?'

'Yeah.'

From where they were standing, his view of the youths was obscured by a large tree that stood between the road and the beach. The smoke further obscured them too – a literal smokescreen – but their silhouettes flickered in the glow from the fire. It looked like there were three of them.

They must have seen Mel arrive home, because the next thing Calvin knew, the volume of the music had been turned down to be replaced by a chant.

'But-ters. But-ters. But-ters.'

This was followed by a roar of laughter.

Mel's face went pink and he saw her jaw tighten. She was about to start crying again and he squeezed his hands into fists.

'I'm going to talk to them,' he said, starting towards the road.

'No.' She grabbed his forearm, holding him back. 'They're dangerous.'

He stepped a little to the left, so he could get a better look past the tree, and saw that one of them – DJ, presumably – had come forward and was standing beside the front of the car the music was emanating from. He was stretched to his full height, peering over at Mel, a big grin on his face. He held up a can of lager in a mocking toast.

'I bet they're all mouth and no trousers,' Calvin said. His blood was up and Mel was looking at him like she'd never seen him properly before. Well, she hadn't seen this side of him before. Few people had. 'Wait here.'

Before Mel could protest again, he strode across the road towards the beach.

Seeing him coming, the three youths laughed again and one of the girls said, 'It's Butters's bae,' which made them erupt with mirth and start chanting 'Butters's bae, Butters's bae.' Calvin had no idea what 'bae' meant and he didn't care. Their tone was enough to tell him all he needed to know.

They fell quiet when Calvin reached them. The guy closest to the car, the alpha male, was obviously DJ. He was about twenty-one, with sandy-blond hair and a chiselled jaw. A good-looking kid, Calvin thought. DJ's pupils were dilated and Calvin realised that, along with the bonfire smoke, the smell of cannabis hung in the air.

The others were sitting around the fire. A girl with a septum ring and a boy who, even sitting down, appeared to be enormous – both big and tall. They both looked a little younger than DJ, maybe seventeen, and they were grinning with that stoned, happy look he recognised from his student days.

'Butters's bae,' said the girl with the septum ring, and the boy giggled.

'Who's this?' said a female voice behind him, and Calvin turned to see a young woman walking towards them from the edge of the lake, where he assumed she'd been answering a call of nature.

He did a double take. *Freya.* For a moment, he found himself frozen, unable to speak. It was her, back from the dead. The smattering of freckles across her nose. The straightened teeth. The amused, lightly mocking expression. It was his sister.

But of course it wasn't his sister. This girl, or young woman – she must have been eighteen or nineteen – had hair a shade darker, broader shoulders, a different-shaped nose.

'Why are you staring at me like you've seen a ghost?' she said.

'I'm sorry. I . . .' He tried to regain his balance, turning to their leader as the new arrival took a seat beside her friends. 'You're DJ, right?'

'You're famous, bruv,' said the other boy, who had to be at least six foot four.

'Shut up, Kai.'

DJ's smile had disappeared, and Calvin realised he should be afraid. There were four of them, including the enormous Kai, and he knew, from his threat to drown Mel in the lake, that DJ had a violent streak. It wasn't the sensible thing to do – striding over here trying to be the big hero.

But at times like this, Calvin was far from sensible or rational. The heat inside him took over. That too-familiar itch. The whoosh of blood in his ears. The cortisol flooding his body.

'You're going to leave her alone,' he found himself saying.

DJ paused for a second, as if he was surprised that this older man appeared so up for a fight. Then he said, 'Who – Butters?' He nodded across the road at Mel. From this distance she was just a small figure with indistinguishable features. But they could all tell she was looking in this direction.

DJ waved at her, a stupid piss-taking grin on his face which made Calvin want to punch him.

'That's not her name,' said Calvin.

'No shit,' said DJ. 'I thought it actually was.'

'We know *your* name,' said Septum Ring. 'You're that chef. The one who owns that bakery in the village.'

The other girl, the one who looked so much like Freya, had her phone out, and she held it up to show the famous video. 'It's better than sex,' said Maud on the screen, and the two girls and Kai laughed.

DJ said, 'You're Chef Calvin?'

That was what everyone called him on social media.

'I went in there with my mum,' said Kai. 'Ten out of ten, would recommend.'

'And Butters is your mate?' DJ asked, looking over towards where Mel stood watching.

'She works for me.'

'Works under him,' said Septum Ring, which made them all splutter.

'Listen, mate,' said DJ, his voice and attitude softening a little. 'We're only fucking with her. It's a laugh, yeah? She gets it.'

'She doesn't *get it*. She finds it scary.'

'For real?' He seemed astonished.

Calvin almost said *For real* back, but stopped himself. DJ's change in attitude was allowing Calvin's blood to cool a little. 'Yes. Do you really think it's big and clever to call a woman ugly and chant it at her? You might think we're ancient, but we can decipher modern slang.'

'Translation: he knows how to use Google,' said Kai out of the side of his mouth.

DJ glanced over at Mel again, then produced a spliff from his pocket. He lit it and took a lungful, exhaling it in Calvin's direction. 'Want a bit?'

'No, I don't. And don't blow it at me. That's another thing – your bonfire smoke blows directly at Mel's house.'

Calvin realised he might have just given away Mel's name, but DJ didn't flinch, which made Calvin think he probably already knew it.

'Yeah,' he went on. 'It gets inside her windows. Makes the whole cottage stink.'

'So what are we supposed to do?' Kai asked.

'Take yourselves somewhere else. There must be plenty of places around here that aren't near houses.'

'Huh. Not many. And we like it here.'

'Why don't you go to Drigg Beach? It's not that far. The point is, you need to stop harassing her.'

'All right,' said DJ, with a hint of a sneer. 'I hear you. We won't call her Butters anymore. We'll call her Mel.'

'I don't want you to call her anything. You need to leave her alone.'

'Or what's going to happen?' Kai asked.

'What always happens to dickheads like you.'

Kai turned to DJ. 'Can you believe this old guy is actually threatening us? We ought to—'

But to Calvin's surprise, DJ said, 'Yeah, whatever. We'll leave her alone.' Kai started to protest and DJ said, 'Shut it. It's cool. It was getting boring anyway.'

Calvin was taken aback, but pleased. 'Good. If it happens again I'm going to make sure she calls the police and that they take it seriously.' He looked at Kai and the two girls, whose names he hadn't yet learned. 'And I'll talk to your parents.'

'My mum won't give a fuck,' said Septum Ring.

'Mine neither,' said the Freya lookalike.

From the lack of conviction in their voices, Calvin didn't believe either of them.

As he was about to walk away, DJ said, 'Hey, can I ask you something?'

'I suppose so.'

'Do you believe in Heaven?'

'What?'

'Heaven. Is it a real place?'

'It definitely is,' said Kai. 'It's between Jessica's legs.'

'Fuck off!' the girl with the septum ring yelled, punching Kai on the upper arm. 'You're disgusting.'

But DJ wasn't laughing. He seemed serious, still waiting for an answer.

'Why are you asking me that?' Calvin asked.

'Just wondering, that's all. Because if you believe in Heaven, you have to believe in Hell, right?'

Calvin stared at him, a horrible, swirling sensation in his guts. He noticed that the Freya lookalike was watching him, a deep frown making the resemblance to his sister even stronger. He had to get out of here. Now.

'Goodnight,' Calvin said, and he walked away, trying to look like he was unruffled and calm.

21

Mel was standing by her front door, twisting her hands together, her face as white as bone.

'What happened?' she asked in a half-whisper. 'What did they say?'

He shrugged. 'I had a word with them. I don't think they'll bother you again.'

Her voice dropped further, eyes widening. 'Did you threaten them? Scare them?' She seemed disconcertingly thrilled by the idea.

Calvin, on the other hand, was still shaken. 'No, of course not. I explained to them that if they keep doing it we'll go to the police.'

'Oh. Right. What . . . did they say about me?'

He hesitated for a second, trying to decide whether to be honest. 'Nothing, really.'

A moment of silence, broken by Mel saying, 'Do you want to come in?' There was the faintest tremor in her voice. The aftermath of the tension she must have felt waiting for him to return. 'For a cup of tea?'

He looked at his watch. It was just after seven. 'I ought to get back. Vicky will be home soon.'

'Please, Calvin. Just for ten minutes. What if . . . what if they come over the moment you leave?'

'They won't.'

She looked at him with big, fearful eyes, glancing over towards the beach. Could he really just leave her here, terrified? He double-checked his watch. Vicky wasn't due home for another hour. And he owed Mel, didn't he, for everything she'd done to help get him through this crazy, busy period? He followed her gaze towards the beach. It looked like DJ and his friends were packing up their stuff, but there was a chance they might come over to harass Mel as soon as he left, wasn't there? Calvin wanted to go home. But she looked so worried. He couldn't say no.

'Okay. A cup of tea. But I can only stay for ten minutes.'

'Of course.'

He followed Mel into the cottage. It was an old place, with low ceilings and narrow hallways. He even had to stoop a little to get through the front door.

'Was this place designed for Hobbits?'

'Luckily I'm only little,' Mel said, leading him into a tiny kitchen that was dominated by an Aga. She lifted its cover and placed an old-fashioned kettle on the hotplate. The whole place was sparkling clean, so much so that it barely looked lived in. Beside the sink was a draining board that contained a single plate and mug.

Calvin yawned.

'Tired?'

'I'm *exhausted*. It's been a crazy week.' He could also feel the adrenaline draining from his system after the confrontation with DJ and friends.

'Why don't you go through to the sitting room?' Mel said. 'This will take a while to boil.'

He was itching to leave, but found himself trapped by politeness.

'Can I use your loo?' he asked.

'Of course. It's at the end of the hallway.'

As he went into the downstairs toilet – it was literally the size of a closet, with a loo that looked ancient and a miniscule basin, and the smell of damp seeping out of the walls – his phone pinged. It was Vicky.

Where are you?

He hesitated. Vicky was weird about Mel. He really didn't want to tell her he was in her house. But he never told lies to his wife, not even little white ones. She would understand when he told her he'd come here because Mel was being harassed by some yobs. She should be proud of him, even though he knew exactly what she would say. *Playing the knight in shining armour again.* He bristled as he imagined the conversation. Someone had to stand up to the bullies of this world, didn't they? Even if . . .

He didn't allow himself to complete the thought.

At Mel's. About to head back. Are you home already? x

Three dots appeared, showing she was writing a reply. Then they vanished. He waited, then sent another message.

Hello?

No reply. Sighing, he tapped out a final text:

See you soon. Love you xx

He peed, washed his hands using the tiny sliver of soap on the basin, then checked his phone. Again, no reply. His last text hadn't even been read.

He went back towards the kitchen, deciding he wasn't going to have time to drink a cup of tea here. He needed to get back, talk to Vicky, tell her what had happened.

But as he reached the kitchen Mel appeared holding a tray containing two mugs and a plate of cookies. 'I thought you might like to try these oatmeal cookies. I baked them myself last night. I know, I spend all week baking then come home and do it. I'm obsessed.'

This all came out in a single breath.

'I'm sorry, Mel. They look great but I've got to go.'

Her face fell. 'Really? You don't want your tea?'

'Vicky just texted me. I think she's at home already.'

'Oh. I see. You're one of those men.'

'What does that mean?'

'Under the thumb. They call, you come running.'

He was shocked. If Mel had got her first proper glimpse of him this evening, he was also seeing a different side of Mel.

But then she laughed and said, 'I'm just kidding. But I'm sure Vicky can wait another five minutes. Come on, sit down, try a cookie. I really want your opinion.' Another laugh. 'I promise I'm not going to keep you prisoner.'

She set the tray down on the coffee table and the smell made his stomach growl. He was thirsty too. And he *wasn't* the kind of guy who said 'How high?' when his wife said 'Jump'.

'All right. Five minutes.'

Like every other room he'd visited in this cottage, the sitting room, as Mel called it, was small. Cosy, if you wanted to be kind. There was a small sofa and an armchair, a TV, and a real fireplace that didn't appear to have been used for a while. Mel set the tray on the coffee table and gestured for him to take the sofa while she sat in the armchair. He picked up his tea and took a sip.

'Are you going to try a cookie?'

He bit into one. It had an almost-burnt smell, crisp edges but a soft, buttery centre, sugar hitting his tongue as he chewed it.

'Mmm. That's really good.'

She glowed. 'It's an old family recipe.'

'You should bake some for the coffee shop. I think they'd be big sellers.'

'Really?' She looked like she might burst with happiness. 'I'm sure they're not good enough. They're not as nice as yours.'

'I think they are.' He talked with his mouth full. The cookie really was delicious, and he was hungry and tired, craving sweetness. 'Do you mind if I have another?'

'Oh no, of course.' She held out the plate. She was glowing with pride. 'Help yourself.'

He took a second and ate it more slowly this time, washing it down with tea. He stood and went over to the window, which gave a view of the lake. The sunset was in full effect now, pink and orange shimmering across the water.

'Wow. I can see why you live here.'

'It's beautiful, isn't it?'

The other cottages were dark, seemingly unoccupied. Calvin commented on it.

'They're Airbnbs,' Mel said. 'Like so many places in the Lakes now. It's like a plague. These second-home owners who buy places just to rent them out. They stand empty for most of the winter. That's why DJ and his mob target me. I'm the only one actually living here.' She paused. 'Are they still out there?'

'No, it looks like they've gone. So DJ lives on the caravan park?'

Mel took a sip of her own tea. 'I think so. I guess he can't afford to live somewhere proper.'

'Not everyone's lucky enough to have a house.'

Mel frowned. 'If he got himself a proper job. Tried to make something of himself.'

She said something else but Calvin was finding it hard to concentrate. He was so tired. He knew he really ought to get going, but he couldn't get his legs to move.

He could hear Mel still talking, saying something about DJ and drugs, accusing him of being a dealer, but it was like she was a radio that was playing far away. It had come on suddenly. The wooziness. The thickness of his tongue in his mouth.

Mel leaned forward, eyes wide with concern. 'Are you okay?'

'I need to go.' He tried to get up, but he couldn't move. His body felt like it weighed twice as much as it should. He couldn't speak either. He had a sudden, desperate longing for a bed and a pillow.

'Calvin?' Mel's voice was coming from far away. 'Hello?'

A huge yawn made him stretch his jaw open like a python about to consume a pig. He was so tired. So very, very tired.

'Let me get you some water.'

Mel stood and he tried to say 'Yes please' but nothing came out. A moment later, he was gone.

22

Vicky sat on the edge of the bed, the necklace with its broken clasp cradled in her palm. Her hand was shaking so hard that the edges of the object had become blurred. She squeezed her eyes shut.

Somebody else's necklace. In Vicky and Calvin's bed. The kind of necklace that only a woman would wear.

A woman like Mel. Because she wore chains with animal pendants, didn't she. She'd had one on when she'd come to the pet shelter. Not a bee but some other creature. A turtle, was it? Something like that. This bee pendant was exactly the kind of thing she'd wear.

There had to be an explanation. An innocent explanation.

Oh yeah. Another woman's necklace in your bed. What possible innocent explanation could there be for that?

This hadn't been left in her bed by accident. Mel had done this deliberately. She wanted Vicky to know she was fucking her husband. She wanted to blow things up. This was a declaration of war.

Maybe it wasn't Mel's? But who else's could it be? Vicky had no other suspects. Mel had come into their lives like a whirlwind. This time last week neither she nor Calvin had even heard of her. She was an astonishingly fast worker. Less internet shopper, more heat-seeking missile.

She sat there, trying to decide what to do, how to react. Her thoughts were moving too fast, tumbling over one another in a stream not of consciousness but of nonsense. Beneath the tumble of images – a naked Calvin, straddled by Mel; Mel deliberately pulling off the necklace and leaving it here; the two of them in the kitchen at the coffee shop, leaning close, laughing at Vicky – there was a strange noise, the rush of water.

It wasn't in her head. It was coming from the bathroom.

She leapt up and ran into the en-suite. The tub was full to the brim, overflowing, and she almost skidded on the soaked bathroom floor. She lunged for the taps – why did it take so long to turn them all the way off? – and yanked at the plug. Slowly, the bathwater drained away.

At least cleaning up was a distraction from the pain in her chest. She went out to the cupboard where they kept the gym towels and all the other old ones that she'd thought might come in handy one day, and spent the next twenty minutes using the towels to soak up the water, wringing them out in the now-empty tub. Finally, when the floor was merely damp, she left the extractor fan running and shut the door.

She went back into the bedroom, trying not to cry.

Her suitcase was there on the bed, still packed, and she pictured herself putting it back into the car and driving away. She would check herself in to a hotel somewhere and wait. Let Calvin sweat. Make him worry about her. She knew that if she disappeared he would be frantic, desperate to find her. It almost made her happy, picturing him tearing his hair out, searching for her, checking his phone every two minutes, going insane with worry.

Except maybe he wouldn't worry. Maybe he'd be glad she'd gone. Perhaps if she ran she would simply be giving him space to carry on his affair with Mel.

Imagining Calvin frantically checking his phone made her retrieve hers from her bag. She texted Calvin: *Where are you?*

She didn't add a kiss. She wondered if he'd notice this pathetic passive-aggressive act.

He replied quickly.

At Mel's. About to head back. Are you home already? x

She bent over and put her head between her knees, gulping back air. *At Mel's.* At least he was being honest. Or was he preparing her for the blow? That he was going to come home and tell her he was leaving her? Or perhaps he would confess and beg for forgiveness. *It didn't mean anything. It was just sex.*

She started to write a reply but had no idea what to say, so she deleted it and put the phone down on the bed.

Of course. She needed to check the security camera's app. Because if Calvin had brought Mel or any other woman into the house, it would be on there.

Her laptop was in the spare bedroom, the one they used as a study. But opening her laptop she found it was dead, on zero per cent. She plugged it in but couldn't sit there staring at it, waiting for it to wake up. It was an old machine that took ten minutes to boot up if you allowed the battery to drain.

She needed a drink.

She left the study and headed for the kitchen. The sun was setting outside and the light in the house was fading, so she switched on the lights then opened the fridge and fished inside for her emergency bottle of Chardonnay, the one Calvin was under strict instructions not to drink.

If he's shared it with that bitch, she thought, *that will be it. The point from which there will be no return.*

Which must mean, she supposed, that she believed there was still a way back from this.

The wine was there, behind a lettuce that was going brown and a jar of chutney that she kept meaning to throw away. She opened the bottle and filled a glass almost to the brim. The glass, she noticed, still bore white marks from the dishwasher. They needed a new dishwasher; the current one had begun to make a grinding noise. They'd bought it when they moved into this house back—

Why the hell was she thinking about dishwashers?

She swallowed a mouthful of wine, then another, then heard a noise outside.

She went to the front window and looked out, unable to see anything in the darkness.

Back in the kitchen, Jarvis appeared and jumped up on the counter. She stroked him as she sipped her wine.

'What am I going to do if I find something on the camera, Jarv?' she asked him as he rubbed his head against her hand. She took another sip of wine. The laptop might have enough charge now but she hesitated, putting it off.

If her life was about to change, she wanted to finish this glass of wine first.

23

In the dream, Calvin was lying on a beach. Through his closed eye-lids, patterns of light danced across his vision, the hot sun kissing his face, the sand warm beneath his bare back. He tried to open his eyes but the sun was too bright and it burned, forcing him to keep them shut. Then someone was kissing him. Unfamiliar lips against his. A tongue probing, encouraging him to part his lips, then that tongue in his mouth, and he was returning the kiss in full, though he didn't recognise the taste, the smell, the feel of the person he was kissing. The dream lurched forward like dreams do and he was tearing off his clothes, no longer on the beach but on a path that led through some woods, aware of something terrifying down the slope from where he stood, something he didn't want to look at, didn't want to think about, and DJ was there, watching him and saying, 'Do you believe in Heaven?'

He jerked upright, his head banging against something. It was like a star going supernova inside his skull. A flash of white; a thermonuclear blast of pain. Struggling to open his eyes, he saw a figure staggering backwards, clutching their own head. It was Mel.

It all came back to him. He was at Mel's house. He looked down at himself. He was lying on her sofa, a wool blanket draped over him. His mouth felt like a cockroach had crawled inside it and died, but at least the pain in his head was ebbing away, even if the confusion wasn't.

He sat up fully and threw the blanket aside even though it was cold in the room. Mel was standing with her back to the window, still rubbing her forehead and wincing.

'Are you okay?' he asked. 'I don't even know what happened.'

'We clashed heads.'

'That was your head?' He was so disoriented, still emerging from the dream, the images mercifully slipping away.

'It was my own fault. I was leaning over, trying to wake you up.'

What she was saying didn't make much sense. 'I don't understand.'

'You fell asleep. I went to the kitchen to get you a glass of water, and when I came back you were zonked out. Snoring.'

'And you didn't wake me?' He rubbed his eyes. There was still half a plate of cookies on the coffee table. It was dark beyond the window. He remembered coming here, the confrontation with DJ and his friends, Mel persuading him to come in for tea.

And then he remembered. Vicky. She was home. She had texted him, hadn't she? Asked him where he was.

'What time is it? How long was I asleep? And where's my phone?'

Mel had gone over to sit in the armchair. 'It's only ten thirty. You've been asleep for about two hours.'

'What? Oh my God. And you let me sleep?'

He realised from her shocked reaction that he was shouting. He turned the volume down.

'I mean, you didn't try to wake me up earlier?'

'I did. I mean, I tried, but you were out for the count. You looked so peaceful and I knew you were exhausted, and I thought that maybe you'd inhaled some of DJ's cannabis smoke.'

Had he? Was that even possible, to get passively stoned from someone else's smoke?

'I thought I'd let you sleep for a bit. I'm so sorry, Calvin, if I did the wrong thing.'

She looked terrified that he was going to shout at her, and it made him catch hold of his temper.

'It's fine, Mel. I shouldn't have fallen asleep.'

'I really did try to wake you.'

'It's okay.' He had always been a heavy sleeper, the kind of person who could nod off anywhere. He had been known to sleep through alarms, and often had to be shaken awake by Vicky. And he had been exhausted. He should never have come in and accepted Mel's offer of a cup of tea.

He looked around again. 'I can't find my phone.'

'You left it on the coffee table. I plugged it in to charge for you. Was that the wrong thing to do? Let me get it.'

She headed off to the kitchen, and he stood up and stretched, rubbed at his stiff neck, relieved that his headache had shrunk to nothing more than a dull throb. He also needed to pee, and went towards the downstairs toilet, bumping into Mel in the dark hallway.

'Here's your phone,' she said, handing it to him. She was still acting nervous, like he was angry with her. Unable to deal with her right now – he didn't have the energy to reassure her, especially when he was a little mad that she hadn't tried harder to wake him – he went straight into the loo and locked the door behind him.

He was almost too afraid to check his phone, imagining a torrent of texts from Vicky asking him where the hell he was. How was he going to explain this?

But there were no texts. No missed calls. Nothing since he'd replied to her message three hours ago.

He left the toilet and found Mel in the kitchen, her arms wrapped around herself.

'I need to go home.'

'Of course. I'll show you out.'

At the front door, she said, 'Please apologise to Vicky from me. I would have called her to let her know you were asleep, but I don't know her number and I didn't want to use your phone.'

'It's fine. I'm sure she'll see the funny side.' He attempted a smile. 'She'll be teasing me about it for months. Her idiot husband, falling asleep and failing to get home.'

He looked across to where DJ and the others had been earlier. The bonfire was fully extinguished now.

'I'll see you in the morning,' he said to Mel. 'And listen, I'm not mad with you. I obviously needed that sleep. It was my body forcing me to recharge my batteries.'

He drove away, following the road that hugged the edge of the lake. He put the radio on, needing noise, although he was wide awake now. It was the late-night rock show and they were playing 'Enter Sandman'. He turned it up and put his foot down, only slowing down at the points where he knew the speed cameras were. Not the kind of thing he would usually do, but the roads were empty and he was desperate to get home so he could explain to Vicky why he was so late and put it behind them.

It took just under half an hour to get home. When he pulled up outside his front door he noticed immediately that her car wasn't in its usual spot. That was worrying. He found his key in his pocket as he jogged up the front path to the house. Once inside, he headed straight upstairs.

It was dark, and as soon as he went into the bedroom he could tell it was empty. He turned the lamp on in the hallway, so it cast enough light into the room for him to make out the bed. Vicky definitely wasn't in it.

He checked the en-suite. The light and extractor fan were on but it felt damp, the floor and walls wet to the touch. There were several soggy towels in the bathtub.

So where was his wife?

He checked the spare room. The living room. The kitchen. He turned on all the lights.

'Vicky?' he called, even though he knew he wouldn't get an answer.

She must have been so angry with him that she'd gone to a friend's. Or maybe she was just driving around, as she did sometimes when she was in a bad mood. He went outside to double-check her car was definitely gone and not parked further up the road. There was no sign of it.

He stood in the front garden, trying to think, then took out his phone and called her.

A phone rang somewhere in the near distance, muffled but clearly audible. Leaving it ringing, he went back inside and followed the noise upstairs.

There was her phone, on the bed, beside her bulging suitcase. Still ringing. Why would she go out without her phone? She was never without it.

With a gnawing sensation beginning to grow in his stomach, he went back downstairs. There was an empty wine glass on the counter.

She had come home. She had stayed here for a little while.

So where the hell was she now?

PART TWO

24

AUGUST 1995

Calvin knew something was wrong the moment he opened his eyes. It was there in the energy of the house, in its balance. Something off kilter.

Someone missing.

He had fallen asleep on top of the covers because it was too hot for him to bear even a whisper of fabric on his body. A fan whirred, but all it did was push the thick, muggy air from one side of the room to the other, and the sheets beneath him were damp. And it was still dark outside, which didn't make sense. Hadn't he slept through the night?

He found his glasses – this was a decade before he had laser surgery to correct his vision – and the digits on his clock radio came into focus. 01:37.

Calvin sat up and, naked, went to the window to look out at the garden. The moon was a sliver shy of fullness, and the garden was cast in moonlight. Something slunk along the rear wall: next door's cat or a small fox. The lounger his mum had sunbathed on for much of the afternoon was still out. There was no sign of the promised storm that would break the weather and blow away the heatwave. All was quiet and still.

But something wasn't right.

Pulling on a T-shirt and boxer shorts, Calvin left his room and – quietly, not wanting to wake his parents – crept downstairs. In the kitchen, he went straight to the sink and downed a glass of water, which made him feel slightly more human. He looked around. The kitchen was clean and tidy, no dishes in the sink, no food left out on the counter. There was also no bag on the table. No jacket slung over the back of a chair or shoes on the floor.

He went out into the hallway. Freya had a pair of red Adidas Gazelles that she lived in during the summer, swapping them for Doc Martens in the winter. Every morning, one of their parents would tut as they picked them up off the kitchen floor and put them on the shoe rack by the front door.

The trainers weren't in the kitchen and they weren't on the rack. There was no sign of her bag either. What about her jacket? That was hanging on the peg above the rack, but it was so hot that she'd probably just gone out wearing her vest top and shorts.

It was two in the morning and she wasn't home.

She's seventeen, he told himself. *It's totally normal for her to stay out with her boyfriend.*

Because that's what Milo was now. Since Duchess's gig at the Cricketers three weeks ago, Freya had been infatuated. That night, Calvin had watched the gig, standing at the back with his arms folded, James next to him, as Duchess ran through their set. Milo was the lead singer and guitarist, with his brother Simeon on drums and sister Piper on bass. Their set was a mix of originals – if you could use that word to describe the derivative songs that sounded like bad Blur B-sides – and covers. They did 'Yellow Submarine' and 'Waterloo Sunset', then finished with their own version of Oasis's 'Cigarettes & Alcohol'. The covers, Calvin had to admit, went down a storm with the crowd, drunk on heat and cider. Piper, with her bright-red hair and massive boots, looked like an indie icon. Simeon had that Animal-from-*The-Muppets* thing going on, drumming like the world would end if he stopped, his bright-ginger hair flopping around as he bashed away. Milo was a committed frontman too, leaping around and throwing rock-star shapes, turning around to shake his skinny behind, which drew screams – ironic, surely? – from the audience. But they were so unoriginal and their own songs so weak that Calvin couldn't see them ever being anything more than a pub band.

'You having a good time?' Milo asked at one point, to half-hearted cheers from the audience. He was trying to put on a working-class accent. 'I'd like to dedicate this song to a fit bird I met tonight. This one goes out to Freya.'

Calvin groaned as James elbowed him in the ribs. He could see Freya down the front with Emily, their arms linked. She had her back to him so he couldn't see her reaction, but he heard a squeal of excitement from Emily.

'Why do girls always go for dickheads like that?' James shouted in Calvin's ear. He had no answer.

Duchess launched into an original called something like 'She's a Superstar', and Calvin couldn't take any more.

He went into the beer garden, where he found Camilla with her friends, sitting around a trestle table, smoking.

'How are they?' Camilla asked.

'Like Liam Gallagher if he'd gone to finishing school.'

The girls around the table launched into the chorus of 'Common People'.

'I think your sister likes him, though,' said Camilla.

'He is quite cute,' said one of the other girls, whose name Calvin didn't know.

'I heard he's a smackhead,' said another, a girl called Suzy who was in Freya's year at school.

'Heroin?' Calvin said, and they all laughed at his shocked tone. He had never knowingly met anyone who had done heroin or any of the 'big' drugs, like crack or cocaine. Around here, plenty of kids smoked weed, and sometimes they went to parties and dropped acid or E. Calvin had never done any of them except for trying weed once, and it had made him feel so sick he'd decided it wasn't for him.

'That's what I heard,' said Suzy. 'They smoke it. Chasing the dragon. I guess they think it makes them cool and bohemian.'

He remembered what Camilla had said about the Duchess siblings' hippie upbringing. He could imagine Milo skim-reading *Trainspotting* or *Naked Lunch* and taking away the message that heroin was cool.

'Oh, look, Calvin's getting all protective,' said Suzy. 'Doesn't want his sister getting off with a druggie.'

'Would you?' Calvin asked.

Camilla put a hand on his forearm. 'Chill out. Freya's sensible. She might get off with him after the gig, but I doubt she'll see him again after tonight. He'll be at another gig tomorrow night, dedicating a song to a different girl.'

Except that hadn't happened. Calvin had hung around after the gig, intending to walk Freya home, but she'd vanished. James had already gone home in a bad mood. After a while, Emily came over and told him that Freya had said not to wait for her. So he walked back with Camilla, talking about their university applications and pending A-level results, though all he could think about was kissing her, wondering if she wanted him to make a move. In the end, standing on Camilla's doorstep, he totally blew it, dithering so long that her dad appeared, asking her if she was going to stand out there all night.

He went home, asking himself why he was such a loser. He put the telly on and watched an old movie in which the hero kissed women like he was doing them a favour, which made Calvin feel even worse. At around one, Freya came in, kicking her shoes off in the kitchen and dumping her bag on the table.

She poked her head in the front room. There was a big grin on her face and all her lipstick had been rubbed off. 'Night,' she said.

'Wait.'

She paused in the doorway.

'That guy, Milo. I heard he's a junkie.'

'Who from?'

'Suzy and Camilla.'

Freya scoffed. 'Suzy's just jealous because she fancies him. She was giving me dirty looks all night.'

'So he's not on heroin?'

'What's it got to do with you?'

Calvin was standing up now. 'I really don't think it's a good idea for you to start seeing a heroin addict.'

She made an incredulous noise. 'Oh my God. Who made you my keeper? You're actually worse than Mum and Dad. Also, he's not a junkie.'

'You're sure about that?'

She rolled her eyes. 'I've had enough of this. I'm going to bed.'

'Freya.' She paused. He noticed as she hung on to the door frame that she was swaying. Drunk. 'I know I'm not your parent, but if he offers you heroin . . .'

'All right. I'm not an idiot.'

With that, she'd gone to bed. And the next day, contrary to Camilla's prediction, Freya had announced that she was going over to Milo's house. She had been to see him every day since, either going over to his house on the outskirts of the village – the huge place Camilla had described – or travelling with him to Duchess gigs in the local area.

One afternoon last week, Freya had phoned asking to be picked up, and Calvin, who had passed his driving test earlier this summer but didn't yet have his own vehicle, borrowed their parents' car and went to collect her.

The house – which had a name rather than a street address – was elusive, and he found himself going round in circles like a character in a horror film. In the end, he pulled over and asked an old guy out walking his dog, who told him exactly which lanes to drive down. Even though he knew that, as the crow flew, this house was only a forty-five-minute walk from the Cricketers pub, it seemed remote, like he was traversing the wilderness, the roads potholed and narrow, swarms of gnats splatting against the windscreen as he drove. Finally, he spotted a gate with *ELYSIAN FIELDS* etched into the wall beside it. Of course Milo would have grown up in a place with a pretentious name.

The house appeared at the end of a long winding drive, and when Calvin saw it, he laughed. It was exactly as Camilla had described it. Not quite a mansion but not far off. A grand, stone place with pillars out front, and enough windows to keep a cleaner busy all day. There was a gravel courtyard with a fountain, and instead of a garden it had grounds that stretched as far as Calvin could see. Just beyond the house was a swimming pool, inflatables floating on its shining surface, with a few loungers set up around it.

Calvin pulled up next to the vehicle that the band used to transport their equipment to gigs. It was a black Transit van with a licence plate that told him it was twelve years old. He was surprised they didn't have something newer, but maybe it was part of the image. Or perhaps the family didn't actually have that much money. He'd heard that a lot of the people who lived in big old houses like this were actually broke and had very little income. He had no idea if Milo's mum still made money from the estate of her dad, the famous writer.

As soon as he got out of the car, a pair of fluffy white dogs appeared from the side of the house and ran up to him, yapping and jumping up. They were followed by Milo's brother, Simeon. He was still wearing his army coat and Calvin smiled to himself, wondering if the zip was stuck. The poor guy probably had to sleep in it.

'Can I help you?' Simeon asked, the dogs running around his feet.

'I'm here to pick up Freya.'

'You're a taxi driver?'

Calvin gave him a contemptuous look. 'I'm her brother.'

'Oh. Yes, of course. She talks about you a lot.' He was smiling now, being pleasant. Unlike Milo, he made no attempt to disguise his cut-glass accent. It was as if a young member of the royal family had gone into rock 'n' roll.

'Really?'

'Yes, all the time. Family's the most important thing in the world, isn't it? Speaking of which . . .'

Milo appeared, with Freya just behind him. Milo was wearing round sunglasses, swimming shorts and a shirt that was unbuttoned, hanging open to expose the smooth skin of his puny chest. Freya was wearing a bikini, with a sarong tied around her waist. Her hair was wet. Seeing them, the dogs started yapping again, running up to Milo then back to Calvin.

Milo yelled at them. 'Aldous! Crowley! Leave him alone. He's harmless.'

One of the dogs flipped on to its back and looked at Calvin imploringly, hoping for a belly rub. He crouched to oblige.

'I'm impressed you found us,' Milo said. 'We were having a swim in the pool out back.'

Calvin just grunted, getting to his feet. 'You ready?' he said to Freya.

'Want to hang around for a bit? Have a swim?' Milo asked. 'The water's lovely. Or a smoke?' He patted the top pocket of his shirt and Calvin looked at him, then at his sister. They both had dilated pupils, sleepy eyes. Dopey grins. 'Piper's seeing this guy who gets the *best* shit. Actually, where is Piper? Have you seen her, Simeon?'

'She's in her room, hiding from the sun.'

'Total vampire,' said Milo, and Freya giggled.

'You're stoned,' Calvin said to her.

'No I'm not,' she said with another giggle. 'I'm as sober as . . .'

She trailed off, unable to think of something that might be sober.

'Is that all you've been doing?' Calvin asked. 'Smoking weed?'

'Give her a break, man,' Milo said. 'She's an adult.'

'Actually, she's not. She's seventeen.'

Freya looked at him like he was the most embarrassing person on earth. 'You're so annoying.'

He sighed. He really didn't want to argue.

'Come on, let's go,' he said.

'I'll see you tomorrow,' Milo said, and he pulled Freya into a sloppy, open-mouthed kiss. Calvin averted his eyes and saw Simeon watching him, like he was fascinated to see what Calvin thought of this scene.

When they finally left Elysian Fields, Freya didn't speak to him, all the way home. In fact, she'd hardly spoken to him at all since that day.

Now, on this day at the end of August, with the clock ticking past 2 a.m., Calvin sat at the kitchen table and tried to ignore the gnawing sensation in his belly. Freya was fine. She would have gone back to Milo's, that was all, after their gig in Carlisle. She was seventeen and he needed to stop being so overprotective. He didn't need to wake their parents up. He certainly didn't need to drive out to Elysian Fields to check she was okay. All that would achieve would be to make Freya hate him.

He yawned. He would go back to the stinking, overheated pit of his bedroom and try to sleep.

It was only when he was awoken at five the next morning, and he heard his mother cry out, that he realised he hadn't been protective enough.

25

Calvin was still awake when the sun came up.

He'd spent the entire night pacing around the house, looking at Vicky's phone – they were the kind of couple who knew each other's passcodes and PIN numbers – and watching out the front window, praying her car would pull up outside. It was impossible not to be thrown back to that night twenty-eight years ago, the night when he'd got up at 2 a.m. and convinced himself his sister would soon come home. The night that ended at dawn with his mother's scream.

The minutes slithered by. He searched through Vicky's suitcase and drawers, as if they might contain clues that would tell him where she was. He stood in their bathroom for a long time, looking at the wet towels in the bath and wondering what had happened. He kept returning to the empty wine glass sitting on the counter in the kitchen. Vicky was extremely strict about drinking and driving, even if she'd only consumed a few mouthfuls. So why had she ignored that rule and gone out in the car?

He returned to their last message exchange again and again, like a tongue returning to a wobbly tooth. The exchange had happened at 7.31 p.m. *Where are you?* No kiss at the end of her message. Did *that* mean anything? She almost always left kisses on her texts to him, unless she was angry about something or in a huge rush. He understood that she might be angry with him for going to Mel's, even if that anger was irrational, but that first kiss-free text had been sent *before* he'd told her where he was. Had she suspected for some reason? And had his reply made her so pissed off with him that she'd decided to punish him by hiding?

That had to be the most likely explanation, and it caused his emotions to swing between fear and frustration.

She was doing this to punish him for something he hadn't even done.

No, she would never deliberately punish him like this. Something must have happened to her.

She was angry that he hadn't come home and wanted him to pay.

But she hadn't made any attempt to call him when he was asleep at Mel's.

She was so hurt that she couldn't bear to stay in the house they shared.

He had a sudden, almost overwhelming fear. What if she'd driven off in a blur of pain and rage, perhaps to come and find him, and in her furious, agonised state, and with wine in her blood, she hadn't driven carefully like she usually did?

The image was so clear. A fox or badger running across the road. Vicky swerving, smashing into a tree or losing control, careering down a slope into a ditch in the pitch-black. No one around on these quiet roads to have seen the accident.

Fighting back panic, he called the nearest hospital to see if any road accident victims had been brought in. He called the police too, to ask if there had been any accidents in the last few hours. In both cases, he was told no. He put the phone down feeling a little relieved but still fearful her wrecked car could be in some concealed spot. This part of the world was ninety per cent concealed spots.

Forcing himself to move away from this car-crash narrative, he searched on Google to see if there were any all-night cafes or petrol stations nearby, then phoned the couple he found, asking them if a woman matching Vicky's description was there. They both reported that they were either empty or that the only customers present were lorry drivers. In each case, he left his number and asked them to give her a message if she came in.

Finally, when the sun came up at six, he sat down with Vicky's phone and started to call her friends, starting with those who lived in the village then spreading outwards. Most of them were still in bed, answering groggily. To prevent alarm – he didn't want mass panic to break out among Vicky's social circle – he tried to tread lightly, for now at least.

'We had a little bit of a row and I can't get hold of her. I wondered if she'd come to stay with you.'

They all said no, they hadn't heard from her.

At least two of her friends said, 'I expect she's just trying to make you sweat.' As they said it, he believed it. Making him sweat. She was certainly succeeding. She'd be home any minute now, point made, and he would be so relieved to see her that he wouldn't shout at her for scaring him to death.

But as soon as each call ended, he was plunged back into a state of abject fear and confusion – and guilt. Self-blame. *If I hadn't gone to Mel's. If I hadn't fallen asleep.*

He messaged the neighbourhood WhatsApp group, asking if anyone had seen her or her car, but they were all still asleep.

By the time 7 a.m. rolled around he was half crazed. And something else had occurred to him before becoming the dominant thought in his head.

Vicky knew what had happened to Freya. Even if she was angrier than she'd ever been before, would she really do this to him?

He couldn't see it.

Couldn't see her hating him this much.

Jarvis appeared, jumping on to the counter and meowing for breakfast. Calvin watched him eat then allowed the cat to rub his face against his cheek.

'Where is she, Jarv?' he asked.

Then it came to him. Of course. The animal shelter. Surely that was the place she was most likely to have gone. She had keys, it was warm there, and she'd take comfort from being with the animals. She might even have decided that, unable to sleep and not having been there for a few days, she could catch up with some work. It made sense. He couldn't believe he hadn't thought of it earlier.

He snatched up his keys and phone – grabbing Vicky's phone too, knowing she'd want to be reunited with it – then ran out to the car.

ⱳ

He arrived at the shelter at seven thirty. As he pulled up out front, another car arrived behind him, a black Toyota. It was Louise. She got out of her car and came over. She was dressed in her usual uniform of jeans and a sweatshirt. Today's had a picture of Phil Collins cuddling a cartoon cat, with the legend *So take a look at miaow*.

'Hey Calvin,' she said with a smile, looking past him into the Qashqai. 'No Vicky?'

'No, I'm hoping she's here.'

That caused a raised eyebrow. 'Oh?'

'I think she might have come in early.'

'Sounds like her. Two days away from this place and she's desperate to get back to the moggies. Although . . . her car's not here?'

That fact had already struck Calvin.

'I know. Can we just take a look, please?'

'You're making me worry now. What's going on?'

He found his mouth was too dry to reply.

Louise approached the front gate, unlocking it with a key that she fished out of her pocket. She had huge bunch of them, like a jailer. They walked together to the reception building and Louise unlocked that too, switching the light on. Vicky wasn't there. The computer was off and there was no sign anyone had been in here since yesterday.

'Can we check the cats' quarters first?' he asked.

'What's going on, Calvin?' Louise said again.

'I just need to make sure she's not here.'

Louise beckoned for him to follow her through the door that led out of the rear of the reception building, and down a narrow path to a large wooden structure with another locked door. Calvin could already hear mews, a sound that increased in volume and intensified as they stepped inside. The dogs were housed in the next building, and they all started barking as they heard people in the vicinity.

Calvin and Louise went into the first building, and Calvin was smacked in the face by the smell of cat pee and disinfectant, the stink of dozens of litter trays that needed to be emptied. The cats were kept in pens, one on of top of another, stretching along both sides of the space with a walkway between.

Calvin knew straight away that Vicky wasn't here, but he called her name anyway and walked between the pens to the door at the other end of the building. As he went, some of the cats raised their heads to look at him, green eyes glinting, while others pressed their furry bodies against the bars, desperate for attention and food. He didn't like coming here. It hurt his heart, seeing all these poor animals who had been neglected or abused. It made him lose any faith he might have had in human nature; reminded him how cruel or thoughtless people could be.

How evil.

'She's not here,' Louise said, stating the obvious. A cat beside her was going crazy, bashing itself against the wire mesh of its pen. Calvin stared at it, wishing it would be quiet, thinking he might be sick.

She's dead, said a little voice in his head, and he started to shake uncontrollably.

Dead.

Like Freya.

26

The police turned up on their doorstep a few minutes after five. There were two of them, a man and a woman, both in uniform, standing in the hall, talking to his mum and dad. Calvin crouched on the landing at the top of the stairs and watched from behind the balustrade. The cops were holding their hats in front of them and their lips were moving, but all Calvin could hear was blood rushing in his ears and the echo of his mother's wail. She was clutching at his dad, who looked like he was about to collapse himself.

The female police officer noticed Calvin watching and caught his eye. He had to hold on to the banister as he came downstairs, to stop himself from falling.

His dad turned his head as Calvin reached the bottom step. His eyes were red and he looked ten years older.

'Oh, son,' he said. Then, 'It's Freya.'

Drugs. They were going to say she'd died from taking drugs. Milo had persuaded her to inject heroin and she'd overdosed. Or he'd given her ecstasy or acid and she'd had a bad reaction to it or done something stupid. A guy in a band Calvin had liked when he was younger, The Shamen, had drowned after taking MDMA.

Calvin had heard of people jumping off buildings after taking LSD, thinking they could fly.

He'd tuned out, thinking about all the ways Freya might have died from taking drugs, when he heard the female police officer saying his name. He stared at her. She had acne scars, and that sent him into another reverie: Freya complaining about the spots on her face and their mum telling her not to pick at them or she'd get scars.

The policewoman was saying something about a van.

'Pardon?' he said, snapping back to attention.

'I was telling your mum and dad, the van crashed on the way back from Carlisle, following this gig . . .'

A crash? Not drugs?

The officer went on, but he interrupted her. 'Who was driving?'

The officers exchanged a glance, as if they weren't sure how much information they were allowed to impart. The male officer said, 'Simeon Stewart.'

The first thought that entered Calvin's head was: *I wonder if he was wearing his army coat.*

'Who's that?' Calvin's mum asked.

Calvin heard himself say, 'Milo's brother. Is he okay?'

The male cop squirmed a little. 'A few cuts and bruises but he's fine.'

'What about the others?' Calvin asked. He could hardly get the words out. 'Milo and Piper.' To his parents he said, 'Milo's sister.'

'They're fine too.'

Of course they were. Of course they fucking were.

ω

The next day, the weather broke. A storm that seemed like it would tear the world in two – oh, how Calvin wished it would! – ripped through the Lake District overnight. On the news the following morning there were reports that a man had been struck by lightning, and Calvin wondered if they were talking about him, because that was exactly how he felt. Like a bolt had come from the sky and changed his life in a moment, and now he was filled with a new energy. A dark, simmering anger, mixed with an electric dose of despair. If the temperature hadn't decreased he was sure he could have spontaneously combusted.

He felt a fresh wave of sadness. Spontaneous human combustion was a fear he and Freya had shared when they were little. That, and drowning in quicksand. He wanted to be able to joke with her about it, to see her cringe at the memory of how silly they'd been. He had a feeling that, going forward, this would be a recurring event. That he would hear that one of Freya's favourite bands had a new album coming out, or Mum or Dad would say something embarrassing, and he'd want to share it with her.

But she would never be there to share anything with again.

ω

It was Friday, two days after the police turned up with the terrible news, and Calvin was at the pub with James. Not the Cricketers – there were too many recent memories of Freya there – but the less popular pub on the other side of the village, the Three Crowns. They were sitting indoors, in the snug. Calvin was halfway through his second pint. He went over to the cigarette vending machine, put in some coins and grabbed the pack of Marlboro Lights.

'You're smoking?' James asked when Calvin got back to their table.

'Yeah. Want one?' The cigarette tasted foul and burned the back of his throat, but he didn't care. He wanted to do something self-destructive.

James shook his head. He looked almost as wretched as Calvin felt. He wouldn't stop fidgeting and had torn all the beer mats on the table into shreds, hardly seeming to notice what he was doing. Because Freya was so close in age to Calvin, she had always been there when he and James were kids. They had all gone to the playground together, learned to ride bikes around the same time. When they built camps in the woods, she was there. They went to the same birthday parties, played out on the street together. Of course James was upset.

'How are your mum and dad coping?' he asked.

'My dad had to go and identify the body. He's looked like a ghost ever since. My mum is in a terrible state. She keeps looking at me like she wishes it had been me.'

'Oh, mate,' said James, pushing his floppy fringe out of his face. 'I'm sure she doesn't think that.'

Calvin wasn't so sure. Freya had always been their favourite.

'Have you . . . heard anything from Milo?'

Calvin felt the heat rise in his blood. 'No. Nothing.'

'But do you know what happened?'

Calvin stared at the surface of his pint. 'According to the police, Simeon was driving and Freya was in the passenger seat. They said she wasn't wearing a seat belt. Milo and Piper were in the back with the equipment. The police said that Simeon told them an animal ran into the road and he swerved, clipped the kerb and spun into a tree.'

They said Simeon wasn't even sure what kind of animal it was. Something halfway between a fox and a deer, and Calvin couldn't even think what animal that might be. A large dog, loose on the road?

'Did they breathalyse him?' said James.

'Yeah. He was under the limit. Hadn't been drinking at all. They're not going to prosecute him.'

'Jesus.'

Calvin picked up his pint and took a long swallow, trying to prevent his hand from shaking.

'Do you know . . . why she wasn't wearing her seat belt?' James asked.

Calvin shook his head. He would love to know. He was intending to ask Milo, because presumably he would be at the funeral next week, even though Calvin didn't want him there. He didn't want any of the Stewarts there.

'It's my fault,' he said.

'What are you talking about?'

This was his torment. The truth that haunted him.

'If she hadn't been going out with that arsehole, she wouldn't have been in their van. I should have stopped her from seeing him. I knew he was bad news. I knew it was going to end in some terrible way.'

'But Cal,' James said, 'how could you have stopped her? She had her own ideas. And it wasn't your responsibility to stop her, in any case.'

'I shouldn't have let her come to the Cricketers. Shouldn't have bought her a drink. I enabled her, didn't I?'

'No. It wasn't your fault.'

He had known, though. He'd thought it would be drugs, not a road accident. But he'd had that premonition that first night. He should have tried harder. Told his parents about his misgivings. He could even have offered to drive Freya to the gig himself.

Why hadn't she been wearing her stupid seat belt?

Calvin felt the wetness on his cheeks and realised he was crying. James looked stricken, mouth opening and closing, unequipped to deal with any heavy emotional shit. Neither of them were equipped.

He couldn't bear this. To sit crying in front of his mate. It was weak, embarrassing. And it didn't reflect how he really felt, which was angry. Furious. Overflowing with rage that filled him up, then burst out and flowed in every direction. Anger at himself. Anger at the world. Anger at Freya for getting in that van with those fuck-wits. Anger, most of all, aimed at Milo Stewart.

He slipped off to the gents, where he washed his face and blew his nose. When he was ready, he went back out. James was sitting with his back to Calvin and his shoulders were shaking. Calvin walked around to look at him and saw James was crying too.

He looked up at Calvin, eyes red, snot running. 'I'm sorry. She was just . . .' He sucked in a shuddering breath. 'She was the best of us.'

This was weird. Seeing James cry helped Calvin pull himself together. He went back into the gents and grabbed some toilet paper, which he handed to James, who blew his nose loudly.

'Sorry,' he said again. 'I need to pull myself together.'

'Let's change the subject.'

They both sat there, silent. Finally, James said, 'I'm going to miss you, man.'

'Huh?'

'When you go off to uni.'

They'd got their A-level results two weeks ago. James had failed his but, in his usual laid-back way, didn't seem particularly bothered. 'I'm happy staying here,' he'd said when they came through. 'It's a cool place to live and I don't understand why anyone would want to have to do more studying.' He'd never been academic.

Calvin, though, had got the grades he needed to study Sociology at John Moores University in Liverpool.

'I'm not going,' he said now. 'How can I? I can't leave my mum and dad. They're going to need me.'

Later in his life, Calvin would wonder what he would have chosen to do if someone wise, maybe even one of his mates, had tried to persuade him to go, told him that he couldn't sacrifice his own future. It wasn't just the idea of leaving his parents alone.

He couldn't imagine moving to a new place, trying to make new friends. He couldn't imagine feeling positive about anything.

Maybe if James had given him a big motivational speech he might have found the strength to go. And he might have enjoyed it, once there. His life could have taken a different path.

But it was almost as if fate had already made its mind up and set him on the course he was about to follow. And set James on his, too.

James didn't say anything inspirational. Instead, he bought them both more drinks. They got pissed. And eventually, when he couldn't stay out any longer, Calvin staggered home.

27

Calvin got to the police station thirty minutes after leaving the animal shelter, and went straight up to the desk.

'I need to report a missing person. My wife.'

He sat on a hard chair in the waiting area, rubbing at his scratchy eyes and craving coffee. He kept checking his phone, before remembering once again he had Vicky's mobile in his other pocket. He got up and paced back and forth, unable to sit still. Why was this taking so long? He went back to the desk and asked how long he'd have to wait. He hated being here. Even now, more than two decades on, being around police officers sent him back to that morning when two of them turned up on his doorstep to break the news about Freya.

Finally, a man who looked freshly shaved and impossibly young came out and said, 'Mr Matheson? Would you like to come with me?'

The police officer introduced himself as PC Steve Milner. He wasn't in uniform, which was a little confusing. Wasn't it only detectives who wore plain clothes? The room was tiny and contained just a desk and a pair of plastic chairs. There was a plastic window with a view of the hallway, which was lined with public information posters left over from the pandemic, advising people to wash their hands and wear a mask. The words *HANDS FACE SPACE* swam before Calvin's eyes.

'Do you work on the missing persons team?' Calvin asked.

'We don't have a dedicated misper unit here, sir. They're based in Carlisle. I'm afraid we're only a small team and most of us—' He stopped himself.

'What were you going to say?' But he had already guessed. It would explain why this young cop wasn't in uniform. He was only pretending to be a detective. 'The proper detectives are all working on that case with the buried guy, aren't they?'

Milner didn't blink. 'That is one of the cases we're investigating, yes. But please' – he opened a folder on the desk and searched through it for a form – 'I need to take some details about . . . your wife, is it?'

He took down all of Vicky's details. Biographical information, when Calvin had last seen or spoken to her, what he'd done so far to locate her. The car she drove: a red hybrid Toyota Yaris. He wrote it all on his form, diligently filling in the blanks. It was like completing a mortgage application.

'Do you have a recent photograph of her?' Milner asked. 'Can you email it to me?'

Calvin rocked on his chair, almost exploding with frustration. He'd known the police wouldn't leap into action and immediately despatch vans and helicopters to look for her – even though that's what he wanted them to do – but this young cop's attitude was so casual that Calvin wanted to grab and shake him.

'Are you taking this seriously?' he said, forcing himself not to shout.

Milner looked up from his form. 'Sir?'

'My wife's missing and you don't appear to give a shit.'

It was taking all Calvin's self-control, everything he'd learned from the self-help books he'd read, to keep his anger in check. If he'd had a moment to reflect, he might have marvelled at how quickly the shell of calm he'd built around himself over the last twenty-five years had cracked. He'd believed himself to be cured of the anger that had consumed him after Freya's death, that it wasn't even simmering inside him. But, in reality, he hadn't been tested. Now he was in this situation, terrified that something had happened to the second woman he'd loved – and of course it was a different kind of love, but it was still love – the fury he had suppressed for so long was all at once at full boil again.

A woman walked past the room, a deep frown on her face, creasing her forehead. She moved fast, like she was in a hurry to get somewhere. It took Calvin a second to realise where he knew her from. That red hair. The cheekbones. It was her, the detective from the telly. Imogen Evans. An actual professional. He'd followed the Viper case that she'd been so heavily involved with, and he and Vicky had watched the dramatisation together.

He didn't hesitate. He leapt up and went to the door, snatching it open. Imogen Evans, who was by this point almost at the end of the corridor, looked back over her shoulder and paused.

'Hey. You're Imogen Evans, aren't you?'

Milner was at Calvin's shoulder. 'Mr Matheson? Please, come back into the room.'

Calvin ignored him. 'I assume you're this kid's superior? I'm trying to report my wife missing and he's acting like I'm applying for a bank loan. I want someone who actually knows what they're doing. Unless you're too busy trying to find out what happened to this bloke on the beach. My coffee shop got broken into the other day, my assistant was injured and did your lot do anything? Did they hell.'

Detective Evans, who, until this point, had looked almost as tense as Calvin felt, closed her eyes for a second. When she opened them again it was as if she had shifted from one mode to another.

From stressed to calm. She walked straight towards him and ush-
ered him back into the room, shutting the door behind her. Milner
went to protest but she held up a hand, placating him.

'Mr Matheson, is it?'

'Yes. Calvin.'

'Calvin. And you can call me Imogen.' Her voice was soothing
and he immediately felt calmer. It was quite a skill she possessed.
'Calvin, I can assure you that we treat all serious cases equally. Tell
me what the problem is.'

'My wife was at a spa Sunday and Monday. When I got home
last night, after dark, her suitcase and phone were on the bed. There
were signs she'd had a bath and opened a bottle of wine. I've checked
with the hospital. I've called all her friends and been to her place of
work. She's vanished. And I can't believe she would have just driven
away from our house, leaving her phone behind, and . . . disappeared
into the night.'

'Let's all take a seat, shall we?' She pulled a chair towards her
and motioned for Calvin to sit opposite. 'I need you to answer
some sensitive questions, Calvin. You're going to have to be honest.
Okay?'

'Yes, of course.'

'Does Vicky drink or take drugs?'

'No! I mean, she enjoys a glass of wine, but that's all. I told
you, there was an empty glass in the kitchen and she definitely
wouldn't have driven her car if she was drunk. I've never even
known her to drive after *half* a glass, and as for drugs, that's a big
no. It's difficult to even get her to take a painkiller when she's got
a headache.'

'So she's not on any medication?'

'Are you asking me if she has mental health issues? No, she
doesn't. I think she's actually the most . . . mentally healthy person
I've ever met.'

Imogen had picked the pen up again while he said this and made some more notes on the form. He knew from seeing news reports that the police treated missing 'vulnerable' people differently. He also believed they made certain assumptions about what might have happened to them. Vicky wouldn't be in that category. But did that mean they wouldn't try to find her?

'She wouldn't have hurt herself,' he said. 'I know that for a fact.'

'What do you think has happened to her, Calvin?'

She had the kind of voice that made you wonder if you were making a big fuss about nothing. He noticed the young PC gazing at her with a kind of awe.

'I think someone has taken her. Abducted her.'

It was only when he said it that it really hit home. It shook him. Abducted? Was that really what might have happened?

'And what makes you think that?'

'Because I know she wouldn't go off like this, leaving me worried sick, even if she wanted to punish me.'

He regretted saying it the second the words left his mouth.

'Punish you?'

He floundered.

'Tell me why she might have wanted to punish you.'

'I haven't actually done anything wrong, before you jump to conclusions.' That caused a raised eyebrow. 'But Vicky isn't a big fan of this woman I've just started working with.'

'You said you work in a coffee shop?'

'Calvin owns that new place in Elderbridge,' Milner said. 'Therapy.'

'Oh yes? I've heard good things. Who's this woman?'

'Her name is Mel, and Vicky thinks she has a thing for me, and that there's something strange about her. We've had a couple of arguments about it. Vicky doesn't like Mel working for me.' He clenched his fists. 'Vicky was away this weekend, as I've already explained to Constable Milner here, and when she got home – I mean, I'm assuming she was home – she texted me to ask where I was.'

'And you were with this Mel?'

'Yes. I was at her house, in fact.'

'I see.'

'For God's sake. I'm not sleeping with her. I have no interest in her like that whatsoever. I was helping her because she's being harassed by these yobs – another thing the police have done nothing about, by the way. I went home with her because she was scared and I wanted to have a word with them.'

'And did you?'

'Yes, I did. I warned them off – in a friendly way, before you start accusing me of being a vigilante or something – and then Mel asked me in for a cup of tea. Just a cup of tea and a biscuit.'

He watched Imogen's face for signs that she didn't believe him. Like she was thinking, *That's the first time I've heard it called that.* But she was a closed book.

He, on the other hand, was aware of his cheeks burning and probably turning pink. 'I fell asleep on the sofa. This was after Vicky had texted me and I'd told her I was at Mel's. I woke up at ten and drove straight home.'

Imogen wrote all this down in a notebook then sat back.

'I have to say, Mr Matheson, that it does sound very much as if your wife has simply gone away to calm down. Perhaps, as you say, she wants to make you worry. Or maybe she wasn't really thinking about her motivation – she just needed to get away.'

'That makes sense,' said Milner.

'So why leave her phone behind?'

Imogen looked up towards the ceiling, thinking. 'I'm picturing a woman getting a text from her husband telling her that he's with a woman she's suspicious of. She's upset. She throws the phone down, maybe unable to bear holding the object that contains this hurtful message. Then she leaves.'

'I can see that too,' said Milner.

Calvin took a deep breath.

'Can you give me Mel's surname?' Imogen asked.

'Why?' He realised quickly. 'So she can back up my story? Hold on, you think I might be responsible for my wife's disappearance? That I've murdered her so I can start a new life with my mistress?'

'Calvin, I don't even know if your wife *has* gone missing. It's still very early days. But I will need this Mel's details for my report.'

'Fine.' He gave her Mel's details.

'And what about these "yobs" who were harassing her?' Imogen asked. 'Do you know their names?'

He guessed why she was asking this. If Vicky didn't come home and Calvin fell under suspicion, they'd want to talk to everyone who had seen him. But he had nothing to hide.

'The oldest one is called DJ.'

He could almost see Imogen's ears prick up. 'DJ? Can you describe him?'

'About twenty-one. Blond hair. Smells of cannabis.'

'DJ O'Connor,' said Milner, with both eyebrows raised.

Imogen tapped her pen on the desk. 'Who were the others?'

'An enormous younger kid called Kai and a couple of girls. I didn't get their names but one had a ring in her nose, you know, her septum, and the other one was . . .'

He trailed off. He could hardly say she looked like his long-deceased sister.

'She was normal. Pretty.'

There was a beat of silence. He shouldn't have described the girl as pretty. They would think it weird, wouldn't they? But he didn't want to have to go into the whole Freya thing.

'So what happens next?' he asked.

'The first thing we'll do is carry out a risk assessment. I am going to send this form through to one of the missing-from-home managers in Carlisle. But in most cases like this, the missing person turns out not to be missing at all. They come home within twenty-four hours.'

He so desperately wanted Vicky to be one of these people. The majority.

'And if they don't?'

'It's simple. We do everything we can to find them.'

28

Imogen and Steve left the station together and drove back to Drigg in Imogen's car. The child seat was still in the back and the footwells were full of discarded Happy Meal toys that had never made it home, packets of baby wipes and other assorted junk. She needed an extra day in the week to sort her life out. Clean the car. Spend a little quality time with her family. When this case was cleared up she was going to take some leave, go on holiday. Somewhere hot with a swimming pool and sun loungers, a bottle of wine on the terrace after Ava had gone to bed. Sex, even. She found herself drifting into a pleasant fantasy.

'Penny for them,' Steve said.

'I'd charge a lot more than a penny for these thoughts.' She hoped her smile was enigmatic. 'What did you think of Calvin Matheson?'

'Hot-headed. Kind of annoying. Not a big fan of the police, is he?'

'Who is, these days? His wife, though. What do you reckon?'

'I don't know. It's too early to say, isn't it? I don't have much experience with mispers.'

'It's not something I've ever specialised in either. But my feeling is that she's gone off somewhere to lick her wounds or plot revenge. Maybe she's already *getting* revenge, with a secret lover.'

Steve laced his fingers together. 'Gotta say, I believed Matheson when he said he wasn't shagging this other woman.'

'Bros stick together, huh?'

He looked offended. 'I'm really not a bro, ma'am.'

'Please, call me Imogen. And I apologise. My reflex is always to tease.' She took a right turn, towards Drigg. There was the familiar shape of the power station in the distance. 'I honestly don't know if Vicky Matheson has any reason to be suspicious of her husband and this woman. The important thing is that she thinks she does, and when she gets home from a weekend away to find her Calvin at this Mel's house . . . I think it probably played out exactly as I said. She was upset, horrified even. Threw her phone down, got in the car and drove away. Now she's staying away because she's angry, embarrassed or distraught. Possibly a little of all three. She'll be home by tomorrow at the latest. The most interesting part of that whole conversation was when he mentioned DJ.'

It was yesterday morning that Imogen had spoken to DJ in his caravan.

'I was starting to think he was a reformed character,' Imogen went on. 'Reverend Delaney talks about him as if he's the Handyman from Heaven, and DJ himself acts like he spends all his free time playing video games with his cute dog. But now we know he's hanging out with teenagers, smoking weed and harassing people.'

'Is that where we're going now?' Steve asked. 'To talk to him again?'

'No. Not right now. We're going to talk to Billie Whitehead's parents.'

She filled Steve in on what DJ had said about Leo being a 'nonce'. *Some old paedo who lives in the woods waiting for Little Red Riding Hood to stumble past.*

'Wait. You think he had a relationship with Billie? That her parents found out and killed him? She swore there was nothing like that, didn't she?'

'Teenage girls lie, Steve. I used to be one. My parents didn't know half the stuff I got up to.' She had put the Whiteheads' address in the satnav and it told her to turn left on to the new housing estate on the outskirts of Drigg.

'So you're taking what that scumbag DJ said seriously?'

They stopped at a zebra crossing, waiting for an elderly couple, and Imogen turned to Steve. His eyes widened and she realised that, despite her constant best efforts, the stress must be evident on her face. 'You're not privy to my conversations with the chief constable, but let's just say his patience is starting to run out. He wants to see some movement. Something to show that we're not spending our days building sandcastles on the beach.'

'But we're doing what we can!'

'Yeah, I know that and you know that. But did you see that article this morning? In the paper?'

It had been in one of the tabloids. SUPERCOP OR SUPERFLOP? HOW THE VIPER CATCHER RAN OUT OF IDEAS. Hilariously, they had used a big photo of the actress who played her, with the real Imogen inset – a photo of her coming out of the station, head down, flustered and unhappy. *Cumbria's police, led by 'supercop' serial killer catcher DI Imogen Evans, appear to be all at sea with their efforts to catch the twisted murderer of Leo James aka the Man on the Beach.*

'I memorised a bit,' Imogen said. 'How did it go? "It's as if Manchester City signed Lionel Messi only to discover his goal-scoring abilities had deserted him." And please don't say it's tomorrow's chip paper.'

'Eh? I've never heard that expression before.'

'Oh my God, you are so young.'

Steve clenched his fists. 'It makes me so angry. They're just arseholes. I think you're amazing.' As he said it he went bright pink.

Imogen wasn't sure how to react to that. 'Well, anyway . . . the Whiteheads. The possibility that Billie and Leo did have a relationship, or perhaps her parents thought she did. To be totally honest, right now it's the only idea I have. Maybe he was attracted to much younger girls.' The elderly couple finally reached the opposite kerb and Imogen drove on. 'I don't want to come across like an armchair psychologist, but if Leo's art means anything, it tells us very clearly that he was tormented by something from his past. Perhaps that's why he was living off-grid. And it could be something he did, or something that happened to him.'

'Maybe both.'

'Yes, if you're referring to the fact that most abusers were victims themselves. Maybe he was an abused child and whoever did it to him told him he would go to Hell for what he did. Or that he'd go there if he told someone what was happening to him.'

'What about the phobia of water Billie told us about?'

'I don't know. I mean, I can think of a few horrible scenarios but don't want to say them aloud till we know more.'

The Whiteheads' house was at the end of a cul-de-sac. Like all the houses on this estate, it was less than twenty years old. Red-brick with a neat front garden and little character.

Only Billie's dad, Adrian, was at home. He opened the door with an air of reluctance and Imogen suspected that if they hadn't seen him through the living room window as they'd approached the house – and he hadn't seen them seeing him – he would have pretended to be out.

'If you're looking for Billie, she's out,' he said after they'd introduced themselves and before the door was even fully open.

'I'd like to speak to you,' Imogen said.

'I don't know anything.'

She smiled sweetly. 'It will only take a minute.'

Adrian Whitehead was a wiry, short guy with a few strands of hair scraped over his scalp. He looked like he hadn't visited a dentist in a long time. He took them into the kitchen, which smelled of bleach but was almost as messy as Imogen's own. He offered them a cup of tea, so begrudgingly that Imogen almost said yes just to annoy him.

'Billie's out shopping with her mum.'

'That's nice. Whereabouts?'

He acted like she'd asked him to tell her the square root of 1,156.

'Er . . . Carlisle? Or maybe Penrith. I'm not sure.'

He wiped his forehead with his shirtsleeve. He was sweating. Imogen exchanged a glance with Steve. Something was definitely up here. Was he one of those people who couldn't handle talking to the police – or could DJ have actually sent them in the right direction?

'Teenagers,' Imogen said with a smile. 'Expensive, eh? My daughter's only little at the moment and we're kind of dreading her getting older on that score.'

Adrian grunted. He stood with his back to the sink, not offering Imogen and Steve a seat.

Still wearing her reassuring smile, Imogen gestured to a family portrait on the wall, taken when Billie was five or six. Adrian and Billie and Michelle Whitehead. Father and daughter were smiling – Adrian had actually been handsome back then – but Michelle had a sad, faraway look in her eye. She was also gorgeous. Blonde with large eyes and cheekbones to kill for, and seemingly about a decade younger than Adrian.

'Bet you wish she was still that age, eh?' Imogen said.

Was she imagining it, or were there tears in Adrian Whitehead's eyes? When he spoke, his voice dripped with self-pity.

'Yeah. She loved me back then.' He swallowed hard, Adam's apple bobbing in his skinny throat.

Imogen had got that tingle. They were on the right track.

'Not so close now?' She used her softest tone, making it sound like she was on the verge of giving him a hug.

He swallowed hard again. 'No. These days when I walk into the room and she's there it's like walking into a fridge.'

Imogen tutted with sympathy. 'I suppose that means Billie didn't tell you about her friendship with Leo James?'

He frowned. 'Did she hell.'

'What about your wife? Michelle, is it? Is Billie more open with her?'

A long pause. 'She used to be.'

'Until?'

He stared into the middle distance, his jaw working, muscles flexing in his cheeks. Imogen noticed a tremor in his hands. Finally, he said, 'They were close until Michelle did what she did.'

Gently, Imogen said, 'And what was that?'

He met her eye as if daring her to side with his wife. 'She went off with another bloke. Until she realised the grass isn't greener on the other side and came crawling back with her tail between her legs. It hurt Billie more than it did me.' This was clearly a lie. 'Wrecked the trust between them.'

'So Michelle didn't know about Billie being friends with Leo either?'

Adrian opened his mouth to speak but seemed to think better of it. He was so tightly strung that she feared he might pop an artery.

'Are you trying to insinuate something?' he asked. 'About my daughter and that . . . man.'

He had obviously wanted to use a very different word to describe Leo. Imogen flicked her eyes at Steve, trying to give him the signal that now would be a good time for him to say he needed the loo, so he could take a look around. But he didn't take the hint.

Imogen said, 'Did you ever meet Leo James?'

Adrian glowered. 'No, and he's lucky I didn't.'

Imogen noticed how, down by his sides, he clenched his fists.

'But have you spoken to Billie about him since we interviewed her after the cremation? We're trying to find out what we can about him. What do you know about their relationship?'

'Their relationship? There was nothing going on between *Billie* and Leo James! Or did she tell you different?'

A thump came from above them.

Imogen and Steve looked at each other, then at Adrian.

'What was that?' Imogen asked.

Beads of sweat had broken out on his forehead. He had gone from looking furious to anxious. 'It must have been the cat.'

There was no sign of a cat food bowl in this room. No cat flap in the door.

'Mr Whitehead,' Imogen said, 'I'm going to take a look upstairs, okay?'

She turned around and moved towards the door, but Adrian dashed away from the sink, passed her and stepped into her path, blocking her. 'No.'

She glanced at Steve, who had turned so he too was facing Adrian. The sweat was pouring off Adrian now, and his hands were shaking like he'd been plugged into an electric socket.

'It was a cat!' he shouted, and before Imogen could react, he lunged for the knife block on the counter, pulling out the biggest, sharpest knife.

Very occasionally, not often, Imogen wished the British police could carry weapons. In situations like this, facing a clearly unhinged man with a knife, the odds felt very much stacked against the cops, even if there were two of them and one of him.

'Mr Whitehead,' she said, using her most calming tone, the one she'd used on Calvin Matheson earlier. 'Let's all just take a moment. Please put the knife down.'

He stared at her, eyes popping out of his head, holding the knife out in front of him. He was still shaking as though he would fly apart, the tip of the blade moving so fast it created a blur.

'Mr Whitehead.'

There was another thump from above, and Adrian lunged at her.

He was too fast for Imogen to get out of his way, but she didn't need to. Steve jumped into her path just as Adrian slashed at the air with the knife. The blade sliced across Steve's midriff, just above his belly.

'Steve!' Imogen yelled his name as the front of his shirt instantly turned red. Steve stood there for a second, staring at himself, at his blood-covered hands, then crumpled to his knees, clutching his upper abdomen, staring at his own belly in disbelief.

Adrian Whitehead had scuttled backwards and now had his back pressed against the counter, eyes out on stalks, staring at what he'd done, the knife still trembling in his hand. Imogen was torn, wanting to help Steve, whose hands were already slick with blood, but needing to neutralise Adrian. To disarm him.

She prided herself on being able to calm others. She was going to need to use all her powers now.

'Adrian,' she said in her most soothing voice. 'Put the knife down.'

He stared at her, still bug-eyed, gripping the handle of the knife until his knuckles turned white. She looked over at Steve. There was so much blood, but how deep was the wound? There was a hand towel hanging from a hook on the wall, just within reach. She grabbed it – it looked clean – and threw it to him. 'Hold that against the wound.'

She turned her attention back to Whitehead. He appeared to have gone into shock.

'Come on, Adrian. Put the knife down. Then we'll go about fixing all of this, okay?'

He looked at the knife like he could hardly believe he was holding it.

'I couldn't let her leave me again,' he said. 'Neither of them.'

'You mean Michelle? And Billie? Is it them upstairs?'

He nodded, the most pathetic man she had ever seen, so pathetic it was as if his body was deflating as all the fight went out of him.

He looked at the bloody knife again. Then he lifted it and – before she realised what he was about to do, certainly before she could act – drew it across his own throat.

29

After reporting Vicky missing, Calvin drove home, palms sweaty, sticking to the steering wheel. Would Vicky be home, waiting in the kitchen? Would they have a big chat, straighten everything out, hug and maybe cry a little? He would almost certainly weep with relief. He jumped out of the car and ran through the back door, calling her name.

She wasn't there.

He walked around the house, Jarvis at his heels. Then he went around the neighbourhood in person, knocking on doors and asking if anyone had seen Vicky. Had they heard her car last night? Seen anyone else near his house? No one had seen anything. They were all either pensioners or workers who had to get up early, and it left him wishing he lived next door to some young party animals or a curtain-twitching nosy neighbour.

He went back inside. Jarvis wouldn't settle; he kept jumping from one counter to another, yowling. It was as if he wanted to tell Calvin what had happened, what he'd seen. Calvin sat down then got up again. He couldn't relax. Couldn't stay here.

He decided to go to work.

As soon as he walked in – it was busy again, every table full – Mel almost jumped on him, dozens of words rushing out of her in a single breath.

'What's going on? Where have you been? I've got the new temps here, they're in the kitchen, but look how busy it is, I've been struggling to cope and I was really worried because you didn't turn up and I couldn't get hold of you and I thought something might have happened to you or you were angry with me—'

He held up a hand. 'Please. Mel.'

But in a way, he was grateful for this, because it gave him something to focus on. Something other than his fear over what had happened to Vicky. It was still there, constant and unwavering, but at least his body and brain had something else to do.

'I'm going to the kitchen to talk to the temps. I'll explain everything after that. Okay?'

There were three temps: two young women called Caz and Shamira, and a young man called Ade. Calvin introduced himself then took charge, leaving Ade and Caz in the kitchen, preparing food, and instructing Shamira to work with Mel out front. He moved between the two and was soon swept up in the rhythm, the movement, like a conductor directing an orchestra. It was discordant at first, the new players struggling to gel, but then, as if by magic, everything clicked. From the baking in the kitchen to the service out front, the music was sweet and smooth. The customers' impatience vanished as coffee was served and cakes were consumed. The tip jar rattled with coins. The anxiety caused by Vicky's absence was still there, an ache in his stomach, but otherwise it could have been an ordinary day. Or rather, an *extraordinary* day, compared to how business had been only a week ago.

Midway through the afternoon, there was a lull.

Mel came up to him. 'Calvin . . .'

He'd felt her watching him all day, a mixture of curiosity and concern with a dash of guilt. Every time he turned towards her she would quickly avert her eyes, then flash him a little smile. It was beginning to get on his nerves. Why hadn't she woken him?

But he needed to tell her what was going on. He gestured for her to accompany him up to the office, leaving Shamira – who had picked everything up remarkably quickly – to run things downstairs.

'When I got home last night, Vicky wasn't there. She still hasn't come back.'

Mel's mouth dropped open. 'You're kidding.'

'Unfortunately not.' He explained about how he'd been to the police, who had, so far, done nothing.

'Then what are you doing here?' Mel asked. 'If Vicky's missing?'

'I can't stay at home on my own all day. I'd lose my mind if I was there.'

'I understand. I mean, I can imagine.' She twisted her fingers together. 'I'm so sorry I didn't wake you last night.'

'Did you try?'

'Yes. Of course, I mean . . . You were out of it. But I should have tried harder.'

He grunted, trying to fight back the irritation he felt. She sounded so contrite that it was hard to stay angry. Yes, she should have woken him, but it was still his own fault for falling asleep in the first place.

'Has she ever done this before?' Mel asked in a tentative tone.

'What do you mean?'

'Gone AWOL. Vanished into the night.'

'You think that's what she's done? Run off?'

Her fingers twisted together faster and tighter. 'Do you think . . . she's angry with you for coming over to my place? That she's gone off in a rage?'

'A rage?'

'Yes. I mean, she seems like an angry person to me. I can see it behind her eyes. A fury.'

Calvin blinked at this. He had never thought of Vicky as an angry person. Sure, she got mad with people who were cruel to animals. She was a passionate person who wasn't afraid to speak her mind. But angry? No, he was the one with the innate anger; the rage he had fought so hard to lock up tight.

Vicky was principled, though. Intolerant of other people's bull-shit, and not prepared to be made a fool of.

'I can see her storming off,' he said, voicing some of the thoughts that had come and gone since Vicky had vanished. 'Can picture her staying out for the night. But I can't see her leaving me to worry like this for so long. Also, why would she leave her phone behind? It's surgically attached to her most of the time.'

Mel looked like she was holding back words she wasn't brave enough to say.

'What is it? Come on, spit it out.'

'Well. Maybe she has another phone?'

'Why would she have a second phone? She's not a drug dealer!'

'I know but . . . it's not only criminals who have burners. It's also people who are . . . in secret relationships.' She cringed as she said this, glancing up at him through her eyelashes, braced for his reaction.

'You . . . you think my wife is having an affair?'

'I didn't say that.' A pause. 'But it's often guilty people who accuse their partners of cheating.'

He was momentarily speechless. 'What makes you think she accused me of cheating?'

Mel looked confused for a second before recovering her composure. She had stopped the finger-twisting now. 'I know she doesn't like me, Calvin. That she's suspicious of me. I overheard her when she came here.'

So Mel *had* been listening to them. He tried to recall exactly what Vicky had said. Something about how he had a thing for helping damaged women. He thought she had probably mentioned Freya.

'I wasn't eavesdropping,' Mel said hurriedly. 'I just couldn't help but overhear. And I wonder if she was accusing you because she has a guilty conscience. I mean, do you even know for certain that she went to this spa?'

'Oh my God. You think she spent the night with her lover?'

There was a significant pause before Mel said, 'I'm sure that's not what's happened. But it's worth checking, isn't it? Finding out who the last person to see her was?'

Calvin had to sit down. This was crazy. Vicky wasn't having an affair. He, Calvin, had organised the spa break for her. It hadn't even been her idea. She had shown absolutely no signs that she was interested in anyone else.

Why was Mel suggesting it? Did she want him to believe Vicky was cheating on him?

He needed to get out of here. To get away from Mel, go home. Maybe Vicky would be waiting there for him.

30

Imogen left Steve asleep in his hospital bed, thanking God that the knife hadn't penetrated the abdominal wall. The doctors kept telling her how lucky he was. The knife had sliced through the thin layer of skin that covered his belly and he'd needed stitches, but he was okay. They were going to discharge him tomorrow and send him home.

He was okay – unlike Adrian Whitehead, who had died right there at the scene. Imogen had never seen so much blood. When she closed her eyes now she saw crimson, shining and gushing from the slit in his throat, saturating his clothes as he dropped to the kitchen floor. Steve had scooted backwards, flat on his back, holding the tea towel against his stomach. She had found him a fresh one then got back on the radio.

'Where's that ambulance?' she'd almost yelled. 'I need it here *now*.'

She also needed to see what was going on upstairs.

She crouched beside Steve. 'Are you going to be all right?'

He nodded.

'You're not going to pass out? You need to keep that towel pressed against your wound.' She spoke into her radio. 'I'm going upstairs.'

At the top of those stairs, she called out. 'Billie? Michelle? This is the police. Can you give me your location?'

A thud came from the far end of the landing. The last room. There were bolts across the top and bottom of the door. She drew them back, noticing the streak of drying blood on the back of her hand. She paused for a moment. Could this be some kind of trap? Could Adrian have an accomplice? For all Imogen knew, Michelle Whitehead might be sitting in here with a gun trained on her daughter.

But Imogen's instincts told her otherwise. She pushed open the door to reveal a room cloaked in gloom, the curtains closed. There were two women in there. Michelle was on the floor, both hands cuffed to a radiator, her ankles tied together. There was a ball gag in her mouth and a blindfold covering her eyes. She hardly stirred when Imogen entered the room.

Billie was on the bed. She was gagged too – with a piece of cloth rather than the hideous S&M monstrosity her mother had in her mouth – but not blindfolded. Her wrists were secured to the bed posts with handcuffs but her legs were free. Imogen guessed it must have been Billie who had made the noise, by kicking the wall.

Imogen went to Billie first, removing the gag. The girl sucked in a breath and tried to speak but her mouth must have been too dry. There was a bottle of water beside the bed but Imogen didn't know if it contained drugs and didn't want to risk giving it to her. As she crossed the room to Michelle, she got back on the radio, describing the situation.

She removed the ball gag and the blindfold and spoke softly to Michelle. 'It's fine now. You're safe.'

Michelle opened her eyes, but even this low amount of light must have hurt – how long had she been blindfolded? – because she immediately squeezed them shut again.

'Where is he?' she managed to say.

'He's not going to hurt you anymore,' Imogen had responded.

Now, after leaving Steve's hospital room three hours later, she wanted nothing more than to go home and take a very long shower – but she also needed to talk to Michelle. Mother and daughter had both been too distressed to talk in the immediate aftermath and, once she'd known they were safe, Imogen had needed to leave them so she could return to Steve and the bloody scene downstairs. When the ambulances and police cars had turned up, mercifully quickly, the surviving Whiteheads had been led out first, put in an ambulance and brought straight here to the hospital.

Imogen found Dr Hosseini, who had examined Michelle and Billie. She was a thirty-something woman with the kind of brisk, efficient manner Imogen looked for in her own doctors, and Imogen caught her coming out of the ward.

'How are they?' she asked.

'Not too bad. Dehydrated and shaken, but they're not injured beyond some bruising and soreness. It sounds like they had only been in that room for twelve hours or so before you found them.' Dr Hosseini looked Imogen up and down. 'You're something of a hero, aren't you?'

'Or a magnet for human shit.'

'An unpleasant thought.' The doctor wrinkled her nose. 'But it sounds to me like Cumbria Police are lucky to have you.'

The compliment bounced off Imogen without leaving a mark.

She found Michelle Whitehead sitting up in bed, dressed in a hospital gown, staring into space. Billie, apparently, had been put in a private room and was currently asleep.

Imogen pulled up a plastic chair beside Michelle's bed. 'Do you mind if I ask you a few questions?'

'Sure.' Michelle's voice was still croaky and she looked drained, like it was her who'd lost pints of blood. Despite that, as she spoke Imogen detected a hardness that would hopefully go some way to protect her from the effects of the psychological trauma she'd just been through.

'Adrian told me you'd recently returned home after living with another man for a period. Was that man Leo James?'

There was a moment of hesitation, then Michelle nodded.

'I'm sorry for your loss,' Imogen said, noting the flash of surprise on Michelle's face.

'Thank you.' Another long pause. 'I couldn't grieve. I couldn't even go to the funeral.'

'Adrian wouldn't let you?'

'I was supposed to be working on my marriage. For Billie's sake. And nobody else knew about Leo and me. I don't have any friends around here, detective. Adrian didn't like me having friends.' She swallowed. 'Leo was my only friend. For a time, anyway.'

'Hold on. Did you know Leo before Billie met him?'

'Yes.'

That was news. Imogen's brain tried to race ahead, to figure out what this meant, but she forced herself to put the brakes on. To listen.

'We met on the beach. I used to go down there to think. And to sketch. To dream. I kept seeing Leo. This mysterious character who lived in the woods, who everyone speculated about. The hermit. The weirdo. It intrigued me and made me think . . .'

'Made you think what?'

'That maybe we were alike. Two lonely souls. So one day I went up to him and struck up a conversation. It was funny – he was so startled he almost ran away. But I think he was desperate for friendship too. Someone to talk to.'

'And one thing led to another?'

That brought a little smile. 'One day we just ended up going back to his cottage. And I didn't leave. I got a message to Billie telling her I was safe but that I didn't want her dad to know where

I was. Then I turned my phone off.' She shook her head. 'I know, it sounds mad but . . . I was so desperately unhappy in my marriage. So trapped. And Leo listened to me. He made me feel like I wasn't worthless or ugly or stupid. I just hid out with him in his house, and he cooked for me and listened and made love to me like, well, like a starving man. He made me feel human again. Made me feel loved.'

'But you came home?'

'Yeah. I went back to Adrian. It was the guilt over Billie. Plus I missed her. I thought about setting up a secret meeting with her but knew there was too much risk that Adrian would follow her and that he'd hurt Leo. Attack him. So I left. Went home.' She paused. 'It wasn't just that. Leo wasn't always easy to be with. He was tortured. He'd wake up in the night, panting and acting like he was being attacked. It was scary. A few times I'd catch him staring at me like he didn't know who or what I was.'

Imogen tried to make sense of everything. 'When did all this happen?'

'I went home just after Christmas. Adrian didn't even ask me where I'd been. It was . . . unsettling. But not a huge surprise. Adrian doesn't like to ask questions he doesn't want to hear the answers to. He didn't want to know I'd been with another man; would rather believe I'd been off on my own. But Billie kept bugging me, asking and asking, and in the end I gave in, knowing she wouldn't tell her father. And I guess she went to see Leo. Struck up her own friendship with him.'

So Billie's story about meeting Leo on the beach was a lie.

'Did you know? About her going to see him, I mean?'

'No, of course not. I would have stopped her. I was scared Adrian would find out. And then Leo was killed, in that awful, awful way, and bloody Billie went to the funeral and you saw her and everything came out. Billie told her dad about me and Leo, and Adrian went mad. Locked us in that room. Said he wouldn't let either of us leave him again.'

'Wait,' Imogen said. 'Are you telling me Adrian didn't know about Leo until after the funeral?'

'Yes. I mean – he definitely didn't know Billie had been friends with him.'

'But what about you and Leo? He hadn't found out about you?'

Again, her mind tried to race ahead. She had been sure they'd found their murderer. That Adrian Whitehead had found out about Leo's involvement with his wife and friendship with his daughter, which he had probably suspected to be more than platonic, and decided to punish him. Adrian was capable of locking up his own wife and daughter. He had cut Steve, then taken his own life. He was certainly capable of violence. Surely he was the murderer? Surely the case was about to be closed, all the pressure off, no more superflop, back to supercop?

Michelle's next words made Imogen's stomach twist with disappointment.

'Detective, I'm certain he didn't know about us until last week. I was always worried he might find the photo of Leo that I kept hidden on my phone, but I'm sure he never did.'

Imogen, who had been trying not to let the despair show on her face, leapt on this piece of information. 'You have a photo? A recent one?'

'Yeah. I took it. It's a nice one of him sitting in bed. I kept it in a hidden folder.'

'I'm going to need you to forward that to me.'

'Of course.'

Imogen went back a step in the conversation. 'You really don't think Adrian could have murdered Leo?'

'I *know* he didn't do it. It was the Sunday before last, wasn't it? And Leo was found Monday morning? Adrian was with me that whole day and night. Ever since I went home, Adrian wouldn't let me out of his sight.'

This was not what Imogen wanted to hear.

'You said Leo listened to you a lot, but did he talk, tell you about himself? You know we haven't been able to find out anything about him, where he's from, anything.'

Michelle closed her eyes for a second. 'I know. I saw the news reports. Your appeals. And I'm sorry, detective, but I talked, he listened. He never volunteered anything about himself.'

'And you didn't ask?'

'I tried. But he just kept saying there was nothing to tell.'

Imogen wanted to kick something. She'd found a woman who'd been sleeping with Leo James and even *she* didn't know anything about him, except for the extremely unhelpful fact that he made love like a starving man. At least they would have a photo now, though.

'Did he seem afraid of anyone? Act like he was in hiding?'

'No.'

'Did he ever have any visitors?'

'No.' There was a pause. 'There is one thing. I don't think Leo was his real name.'

Imogen looked at her.

'Sometimes I'd say his name and he wouldn't react until I'd said it again, and then he'd kind of blink at me before it dawned on him I was talking to him.'

'But you don't know what his real name was?'

'Sorry.'

Imogen said goodbye to Michelle and headed to Billie's room. Billie had just been through an ordeal but Imogen now knew she'd been, at the very least, withholding information. She needed to talk to her again.

But her room was empty, a nurse changing the bed sheets.

'She's gone,' the nurse said. 'Discharged herself. Said she was feeling fine and just wanted to go home.'

'What, you just let her go?' Imogen sucked in a breath, then marched away, furious.

On the way out of the hospital, Imogen saw a familiar face. Karen Lamb, the pathologist. Imogen tried to hide but it was too late. Karen saw her.

'I hear I've got another one of yours waiting for me,' she said. 'Leo James's murderer, I hear. Congratula—'

'The only person Adrian Whitehead killed is himself.' Imogen turned her face towards the nearest window. It gave a view of the hospital car park and the town. But beyond that, the lakes and hills and beaches and woods. All the places someone could hide, in dark places or plain sight. 'Leo James's murderer is still out there.'

31

Tuesday night was the worst of Calvin's life to that point. Worse even than when Freya had been killed. He got home from Therapy and got straight on the phone, calling all Vicky's friends again, asking if anyone had heard from her. Then he messaged the neighbourhood WhatsApp group. When they came back with nothing but confused concern, he went on to Vicky's Facebook page and messaged the friends she only communicated with online. One of them suggested he should create an appeal post and ask everyone to share it. That was, he thought, a good idea. He posted a recent photo of Vicky on her page, explaining when she'd last been seen, then asked everyone to share it.

Have you seen this woman?

The comments began to appear immediately, but none of them were particularly helpful. It was just lots of people telling him they'd shared it, along with their thoughts and prayers. Someone offered to give him the name of a psychic who had helped her mum find her missing cat and Calvin blocked them, not being in the mood for any bullshit.

He left that running, then logged in to his Therapy social account, which had a much larger potential reach than Vicky's

Facebook circle. Tara was still in charge of this account but he could do this himself. The platform didn't allow you to post a single still image so he posted a few still pictures of Vicky from his phone, accompanied by some maudlin piano music and text explaining who she was. He hit post with a little surge of hope.

Somebody out there must have seen her. Somebody, he was sure, must know where she was.

But all he got on his post was a flood of heart emojis, people saying 'Hope you find her' and a couple of people asking him what he'd done to drive her away, followed by the crying-with-laughter emoji.

He had always known it. Social media was a playground for weirdos.

Frustrated, he put the phone down and went upstairs to go through Vicky's suitcase again, futilely combing through it for a clue.

Lingerie. From her dirty night away.

He pushed that thought away immediately, ashamed of himself and angry with Mel for putting the idea in his head. He made himself dinner but he was so distracted he burned it, and he didn't have any appetite anyway. He wanted a drink but he also needed to keep a clear head. And what if he was required to drive? He paced and paced, watching the minutes crawl by, jumping at every noise. At one point his phone rang and he snatched it up, pleading silently for it to be her, but it was one of her friends, phoning to see if he'd heard from her. He couldn't help it: he was rude, hanging up on her, not wanting the line to be engaged unnecessarily.

Eventually, he went to bed, but he didn't sleep. He thrashed around in the giant, empty space all night, feeling like there were fat worms in his head, squirming against the inside of his skull. His skin was too tight, his armpits prickled. He sweated then shivered as the sweat cooled. He imagined an entire funeral for his wife, modelled on the terrible farewell they'd given Freya years before, when his mum had been catatonic and his dad had wept and flung himself on the grave, the other pallbearers having to pull him up and hold on to him until he got himself together. In this new fantasy, it was Calvin who threw himself on to the grave, even though the coffin was empty because Vicky had never been found. He crawled in the mud and sobbed, and someone stood over him, a silhouette with a voice he hadn't heard in a long time, telling him this was karma. This was his comeuppance.

ϖ

He was woken by a knock at the door. His first thought: *Vicky*. She was home. The nightmare was over. He ran down the stairs, wearing the T-shirt and boxers he'd fallen asleep in, and flung the door open.

It wasn't Vicky. Of course it wasn't. It was the young woman who had been with DJ outside Mel's house. The one who looked like Freya. It was a warm day, the sky cloudless and blue, and she was dressed in a vest top and a short skirt, her hair tied back into a ponytail. How old was she? Anywhere between seventeen and twenty.

'Chef Calvin?' she said. 'Can I talk to you?'

'What is it about?' His immediate thought was that it must be about Vicky. Did she know something?

She glanced behind her, nervous, like she was afraid of something.

'Do you want to come in?' he asked.

Her expression reminded him of what he must look like, standing there in his T-shirt and boxer shorts, hair sticking up, crumpled from sleep. Of course she didn't want to come in. In fact, she retreated a little way down the garden path and said something he couldn't hear.

'What's going on?' he asked.

She looked even more nervous now, eyes darting around. He looked down at himself. Okay, he was in his underwear but the shorts were baggy and stopped just above his knees; nothing was on display. He left the house and took a few steps towards her.

'Is this about my wife? Do you know where she is?'

'Huh? Oh . . . No. I've just got a message for you.'

'From Vicky?'

She looked around again, glancing towards the entrance to the woods at the end of the cul-de-sac, about twenty feet away. Was that the way she'd come?

'What's your name?' he asked.

She hesitated. 'Billie.'

'And what's this message, Billie?'

'I need to whisper it.'

Before he could react, she stepped forward and put her hand on his chest, which made him feel extremely uncomfortable, then leaned in so her lips were close to his ear.

'This is the beginning of the end,' she said.

He jerked away. 'What?'

But she was already walking away, fast, towards the trees. Calvin was about to chase her when his next-door neighbour, Margaret, came outside. She was a woman in her sixties, a widow and retired librarian, who Calvin hadn't seen for a while. She'd been on holiday for the past couple of weeks, he remembered, and must have just got back. She gave him and the departing Billie a curious look, taking in his bare legs and feet and raising her eyebrows. It wouldn't look good: a middle-aged man in his underwear, chasing a teenage girl. He had no choice but to hold back, watching her go. She slipped into the trees.

Was it his imagination or did he hear her say something? And someone speak back? A male voice.

He was still staring at the woods when Margaret said, 'I saw your messages about Vicky on the WhatsApp. How worrying. Is she still not back?'

He shook his head. His mind was racing and he wanted to run inside and get dressed, pursue Billie and whoever she was with. But Margaret was still talking.

'If there's anything I can do to help—'

He cut her off. 'Thank you.'

He went back inside. It was too late to chase after Billie now. She'd be long gone.

He didn't understand what had just happened. *The beginning of the end.*

What did that mean?

ϖ

He phoned Louise on the way to the coffee shop to check Vicky hadn't turned up at work. He left a message for DI Evans too, asking her to call him. He needed the police to take Vicky's disappearance seriously.

He spent most of the morning in the kitchen with the temps, preparing food. When he went out front, he found Mel behind the counter looking bored, and noticed a few customers staring at him, frowning. One woman shook her head, apparently disgusted about something.

Then, at lunchtime, a voice said, 'Calvin?'

It was Tara, poking her head into the kitchen.

He went to the doorway to give her a hug, being careful not to bump her wrist, which was still in a cast.

'How is it?' he asked.

'Itchy as hell. I am also dying of boredom at home. I've completed Netflix, Prime and Disney Plus. Watched everything. Twice.' The grin that accompanied these words slipped away. 'But there's something I need to talk to you about.'

'Oh?'

She glanced behind her, towards the counter, where Mel stood, apparently minding her own business. 'Can we go to the office? I don't want anyone to overhear.'

Once upstairs, Calvin insisted that Tara should have the only seat. Her first words were, 'Is there any news about Vicky?'

'You heard about that?'

'Calvin, I saw your post.'

'Oh. Yes.'

'Besides, the whole village knows. The whole county. What I don't understand is what happened. Did she make it home from the spa?'

He explained, as succinctly as he could, about the events of Monday night. Tara looked faintly appalled when he told her he'd fallen asleep on Mel's sofa and said, 'Oh God, Calvin.'

'I already feel shit about it.'

She gave him a look that told him he deserved to feel crap, then produced her phone from the pocket of her hoodie. '*This* is what I wanted to talk to you about. Have you looked at the Therapy account this morning?'

'Not really. I mean, I skimmed through the comments but it was mostly nonsense. Nothing useful.' Hope flared. 'Why, has someone said they know where she is?'

'Sorry, no.' She paused. 'You haven't checked the message inbox?'

'No.'

'Good. Because I would stay out of it if I were you. There's some . . . unpleasant stuff in there.'

'What kind of stuff?' He couldn't resist. He immediately found his own phone and opened the app that, just a week ago, he'd been addicted to.

'Calvin, don't.'

But it was too late. He had already opened his inbox, which was full of messages from accounts he didn't recognise.

I know you did it.

MURDEROR YOR GOIN TO BERN IN HELL!!!

I was so sorry to hear about your wife but you can tell me in confidence if it was you and if you need someone to come over to comfort you. DM me back for pix

You think you are a good man don't you but you are just another lethal misogynist and your cakes taste of shit. You had better get out of this village or YOU WILL BE THE NEXT TO DIE.

'I told you not to look,' said Tara. 'Some of them are pretty crazy.'

'*Some* of them?'

'I also have to tell you there are a lot of posts about Vicky's disappearance. Amateur sleuths speculating about what might have happened to her. I hate to tell you this, Calvin, but the social mob's consensus is that, well, she's dead and that you did it.'

Again, Calvin couldn't help but look. He found posts in which he'd been tagged; posts in which people he'd never heard of talked about how Calvin looked 'sus' – short for suspicious, he guessed – and that there was 'something dark' about him. There were lots of stats about how a high percentage of missing women were found to have been murdered by their partners, which led to an argument on one post about how men always got the blame for everything, culminating in the use of the word 'feminazi' and someone being called Hitler.

'Some people have been posting maps of the area and pictures of your street, most of it taken from Google Maps and Street View.'

He went cold. 'You mean, there are pictures of my house? With the address?'

'I haven't seen anyone post your actual address but it's quite easy to work out from the maps and images. Then there are lots of people fighting about whether doxxing is ever ethical.'

'What-ing?'

'Doxxing. It's when you publish someone's private information online. I'm sorry, Calvin. This is the dark side of social media.'

He needed to sit down, but the only seat was taken. The next best thing was to lean back against the wall.

'People think I've murdered Vicky? And what, buried her in the back garden or something?'

'Or in the woods near your house. Or filled her pockets with pebbles and thrown her into a lake. That's probably the most popular theory.'

He unlocked his phone again and started tapping at it.

'What are you doing?' Tara asked.

'Posting a statement about my innocence.'

Tara sprung up and, using her good hand, snatched his phone from his grip. 'Don't be an idiot. You need to stay quiet. Every single word you post from now on will be pored over, dissected, turned against you.'

She was looking at his phone as she said this, scrolling with her thumb. Her face told Calvin she'd seen something horrible.

'What is it? What's happened?'

'It's just . . . a comment.'

She handed the phone to him and he read what a user called caravan_rubbish had written:

> *I know for a fact that Chef Calvin is screwing this female who works for him. Monday night (the same night his wife 'disappeared'!!) he came home with this woman and went into her house for hours. I also heard this isn't the first time he cheated. He's mostly into much younger girls. Looking at this female he's screwing now he isn't that fussy about where he sticks it. PS this female's name is Mel.*

Calvin read it twice. There were already multiple responses and follow-up comments.

> *I knew it!*

> *Oldest story on Earth. Chef Calvin's gonna burn for this.*

> *Great intel caravan_rubbish!*

'It has to be DJ,' Calvin said, half to himself. It felt like there was a fist in his stomach, squeezing, and his voice came out sounding strangled. 'Or one of his friends. They're trying to set me up – revenge, for me telling them off.' His eyes popped wide. 'What the hell *is* this? "Into much younger girls"?'

He flashed to an image of the Freya-lookalike standing outside his house. Billie. *The beginning of the end.* Is this what she'd been telling him? That DJ's revenge plot against him was about to kick off? He thought he might vomit.

'DJ is the guy with the bonfire?' Tara took the phone back and scrolled through the comments. 'Jesus, Calvin, this is blowing up.

People love this kind of stuff. The McCanns. Amanda Knox. It can go on for years.'

Calvin didn't need to look in a mirror to know he'd gone completely white.

'You need to nip this in the bud asap. But not by going online and pleading innocence. You need to act.' She dropped her voice. 'You should start by firing Mel.'

'What? Won't that make me look guiltier? Like I'm reacting to the gossip rather than ignoring it because it's ridiculous?'

'Is it ridiculous?'

'What are you asking?'

She glanced towards the stairs. 'You're not sleeping with her, are you?'

'No, I'm not! I told you, I went into Mel's house, nothing happened. I had a cup of tea and a biscuit and fell asleep on her sofa.'

There was a long moment of silence. 'Right.'

'What do you mean by that?'

'Just . . . it doesn't sound plausible. You passed out on her sofa halfway through your cup of tea?'

'That's what happened.'

'And why didn't she try to wake you?'

'She says she did.'

Tara shook her head. 'Calvin, I know I'm your employee, but I like to think of myself as your friend too.'

'You are.'

'Then tell me the truth. Are you sure it wasn't her bed you fell asleep in?'

He thumped the table, almost exploding with the frustration. The innocent man accused of a crime he didn't commit. 'I didn't go anywhere near her bed!'

Tara raised her palms. 'All right. I believe you. It's just . . . weird. Don't you think?' She dropped her voice. 'Have you ever done anything like that before? Nodded off like that?'

'I . . .'

He thought about it. Had he? He'd dozed off on trains plenty of times. He often nodded off on the sofa while reading or watching TV. He'd fallen asleep in the cinema a couple of times. But he'd never done it in company like that before, in someone else's house. He'd put it down to exhaustion at the end of a hard week. The adrenaline crash after the confrontation with DJ. But was there something he was refusing to admit to himself? He thought about the dream he'd had. Kissing Mel. And how their heads had collided when he'd woken up. He remembered her reaction when he'd touched her on the shoulder. Vicky telling him to be careful around her. How keen Mel had been to get him into her house.

Oh God. Could she . . . ? Surely not.

Could she have drugged him?

Kissed him while he was asleep?

'Oh fuck,' he said to himself.

'What are you thinking?' Tara asked.

He didn't want to say it out loud. It couldn't be true. Maybe Mel had a bit of a crush on him but she wouldn't *drug* him. She wouldn't assault him while he was asleep.

'I was exhausted,' he said finally. 'I zonked out.'

Tara studied his face. 'I really hope you're telling the truth, Calvin. Because if Vicky doesn't come back, the police are going to be the ones asking these questions.' She looked towards the stairs. 'On top of that, it's quieter here today, isn't it? This stuff could already be having an effect. Driving customers away.'

'Surely it's just a blip.'

'I don't think so. I'm sorry, Calvin, but you need to get rid of Mel. All the time she's here working with you, tongues are going to wag.'

'But I haven't done anything wrong – and neither has Mel.' He had to believe that. Anything else was too crazy, too frightening. 'She's done nothing except help me out, Tara. And I did one thing to try to return the favour and everything has gone insane.'

'All right. Forget the police and your customers for a minute. Think about Vicky. If she comes back, all of this goes away. What if she's hiding out, waiting to see what you do, trying to persuade herself that you're not having an affair? Getting rid of Mel would be a step towards proving your loyalty. You don't need Mel here anymore, now you've got your temps. And I can come back too. I might only have one working arm but I can help out, take orders, do the admin. If you feel awful about firing her, pay her a bonus. You can surely afford it, the way things have been going. And I bet she'll understand. She knew it was only temporary.'

He got up from the chair and went over to the tiny window, with its view of an alleyway between the cafe and the shop next door. To his surprise, Mel was standing there, outside the back door, next to the bins. He could only see the top of her head but it was definitely her. Was she smoking? No, she appeared to be simply standing there, staring into space.

Tara came over and followed his gaze.

'What's she doing?' she asked him.

'I don't know. Getting some air, I guess.'

He still couldn't believe that Vicky would disappear because she thought he was having an affair. Shout at him, demand a divorce, instigate long, painful conversations, drag him to see a couples therapist. Even vanish for a few hours. But to hide out for what was getting on for two days? It just wasn't her – which meant that firing Mel wouldn't do anything to help bring her back.

Mel was still in the alley and he could see that her head was dipped, staring at the pavement. He couldn't help it. He felt sorry for her. He couldn't sack her; she loved working here and it wouldn't feel right or fair, not when she'd done so much to help him. She hadn't drugged him. He was embarrassed that he'd even entertained the idea.

He turned away from the window. 'I'm not firing her. It's not right.'

'I think you're making a big mistake.'

He was tired of arguing about it. Tired of talking. He went downstairs, at the same time that Mel came back inside. He did a double take. Had she been crying? She went straight into the toilet before he had a chance to say anything.

The coffee shop was almost empty, just a couple of elderly customers sipping cups of tea. It hadn't been this quiet for a week.

A movement outside caught his eye. There were two teenage girls with their faces pressed up against the window, gawping at him. As soon as they saw him notice them, one of them mock-screamed, like she'd been spotted by a monster.

They ran away up the street, laughing.

32

The first thing Calvin did when he got home was call Vicky's name, hoping for a miracle, but of course she wasn't there. Almost forty-eight hours had passed now, and there was a war going on in his mind: a war between the more hopeful side of him, telling him she had gone away of her own volition, and the side that said something terrible had happened to her.

He went into the kitchen, expecting to see Jarvis, but the cat was nowhere to be seen. That was unusual. It was 6 p.m. and Jarvis never missed dinner. Calvin quickly went around the house checking the cat hadn't accidentally been shut in a room again, but there was no sign of him.

Normally, Calvin would give it a couple of hours before he started to worry. Cats went off wandering all the time. It was spring. Jarvis was probably sitting over a mouse hole or doing whatever it was cats did when they weren't curled up indoors. But having lost his wife this week, and with his nerves jangling, he knew he wouldn't be able to settle until he had Jarvis in his arms. On top of that, he was sure he hadn't let Jarvis out before leaving for work that morning, although it was possible he'd snuck out when Calvin opened the door.

He went to the back door and called the cat's name, then went out and looked around the garden. The lawn needed mowing and weeds were springing up in the beds Vicky always kept so neat. That hadn't taken long. He had an image of weeks passing, of the weeds choking the flowers Vicky had planted.

'Jarvis!'

He checked the shed, peered over the neighbour's wall, then went round to the front of the house and yelled again. He went into the kitchen and brought out the tin they kept the cat food in. Hearing the lid being removed from this tin always signalled to Jarvis that it was dinnertime. Calvin stood in the back then the front gardens, clanging the lid, waiting, then clanging it again.

He heard a faint meow.

'Jarvis?'

A neighbour a few doors up was playing loud music, and there was traffic going by on the main road, and Calvin thought he might go insane with frustration. But in a moment of silence he heard another mew.

He walked around the garden, listening intently. Where could he be? Was it coming from inside the house? He went indoors again and searched, opening all the cupboards, peering under beds, checking inside the tumble dryer and the airing cupboard. He stood and listened but couldn't hear anything. It was only when he went back outside that he heard it. A faint cry.

He walked down the side of the house to the front and there it was again: louder this time.

Surely not?

He approached the wheelie bin. The dustmen had been yesterday and, despite everything, he had remembered to put the bins out, dragging them back in last night. He hadn't put any rubbish in it since, so the bin should be empty.

But the meowing grew louder as Calvin got closer.

He opened the lid and two green eyes looked up at him.

'Oh, Jarvis!'

Calvin reached in and the cat clawed at his arms as he lifted him out, holding the wriggling animal close. As he did this, he glanced down into the bin and saw an envelope.

He took Jarvis indoors and deposited him safely in the kitchen, then went back outside. He leaned over the wheelie bin, trying not to breathe in, stretching to pluck out the envelope. He opened it to reveal a single word.

MURDERER.

He looked left and right. Peered up the street towards the main road and back towards the woods. There was no one around. No figures lurking at the edge of the trees. No shadowy accuser standing beneath a lamp post. Just a quiet, ordinary street.

He went back into the kitchen and found his phone. He was about to call the police when he wondered if it was worth it. What would they do? They'd done nothing when the coffee shop was broken into, even though Tara had been injured, and so far they'd done zero to find Vicky. He already knew there was no CCTV on the street, and if anyone had seen anything they would have already messaged the WhatsApp group.

He went back into the living room, taking a glass of water and a packet of headache tablets with him. He coaxed the cat out from beneath the armchair and took him over to the sofa. Jarvis settled down on his lap and began to purr.

Calvin opened the social media app and went to his account. There were over a hundred messages in his inbox and so many comments that he scrolled through them for two minutes without getting anywhere near the bottom of the notifications list.

Another cheating piece of shit pretending to be a nice guy. They should bring back the death penalty in this country you are sick and EVIL and I hope there is a place called HELL where you will BURN

Ignore all the crazies Chef Calvin I can see in your eyes that you are a kind man and also a gentle lover and if you want somewhere to hide out you are welcome here with me HAHA JK YOU ARE GUILTY AS SIN AND YOU SHOULD KILL YRSELF

Cheat

Scum

MURDERER

They were all like that. People, strangers, openly accusing him of the worst possible crimes. Most of them didn't even hide behind pseudonyms, and he clicked on a couple of profiles to see what kind of people would send such vicious messages to someone they'd never met. Of course, they were ordinary people. A grandmother. A woman whose feed was full of pictures of her spaniel. A guy who described himself as a 'dad and truth seeker who loves true crime and Taylor Swift'. A young woman whose profile included the hashtag #bekind.

The whole world thought he, Calvin, was guilty. And scrolling through the comments he found dozens of references to Mel, using her name, discussing her attractiveness, asking what he saw in her, speculating about what she must be like in bed. Vile, obscene, misogynistic. He wondered if she was looking at this stuff. His anger flared and he wanted to reply to all of these finger-pointing bastards, tell them what he thought of them.

He almost messaged Mel too. Only just stopped himself. Because although his lifelong belief that the police were useless didn't waver, he remembered Tara's warning. If Vicky didn't come back, they would look at him first. And if they saw he'd been messaging the woman everyone thought he was sleeping with late at night . . .

Tara had to be right about that. And maybe she was right about everything else too.

He went back and forth a few more times, wrestling with his own sense of right and wrong. Not wanting to give in to the social media mob but not wanting this to escalate any further. Someone had already locked his cat in a wheelie bin.

What would be next?

With a heavy heart, he realised what he had to do.

33

He couldn't get to sleep for hours, finally drifting off sometime around four, then woke up with someone ringing the doorbell. Groggy and confused, he sat up. Bright sun was shooting through the curtains like a death ray. He pulled on his jeans and went downstairs, thinking it must be Billie again, but it was the postman, delivering one of Vicky's beauty subscription boxes. Calvin took it and was shocked to see the time. Nine fifteen. He had overslept by hours.

He drove at speed into the centre of Elderbridge, parked then ran down the street to Therapy. As soon as he went inside he saw Tara, sitting at the table closest to the counter, staring at her phone. Shamira was behind the counter. No sign of Mel, and there were only a few customers, all of them lifting their heads to watch him as he came in. Shamira wouldn't meet his eye.

What had happened now?

Tara beckoned him over with some urgency.

'What is it?' he asked.

'Have you been online in the last half hour?'

'No. I overslept.'

'Calvin, I think you need to invest in some caffeine tablets. Give me your phone. You need to look at this.'

Her expression was grim. She tapped at his phone screen a couple of times then handed it to him, saying, 'I came here as soon as I saw this. It was only posted thirty minutes ago but the comments have already gone crazy.'

He didn't need to see the comments to imagine exactly what they might say. The short video clip he was looking at showed him standing in his front garden with Billie, dressed in his T-shirt and boxer shorts. From the angle the video had been shot at – up the street, indicating the cameraperson had been standing just inside the woods – he and Billie appeared to be even closer together than they actually had been. She put her hand on his chest and leaned in close to whisper in his ear. In reality, she had been saying, *This is the beginning of the end.* In this social media post she could have been saying anything. She could even be leaning in to kiss him.

The caption read:

> *Told you he's into younger women! Chef Calvin isn't only screwing his assistant. He's also been hooking up with this nineteen-year-old girl. Anyone still think he's innocent of killing his wife??*

'What the hell is going on, Calvin?' Tara said.

He made a spluttering noise. Comments on the short clip were coming in fast, scrolling up the screen, but he caught a few words and sentences: *sicko, perv, killer, paedo, caught with his pants down, great work caravan_trash!*

'That's Billie Whitehead,' Tara said.

'You know her?'

'Yeah. She lives in Drigg. Went to my school, though she's a few years younger than me. Didn't you hear about her dad? He locked her and her mum up and then killed himself, right in front of the police. Slit his throat. How have you not heard about this?

It only happened on Tuesday. It's replaced the guy on the beach as the thing everyone is talking about. Well, apart from you. And now they're going to be going even crazier, trying to figure how it all fits together.' She paused. '*I'm* trying to figure it out.'

He tried to take all this in.

'Why did her dad kill himself?'

'No one knows. The police won't say, Billie's mum won't talk to anyone and no one has seen Billie. The rumour is that Billie's mum was shagging someone else and he, the dad, found out and went mad. Honestly, I've lived here my whole life and *nothing* has ever happened in Elderbridge or Drigg up to this point. And now we've got a murder, a horrific suicide . . .'

'And Vicky going missing.'

'And here you and Billie are in a video together, connecting two of those things.'

He stared at her, then at the video again, comments still streaming in.

'I don't even know her. It's a set-up,' he said. 'She's one of DJ's friends. This is revenge for me telling them off, trying to stop their fun.' He thumped the counter. 'Fucking DJ. I bet he made her do it. I'm going to kill him.'

The ears of the nearby customers pricked up. Right now, he didn't care. He was so angry he could barely see straight.

At that moment, Mel appeared from the kitchen. She looked from Tara to Calvin, eyes widening.

'Is everything all right?'

'No, it's not all right,' he said. Here she was, walking directly into his sights. Someone who was partly responsible for this mess. Someone to blame. If she hadn't asked him to go to her house he would never have encountered DJ or Billie. If she hadn't invited him inside. If she had only bloody woken him up!

'Have you seen what's happening online?' he asked.

'That stupid gossip? It's nothing to worry about.'

'How can you say that? Look around. All our customers have abandoned us. I'm being accused of murdering my own wife, of being a monster who can't keep his dick in his pants. Whatever I've—' He broke off, got hold of himself. 'When I got home last night, Jarvis was trapped in the wheelie bin. Someone had put him in there with a note that said "murderer".'

'You never told me that,' Tara said, shocked.

He got up from the table and prowled to the area behind the counter, taking a cold bottle of lemonade out of the fridge. He cracked it open and downed it in one swallow, hoping it might cool him down. He dragged his sleeve over his sweating brow.

'I need Vicky to come home,' he said, going back over to Mel and Tara, and he remembered what Tara had said the day before. About how Vicky might be watching, waiting to see what he did. Waiting for him to make this right.

He would deal with DJ and Billie next. But first . . .

'I'm going to have to let you go,' he said to Mel.

She didn't speak at first. She put a hand on her chest like he'd shot her through the heart, but she didn't say anything.

'Mel, are you taking this in?'

There was another long silence. Finally, she said, with a tremble in her voice, 'Yes. You're firing me.'

Tara got up. 'I'm going to leave you to it. I'll be in the office.'

She hurried upstairs. Moments later, the remaining customers got up and went, leaving Calvin and Mel alone. Shamira was in the kitchen.

'You can't do this,' Mel said. 'I haven't done anything wrong.'

Her upset removed the sting from his anger.

'Mel, I'm doing this to protect you from all the gossip and speculation.'

'To protect me.' She shook her head. 'After all I've done for you. This place would have fallen apart the last week if it wasn't for me. I've been – what was it Vicky said? – a godsend.'

That confirmed for certain that Mel had overheard the conversation with Vicky, when she'd accused him of hiring Mel because of his issues with 'damaged women'.

'I know, and I'm grateful. I probably wouldn't have coped without you.'

'Not probably. Absolutely certainly.'

'Maybe you can come back when all this has blown over,' he said. 'When Vicky's home . . .'

'In other words, never.'

He stared at her. She'd just put the sting back. 'What the hell's that supposed to mean?'

Mel's jaw was clenched. 'Nothing.'

'No, tell me. Why do you think she's not going to come back?'

'I don't know.'

But he wasn't going to let her off the hook. 'You must know why you said it.'

Mel stared back at him, and he could tell she was trying to hold back what she wanted to say. But she couldn't. The need to speak the words overpowered any desire she might have had to defuse the situation.

'She's obviously unhinged. Jealous. I know exactly what she thinks of me: that I'm some kind of nutcase who became fixated on you online and decided to worm my way into your life.'

Oh God. She'd overheard even more of that conversation than he'd feared. Although that meant she must have been listening in deliberately. Standing in the kitchen by the door, eavesdropping.

He found himself saying, 'And maybe she was right all along.'

'What? You're saying I'm a stalker? What, you think I'm obsessed with you? In love with you? My God, men and their egos. And their jealous wives feeding those egos.'

'If you hadn't let me fall asleep on your sofa, if you'd woken me up like any normal person would, none of this would have happened.'

'I tried to wake you!'

'Obviously not very fucking hard.'

She reacted like he'd struck her. She pulled her apron off and threw it on to the floor.

'Fuck you,' she said, and not only was there no response to that, but he wouldn't have had time to come up with one, because she stormed across to the door and flew through it, slamming it behind her.

He watched her stomp up the road until she disappeared from view, then slumped forward across the table and put his head in his hands.

'Are you all right?' It was Tara, who had come back down from the office. 'How was she?'

'How do you think? Can you hold the fort? Shamira's in the kitchen. I just need you to supervise.'

'Where are you going?'

He held up his phone. 'To see DJ. I'm going to sort this shit out.'

34

Imogen was getting a cup of vile coffee from the vending machine when Mehmet, who was working the front desk, came in and said, 'I've just had a call from a woman who was swimming in Foxton Water.'

Imogen looked at him blankly.

'It's one of the smaller lakes, the other side of Elderbridge. Near Drigg.' He showed it to her on the map on his phone. There it was, a few miles inland from the beach where Leo was murdered, and not too far from St Bart's church. One day, if she stayed here, she would know the names of all the bodies of water in the county, just as she knew how to get around the London Underground system without having to study the map.

'Please tell me she's found a message in a bottle. A full, signed confession for Leo James's murder.'

Mehmet didn't smile. Not much of a sense of humour, then. Imogen was certain that one of these days a wisecrack was going to get her into serious trouble. 'She says there's a car under the water,' he said. 'And it doesn't look like it's been there long.'

ϖ

It took an hour to get the police divers out to the lake to carry out a preliminary investigation. Imogen wasn't sure if this was going to end up being her case, if it was connected to all the other stuff that was going on, but she had been the most senior officer around when the call came in. Now she stood on the banks of the lake, waiting for the divers to come back up and tell her what they'd found.

If there was a body down there.

The woman who had alerted the police was called Josephine Pope, a tourist who'd come to the Lakes to indulge in her passion for open-water swimming. She was sitting nearby in her car with her husband, trying not to look too excited about her role in this drama. Josephine, who had dived beneath the water because she'd seen something brightly coloured below her feet, hadn't gone close enough to look inside the submerged vehicle, but she had been able to see that the car was small, red and apparently in good condition; not a rusting wreck that had been in the water for years.

Imogen looked to her left. A road ran along the edge of the lake with no barrier between it and the water. There were some houses a little further along and a beach, if that was the right word, where it seemed someone had recently had a bonfire. Depending on what the divers found, they were probably going to have to close that road and bring in a specialist team to pull the car out. Imogen was praying Josephine Pope was wrong about the car's age, that this was a historic dumping.

She watched as the two divers broke the surface of the water and climbed back into their little boat. After what seemed like a century of faffing about – Imogen knew she wasn't the world's most patient person – the divers manoeuvred their way to the shore and got out of the boat.

The senior diver, Mike Higgis, came over.

'Well?' Imogen asked. 'Is there anybody inside the car?'

He shook his head. 'It's empty.'

She breathed a sigh of relief.

'It does look like it's only been there a short while, though,' Mike said. 'It's a hybrid Toyota Yaris.'

He began to recite the licence plate number but Imogen didn't need to check it. She already knew who it belonged to.

'We're going to need to get this car out of here and search the lake,' she said to Mike. 'This car is involved in an active missing persons case.'

Vicky Matheson had been driving a red hybrid Yaris – and Imogen knew she was about to face some difficult questions about why she hadn't taken Calvin's report more seriously. *Well*, she could say, *I was kind of busy trying to solve a murder and dealing with local lunatics slitting their throats in front of me.*

Excuses, excuses.

While Mike called his senior officer, Imogen got back in her car and thought about next steps. The obvious one would be to contact Calvin and let him know his wife's vehicle had been found. But Imogen hesitated to do that, because right now they didn't know if Vicky had driven into the lake by accident – though, in which case, why wasn't her body in the car? – or if a crime had been committed. In the case of foul play, the husband was always the first person they looked at.

Calvin Matheson had seemed genuinely upset when she'd spoken to him. But she knew from bitter experience that murderers could be very good at lying and disguising their emotions. There was little she could do here at the moment, so she left Mike in charge while he waited for the rest of his team to arrive, then headed into Elderbridge.

She wanted to break the news to Calvin Matheson in person so she could look him in the eye and see how he reacted. If he already knew about the car's whereabouts, she was confident she'd be able to see it on his face.

☡

Except Calvin wasn't at the coffee shop where he worked. A twenty-something woman with one arm in a sling was working behind the till and the cafe was almost empty, which seemed odd, especially as the place up the road, Peggy's, was heaving. Imogen ordered a coffee to go and said, 'I was hoping to talk to Calvin.'

'You're that cop, aren't you?'

Imogen often wondered why she bothered to dress in plain clothes. While she waited for her coffee, the other young woman working in the coffee shop asked the woman behind the till a question, referring to her as Tara.

'Are you actually doing something to try to find Vicky?' Tara said, handing the coffee over. She was very confident for someone so young. 'Calvin's going out of his mind.'

'Is he really?'

The woman narrowed her eyes. 'What's that supposed to mean? Don't tell me you suspect him of doing something to her? All that stuff on social media is bullshit. He's being set up.'

This was interesting. 'What stuff?'

Tara looked like she wished she had a zip across her lips. 'Nothing.'

'Are you sure? You know I can take a look myself.'

'Really? I thought the police around here were incapable of doing anything. Someone shoved me down the stairs here and has anything been done about it? Has it hell.'

Imogen sifted through her memory. Did she already know about this? She was in danger of becoming overloaded with too much information about too many different cases.

'We were burgled. Just over a week ago. Whoever did it knocked me down the stairs when I disturbed them and I fractured my wrist.'

Imogen glanced at the cast on Tara's arm. 'Is this coffee shop built on an ancient burial ground or something?'

'What?'

'Well, your boss seems to be attracting a hell of a lot of bad luck at the moment, doesn't he? Do you know where he's gone?'

It was obvious from Tara's face that she did know, but didn't want to say. More frustration. It was vital for Imogen to speak to Calvin before he heard about Vicky's car. With a full police diving crew about to descend on Foxton Water, and the imminent closure of the road that ran along the lake, it would be all over Twitter and Facebook very soon, swiftly followed by the local news and good old-fashioned word of mouth.

'I understand that you're unhappy with the poor response to the incident here,' Imogen said, 'and I'm genuinely sorry about that. I can have someone look into it for you. But I really need to speak to Calvin, and I'd appreciate it if you could tell me where he is.'

Tara tried to fold her arms, which was awkward with one of them in a cast. 'Why should I tell you?' she said.

'Because,' Imogen replied, 'I'm a good person to be friends with.'

35

One of the self-help techniques Calvin had taught himself in an effort to keep control of his anger, having found the suggestion in a book, was to sing along to loud music. Something about the act of singing, the endorphins it produced, or perhaps simply the distraction of it, did always make him feel better. Now, he drove to Drigg Beach caravan park with the radio turned right up, singing along to a Britpop hit that he and James had loved: 'Staying Out for the Summer' by Dodgy. They'd even been to see them, travelling to Manchester in Calvin's car, only a week after he passed his driving test. They'd run out of petrol on the way home and got stranded on the side of the motorway. Calvin's dad had been furious, because he'd had to drive out in the middle of the night to rescue them, muttering about irresponsible teenagers.

Ah, good times.

Freya had liked this song too, and Calvin was pleased that he was able to enjoy this happy memory without getting upset. He had a clear image of them watching *Top of the Pops* together, with their dad being utterly stereotypical and complaining about how all the bands 'these days' were talentless and unoriginal. It had given Calvin and Freya something to snigger conspiratorially about. Listening to all the songs their dad had sneered at, that he and Freya had loved, made Calvin happy now.

But then 'Cigarettes & Alcohol' by Oasis came on and, although Calvin had been a massive fan back in the day, he couldn't listen to them anymore. All he saw when he heard them was Milo, swaggering about onstage, trying to be Liam Gallagher, with Simeon and Piper behind him. Any track that Duchess had covered threw Calvin right back there, to that awful night and morning, to the funeral and to everything that happened afterwards.

He switched the radio off and tried to control his breathing.

Five minutes later he pulled up outside the caravan park. He'd driven past this place a few times, en route to the beach itself, but he'd never had any need to visit it. He had a vague understanding that half the people here were holidaymakers and the other half were residents. He knew that a fair number of the caravans were owned by people who lived inland, in towns and cities, using them as vacation homes, renting them out the rest of the year.

He sat in the car for a while, deciding how he was going to play this. What was his aim? When he'd stormed out of the coffee shop he hadn't thought beyond the desire to punch DJ on the nose, but now he had calmed down a little – the music having drained away some of his poisonous anger – he was able to think more rationally.

He wanted DJ to admit he had been lying about, well, everything he'd posted about him. Calvin and Mel. Calvin and Billie. All this shit about him murdering Vicky. He needed to persuade DJ to remove his accusatory post. Better yet, he needed him to post that it had been a prank. A joke. His fear was that, seeing as DJ had gone to so much effort to set him up – sending Billie to his doorstep a day after her dad had killed himself – this wasn't going to be easy. He couldn't even compute what was going on with Billie. What was she doing taking part in this insane revenge scheme so soon after her dad's death? And did Tara say her dad had locked her and her mum up? Was there something in the water around here, making everyone go mad?

Whatever the truth was, he knew that going in with all guns blazing, making threats, was unlikely to work. Legal threats probably wouldn't get Calvin far either. He didn't, however, know exactly what DJ was looking for. An apology for the way Calvin had spoken to him the other night? Money? Calvin had to hope that DJ could be reasonable. Maybe he would respect Calvin for coming here and fronting up to him.

And if DJ refused to be reasonable and cooperative?

Well, then Calvin *might* need to get heavy. Go to a lawyer. Because surely it wasn't legal to make accusations about people on social media. Was it even legal to post videos of them without their permission? He had no idea, and he wondered if it might have been a good idea to talk to a lawyer first. But that might be expensive. He hoped he and DJ could sort it out between them, man to man.

He got out of the car, screwing up his eyes against the bright sunshine. He could hear voices in the distance: children playing on the beach, a mother calling out to her offspring. Seagulls circled overhead like vultures, waiting for someone to drop their ice cream cone. A beautiful day. Not a day to be feeling like this.

He passed through the gates of the caravan park. A man in a white vest was sitting on a fold-out chair outside the first caravan Calvin saw, and Calvin said, 'I've got a delivery for DJ O'Connor. Can you tell me where to find him?'

The man seemed suspicious – Calvin didn't look like a courier and he wasn't carrying any packages – but he also appeared not to care if Calvin was actually an assassin or an undercover cop.

'Take the second row over there,' the man said, scratching his belly. 'DJ's in the last caravan on the right.'

'Cheers.'

Calvin passed a few more people, including a woman hanging out washing and a family who appeared to be on holiday, looking slightly bewildered and wondering how they'd ended up here. The caravan park had a seedy air, with lots of the mobile homes being in a state of disrepair; others were draped with England flags, an assortment of beaten-up cars parked between them. Calvin found himself at the end of the row, standing outside a static caravan that was about six or seven metres long. There was a plastic table and chairs outside, and no sign of life.

Calvin took a deep breath and, steeling himself for the conversation – or confrontation – ahead, knocked on the door.

Immediately, a dog started making a racket within, a fierce volley of barks that didn't stop.

But no one came to the door.

'DJ?' Calvin called.

No response.

He knocked again, which pitched the dog into even more of a frenzy, then he went over to a narrow window, peering inside. He could see a kitchen, a small sink piled high with dishes, a stack of lager cans on the counter. Suddenly, the dog appeared on the kitchen floor, jumping up and down like its little legs might be able to propel it up to the window. It was one of those French bulldogs that had started to appear everywhere over the last few years. Calvin felt sorry for them, with their squashed faces which made it hard for them to breathe. He felt even sorrier for this one. Had DJ left it on its own? He knew it was fine to go out for a short while and leave a dog unattended, but this French bulldog seemed distressed. It had begun to turn in circles now, barking loudly as it spun.

Was there someone here with a master key to the caravans? Or the tools to break in? Calvin was about to head back to the entrance but decided he should try the front door, just in case it had been left unlocked.

To his astonishment, it opened.

As he pushed the door fully open, he braced himself, expecting the dog to fly out at him. But, instead, it made a whimpering noise and trotted off to the right. *Some guard dog*, he thought, stepping through the door and finding himself in a small living area with a couch and TV, a games console attached. The TV was on but the console appeared to have put itself into sleep mode.

'Hello?' Calvin said. He had a strange feeling that he wasn't alone, that someone was here, hiding. He said it again: 'Hello?'

The dog made that whimpering sound and Calvin looked to the far right, past the kitchen. There was a door, standing open just enough for the dog to get through. Calvin approached it slowly, all his instincts telling him to get out of here but, like a character in a horror movie, unable to resist. He needed to know what was beyond that door.

He pushed it open to reveal a tiny bedroom.

DJ was lying on his back on a narrow bed that was attached to the wall. One arm hung off the bed, knuckles touching the floor. His eyes were open but he wasn't blinking.

The dog sat beside the bed, staring up at Calvin, licking its master's hand in an attempt to wake him up. But DJ was never going to wake up. The T-shirt he was wearing was saturated with blood that was darker and thicker in several spots, above his chest and stomach, where he had clearly been stabbed, at least three times.

A fly landed on him and crawled across his staring eyeball.

Calvin staggered from the room, trying not to throw up. When he heard his name, he thought it was DJ, a dead man talking, and he might have cried out if his brain hadn't quickly told him the voice was female, that there were no talking corpses here.

He turned – and found himself face-to-face with Imogen Evans.

36

Calvin sat opposite Imogen in an interview room at the same station where he'd reported Vicky missing. He wasn't under arrest and had been told he was free to leave, but he sensed that would not be wise, especially when he remembered the words he had spoken about DJ, in front of witnesses: *I'm going to kill him.* That was on top of everything else. The shit that was all over social media, accusing him not only of an affair with Mel but with DJ's friend Billie. The fact that his wife was still missing. Right now, Calvin felt as if he were inside a wrecked building, during an earthquake, and that one wrong move, one more stupid decision, would not only make the ceiling collapse on top of him but make the floor crack open at the same time. Talking to the police could only be a good idea – especially as he needed them to find Vicky.

'Don't you usually do this in pairs?' he said. 'Where's the young cop I talked to the other day? The constable?'

'You haven't heard? It's been all over the news.'

He shook his head. 'I've been slightly preoccupied, trying to find my wife.'

'What were you doing in DJ O'Connor's caravan?' Imogen asked, still not telling him what had happened to the constable – whose name, Steve Milner, came back to Calvin as he mulled over how to reply.

'I told you all this at the scene.'

'Please, Mr Matheson. I need you to take me through it all again.'

He muttered a swear word. 'I was worried about his dog.'

'Lola.'

'Sorry?'

'The dog's name is Lola.'

While Calvin had waited in the back of Imogen's car, outside the caravan park, he'd overheard her make a call to the dog warden. Lola would almost certainly end up at Vicky's place and he had been tempted to tell Imogen to cut out the middleman and call Louise. But he understood there were procedures that needed to be followed.

'Poor Lola,' he said.

'Poor DJ.'

He nodded, seeing DJ's blood-drenched body in his mind's eye. His trailing hand, the dog licking it.

'I was actually at DJ's caravan because he posted something about me on social media, and I went there to talk to him about it. There was no answer when I knocked, but the dog started going mental. That's why I went in. Lola led me to his body. The door was unlocked, by the way.' A pause. 'Do you have any suspects?'

Imogen gave him a meaningful look.

'Come on. You must know I didn't do it. Where's the weapon? Why is there no blood on me?'

'Have I said you're a suspect for this, Mr Matheson?'

'No, but I'm guessing I will be because I had a good reason for disliking DJ. I might as well tell you before you hear it from a witness: I said I was going to kill him. But it was just a turn of phrase.'

'And why did you say that? Because he harassed your friend? Mel?'

'She's not my friend. She worked for me.'

'Worked? In the past tense?'

'Yes. And no, that's not the main reason for me not liking DJ.'

Imogen had a can of Diet Coke on the table which she cracked open. She'd already offered him one and he'd declined, choosing water. He didn't need any more caffeine in his system.

'I think you'd better tell me everything,' she said.

So he did, starting with what he'd already told Imogen when he reported Vicky missing two days earlier: the conversation with DJ and his friends outside Mel's place, how he'd fallen asleep then gone home to find Vicky missing. His attempts to track her down, including the posts on social media. Finding Jarvis in a wheelie bin with a note that accused him of being a murderer. Then the lies that had been spread about him that had led him to the caravan park this morning. He told her, too, about how he'd decided to let Mel go and the argument that had led to. Finally, he showed her the post by caravan_rubbish purporting to show him in a secret liaison with Billie.

'I've only ever spoken to her twice. Once outside Mel's place, when DJ and their other mates were there, and this encounter in my front garden. I didn't touch her. I've never touched her. It's not something I'd do. She touched me – put her hand on my chest.'

Imogen looked pained.

'Is she – *was* she – DJ's girlfriend?'

Imogen didn't reply, but she looked like she was wondering the same thing.

'It just seems mad that she would be on my doorstep, taking part in what I assume to be a social media prank, the day after her dad locked her up and then killed himself. That's what happened, isn't it?'

Imogen Evans was wearing the expression of someone who was trying to defuse a particularly tricky time bomb.

'Do you think all of this is connected to Vicky's disappearance?' he said. 'Was that part of DJ's scheme against me? Did he abduct Vicky while I was asleep at Mel's? And who killed him? And where is Vicky now? You need to question Billie—'

'Please, Mr Matheson. There's something I need to tell you.'

Her tone sent a shiver through him. The bad kind of shiver.

'Is it something to do with Vicky? Oh Jesus, have you found—'

'Calvin, Calvin, please. Don't panic. We don't know where Vicky is.' A pause. 'But we've found her car.'

He sat up straighter.

'It was in Foxton Water.'

He felt like he'd been punched in the stomach. But before he could say anything, Imogen spoke quickly to reassure him. 'There was nobody inside the car, and so far, well, there's no sign that anyone has come to harm. We do, however, have a team exploring the lake at the moment. Just in case.'

He went to speak and she held up a hand. 'Let me finish. The doors were locked and the windows were up. No one was in the car when it went in the water. The team called me shortly before we came in here and they believe the car was pushed down a bank from the road. We believe it's unlikely that your wife is in the lake too. She certainly didn't drive it in there.'

His thoughts went in about a hundred places at once – all coming back to the same point. 'So where is she?'

'We don't know.'

He had the feeling he had passed some sort of test. He guessed she had wanted to study his reaction, see if he looked shocked and horrified when she told him about the car.

'Obviously,' Imogen said, 'this means that your wife's missing person case just moved up to another level.'

'From the level where you weren't bothering to do anything, you mean?'

'All right. That's fair enough. Although we have to bear in mind that it could very well be Vicky who put the car into the lake, that it's all part of her plan to disappear.'

'Why would she do that? It doesn't make sense.'

'Maybe not. But we have to keep all options open at the moment.'

He stood up. All of a sudden he felt like a caged animal. 'We need to get out there. Search the whole area. She could be hurt. Someone might have her.'

'Who?'

'*I* don't know! Isn't that your job, to figure that stuff out? Maybe it was DJ and Billie. Where is she now? At home? You need to talk to her. I'll fucking talk to her.'

'Please, Calvin, sit down. Stay calm. I'm going to talk to Billie next.'

Like last time, something about her demeanour helped dampen the flames of his anger and panic, soothing him. Wouldn't it be useful, he thought, to have a miniature Imogen Evans to carry around in his pocket, to calm him down when he was stressed? It would work better than any of his self-help techniques.

Something occurred to him. 'Why were *you* at DJ's caravan?' he asked.

'I was trying to find you so I could tell you about Vicky's car.'

'Hmm. When I mentioned him before, when I reported Vicky missing, you definitely knew who he was. You said his full name. That was before this thing with Billie's dad. Was DJ connected to the other case? The murder on the beach?'

She didn't respond but it was obvious he was on the right track.

'Do you know why this beach guy was murdered? What was his name again?'

'Leo James. And no, we still don't know the motive.'

'But was DJ connected? What about Billie?' Again, Imogen didn't deny it. 'She is, isn't she? How?'

'I can't tell you that.'

'But what if that murder has something to do with Vicky's disappearance? I mean, it has to all be connected, doesn't it? All this crazy shit happening here, in this tiny area of Cumbria? And Billie – and DJ? – linking everything? The person who murdered this Leo James guy has to be the number-one suspect for killing DJ, right? What if they've got Vicky too? What if it's Billie? You need to get her in an interview room now!'

'Calvin, please, slow down.' Imogen took a deep breath. 'Does Vicky know Billie?'

The question took him aback. 'I don't think so, but she grew up in the next village to her. Plus she comes into contact with lots of people around here through her job. Does Billie have a cat or dog?'

'Not that we know of.'

'What about this Leo James? Did he have one?'

Imogen shook her head. 'There's no evidence to that effect.'

'She might have known him, though. Maybe *I* know him. Have you got a picture?'

'Yes, we have now.'

She picked up an iPad, tapped at it a few times, then turned it around to show him.

'A woman he was friends with just sent it to us. It's the only one we have. We're about to start circulating it to help us identify him, see if anyone knows him . . .'

Her words had faded as he stared at the photo, growing fainter until they eventually dwindled into nothing, replaced by a humming in his ears. He squeezed his eyes shut then opened them again, unsure if his mind was playing tricks on him because of all the stress.

He realised Imogen was asking him a question and managed to tune back in. 'What is it? *Do* you know him?'

He lay the iPad flat on the table, unable to take his eyes off the photo. His hands shook.

'Yeah. I know him.'

She waited.

'But his name isn't *Leo* James. James is his first name. James Sullivan.' There was absolutely no doubt about it. He was looking at a photo of someone he hadn't seen for nearly thirty years. 'He was my best friend.'

37

SEPTEMBER 1995

It was the last week of September, a month since Freya's funeral. The last night before lots of their friends headed off to university. Calvin walked round to James's house trying to fight off the waves of regret that had been threatening to drown him all day. James's mum, Mrs Sullivan, greeted him at the door.

She was long-divorced, an art historian who drove to her museum job in Penrith in a vintage 2CV. A cool, quirky mum, whose house was full of art. Some of it was embarrassingly sexy – trying to have a conversation with Mrs Sullivan beneath the giant Modigliani nude in the living room was a squirming challenge – and some was disturbing. The dining room walls had been freshly adorned with prints of paintings by Hieronymus Bosch. Writhing, tortured bodies on what appeared to be a vast battlefield, tormented by weird animals and bizarre contraptions.

'It's a vision of Hell,' Mrs Sullivan explained when she saw he'd tumbled into the images. 'These used to hang in the upstairs hall-way, but poor James asked me to move them because they scared him to death if he needed to get up in the night to use the loo. It's all so fascinating, though. We're putting on an exhibition of art inspired by Dante's *Divine Comedy*, if you're interested.'

Calvin wasn't. And he couldn't blame James for being scared of these pictures, especially as Mrs Sullivan had taken James to church every Sunday through primary school. The village had a vicar who was properly old-school hellfire-and-brimstone, terrifying the kids and thrilling the adults with his warnings about what awaited sinners. There was a lot of talk of red-hot pokers. When James was twelve he'd told his mum he didn't want to go anymore, and then the hellfire vicar had died and she'd stopped attending too.

'James told me you decided to take a year out?' she said to him.

'Yeah.'

'Do you know what you're going to do after that?'

'I don't know. Maybe catering college.'

She beamed. 'That's a wonderful idea. Perhaps you could give James some cooking lessons.'

Calvin went up and found James leafing through that week's *Melody Maker*. The Charlatans were on the cover.

'I'm so bored,' James said. 'What do you want to do? I've got some weed.'

'You know it makes me throw up.'

'We could rent a video?' He paused. 'Or we could go to the pub.'

Since that afternoon in the pub a few weeks ago, they hadn't been out at all. Calvin hadn't felt like going out drinking, being around people who were laughing and carrying on like everything was normal. He wanted to tell everyone that his lovely, clever young sister was dead at seventeen with her whole life ahead of her. How could they drink and laugh and watch football and listen to upbeat songs when Freya's ashes were sitting in an urn in Calvin's house, and his mum was a zombie and his dad kept waking up sobbing in the night?

'You know Camilla's leaving for college tomorrow?' James said.

'I know.' He had been trying not to think about it.

'Have you spoken to her recently?'

He shook his head. He'd blown his chance weeks ago.

'You don't want to see her? Try to get a goodbye kiss?'

'Is that what you want to do? Go to the pub?'

James shifted awkwardly. 'I think . . . we can't just sit around hiding from the world forever. If we stay here, Mum might make us go downstairs and watch *Pride and Prejudice* with her.'

'Oh God.'

They were both silent for a minute until James said, 'Freya wouldn't have wanted you to curl up and die. To hide away forever.'

'How do you know what she'd have wanted?'

James shrugged. 'Obviously I didn't know her like you, but she wasn't that kind of person. I reckon she'd tell you to get back out there. Try to get a sympathy shag out of Camilla.'

'Hey!'

But it made him laugh. And then, possibly because he couldn't stand the thought of being stuck indoors all evening, he said, 'All right. It will be fun.'

Later, he would look back at those four simple words – *It will be fun* – and laugh bitterly. They should have stayed at James's house, got some cans in, maybe bought some E from the dodgy bloke who always hung around the back of the Co-op.

Whatever they did, they shouldn't have gone to the Cricketers.

38

Imogen sat on the armchair in Steve's living room. He was moving gingerly because of the wound in his stomach but looking a lot brighter than he had two days ago at the hospital. Maybe even a little high from the painkillers he had been given.

'I've been signed off for two weeks,' he said with a shake of the head, like this was the worst thing that had ever happened to him.

'Do you know how much I would love to have two weeks off?'

'Yeah. But you've got a family. I live on my own. All I've got is the job.' He stared out the front window. He lived on a street that was so quiet you could almost hear the snails slithering along the pavement.

'Flipping heck, Steve. You need to find yourself a girlfriend pronto. Or boyfriend?'

'I'm straight.'

He wouldn't meet her eye and had gone bright pink. Oh God, she thought. Surely he doesn't . . . ? She pushed the notion away. Right now she had too many other things to worry about. Dealing with Steve's puppy-like feelings was very low on her list of priorities.

An hour had passed since she'd let Calvin leave the police station, having got as much information about James Sullivan out of him as she could. She could hardly believe it. They finally knew who Leo James was and where he came from: Reyton, a village on the other side of Cumbria, just thirty miles away. The place where Calvin had grown up.

'If only Michelle had come forward a week ago,' Steve said now, after she'd updated him.

'I know. Calvin seemed quite shocked by how old Leo looked in the photo – I mean how old *James* looked – but he recognised him straight away.'

'You don't think Calvin Matheson is a suspect?'

'No. I mean, he doesn't have an alibi, not with his wife missing and unable to vouch for him. But he was genuinely shocked when I told him about Vicky's car being in the lake, and seemed even more shocked when he saw James's photo. And he wouldn't have identified him for us if he was the murderer.'

'He has to be involved, though, right? Somehow?'

Imogen nodded. 'I just can't figure out how.'

This was why she had come here. Of course she wanted to see how Steve was doing, but she needed someone to talk it all through with too. Apart from her, Steve knew this case better than anyone else.

'Are you feeling up to this?' she asked.

'God, yes. I'm going insane with boredom. Did you bring a whiteboard with you?'

She smiled. 'Sadly not. We're going to have to make do with a pen and paper.'

Over the next hour they went through it all, sitting at Steve's dining room table and writing down everything that had happened and what they knew so far. She started by drawing a line down the middle of the page and giving both columns a heading: *James Sullivan murder* and *Vicky Matheson disappearance*.

'Okay. So the main players in the James column, along with Calvin, are Michelle, Adrian and Billie Whitehead. Michelle had a romantic relationship with James, who she knew as Leo, starting in autumn last year, returning home to Adrian just after Christmas. Billie found out about the relationship and sought out Leo herself shortly after that.'

'Who else had contact with James? Just Reverend Delaney?'

'Yep. Which connects us to DJ, the vicar's handyman.' She wondered if Delaney had heard about DJ's death yet. They had sealed off the caravan park while the forensics team gathered evidence, but they had chosen not to release any information, although social media was abuzz with rumours, as was the local grapevine. It would probably be Delaney conducting the funeral, Imogen thought. They still needed to locate and talk to DJ's next of kin too.

Her to-do list was getting out of control. She needed people to stop dying.

'DJ connects the cases because of his contact with Calvin, via this woman who worked for him. Mel.'

She underlined DJ's name, twice. His link to James was tenuous, circumstantial really. It was a small village; the vicar was a public figure. They had no evidence that DJ had ever even met James.

'Let's go back to Billie Whitehead,' she said. 'She's the main connection to Calvin and Vicky Matheson.'

Steve looked confused.

'We know that she was friends with DJ, at the very least, and she's involved with what appears to be some kind of revenge scheme against Calvin. An attempt to ruin his reputation. He swears blind that he's only met Billie twice: yesterday when she turned up on his doorstep, and Monday night, with DJ, outside the home of this woman who worked for him. Mel.' She wrote Mel's name down on the sheet of paper. 'I went to the Whiteheads' house on my way here but they were out, and Billie isn't answering her phone. I've left her a message to call me urgently.'

'Do you think she might be a suspect? For DJ's murder, I mean?'

'I don't know. I can't see it, though. Can you?'

'To be honest, Imogen, if aliens landed on Drigg Beach this evening and told us they were responsible for everything, I wouldn't be that shocked.'

She smiled. 'Always good to keep an open mind, Steve. You'll go a long way.'

He flushed pink again – goodness, the boy had a hair trigger – then cleared his throat and said, 'Do we know anything else about Leo? Anything that might be relevant? Like, why did he change his name and start living off-grid?'

'We still don't know that. But I think it has to be something to do with his preoccupation with sin and punishment. The paintings. The obsession with Dante's *Inferno*.'

Steve's eyes rounded and he gave his head a slow shake. 'Curiouser and curiouser.'

'Indeed.' She tapped the paper with her pen nib, making a series of tiny dots. 'It has to be that he was hiding from something.'

'Something that he did.'

'A sin he committed.'

They were both quiet for a moment, pondering this.

'I need to go back to Calvin and ask him about that,' Imogen said. 'Was he aware of anything in James's past that would torment him?'

'Something big enough to make him go off-grid.'

She had written Calvin's name in block capitals. He was the only other strong connection between the cases that they knew about. His wife missing, his former best friend murdered – and the guy who had been harassing him online now murdered too.

'Another thing that makes a good cop,' she said, 'is admitting when you're wrong. And I made a big mistake about Vicky

Matheson. I should have seen it before we found her car dumped in the lake. This woman runs an animal shelter. Has dedicated her life to helping cats and dogs. It's possible she might run out on her husband, or even leave the animals for a few days – but completely abandon them, without making arrangements for their care? Calvin thinks someone's got her.'

'Do you agree?'

'Like I said, I just can't see her abandoning the animals. I certainly can't see her dumping her car in a lake. I hate to say it, but I think either someone has got her, or she's dead.'

'But where's the body? Why wasn't it in the lake with the car?'

'That's why I'm swaying towards her still being alive. There's another thing too: assuming we only have one killer running around, why did they make such a big display of Leo's – sorry, James's – body, while DJ's was just left in his caravan and Vicky hasn't even been found? It's like all these crimes have different motivations.'

'So maybe there are two murderers. Or three.'

'I'm starting to hope it's the aliens you mentioned.'

She circled James's name with her pen. 'His death was so . . . *showy*. Staged, as if it was intended to deliver a message.'

'What kind of message?'

'Maybe "warning" is a better word. It's almost like one of these gangster killings. This is what happens if you step out of line. Except that doesn't feel right. I'm sure this is a personal crime. Not a crime of passion, but emotional, definitely. The darkest emotions.'

Steve rubbed his arms as if a chill had blown through the room. 'A warning to who? We know it wasn't Adrian Whitehead delivering a message to Billie or Michelle. Who's the only other person connecting the cases?'

'Calvin Matheson. I'm wondering if the method of James's murder was part of the message to Calvin. The drowning. Billie said James was terrified of water.' Imogen grabbed the pad again and scribbled down some words. 'I need to ask Calvin about that, find out if that was always the case.'

She was a little breathless. All along, this case had been an impossible puzzle with no clues, no way in. They were finally making progress, but it didn't make her feel any better. Because it seemed almost certain that whoever had taken Vicky must have plans for her, perhaps to deliver the second part of this warning to Calvin.

They weren't just trying to find out who the killer was.

They were trying to stop them from killing again.

Imogen picked up the notepad. 'I need to talk to Calvin, urgently. I also need to talk to James Sullivan's mother. We've found her address but I need to find the time to drive over to Reyton.' It was over an hour's drive from here.

Steve touched his stomach lightly, where he had been slashed. 'I could go and talk to her.'

'No. You need to rest. He's been dead over a week now. A few more hours of blissful ignorance might not be a bad thing for her.'

'Yeah. But I wish I could come with you to talk to Calvin.'

There were CSIs at the caravan park. Divers at Foxton Water. A woman still missing and a fresh body in the morgue. It felt like the last couple of days of the Shropshire Viper case.

'Believe me,' she said as she headed for the door, 'you're better off at home.'

39

Calvin hadn't been back home to Reyton since his parents died. His mum had died of liver failure ten years ago, which hadn't surprised anyone who saw how hard she hit the bottle after Freya's death. His dad was diagnosed with Alzheimer's shortly afterwards. It was an awful time which Calvin didn't like to think about. Sometimes he would wake at 3 a.m. and torment himself with regrets. He should have tried harder to remain close to his parents. He could have done more to drag them out of the swamp of grief they'd got stuck in.

Driving into Reyton now, ninety minutes after he'd left the police station in Elderbridge, he was still shaking. James, dead. Not only that, but he had been living just a few miles from Calvin all this time, using a different name. A hermit, to use an old-fashioned term. Imogen had told Calvin about the life James had created for himself there, living in complete solitude until last year, when it appeared he'd briefly experienced a connection with two members of the same family: mother, then daughter. Michelle, who Calvin had never met, and Billie. Imogen had told him about the paintings too, and she'd asked him if James had been religious when they were growing up.

'When he was at primary school. And his mum had all these religious paintings in the house. Creepy things. Bosch? Is that what his paintings were like? When he was a kid he mostly drew robots and, well, women with big boobs.'

She showed them to him on the iPad. Hellish scenes of torture, souls being tormented by devils, fire and brimstone and suffering. Just like the Bosch paintings that had hung downstairs at James's house, and a very long way from the pictures James used to draw when he was a teenager.

'Any idea why he might have developed such an obsession with these themes?' she asked.

'No.'

He had to fight back the nausea. Sitting there in the interview room, staring at James's picture, he felt like the bomb he'd been carrying around with him his whole adult life had finally gone off. James murdered, Vicky missing, DJ dead, Calvin targeted. Nothing made sense and everything made sense.

He had to resist the urge to tell Imogen Evans the whole truth. Part of him thought that if he confessed all, she would make it better. But even though he was desperate to find Vicky, and the rational part of him told him Imogen would only be able to help if she knew everything, he couldn't do it. He was too scared. He'd lived with this fear for so long that it still controlled him.

He passed the Cricketers pub. He hadn't been there since the night before Camilla left for university, which was one of the last times he had ever seen James. 1995. A lifetime ago. Sometimes he would hear that it was the twenty-five- or thirty-year anniversary of some album he'd loved when he was a teenager, and his first instinct would be horror and shock. How could the years have passed so quickly? But then he'd think, yes, it was a long time ago. He had been a different person then. He had been a boy. He and James. They'd been kids, really. Stupid kids.

The house where James had lived, in which Calvin had spent so much time as a teenager, looked exactly the same. The car that Mrs Sullivan had driven, an elderly Citroën 2CV, had been replaced by a tiny Smart car, just big enough for two. It was exactly the kind of car he could see James's mum driving. But could she really still live here? Was she still alive?

He knocked, and a minute later, seeing her, he wondered why he'd thought she might be dead. She'd been a young mum when they were teenagers, only in her early forties, which meant she wasn't yet seventy. Time had been kind to her too. Her hair was streaked with silver but she looked fit and healthy.

She tilted her head when she saw him. 'Calvin Matheson?'

'You recognise me?' His threshold for shock had risen to new heights in the last few days, but he was still taken aback.

'Of course I do! You haven't changed at all.' She frowned. 'I was so sorry to hear about your mum and dad.'

Unexpectedly, he felt tears prick his eyes. 'Thank you.'

'Too young.'

He studied her face for signs of upset. Had the police been in touch to tell her they had identified the body on the beach as her son? It seemed not. That meant he was going to have to tell her.

She must have seen upset on *his* face. 'What is . . . It's James, isn't it? Oh goodness. You'd better come in.'

They went into the living room, and Mrs Sullivan, who insisted that Calvin call her Theresa, also insisted on making them both a cup of tea. As she clattered in the kitchen he looked around the living room. There were photos of James everywhere: as a baby, a toddler, a little boy with no front teeth. There was a picture of teenage James which also featured Calvin. He winced at his hair – he'd had curtains – then again felt tears prick the backs of his eyes. Apart from Vicky, James had been the best friend he'd ever had. Apart from his wife, he'd never made any proper friends as an adult.

There was no sign of the Bosch prints that had given the young James nightmares. The ones that had clearly made such a lasting impression on him.

Theresa came in with the tea, served in huge, brightly coloured mugs. He noticed that her hands were trembling and he hurried over to help her. She sat down on the sofa and gestured for him to sit next to her. He angled himself so he was facing her.

'What's going on, Calvin? Why are you here? I've been worried since James's Instagram account disappeared just over a week ago.'

James was on Instagram? Imogen hadn't mentioned that. Had she known?

'Calvin?'

He had come straight here from the police station. Imogen, or some other cop, might turn up on the doorstep any minute, come to deliver the bad news. He had to tell her first, no matter how badly the words stuck in his throat.

'Theresa,' he said. 'James . . . He's dead.'

'Oh. Oh . . .' She made a strange whimpering noise. 'I knew it. Oh God, I knew it.'

'I'm so sorry. I only found out it was him today, but he died last week. He was . . . he was murdered.'

She recoiled at this, pressed her hand to her mouth. '*Murdered?*'

'Have you seen on the news – the guy on the beach?'

'Oh. Oh my God.'

Calvin briefly explained that the police hadn't been able to confirm the true identity of the body, that they'd only just come into possession of a recent photograph.

'I need to—' Theresa got up from her chair and hurried from the room. He heard what was presumably a bathroom door shutting. A toilet flushing, taps running. He sat there, twisting his hands together, until she came back. The skin beneath her eyes was damp, her nose pink.

'I'm so sorry,' Calvin said again.

She sat back down, picked up her cup of tea, and stared at it as if she didn't know what it was. She placed it back on the coffee table.

'Have they . . . have they buried him already?'

He hung his head. 'A cremation.'

That brought on another wave of tears. Calvin reached out to awkwardly pat her shoulder.

Abruptly, she stopped crying, waved him away. 'I'm fine. I'm fine. He's been gone a long time.'

She clearly wasn't fine, but Calvin didn't know what else to say. 'Theresa, I need to ask you some questions. I think the person who did this has Vicky.'

'What?'

'My wife, Vicky. I don't have time to get into it, but there are things I need to figure out. You might be able to help.'

She nodded.

'You said James was on Instagram?'

'Yes, just for the past few months. Sandpiperphotos. He . . . he took some lovely shots of the beach where he lived. Drigg. You know we used to go there when he was little? We started exchanging messages and he told me he'd been living there years, that he'd started out as some elderly woman's lodger, and then when she died he kept waiting for someone to kick him out but they never did.'

Calvin remembered Imogen telling him that the house's owner had died with no relatives. James had effectively been squatting there for years – and, it seemed, had fallen through the legal cracks.

'And he contacted you?'

She produced a tissue and blew her nose. 'Yes. He said in his first message that it was the first time he'd ever used technology like that. But a young woman was helping him.'

Billie, Calvin assumed.

'It was the first time I'd heard from him in years. At first I didn't believe it was him and had to ask him lots of questions to get him to prove it. He told me, via direct message, that he'd been through a very dark time but that he was starting to feel a little better. I wondered if it had something to do with the woman who'd got him to join Instagram.'

'I think it was her mum,' Calvin said.

'Oh?'

'He had . . . a girlfriend, briefly. Then her daughter befriended him. That's what I was told today.'

Theresa appeared to take some comfort from this. 'He was still troubled, though,' she said. 'He said he hadn't been in touch because he was living with too much shame and guilt.'

Calvin swallowed. 'Did he say why?'

'No. But I know—'

Calvin went cold.

'—it was something that happened that summer. When you finished school. Around the time Freya died. I know how badly it affected you and your parents, but that's when he changed too. Especially at the end of that summer. Whatever it was still haunted him, nearly thirty years on. I asked him to tell me, to unburden himself, and he said he couldn't, it was too awful. He clearly wanted to talk to someone, though.'

She was watching Calvin carefully as she spoke. She obviously knew he had been involved in whatever it was too.

'I said that perhaps he should talk to a man of the cloth. Or woman. We're not Catholic, so it's not as if we can go into a booth and confess, but I always found it comforting when I went to church, back when James was young, talking to our vicar. James did too. There was one time when he was nine when he was worried about something he'd done. He'd shoplifted a cassette or something from Woolworths and thought he was going to go to Hell for it. He spoke to our vicar and felt a lot better for it.'

'And did . . . did he take your advice? Now, I mean?'

'I think he did. He messaged me to tell me he wished he'd unburdened himself years ago. Said he thought he might soon feel well enough to visit me. That he might even be able to tell me what he'd done.' There was a pause. 'That was the last message I received from him.'

'What was the vicar's name?' Calvin asked, feeling sick. Somebody knew what they had done.

'Reverend Delaney.'

That was the vicar in Drigg, wasn't it? Of course. Hadn't James's secluded cottage been only a stone's throw from St Bart's? Then, with a jolt, Calvin remembered something else. Hadn't Imogen told him DJ had been working as a handyman for the local vicar?

Had DJ overheard James talking to the vicar? Confessing?

Had James told Delaney *everything*? Had he used Calvin's name?

He became aware of Theresa scrutinising him, trying to read his face.

'What happened, Calvin?' Theresa asked. 'What did the two of you do?'

40

September 1995

The Cricketers was packed and it didn't take Calvin long to realise why: it seemed like everyone from sixth form was here, assembled in groups of friends who were going off to university or saying goodbye.

He bumped into Camilla, who was coming back inside, cigarette smoke clinging to her clothes. Here was another reason to feel regret, although if they had been boyfriend and girlfriend it would be even worse watching her head to UEA to read English and start the pursuit of her dream to be a novelist.

'Do you think you've made the right decision, staying around here?' she asked. She was drunk and didn't care what she said. 'Because I don't. I think you're making a stupid mistake.'

'My mum and dad need me.'

'Do they, though?' She put her arms around him and kissed his cheek. 'Oh, I don't know. You're a good guy, Calvin. I just hope you don't regret it. Small towns can suck all the life out of you. They can kill you.'

She kissed his cheek again then staggered away, back to her group of friends.

Calvin made his way over to James, who had managed to grab a small table in the corner.

'I saw you talking to Camilla,' said James. 'What exactly happened with her?'

'Nothing happened. I blew it.'

'Are you not going to try to make something happen before she— Hey, are you listening?'

Calvin wasn't. Because while James had been talking, the crowd around their table had shifted to reveal Milo Stewart standing by the bar, waving a £10 note at the barmaid, trying to get served.

'What is it?' James asked. Then he saw Milo too. 'Oh shit. What's that wanker doing here?'

The way Milo was leaning on the bar, flapping his money, he looked wasted. Drink, or drugs? Both, probably. Calvin craned his neck but couldn't see any sign of the other Stewart siblings, Simeon and Piper. He knew that if he saw Simeon, who had been driving the van, he might not be able to control himself, even if it had been an accident and Simeon had been sober.

'He didn't even come to the funeral,' Calvin said, still staring at Milo. Calvin still couldn't believe it. What kind of dickhead wouldn't go to his own girlfriend's funeral?

'Maybe he thought he wouldn't be welcome,' James said.

'Are you trying to defend him?'

'No. Course not. I guess you don't need a reason when you're a druggie dick like Milo.'

James glared at Milo with loathing, like he hated him as much as Calvin did. It had slowly dawned on Calvin since Freya's death that perhaps James hadn't merely seen Freya as his best friend's younger sibling. He had liked her.

He had to ask. 'Did anything ever happen between you and Freya?'

'What? Of course not!' But James had gone pink. He had obviously wanted it to.

'You should have asked her out,' Calvin said. 'If she'd been going out with you she might never have got together with that twat.'

'I didn't think you'd want me to. You were always, you know, really protective. I thought you'd beat me up if I made a move on her. Anyway, she was out of my league.'

Calvin sipped from his pint. 'She was definitely out of Milo's league. And I wasn't protective enough, as it turned out, was I?'

The singer left the bar and Calvin lost sight of him. More and more people packed into the pub and it got so loud it was hard to hear anything. Calvin found himself leaning over the table, shouting, with James shouting back. But it was such an effort that after a while they gave up trying to talk and concentrated fully on drinking.

The more he drank, the less he thought about Freya and the better he felt. It was almost closing time and the crowd had thinned out, most people dispersing, heading back to their beds. Camilla was still in the pub, though, laughing with her friends, head tilted back to expose her throat, and he thought about walking over and kissing her, taking James's advice and asking if they could spend one night together before she left. That might help him not think about Freya too.

He got up from his seat, swaying a little, and halfway across the pub he realised he needed to pee. Badly. Like, if he didn't go immediately something embarrassing would happen. So he changed course, heading towards the gents. Standing at the urinal, he fixated on Camilla. Should he go up to her? His drunk brain convinced him it was a great idea that she would welcome.

But when he left the toilets he looked over to where she had been standing with her mates and saw she wasn't there. She must have gone out for another cigarette. He headed for the exit and went into the beer garden. It was empty. No smokers. No little orange dots dancing in the darkness.

He'd missed her.

'Bollocks,' he said loudly.

'Bad night, yeah?'

The voice made him jump. Peering into the gloom, he saw there was someone sitting on the ground, back against the wall of the pub, knees pulled up to his chest. Calvin took a step closer and the figure stood up, stepping forward into the light.

It was Milo.

Calvin stopped dead. 'You.'

'Yeah. Me.' Milo seemed as out of it as Calvin, but with a different energy and dilated pupils. He was stoned. He leaned back against the wall and closed his eyes for a second. When he opened them again he said, 'You all right?'

Calvin stared at him. 'What do you think?'

Milo's chin dipped, then he searched in his pockets until he found a pack of Marlboro Lights. 'Oh, yeah. Freya. Bad fucking times.'

Calvin had never really hated anyone before. Sure, there were celebrities he couldn't stand, who set his teeth on edge. There was the aunt who used to pick on Freya – and her husband, their uncle, who was a loud-mouthed snob. Calvin had an allergic reaction to that pair of idiots. There had been sadistic teachers and playground bullies. Plenty of people who Calvin disliked and did his best to avoid. But hatred? Sheer, animal hatred, the kind that made your stomach tie itself in knots, that made your blood heat up and your fists clench involuntarily? That was new.

He'd never liked Milo. He was a poverty tourist. A rich kid pretending to be working-class. A pretentious, swaggering druggie who thought he was cool when he was actually an idiot.

None of this would have mattered, of course, if Milo hadn't started going out with Freya. Calvin had known straight away that he was bad news. He'd foreseen a story in which Freya was messed around and screwed up, very possibly heartbroken. He had feared Milo would get her into hard drugs. And yeah, he knew that none of it was his business, really. Freya had to live her own life, make her own mistakes.

Except now she was gone. She'd made one big mistake – going out with Milo – and that was it.

With loathing bubbling and roiling in his gut, he jabbed a finger towards Milo's face and said, 'Bad times? She'd be alive if it wasn't for you.'

He half expected Milo to hang his head or attempt an apology. That's what any normal person would do. Instead, he said, 'I'm upset too, you know.' He thumped his own chest with a closed fist. 'It hurts, man. Right here.'

He sounded like he was talking about losing a pet hamster.

'She was a special girl,' he said.

Calvin shook his head. 'Is that all you have to say?'

'What do you *want* me to say?'

'How about "Sorry"? You didn't even come to her funeral. You didn't give a toss about her.'

Milo's pupils were so wide Calvin thought he might fall into them and disappear. 'Chill out, Calv. You're really killing my vibe, mate. I did give a toss. I gave a very big toss. She was a top bird.'

'A *top bird*?' It took all Calvin's self-control not to punch Milo in the face.

Milo nodded. He was, Calvin realised, so stoned he could hardly stand up. His cigarette had turned into a column of ash between his fingers.

'I'll never forgive myself,' he said. 'But it was the dog. This massive fucking dog, man. It just ran into the road. I think it might even have been a wolf.'

'What are you going on about? A wolf?'

'It just ran into the road in front of me.'

And it was only then that it struck Calvin what Milo was saying. He realised, at the same time, that James had emerged from the pub and was standing behind him, watching and listening. Milo didn't appear to have noticed him.

'It was you!' Calvin said. 'You were driving, weren't you? Oh Jesus. Oh, fuck me. And I bet you persuaded your brother to say it was him because you were drunk or stoned like you are now.'

'No, no.' Milo waved his hands like he was trying to erase the mistake he'd made, to rub it out. 'Simeon was driving. I was in the back.'

'You're lying. You're *lying*.'

Milo looked like he was about to say something else. But all he said was, 'Whatever. Screw this.'

He lurched away towards the gate that led out of the beer garden.

James appeared at Calvin's side. He had that glassy-eyed look he always got when he'd had too many pints. 'What's going on? What was he saying?'

'It was *him*. He was driving the van.'

'When Freya was killed?'

'Yes! He killed her.'

James gawped at him, then they both watched Milo disappear into the darkness. Just beyond the pub was a lane that led deeper into the countryside. Calvin knew, from the day he'd driven out to pick Freya up, that Milo's house was a couple of miles from here, in that direction. Milo must be planning to walk home down the country lanes.

'Let's go after him,' Calvin said.

41

Calvin stood in the churchyard with the vicarage behind him, looking at St Bart's. He'd never been here before, but after talking to Theresa, he was convinced the vicar here, Reverend Delaney, held the key to understanding what was going on. Theresa had told him James had unburdened himself. Shortly after that, he'd been murdered.

Right now, Calvin's theory was that DJ had overheard the confession, then set himself up as some kind of avenging angel, for reasons Calvin couldn't understand. Maybe he'd tried to blackmail James but it had gone wrong so he'd murdered him, then targeted Calvin. Had he been planning to blackmail Calvin? Why had he abducted Vicky? And who had killed DJ? There were still so many unanswered questions, but the most important was not why or who. It was where. Where was Vicky?

He ought to go back to Imogen Evans, tell her everything. But there still had to be a chance he could find Vicky without condemning himself to spending the rest of his life in prison. Driving here, he had made his mind up. He would talk to Delaney and then try to find Billie, who had to be working with DJ. She might know where Vicky was being kept. And if neither Delaney nor Billie could help him, then he would give up and go back to Imogen. Tell her everything. If he ended up in prison, so be it.

The church door was open and Calvin slipped inside.

Despite the rain outside it was warm, but it was cool here in the church. Cool and quiet. In that near-silence, Calvin could hear a voice coming from somewhere up ahead. Calvin walked up the aisle towards the altar. Just behind the organ, to the left, was a little room. The vestry, he thought it was called. The voice, presumably Reverend Delaney's, was coming from there.

Calvin cleared his throat and Delaney immediately appeared out of the vestry.

He smiled pleasantly. 'How can I help you?'

Calvin froze for a second. He wasn't sure he was doing the right thing coming here. But he had to know if the vicar knew. If his theory about DJ was correct.

'My name's Calvin Matheson,' he said. 'I was a friend of James Sullivan. You knew him as Leo James.'

Calvin searched Delaney's face for a sign that the vicar knew what he'd done. But instead, he just looked sad.

'I heard he'd been identified at last. I'm sorry you couldn't come to the cremation. It's always terrible when no one is there. But what can I do for you, Mr Matheson?'

'I've just got back from talking to his mum. She told me you had been talking to James.'

He watched Delaney, looking for a reaction that told him he knew about James's past. But the benign smile stayed in place.

'That's right.'

This was agonising. Vicky was missing. The bomb was ticking. Calvin needed to stop being subtle. 'I need to know what James told you. About what we . . . what he did.' He winced, hating himself for trying to put all the blame on his dead friend.

'I'm not sure what you're talking about,' said Delaney.

'Please. Don't lie to me. He confessed, didn't he? Told you about Milo Stewart?'

'I'm sorry, but I have no idea what you're talking about.' Delaney sighed. 'People keep asking me about this, and even though you were his friend, all I can do is repeat what I told the police. Anything anyone tells me is confidential. But I can tell you that Leo, or rather James, didn't confess anything to me. We talked about sin and redemption, but it was all in the abstract.'

Calvin studied the vicar's face. He was telling the truth. Why wouldn't he be? But that meant Calvin was wrong. If James hadn't spoken about what they'd done here, DJ couldn't have overheard.

But Theresa had been sure James had unburdened himself. If he hadn't confessed all to the vicar, then who . . . ?

There was only one possibility, surely. It had to be Billie. The young woman who looked so much like Freya. Was that why James had done it? Had it been like confessing to Freya's ghost? Telling her how they had been trying to do right by her after finding out Milo had been driving?

Was Billie behind everything?

'Are you all right?'

Reverend Delaney was looking at him curiously, waiting for an answer.

'I'm sorry to have bothered you,' Calvin said, already turning away.

He staggered out of the church and back to his car. What should he do? He took deep breaths to stay calm but there were pains in his chest. He needed to get away from the church; it was compounding the feeling that he was being punished, that he deserved all of this. That he was going to be struck down.

He drove a short distance, glad the roads were quiet because his sense of speed and distance was all messed up. He wanted to confront Billie Whitehead, but didn't know her address.

Go to Imogen, said a voice in his head. *Now.*

But then, said another voice, *you'll have to confess everything.*

There was still a chance he could do this without destroying his life. Now he was out of sight of the church, he pulled over on a quiet street and sat behind the wheel, trying to figure out what to do. He squeezed his eyes shut and tried to think. Could Billie, this slight nineteen-year-old, really have murdered James? Abducted Vicky and dumped her car in a lake? Murdered DJ? Surely it wasn't possible for her to do all that on her own.

The obvious suspect had to be DJ. But he was dead. Would Billie really have killed her partner in crime? What if she'd been working with someone else? Who? Her mother? No, surely not. But who else was there?

He thought back to when he'd met Billie and DJ the first time and a chill ran through his blood. Who was it who had brought him into their orbit?

The woman who had appeared in his life at the start of all this. Mel.

Oh God. Had Mel been working with Billie? Maybe with Billie and DJ? *Had* she drugged him? And while he was out cold, had she – or Billie or DJ – gone to his house and grabbed Vicky? Had that whole evening been a set-up?

Had he been an idiot for defending her all this time?

He had no idea what Mel's motivation might be. That was something he was going to have to ask her about.

No, not ask. Demand to know.

He started the engine and set out towards the other side of Drigg. It was time to finally confront her.

42

Imogen parked outside Calvin and Vicky's place, noting that his car wasn't there, and rang the doorbell. Nobody came to the door, which was expected but annoying. She went back to her car and phoned Calvin's number. It went immediately to voicemail, like he had no signal.

What to do?

After her conversation with Steve, she had mulled it all over, examining the theory that James's murder had been a message intended for Calvin. The more she thought about it, the more she believed the message was only part of it. There had been real sadism in James's murder. A slow, terrifying death. All along she'd believed whoever had killed James loathed him and wanted him to suffer. Maybe it was still that, but the more she thought about it the more convinced she became: it was a message that only Calvin was meant to understand. When he'd failed to react – because the murderer had failed to ensure there were photos of James for the police to circulate – they'd ramped things up by taking Vicky.

She could imagine herself in a courtroom, explaining all this to a jury, their mouths hanging open. But she knew from the case that had made her famous that killers, like God, often worked in mysterious ways.

She got out of the car and went back to the house, peering through the front window.

Everything had ramped up today. DJ's murder. Finding Vicky's car. The identification of Leo James. She needed to find Calvin.

Because maybe they've got him too, whispered a voice in her head. Maybe they were going to find his car in a lake in a day or two.

Or find Calvin and Vicky's bodies.

She called in to the station. 'I need you to ask all patrols to be on the lookout for Calvin Matheson.'

Could Calvin be in the house now? Hurt? Her experience with previous cases told her that was a possibility. She needed to find out. She was about to go around the back, to check the back door – before she started breaking anything down – when a woman came out of the house next door. She was in her sixties, with short grey hair, well dressed, sharp eyes.

'You're that police detective,' she said. 'Imogen something.'

'Imogen Evans.'

'I'm Margaret. Looking for Calvin?'

'I am. And it would be helpful for me to get into the house.'

Margaret's eyes widened. 'You think something might have happened to Calvin too?'

'I just want to set my mind at rest.'

At that moment, Imogen heard meowing from inside Calvin's house. There was a cat pressed up against the inside of the window.

'Oh, poor Jarvis,' said Margaret.

'I'm going to break the door down, okay?' Imogen said.

Margaret seemed surprised. 'There's no need to do that. I've got a spare key.' She grinned. 'It's not every day we get celebrities round these parts.'

Finally, an upside to being recognisable.

Margaret went back into her house and came out a few minutes later with a Yale key. Jarvis continued to meow frantically as

Imogen opened the front door, running up to Imogen – who asked Margaret to wait outside – as she entered the house, before realising she was a stranger and shooting up the stairs in a blur of fur.

'Okay, cat, so you're not impressed by my celebrity.'

She went into the kitchen first, looking for signs of a disturbance or struggle. There was nothing. No sign at all that he'd even been back here after leaving the station. Now she was inside, she was starting to think this was a complete waste of time – but she might as well look around.

She checked the living room, then went up the stairs. She poked her head into Calvin and Vicky's bedroom. A suitcase was on a chair next to the bed and the cat was under the chair, green eyes peering out fearfully. Imogen entered the bedroom and crouched, holding out her hand and making kissy noises, feeling foolish. The cat clearly thought she was foolish too, as he gave her a look of feline contempt before strolling past her as if he'd never been bothered by her presence.

There was a silver necklace beneath the chair where the cat had been sitting. Leaning closer, Imogen could see a pendant in the shape of a bee.

She was sure she had seen it before. Not on Vicky, obviously, because she'd never met her.

Standing, she had a quick look at the surface of the dressing table. There was a jewellery box and a stand, on which were strung several necklaces, along with numerous pairs of earrings. They were all gold or rose gold. Nothing silver at all.

The bee pendant certainly didn't look like something Calvin would wear. So whose was it, if it wasn't Vicky's? And what was it doing here?

She crouched again and took a few close-up photos of the pendant and chain, then went back out into the hallway. Now the cat shot out of one of the other rooms, dashing down the stairs.

Imogen followed him. He'd run towards the rear of the house and, halfway, she turned to look over the banister at him.

There was a security camera attached to one of the door frames. Calvin hadn't mentioned that when he'd reported Vicky missing. Imogen went into the hallway to get a better look. It was a tiny little spy camera, presumably connected to a phone. The light was on now, telling her she was being recorded.

'I need someone to come to the Matheson property to pick up a security camera.'

Twenty minutes later, after a uniformed officer arrived at Calvin's house and she explained what she needed off the camera's feed, she drove into Elderbridge and parked outside Therapy.

She went in.

'Sorry, we're closing. It's five o'clock.' This was Tara, who was on her own behind the counter. 'Oh, it's you. Did you find Calvin?'

'I did. But I need to find him again.'

'Careless of you.'

Imogen couldn't help but smile. She liked Tara.

'He's a slippery guy. Has he been back in this afternoon?'

'I'm afraid not.'

Several hours had passed since she'd interviewed him, and she wondered where he'd been if not home or here.

'You look exhausted,' Tara said. 'Want a coffee?'

Imogen didn't usually drink caffeine after 3 p.m., but she had a feeling it was going to be a long night. 'Go on, then.'

Tara went over to the machine, telling Imogen to sit down. The machine hissed and clanked and the smell of coffee filled the air. A few minutes later, Tara brought over a cappuccino, setting it down in front of Imogen.

'Cake? We take the leftovers to the homeless shelter but we have loads left today. It's been so quiet. Calvin's going to have to get rid of the temps if it doesn't pick up.' She placed a slice of carrot cake in front of her and Imogen felt her mouth water. When had she last eaten?

She was about to take a bite when her phone buzzed. She glanced at the message.

'What the hell?'

Tara raised her eyebrows.

'We've got reports of loads of dogs and cats running loose on the other side of Elderbridge. A pack of dogs running across the housing estate. What a day.' She put down the phone. Someone else could deal with the animals. 'Did Calvin say anything about having CCTV in his house?'

Tara scoffed. 'I'm sure he didn't. He hasn't even got it installed here. If he did, we might know who pushed me down the stairs.'

'Yeah. Oh, can I show you something?'

'It depends what it is.'

Imogen smiled and brought up the photo of the necklace and pendant. She held it up so Tara could take a look. 'Do you recognise this?'

Tara scrutinised it. 'Hmm. I'm not sure.'

'Is it the kind of thing Vicky would wear?'

'No way. She only has nice jewellery. This is like something a kid would wear. Or, actually, I know someone else who always wears stuff like this. Mel.' Her hand went to her mouth. 'Is this a clue in Vicky's disappearance? Is Mel involved? Oh my God, why am I not surprised? She wants Vicky out the way so she can have Calvin for herself. I *knew* it.'

'That's . . .' Imogen was sure that wasn't it. And there was a far more likely explanation for this being in Calvin's house. Mel had been there with Calvin. And, what, Vicky had found it when she got back from her trip? And run away after all?

Or she had confronted Calvin, and he'd murdered her?

Had Imogen allowed herself to be taken in by him?

She called the station. 'Have you got the footage off that security camera yet? . . . What do you mean, everyone's gone to round up cats and dogs? Jesus wept. I need it *now*.'

'Do you want another coffee?' Tara asked.

Imogen needed to talk to Mel. She also wanted another coffee.

'Sod it,' she said. 'Can you make me one to go?'

Tara went back over to the machine and Imogen's phone buzzed again. 'I am not going to help catch cats and dogs,' she muttered. But reading the message she said, 'That was quick.'

Tara turned back. 'What is it?'

'They've got the footage off the security camera. A clip from the night Vicky disappeared. They've sent it along.'

She put her phone on the table and was aware of her leg shaking, her heart thumping – where was her famous calmness now? – as she waited for it to download.

43

Calvin was almost at Mel's place, driving along the edge of Foxton Water – the lake where Vicky's car had been found – when he started to get the feeling he was being followed. He slowed and peered into the rear-view mirror. There was a four-by-four behind him. Mel drove a Land Rover. Was it her?

He decreased his speed further and the four-by-four stopped, did a fast U-turn and shot off in the opposite direction.

What the hell? The anger taking hold of him again, Calvin did the same, putting his foot down and firing off after the four-by-four.

Mel. Suddenly he was convinced she was behind all this, that she was the architect of this plot against him, that she had done something to Vicky. He was going to catch her and shake the truth out of her.

The lake sped by on his left. But even smashing the speed limit – he was too far gone to worry about tickets and points on his licence later – there was no sign of the four-by-four. He'd lost it.

He slowed down; thumped the wheel with frustration. If that had been Mel, and he was sure it must have been, there was little point turning round and going to her house as he'd intended. And he couldn't go and look for Billie, because he didn't know where she lived.

A wave of despair crashed over him. A draining of adrenaline.

He was out of his depth. Not just out of his depth but drowning. It was time to go back to the police, tell Imogen Evans everything. That he believed James had been murdered and that he was being targeted by Billie and Mel. That James must have confessed to Billie and that the two women, possibly with DJ's help, up to the point where . . . what? They'd decided they no longer needed him? There were so many holes in his theory – like, what exactly was their motivation for all this? – that he thought Imogen might laugh him out of the station. But it was time to come clean and let the professionals figure it out and pray they were in time to save Vicky, if she wasn't already dead.

He headed back to Elderbridge, and was halfway there when his phone pinged.

He slowed down and picked it up.

It was a text from an unfamiliar number. But opening it, the first thing he saw was his wife's name.

He knew if he tried to read it while he drove he'd crash the car, probably drive it straight into the lake, so he pulled over by the side of the road.

Calvin, the text read. *It's me. Vicky. I'm safe and I can explain everything. I need you to come and get me. I'm going to send you an address.*

He immediately replied: *Why are you using this phone? How do I know it's you?*

> *Because I left my phone at home. I can prove it's me. Ask me something only we would know.*

He thought about it. When their cat had been brought in to the shelter he'd had a different name before they'd decided he was a Jarvis. Only the real Vicky would know that. Taking twice as long as normal to compose the text because his hands were shaking so much, he wrote back: *What was Jarvis's original name?*

The reply came immediately: *Damian. The RSPCA guy who brought him in said he was a devil.*

It was right. This really was Vicky.

I'm sending you the address now. Get here as quickly as you can. Don't go to the police. There's no need for them to know what you did.

The words on the phone screen made him go cold. Vicky knew his secret? Whoever she was with – Billie? Mel? both? – must have told her.

He texted back: *Why can't you come home? What's going on?*

But there was no reply. Just another text with a pin showing him a location on Google Maps.

It was back in Drigg, in what appeared to be some woods, not far from the beach. Also, not that far from St Bart's church.

Was that where James had lived?

Calvin took a deep breath, attempting to slow his heart rate. Vicky was alive. She'd said she was safe. What the hell was she doing at James's place? Was she alone? He knew there had to be a strong chance she had answered that text under duress, that someone was holding a gun to her head – or a knife to her throat – telling her to give the correct answer.

He sat and thought for a moment. He should go to the police. But Vicky had told him not to. It was the wise thing to do, but he had spent almost thirty years protecting the secret. It had become part of his nature. Part of him. And Vicky, under duress or not, had told him not to go to the police. Going to them now might put her in more danger.

He made up his mind. He would go to the location. Take a look. If there was any sign it was a trap he would get out quickly and call the police.

He turned the car around once again.

ϖ

A narrow lane led into the woods, a tangle of trees on either side. Evening was approaching, shadows getting shorter. In the near distance, he heard church bells ring six times.

A bungalow came into view, surrounded by a fence with a gate that was hanging off its hinges. A sign read *PRIVATE PROPERTY KEEP OUT*. He was sure, from what Imogen had told him, this must be James's place. The house where he had hidden away from the world all these years.

He parked and went through the gate. There were remnants of police crime-scene tape tied to the posts, but the cops, he guessed, must have finished here within days of the murder. He went up to the front door and stood there for a moment, listening. All he could hear were birds in the trees. The bells had stopped ringing and there were no sounds coming from inside the house. The silence sent goosebumps rippling across his flesh.

The door was ajar.

He pushed it open and stepped inside. The place smelled musty, unlived in, even though it had been less than two weeks since James had been killed.

'Vicky?'

No response.

He found himself looking at a hideous painting that hung on the wall in the hallway: sinners being tormented by a devil-like creature. It was clearly influenced by the Bosch paintings that had scared James as a child. Seeing it made Calvin feel wretched. While he had been getting on with his life, James had fallen apart. If only he had reached out, Calvin might have been able to help him – though he also knew he might not have responded.

He went into the kitchen. It was empty. The police, presumably, had left it in disarray: drawers and cupboards still open, piles of groceries and papers strewn on the counters. A fat fly struggled in a spider's web that half-covered the window.

What was going on? Vicky wasn't here.

He went back into the hallway, then poked his head into another room, a bedroom. More of those hellish paintings on the wall. He looked in the bathroom, which was filthy, with limescale stains in the bathtub.

There was one room he hadn't been into. Its door was closed.

He hesitated, then pushed it open and stepped into a small living room. A threadbare sofa. Stacks of books but no TV. A boom box with a pile of CDs next to it. Calvin recognised the boom box. It had belonged to James in the nineties. It was crazy that it still worked.

But the house was empty. There were no more rooms to explore. No sign of a basement. Had he come to the right place?

There was another of the paintings on the wall. A huge canvas, five feet across. This one was most clearly influenced by Hieronymus Bosch. A nightmarish battlefield of weird creatures and writhing souls. Calvin took a step closer. At the edge of the frame was a river, the water dark, tinged red with blood. Bodies floated there. Men thrashed, trying not to drown. And devils squatted on the banks, watching, grinning.

'Quite talented, wasn't he?'

Calvin moved to turn towards the male voice, but something metal was jabbed against the back of his head. It had to be a gun. At the same time, he heard an engine. A vehicle pulling up outside.

'Don't move.' He didn't recognise the man's voice, even when he continued to speak. 'I wanted you to see it, the place where poor James lived all this time. At least he felt guilty over what he did. Guilty enough to confess eventually. You didn't give a shit, did you? You just got on with your life. Making cakes. Making fucking cakes.'

'I—'

'Shut up! Don't move.'

'Where's Vicky?' Calvin said, his voice hoarse.

'We were originally going to bury you on the beach,' said the man. 'Like James. But it's too risky. The police are going to be looking for you. We're taking you somewhere more private.'

'Come on, do it,' said a woman from further back in the room. A familiar voice. And then something struck Calvin hard on the back of his head and he collapsed to the floor, unconscious before he hit it.

44

Calvin came to, lying on his side, and was hit immediately by a pain that felt like someone hammering a spike into his skull. He forced himself to open his eyes, despite the agony. There was just enough light for him to make out black shapes. An empty chair. Crates piled on top of one another. A bare light bulb hanging from the ceiling and some stairs leading up to a door. It was a basement. Was this James's cottage? The space felt too big.

He groaned and a voice behind him said, 'Calvin?'

He rolled over. '*Vicky?*'

She was sitting on the floor on the other side of the basement. He tried to get up and immediately felt something tug at his ankle, tripping him and sending him sprawling on to the floor, palms smacking against stone.

Getting back into a sitting position, he realised he was manacled, with a metal band clamped tight around his ankle. Shuffling forward he felt a chain, about four feet long, which was attached to a lead pipe. He tugged at the pipe, as hard as he could, but it was solid and wouldn't shift.

He turned back towards Vicky. She was alive! That was something. A sliver of hope to cling to. She was manacled too, chained to another pipe on the opposite wall.

'Are you okay?' he asked.

She sounded exhausted and weak. 'I'm okay. Hungry. Wondering what the fuck is going on. Who is he, Calvin? Why is he doing this?'

He still hadn't seen the man's face. He didn't know who had done this. The woman's voice . . . Who was it? He couldn't think through the pain.

'What happened?' he asked. 'At the house?'

She told him, starting from when she got home and texted him, asking him where he was.

'Then I found her necklace . . . in our bed.'

'Whose necklace?'

'Mel's!'

He tried to take this in. 'That doesn't make sense. Mel has never been in our house, I swear.'

'It was a bee. That's the kind of thing she wears, isn't it?'

Was it? He had no idea.

'You have to believe me,' he said. 'She's never been in our house. But I think she's part of this. Her and Billie and DJ . . . Well, he was, but now he's dead and—'

'I have no idea who you're talking about.'

He was sure there hadn't been any necklace in the bed on Saturday night or Sunday morning, when he'd slept there alone. He'd have noticed it. Somebody must have snuck in on Sunday while he was at work and planted it there, for whatever reason. Which meant someone had a key to their house.

Presumably the same someone who'd been there a few days before, accidentally shutting Jarvis in their bedroom.

He kept a spare key at the office. Had Mel taken it and let herself into their house during her lunch break, because she wanted Vicky to believe they were having an affair? If so, how did that connect with everything else going on?

Calvin reached up and touched his head, wincing at the pain. There was a tender lump on his skull.

'The person who took me from our house,' Vicky said, 'who locked me up down here – it's a man. About our age. Thinning ginger hair. A kind of manic energy.'

'Just a man? Because there were two of them when they grabbed me. A man and woman.'

Calvin racked his brains. He was sure the woman he'd heard must have been Mel. But who was the man?

'I've only seen the man. I've heard a dog barking, maybe two. Heard him playing music too, up there. But he's barely spoken. Hardly even looked at me. All he's said is that when I find out what you did, I'll understand.'

A man with ginger hair. A man who cared about what Calvin did. He was beginning to get a horrible feeling about how this might all connect up and why this was happening. This was it, then, at last: the shadow that had been hanging over him since he was eighteen. The darkness that had swallowed James was about to swallow him.

'Do you know where we are? How long was the journey?'

'I don't know. Over an hour, I'd say.'

So they couldn't be at James's place in Drigg.

'What does he *sound* like? The man who brought you here?' Calvin asked.

'What? What do you mean?'

'His accent. Is he posh?'

'Yeah. He sounds like, I don't know, Prince Harry.'

Calvin knew for certain who it was. Why this was happening.

He heard the door above them open and someone enter the basement, standing at the top of the stairs. They began to descend down the wooden steps, their face hidden from view at first. Any doubts Calvin might have had were blown away the moment he saw the coat. The green army coat that had been worn even on the hottest days in the summer of 1995. Army coat and ginger hair and a cut-glass accent.

'Gawp away, Calvin. All these years and I can still get into this old thing.' He said this with clear pride, tugging the lapels of the coat together under his chin like a fashion model as he reached the bottom of the steps. 'You know, it actually used to belong to Milo. My brother was always the most stylish member of the family.'

It was Simeon Stewart.

'Go on then, Calvin,' he said. 'Tell your lovely wife what you did to my brother.'

45

September 1995

There were no street lights along the lane, and within a few minutes of leaving the pub's beer garden, Calvin and James found themselves in a world lit only by the bright, almost-full moon.

'Where is he?' James asked, meaning Milo, who was somewhere out of sight ahead of them.

'If you hadn't needed the loo,' said Calvin. Before leaving the pub, James had insisted that he needed the toilet, then proceeded to do the longest pee in history.

'It's fine. We'll catch up with him.'

Calvin hadn't really thought about what they were going to do when they caught him. Ideally, what he would have done was go home and find his old tape recorder, then get Milo to admit what he and his brother had done on tape.

'So Milo just flat-out admitted it?' said James as they walked down the lane. 'That he'd been behind the wheel?'

'Yes. And because he was drunk or on drugs, and Simeon was sober, they told the police Simeon had been driving. The sister, Piper, backed them up.'

'Do you think Freya knew Milo was pissed when she got in the van with him?'

Calvin stopped walking. 'What, are you saying it's her own fault?'

'No. Chill out, Cal. It's just . . .'

'Yeah, I know. A stupid thing for her to do. Stupid of her not to be wearing a seat belt too. But she paid the price, didn't she? Paid the price for getting involved with that dickhead in the first place.'

'And he didn't show any remorse?' James asked, as they started walking again.

'No. He just kept going on about how she was a "top bird". And some nonsense about a wolf running into the road.'

He spat the words out. He was so angry, unlike any anger he'd experienced before. Like red-hot needles inside him. It was all so unfair. Unjust. That Milo had walked away from the crash with barely a scratch on him. That was one thing. The lie his siblings had told was another. But the worst, the very worst, was the almost-certain knowledge that if Milo hadn't been off his face, hallucinating wolves, Freya would still be alive.

Calvin began to walk faster, determined to catch Milo before he got home, and James increased his pace too. Calvin could still feel all the beer he'd drunk sloshing around inside him, like dark and dirty water.

Towards the end of the lane was a gate that led into a field, which sloped downwards towards a small wooded area. As they passed it, Calvin looked to his left and saw a tiny figure almost at the far edge of the field, moving towards the treeline. It had to be Milo. He pointed him out to James.

'Come on.'

He climbed the stile, with James following. A sign pointed out that this was a public footpath. Calvin realised this must be the shortest route to Elysian Fields. As they walked at pace across the field, the downward gradient making it easy-going despite the uneven ground, Calvin glanced up at the clear sky, the moon, the galaxy of stars. A fine, clear night. Under different circumstances he might have appreciated being young and alive in such a beautiful place, at such a good time in history. But right now, all he cared about was catching up with Milo. He was in the power of his own anger, enslaved by his negative emotions. Even if his future self had been able to time-travel and warn the young Calvin that he was minutes away from calamity, his eighteen-year-old self wouldn't have listened. It was too late.

Milo, not too far ahead of them now, disappeared into the woods. A minute later, Calvin and James left the field and entered the trees too. There was only one path, so there were no decisions to make. On one side of the path, dense trees. On the other, a steep bank that sloped down to a wide stream, water glistening in the moonlight.

'He's there,' Calvin said suddenly, his voice hushed – but not hushed enough, as Milo looked over his shoulder and paused for a second before increasing his pace. *He probably doesn't know who we are*, Calvin thought. He must be afraid. Anyone would be alarmed to discover there was someone else in these dark woods, possibly following them.

Calvin broke into a jog, and James did the same.

Milo looked over his shoulder again, then started to run.

Calvin increased his pace. Driven by fury, he was much faster than he normally would have been, and his feet miraculously found the smoothest spots on the ground while, ahead, Milo stumbled over rocks and bumps, almost falling but managing to stay upright.

Calvin caught up, then dashed in front of him, stopping on the path and stretching his arms wide.

Milo skidded to a halt.

'You. What are you doing here?' he demanded through heaving breaths.

James arrived, blocking any chance Milo had to retreat. James and Milo were both panting but Calvin didn't feel out of breath at all. He felt powerful and young and strong.

'This is not cool,' Milo said, trying not to seem afraid, but his eyes were darting left and right, looking for an escape route. Trees to the left, the steep bank to the right.

'No. It's *not* cool, is it?' said Calvin.

Milo smiled nervously. 'What do you want?'

'I want you to go to the police. Tell them what you told me.'

'I don't know what you're talking about.'

Of course, Milo hadn't actually confessed, had he? He'd just given himself away, like the druggie dickhead he was.

'I want you to go to the police. Tell them you were driving. That you were out of your head and that you killed Freya.'

Milo spluttered, 'Fuck that.' He turned back to face James. 'You believe this maniac? He's making it all up. My brother, Simeon, was driving. It was an accident. One of those things.'

'*One of those things?*' Calvin couldn't believe what he was hearing.

Milo half-turned back to him. 'I mean, yeah, it's sad. I really liked her. She was cool.'

'A "top bird", yeah?' Calvin spat. This prick wasn't going to apologise or be reasonable. Calvin was overwhelmed, for the first time in his life, with the desire to be violent. Fuck taking Milo to the police. He was going to mete out his own justice, here, with his fists.

He raised them. Over Milo's shoulder, he saw excitement on James's face.

'Did you undo her seat belt?' Calvin asked.

'What? No, she never put it on. She had sunburn from when we'd been in my pool, and she said the belt rubbed it.'

'So that was your fault too. I'm going to—'

Milo made his move. He swung a hapless, almost laughable fist at Calvin. It went well wide of the mark but made Calvin step back, allowing Milo space to dash down the slope to the right, toward the stream. It was steep, rough with tree roots and ridges and rocks. Milo made it only about ten feet down the slope before he tripped. He went hurtling down the remainder of the slope, crashing head-first into a rock before rolling and landing in the stream at the bottom.

He lay there still, face down.

Calvin had been enshrouded in a red mist, the whole thing – attempted punch, dash, fall – taking seconds. As Milo landed in the water, it was as if a gust of wind blew the mist away and he woke up, re-entering the real world. Milo was lying there in the water, not moving. In the moonlight it was hard to see clearly but Calvin was sure there was a dark, glistening patch on the top of Milo's skull: blood, from where he'd hit his head on the way down. The impact must have knocked him unconscious.

Instinctively, Calvin moved to descend the slope. He needed to get Milo out of the water. Turn him over, at least.

James grabbed his arm.

'Wait.'

Calvin stared at him. 'We need to . . .' He trailed off.

'Do we?' said James. 'Do we really? After what he did to Freya?'

Calvin felt his arm go slack. There was a voice in his head telling him he needed to get down there, turn Milo over, a voice yelling, *He's going to die if you don't do something*. But then the red mist was back. The anger. The hatred. This person had killed Freya. Had lied about it. He didn't even care.

He and James locked eyes, silent, the knowledge of what they were doing passing between them.

They were allowing a man to drown. Removing him from the world.

A cloud drifted across the moon, turning the world dark, and when it passed and moonlight illuminated the woods and the stream again, they knew the figure lying face down in the water was no longer a living person. It was now a body.

'We should go,' James said. 'Before someone comes or before anyone notices we're missing.'

The ground was hard and dry, so they didn't need to worry about leaving footprints. Calvin looked around, making sure neither of them had dropped anything. His heart was thumping so hard it hurt and his skin was cold. Regret was kicking in already. What had they done? What had he done?

He looked to James, seeking reassurance, but James appeared to be regretting it already too. He had gone as white as the moon that hung above them. Calvin felt as if he were in a film and the clouds above had sped up, rushing by in fast motion. The darkness was an extra inky black. The trees leaned in close, whispering. Here, he knew, was a crack in the middle of his life. The 'before' was gone. From now on, everything would be 'after'.

'No one saw us going after him, did they?' Calvin said. His friend didn't react, just kept staring. 'James?'

'I don't . . . I don't think so.' The pub's beer garden had been empty when they'd left.

'Okay. Okay, good. I'll . . . I'll say I spoke to him at the pub, because there were probably witnesses to that. I'll say we chatted about Freya. We both need to say we went straight home. My parents will be in bed. What about your mum?'

It was after midnight.

'Yeah. She goes to bed after the ten o'clock news.' James's voice had gone weak and he looked like he might start crying.

'Okay.' There was a pause. 'We have to make a promise. We can never talk about this to anyone. No confessions to future girlfriends. This is between us. Forever. Understood?'

James nodded. They didn't make a pledge or swear an oath. They didn't spit on their palms and shake. But they had an understanding.

Calvin knew, as well, that this was it, the end of things. Of their friendship. The secret would not unite but divide them.

'Silence,' he said, before they left the body behind and went their separate ways. Home to attempt to sleep. 'Silence for the rest of our lives.'

46

All the way to St Bartholomew's, Imogen's police radio buzzed with news of the great pet escape on the other side of Elderbridge. Residents of the housing estate had been trying to take matters into their own hands and a woman had been bitten by a frightened cockapoo, while a small group of men had a pair of XL bullies cornered in someone's back garden. A cat had clamped its teeth into a child's hand before escaping over a fence, and there were still a dozen dogs running loose. Pretty much every cop in the area – those who weren't at the caravan park or Foxton Water – had been despatched to deal with what, in any normal month, would be the biggest thing to happen around here.

But this really hadn't been a normal month.

'Has anyone spoken to the woman who runs the animal shelter?' Imogen said into her phone as she drove.

'You mean Vicky Matheson?' That was Mehmet, who had been left to hold the fort.

'Shit. Of course.'

Everything kept coming back to the Mathesons.

'What about the woman who works there with her?' Calvin had mentioned her when he'd reported Vicky missing. 'Louise something?'

'Louise Monks. An officer has gone to the shelter but there's no one there. And we can't get hold of Miss Monks.'

'What about the dog warden? Shouldn't they be dealing with this?'

Mehmet sighed. 'I spoke to the council. They only have two people working in that department. One's on long-term sick leave and the other one is recovering from a bite he sustained last week.'

'Another vicious dog.'

'Oh no. It was a parrot. An escaped parrot called Captain Trips.'

'Of course it was.' A call was coming through on her phone. Steve.

She answered it. 'What's happening?' he asked.

Imogen explained what she'd seen on the footage from Vicky's security camera. Two separate clips, one captured on Monday afternoon, when Vicky was at the spa and Calvin was at work, and the other later that night, when Calvin was asleep on Mel's sofa.

The second clip showed a man Imogen didn't recognise. Forties, red hair, a similar colour to Imogen's but going grey. He was creeping along the hallway, looking around as if checking there was no one else in the house. This was the person who had abducted Vicky Matheson, but no one at the station knew who he was.

The first clip showed DJ entering the house, apparently letting himself in with a key. He passed the camera and presumably went up the stairs. A minute later he reappeared and stood directly beneath the camera, a big grin on his face. He spoke to someone – the camera didn't capture sound – and then that person entered the frame and he kissed them.

It was Billie.

'And that's who you're going to talk to now?' Steve said.

'Yes. I think DJ must have been planting that bee necklace in Calvin and Vicky's bedroom. According to Tara at the coffee shop, the necklace is Mel's. They were trying to make it look like Calvin was having an affair with Mel. I need to know why.' She paused. 'And I think Billie will know who the other man is.'

She pulled up outside the Whiteheads' house. Last time she'd come here, a man had died and Steve had almost been seriously injured.

'I need to know who he is, if we're going to have any chance of finding and saving Vicky.'

47

Calvin finished telling the story to Vicky. His confession. The secret he'd carried his whole adult life. Simeon stood there the whole time, listening and prompting Calvin to carry on if he hesitated. He didn't contradict Calvin when he reached the part about how Milo had been driving the van when Freya was killed.

'You murdered him,' Simeon said.

Calvin knew he could argue. That he hadn't murdered Milo, he'd just failed to rescue him. But all these years he'd persuaded himself it had been murder. He wasn't sure what the legal definition would be, but he had caused it. If he and James hadn't been there, Milo would never have fallen down that bank. And then they had deliberately left him to drown when they could have saved him.

'You might as well have smashed him over the head with a rock,' Simeon said.

Calvin said nothing.

'I'd wondered if your version would differ from the one James described when he was buried up to his neck, but it's pretty much identical.' He made a little snorting sound. 'You know, James almost seemed relieved it was all about to be over. It was disappointing, really. I was hoping for more terror, especially as DJ had assured me he was scared of water. Scared of Hell too. But even when he was digging the hole he seemed resigned to it. At peace with the idea of death.'

Vicky had hardly spoken during Calvin's confession. He had expected her to be shocked and appalled, but he guessed she was far more concerned about what was going on now and their chances of getting out of here. If she was disgusted with him, if his story meant she no longer loved him, they would have to deal with that later.

If they survived this.

'Where are we?' Calvin asked. 'Do you still live in the same big house? Elysian Fields?'

Simeon looked surprised. 'You remember.'

'I remember everything. All of it; it's tormented me. And I'm so sorry for what we did. Although, if Milo hadn't crashed the van, if you hadn't lied to protect—'

'Shut up. I don't. Want. To hear. Any *excuses*!'

A noise came from upstairs. A door slamming.

Simeon looked up towards the basement ceiling. 'Piper's home.'

Home. That confirmed it. They were at Elysian Fields.

'Your sister? She still lives here too?'

Middle-aged siblings, still living together. Calvin assumed their parents, who he'd never met, were dead. Hard to see them keeping Vicky locked up down here with their mum and dad here, unless they were in on it too. But he realised the female voice he'd heard at James's house must have been Piper's. He was surprised he was still able to recognise her voice after all these years.

'Time to get this done,' Simeon said. And then he had a gun in his hand. Some kind of handgun. It must have been tucked in the pocket of his ridiculous coat.

He was going to shoot them. Calvin scrambled back against the wall, but that made Simeon laugh. 'Relax, Calvin. It's not going to be that quick or easy.'

He went to Vicky first and told her to put her hands behind her back. He produced a pair of handcuffs and snapped them over her wrists. Then he unlocked the manacle that secured her to the pipe. He came over to Calvin and repeated the process.

'On your feet,' he said. 'Both of you. Vicky, come here.'

She came over and stood beside Calvin. Their eyes met and there were so many things he wanted to say – 'sorry' being the main one. He knew that Simeon was planning to punish him, just as he had punished James. He had to hope Vicky was only here as a witness, or maybe as a means to make Calvin do as he was told. Why would they kill Vicky when she hadn't done anything?

'Up the stairs,' Simeon instructed. 'Go.'

He stood at the bottom as they climbed the wooden steps. The door at the top was ajar. Simeon told them to push it open when they reached it and go through. He followed them up. They found themselves in a bare hallway with an open door to the left.

'That way,' Simeon said. 'To the door.'

It was dark in the hallway. Calvin and Vicky went slowly, with Simeon behind them. They reached the door. Very little light came in. Night had fallen.

'Go out. Vicky first,' Simeon barked at them.

Vicky went outside. Calvin was about to go out too when, from the other end of the hallway, he heard footsteps, followed by that familiar woman's voice: 'I think someone was following me.'

Piper – it had to be her – stood in the gloom, just her outline visible.

'What?' Simeon asked her. 'Who? Not the police?'

'No. A four-by-four. But it's okay, I lost them in the lanes. And it might not even have been someone following me.' She laughed. 'I'm nervy. Jumpy.'

'Well, sort yourself out.' Simeon turned back to Calvin. 'What are you waiting for? Get outside.'

He jabbed the gun at him.

Calvin thought about kicking out at him, attempting to run. But Simeon had a gun, and with his wrists handcuffed behind him, Calvin knew it would be futile. He went out and found Vicky standing there, looking around like she was trying to figure out if she should run. Then Simeon appeared and it was too late.

They were around the back of the house, standing on a concrete area next to a large dumpster. A lawn stretched into the distance just beyond this point, but Calvin couldn't see the entrance gate from here as it was obscured by the corner of the house they'd just come out of.

He hadn't been here since 1995, the day he'd collected Freya, and he'd forgotten how huge the house was. Almost big enough to have wings, east and west. The kind of place where people held country weddings, except shabbier, falling apart. Paint flaked from the window frames and ivy had spread across the walls like an uncontrolled virus.

'I can't believe you never left,' Calvin said as Simeon emerged behind them. He wanted to keep him talking, to delay whatever Simeon had planned.

'Why would we? I mean, once upon a time we dreamed of being rock stars. Travelling the world. But you ruined that, didn't you?'

'You ruined it yourself. When your brother killed Freya.'

'That was an accident.'

'So was what happened to Milo.'

Simeon took a step closer, the gun unsteady in his hand. Calvin was afraid it might go off by accident, or that Simeon would lose his temper and abandon whatever plan he had, end everything with a simple gunshot.

'You let him *drown*,' Simeon said, his voice torn. 'You could have saved him, but you stood there and watched him drown.'

Calvin swallowed. His shame was so great; if he had one wish it would be to turn the clock back, rewind time. Drag Milo out of that stream. But what was the point of saying that to Simeon?

Simeon said, 'Milo was special. He was going to be a star. Your Freya . . . She was just a cheap groupie.'

'Fuck you,' said Calvin, fighting back the urge to spit in Simeon's face. 'Freya was worth a thousand of your brother. He was nothing but a poser. A wannabe.'

'Better that than a cheap slut.'

'I'm going to—'

'Please!' That was Vicky, raising her voice. 'Just stop, both of you. Simeon, why don't you get on with it?'

God, Calvin loved this woman.

Simeon was shocked for a second, then smiled. He lifted the nose of the gun towards Calvin and Vicky.

'Come on, then. Walk.'

He directed them around the side of the big house. The moon was out, just as it had been the night Milo died. The grass was overgrown and the nettles and brambles had taken over the flowerbeds. A broken statue lay on its side on the gravel. If he had stumbled across this place, Calvin would have assumed it was abandoned.

They went around the corner, and the impression of neglect and abandonment was compounded by the site of the empty swimming pool. Freya had swum here that hot summer's day in 1995. The water had sparkled in the sunshine. She'd got a bad sunburn that had prevented her from wearing her seat belt. They had all been young and beautiful and should have had their whole lives ahead of them. Now, the pool was a dark pit, with chunks missing around its edge and a rusted metal ladder leading down into it on the far side.

Simeon went over to the wall and bent down. He must have flipped a switch because, suddenly, a floodlight came on above them, illuminating the entire space with white light.

'Lie down next to the pool. On your bellies. Right by the edge.'

They both did as he said, though it was awkward without the use of their hands. Calvin turned his head to look at Vicky, who stared straight ahead, her chin on the ground. Simeon produced something metallic from a large pot near the pool. He approached Vicky and crouched beside her.

She kicked out at him and he hissed at her: 'Hey!' He grabbed the back of her hair and yanked her head up. 'Try anything like that—'

'Get your fucking hands off her!' Calvin yelled.

Simeon, who had set the gun on the ground beside him, picked it up and pointed it at Calvin again. 'Shut up! Lie flat and stay quiet.'

He scooted further down beside Vicky's feet and Calvin saw what the metallic objects were: two pairs of ankle cuffs. He snapped one pair over Vicky's ankles. Then he did the same to Calvin. There was, Calvin realised, something attached to the ankle cuffs: a kettlebell. Then, finally, he produced a piece of thick rope and used it to connect the two sets of cuffs. They were both hog-tied.

He muttered as he did it. 'This would be so much easier if I didn't want you to suffer. Same with James. You know how long it took him to dig that fucking hole? And to wait for the tide to come in? But it was worth it. Oh my God, it was so worth it.'

He was demented.

'Now. Get up.'

He pulled them both up onto their knees and they knelt there, right on the edge of the pool. Now Calvin could see the hose, leading from a tap at the side of the house and into the pool. Looking closer, Calvin realised the hose was already on and that there was about three feet of water, maybe slightly less, at the bottom of the pool. A shudder went through him.

'That's your plan?' Calvin said. 'You're going to drown us? Like you drowned James?'

'Like you drowned Milo.'

'I'd rather you shot me,' Calvin said.

Without a word, Simeon strode around Calvin to Vicky – and pushed her in.

'No!' Calvin yelled, helpless to do anything but watch.

Vicky hit the water with a splash and, going in sideways, immediately vanished beneath its surface. Calvin called out her name and, for a few moments, time froze. He didn't breathe. She was beneath the water, hands and ankles tied. What if she had hit her head like Milo? In the moonlight, the water where she had landed looked terrifyingly calm.

'Vicky!'

Nothing.

He screamed it: '*Vicky!*'

Suddenly, there she was. She had managed to get upright and on to her knees so her head and neck broke the surface. She gasped and spluttered, spitting out dirty water. With her ankles cuffed and her hands behind her back, it was impossible for her to get to her feet, but the weight of the kettlebell kept her rooted to the bottom of the pool. Calvin realised that the rope that connected the two sets of cuffs would prevent Vicky's body from stretching out as the water rose. She would remain on her knees – if she didn't topple over.

'Keep calm,' Calvin found himself calling to her. 'It's going to be okay.'

'Yeah, *you* keep calm,' Simeon said with a snort. 'You're going in too.'

Before Calvin could do or say anything, Simeon kicked out, shoving him with his foot over the edge of the pool.

He hurtled into the water.

48

Imogen screeched to a halt outside the Whiteheads' house, jumped out and ran to the door, hammering on it. Michelle answered, still looking pale and tired, just as she had at the hospital.

'I need to talk to Billie. Is she here?'

'She's in her room. What's all this?'

'I really don't have time to explain. Just get her. Now.'

Alarmed, Michelle went up the stairs and reappeared a minute later with a scared-looking Billie. She had red eyes like she'd been crying. Imogen took her into the living room and sat her down.

'I know DJ was your boyfriend. I also have a video clip showing you inside the Mathesons' property the night Vicky Matheson vanished. I have reason to believe you were involved in the murder of James Sullivan, known to you as Leo James, and Vicky's abduction. If you help me find Vicky now, then I will help you when this goes to trial.'

Billie's chin trembled, a look of desperation passing over her face. 'I think I need a lawyer.'

'For fuck's sake, Billie.' Michelle stood in the doorway. 'Just do what she asks.'

Tears ran from Billie's eyes. She made no attempt to wipe them away.

'I promise you, if you cooperate, it will look better. It will lighten your sentence. Are you ready to talk?'

Billie nodded miserably.

'Okay. The person who has Vicky – do you know his name?'

There was a long pause. Imogen was thinking she was going to have to make another promise, or threat, when Billie said, 'Simeon Stewart.'

From behind Imogen, Michelle said, 'Oh Jesus.'

Imogen looked over her shoulder. 'You know who that is?'

'Yeah. I know the name. What I don't understand is how Billie knows who he is.'

Imogen took out her phone and opened the video that showed the mystery man at the Mathesons' house. 'Is this him?'

Billie sniffed. 'Yes. That's Simeon.'

'Who is he? How do you know him?'

Billie burst into tears. 'I didn't think . . . I didn't know what it would lead to.' She sniffled, rubbing her nose on her sleeve. But the tears dried up quickly. She looked up at her mum, who was still standing in the doorway. Imogen moved so she could see them both.

'Oh God,' Michelle said. 'You overheard, didn't you?' She turned to Imogen. 'I promised I'd never tell anyone what Leo told me, no matter what.'

Imogen wasn't sure if she was going to have to arrest Michelle too, for impeding an investigation. She would have to let this play out, see what Michelle said.

'Leo – I mean James – came here, this was towards the end of February, maybe the start of March. Yes, early March. Adrian was out, thank God. James said he had something he needed to tell me. He was trembling. He looked terrified and desperate. I had to let him in.' She addressed Billie. 'Where were you?'

'I was in my bedroom. I assumed you thought I'd gone out.'

'Yes. I had. Anyway, James . . . confessed. He told me he'd killed someone. Or rather, let him die. Him and his friend. He told me that was why he was so messed up, why he lived alone. Why he did those paintings. Couldn't help but do them. He said that was why he couldn't make the two of us work. He was too screwed up over what he'd done. Couldn't get past it. He'd been living with it for nearly thirty years, since the summer of ninety-five.'

'And you overheard how much of this?' Imogen asked Billie.

'All of it.' She rubbed her eyes. 'He'd gone, like, really weird on me. Started acting like he didn't want me hanging around anymore? I knew he'd been in contact with his own mum, through Insta, and I thought he'd be more grateful to me because joining it had been my idea.' She said this with a pout. 'But he was even more stressed out. Agitated.'

'He seemed so relieved after he told me,' Michelle said. She had come into the room now and sat in an armchair. Billie sat on the sofa, chewing her fingernails between sentences. Neither looked at the other.

'So what happened after that?' Imogen asked.

Michelle looked questioningly at Billie, who hung her head. 'I told DJ.'

'Oh, Billie.' Her mum's sigh of disappointment was much worse than any admonishment she could have given her.

'We were . . . in his caravan,' Billie went on. Settling in, now, to say all she had to say. 'I wasn't his girlfriend but we'd, you know, hook up occasionally.' Michelle shifted miserably in the armchair. Billie winced a little, began again. 'I wanted to impress him, I guess. I mean, I know I did. I wanted him to like me more. So I told him I knew an amazing secret. I told him everything I'd overheard. And he loved it. He went straight online, looked up the name of the man James said he'd killed.'

'Which was?'

'This bloke called Milo. Used to be the singer in a band called Duchess. Like, a Britpop band? James and his mate killed Milo because Milo crashed his van and killed this girl who was the sister of James's friend.'

Calvin. It had to be.

'DJ looked the band up and found an old piece about bands from the Lake District who'd never made it. There was this blog post about this band called Duchess whose singer had accidentally drowned. It was, like, a family band. Milo and his brother Simeon and their sister. Piper, I think she was called. The article said they were rich kids.'

'And that got DJ's attention?'

'What?'

'That they were rich? That's why DJ tracked Simeon down?'

'Yeah. The sister too. They still lived in their family home, in this place called Reyton. The house has a weird name. Something Fields. DJ called and said he had some information about what had really happened to their brother, if they were willing to pay for it.'

'And they were?'

'Yeah. In fact, they told DJ they'd pay him a lot more if he helped them do something about it. So the three of them came up with this whole revenge thing against James and the other one, the friend. The one they hated most.'

'Calvin Matheson?'

'Yeah. Chef Calvin. Though he wasn't well known back then.'

'What was your involvement in all this, Billie?'

'I was asked to keep an eye on James. I didn't know . . . I didn't know they were going to kill him, I swear. DJ told me he didn't know either.'

'Believe that and you'll believe anything,' said Michelle.

For the first time, Imogen saw a flash of anger on Billie's face. 'Shut up, Mum! I loved him. He was nice to me.'

'So was your father, once. Jesus, talk about patterns. It's all my fault, I suppose.'

Imogen needed to keep this conversation on track. 'What were they doing? What is this "revenge thing"?'

Billie hung her head again, like there was another particularly shameful bit coming up. 'Simeon didn't just want Calvin dead, he wanted it to look like he was the murderer too. Partly so his reputation would be destroyed – any amount of pain Simeon could cause him wasn't enough, he hated him that much – but also so you, the police, wouldn't try to find the real killers. Simeon worked it all out. Came up with the story and promised to pay DJ to make it look true.'

'And what was the story?'

'That James and Calvin were both involved in a love triangle.' She paused. 'With me.'

'Oh my God,' Michelle said.

'Simeon thought it would look worse, with me being so young. The story was that I was supposed to be sleeping with James, but I was also seeing Calvin. And when Calvin found out about me and James, he went crazy and murdered him. And then, in this story, I kept sleeping with Calvin, and when his wife found out, because DJ put my bee necklace in her bed, she would run off, accidentally drive her car into the lake, and, thinking she was dead, Calvin would kill himself out of shame and regret.'

So the bee necklace was Billie's, not Mel's.

'DJ broke into the coffee shop and stole this spare set of keys that Calvin kept there. That's how we got into their house.'

'I cannot believe you went along with this,' said Michelle. 'What the hell is wrong with you?'

'James and Calvin were murderers. They killed Simeon's brother. They deserved everything that was coming to them.'

'They didn't murder Milo,' said Michelle. 'Okay, they let him drown, but . . .'

'It's the same thing.'

'It isn't.'

Imogen interrupted. She didn't have time for this argument. 'Is Vicky Matheson dead? I assume them abducting her was part of the "Vicky running off" part of the plan. But her body wasn't in her car in the lake, which I'm guessing we found sooner than they intended. Maybe she got away.' Imogen tried to think it through. 'No, I bet they still have her. That they're planning to put her body in the lake later.'

Why would they do that? The only answer Imogen could come up with was that they wanted Calvin to watch her die.

She tuned back in to Billie's voice. ' . . . but Simeon said he'd let her go . . .'

'You really are an idiot,' said her mother.

'Shut up!' Billie screamed at her. 'I hate you! It's all your fault. If you hadn't fucked James I would never have overheard him spill his guts and none of this would have happened. And Dad would still be alive!' And like that she was sobbing again, snot streaming. *Teenagers*. 'And I'm probably going to end up in prison.' She made an imploring gesture to Imogen. 'Please. It was Simeon and DJ. Not me.'

Imogen had run out of patience with the both of them. With everyone involved. All she cared about now was finding Vicky.

'You said Simeon and his sister live in Reyton? Can you remember the full name of the house?'

'Sorry, no. Something Fields. A weird word. Like something from the Bible or Harry Potter.'

It didn't matter. Imogen had their names and knew they lived in Reyton. It wouldn't be at all hard to find an address.

'I hope you find them,' Billie said, her eyes flashing with sudden anger.

'Oh, you care, do you?' said her mother.

'Of course I care! They killed DJ.'

'Why do you think they did that?' Imogen asked.

'I guess they'd got what they wanted and didn't want to pay him.' Billie looked up at Imogen. 'There's something else I should tell you. DJ told me the sister, Piper, was around, pretending to be someone else and using a different name. That she'd, like, snuck into Calvin's life. That's how we got into their house. She got a copy of their front door key and she always knew their movements.'

'But you don't know who?'

'No. DJ didn't know either. Simeon wouldn't tell him, in case he accidentally gave it away.'

Imogen mulled this over. It made so much sense – and surely there was only one suspect. A woman who had come into Calvin's life recently, who was at the heart of all this.

Mel.

It had to be Mel.

'What's going to happen to me?' Billie asked as Imogen headed to the door.

'I'm not sure. It might depend if this information helps me save Vicky. Stay here, both of you. Don't go anywhere. Don't talk to anyone.'

Imogen left the house, enormously pleased to be out in the open air, out of that house with its curdled atmosphere and all the echoes of violence and secrets. Perhaps Billie and Michelle would be able to communicate better and rescue their relationship when Michelle was visiting her daughter in prison, but it seemed unlikely.

As she approached her car, she tried to phone Calvin. It went straight to voicemail. Then she saw Steve, waiting for her with his hands in his pockets.

'What are you doing here? You're supposed to be resting.'

'I can't stay at home doing nothing.'

She didn't have time to argue. 'All right, get in the car. You can make some calls while I drive.'

'Where are we going?'

She started the engine. 'Into Calvin Matheson's past.'

49

Calvin was prepared for the plunge. He sucked in a breath as he fell and twisted as he hit the water to avoid banging his head on the bottom. He landed on his side and, like Vicky before him, managed to push himself into a vertical position, on his knees, gasping and spitting out water as his head emerged in the air. Vicky was right there, next to him, face tilted up towards the moon. He tried to move his legs so he could get on to his feet, but the ankle cuffs and kettlebell made it impossible.

It was cold. *So* cold.

'Are you all right?' he asked Vicky.

She just stared at him like she'd gone into shock.

He looked up at Simeon, who was crouching by the side of the pool, peering down at them. Beneath the floodlight, he cast a long, warped shadow.

'Let her out!' Calvin shouted. 'She never did anything.'

'I told you, stop yelling.' He pointed the gun, not at Calvin but at Vicky. 'She's shorter than you. You're going to watch her die first.'

Simeon was right. The water was almost at Vicky's chin. For Calvin, the water was a few inches lower. He would last a little longer. The hose was pumping water into the pool, making the level rise very slowly but steadily.

'Please. Please let her out. She's innocent.'

Simeon shook his head. 'But that's just the point. I need you to know how it feels. I need you to watch her die.' More quietly, half to himself, he said, 'Also, we can't have her around to contradict the story.'

'What story?'

Simeon grinned. 'Let's just say that, after you're gone, every-one will know about you and James and Billie and your sordid love triangle. How you murdered James out of jealousy and then killed your wife to cover it up.' It was like he was back on stage. Calvin could see Milo in him. The performer, hammy and trying too hard. 'Finally, gripped by remorse, you drowned yourself, unable to go on.'

'No one's going to believe that.'

'Oh, I think they will. The juicier the better. They'll lap it up.'

What was the point in arguing with this lunatic? All that mat-tered was getting out of here. Calvin turned to look at Vicky. In the moonlight she looked horribly pale and still.

'Please,' he said again. 'You have to let Vicky go.'

'How many more times—'

Simeon's words were interrupted by footsteps coming towards them from around the side of the house. Piper, it had to be.

The footsteps grew nearer. From his position in the pool, on his knees with only his head above the water, he couldn't see her properly. She was a silhouette.

'You started without me?' she called out, and then she came into view.

She was wearing a sweatshirt that read *Crazy Cat Lady – and Proud!*

He looked up from the sweatshirt to Louise's grinning face.

Calvin couldn't believe it. Louise was Piper? He hadn't rec-ognised her, but how could he have? She looked utterly different to her nineties self, when she had looked so cool, with her dyed red hair and her indie T-shirts and Doc Martens. He turned to Vicky, to see her reaction, and saw stunned disbelief.

Louise – no, Piper – pulled off the sweatshirt, revealing a vest top beneath, and threw it on to the ground.

'My God, I am so happy I'll never have to go back to that bloody animal shelter again. Those horrible cats! I think I'm actually allergic.' She shuddered, then pulled a camping chair over to the side of the pool, sitting down and leaning forward so she had a good view of Calvin and Vicky. 'I set them all free, by the way, Vicky. I couldn't bear seeing all those poor dogs locked up in cages anymore. And the cats, well, maybe they'll run into the road, with a bit of luck.'

'You bitch,' Vicky said.

'A bitch is a female dog,' said Piper. 'So, coming from someone who runs an animal shelter, that's not an insult.'

Calvin shuffled closer to Vicky and they huddled together, the movement making the surface of the water ripple so it lapped over his chin, splashing his lips. The pool filled slowly, millimetre by millimetre. He wondered if Simeon and Piper had known it would take so long for the pool to fill enough to drown them. Maybe that was part of the plan. They wanted Calvin to have a long time to contemplate his and his wife's deaths.

'Please,' he said several times as the minutes ticked by and the depth of the water increased. 'Vicky hasn't done anything. Let her go.'

Each time, the siblings ignored him. Simeon had pulled up a second chair and sat beside Piper, reaching out to hold her hand.

'Do you think Milo's watching?' Piper asked her brother.

Simeon raised his eyes to the sky. 'Maybe. I'd like to think so.'

Calvin couldn't bear to look at them anymore. He shifted his knees and turned his body away from them, facing Vicky.

'I'm sorry,' he said.

She didn't reply. Her head had dipped – her lips were millimetres above the water – and she looked like she was about to pass out.

'Sweetheart, stay awake. Stay with me.'

She lifted her eyes to his. 'I'm so cold.'

'I know.'

'We're not getting out of here, are we?'

'I don't think so.'

She was whispering and, glancing towards Simeon and Piper, he could see this was irritating them. They wanted to be able to hear everything. Well, fuck them. He had spent his entire life half-crippled with guilt over Milo. Fear, yes, but mostly guilt. But here, in the cold pool, with death creeping inexorably towards him, he didn't feel guilty anymore. Milo had killed Freya through his recklessness and irresponsibility, and he hadn't even cared. *She was a top bird. Bad times.* And these two, Simeon and Piper, had lied for him, helped cover up what had really happened. How dare they feel he had wronged them? And how dare they do this to Vicky?

Calvin pulled himself up as high as he could and, inch by inch, restricted by the cuffs on his ankles and wrists, waded through the water towards Simeon and Piper.

'He begged for his life,' he shouted. 'It took three seconds for him to tell me you had lied for him. He volunteered to go to the police, to tell them how you'd lied. And you know what else? He told me he hated you. That he was the only talented one in the band and that you two were passengers.'

Simeon got to his feet. 'You're lying!'

The lies felt good. So good.

'He told Freya that too. She repeated it to me. Milo was planning to break up the band, find some proper musicians. Go solo.'

'No! That's bullshit.'

'He didn't love you, either of you. He thought you were pathetic.'

'Simeon,' Piper was saying. 'Simeon.'

'Shut up!' he snapped. He was right by the side of the pool, the toes of his boots a couple of inches over the edge. His eyes were wide and distressed and he had his gun in his hand. Behind him, Piper was sitting up, looking back towards the house.

'I thought I heard—'

'I told you to shut up!' Simeon screeched it, spittle flying, droplets hitting the surface of the pool. 'Milo would never have left us. He loved us. He needed us.'

'That's not what he said. I did you a favour, Simeon. I froze him in time for you. The perfect brother.'

He screamed 'No!' just as Piper shouted 'Simeon!' and then Calvin heard what she'd heard. A car engine.

A door slamming, then another. Footsteps coming around the side of the house. Then two people, running around the corner.

From his vantage point, looking up out of the pool, Calvin could only see her head and shoulders, but relief hit him when he saw who it was: Imogen Evans. The young male officer was with her. Imogen slowed down as she took in the scene: him and Vicky in the pool, the hose, Piper standing now, Simeon finally turning to face Imogen.

He lifted the gun.

Imogen came to a halt and put her hands up by her shoulders. She spoke in that calm voice of hers. 'Simeon Stewart? Come on, put the gun down.'

'Get off my property!' he yelled.

'I'm Detective Inspector Imogen—'

'I know who you are! I said, get off my property.'

And then Calvin sensed a presence behind him, at the rear of the pool. He turned his head.

There was someone creeping around the back of the pool, a silhouette. A female figure. For a second, she passed beneath the beam of a floodlight and looked straight at him.

327

Mel?

Calvin glanced quickly at Vicky, who was still in the centre of the pool, looking like she was going to pass out at any moment. She hadn't noticed Mel. Neither had Simeon or Piper, whose focus was purely on Imogen and Steve.

Imogen took half a step towards Simeon.

'Just put the gun down and we can talk about all this. I know what Calvin did to your brother. We can arrest him, make sure justice is done. Proper justice. The whole world will know Milo's story. They'll remember him properly. If you kill Calvin and Vicky, people will only ever know about *this*. Milo will be a footnote in a true-crime story, and everyone will think Calvin and Vicky are the victims, not him.'

Simeon shook his head a little. He was trying to think. Trying to make sense of Imogen's words. Calvin wanted to speak, to tell him to listen to Imogen, but he also knew his words might only make the situation worse. Instead, he began to move backwards towards Vicky. He wanted to be next to her. Needed to be. At the same time, he craned his neck to look behind him, where Mel was still creeping around the outskirts of the pool, from the right – closest to the property entrance, and where Imogen and Steve stood – to the back left corner, which was shrouded in darkness.

'Please, Simeon, put the gun down,' Imogen said.

'Don't listen to her,' said Piper.

'But the plan! It's all gone wrong.' Simeon sounded like a small child whose game had been ruined by some big kids. He was at the edge of the pool, his back inches from the edge.

He still hadn't seen Mel. As she continued to make her way around the perimeter, reaching the corner now and moving down the left-hand side, Calvin could barely make her out. She was just a black form. Some dim light found her, just enough for Calvin to see her crouching low in the darkness. Was she going to enter the water, try to pull Vicky out? Or was she here simply to watch? Calvin still didn't know if she was involved in all this.

Simeon was absorbed in deciding what to do. He wasn't watching Mel. No one else had seen her.

Imogen said, 'Please put the gun down. For Milo.'

Calvin traced Mel's hunched form as it passed the pool steps, reached the front corner of the pool and dropped to one knee. Calvin was sure Imogen must be able to see her now she was in the light, but Simeon had his back to her and Piper was only looking at her brother.

Simeon raised his voice. 'I can't let them go. I can't—'

Like a sprinter bursting out of the starting blocks, Mel launched herself at Simeon. He caught her movement in his peripheral vision, but only had time to begin to turn before she drove her shoulder into his abdomen and propelled them both into the pool. Calvin heard a bang, which merged a second later with the sound of a huge splash as they hit the water, Mel on top, and plunged beneath the surface just a couple of metres from where Calvin and Vicky stood, sending water into their faces. Calvin was temporarily blinded.

When he was able to blink the water away and see again, he saw that Piper was slumped in her camping chair, clutching her belly, a stunned expression on her face. There was blood on her hands, shining beneath the floodlight. The bang Calvin had heard in the moment after Mel slammed into Simeon had been the gun going off. The bullet had found Piper.

Imogen ran over to the pool, staring with Calvin and Vicky at the spot where Mel and Simeon had gone under. A moment later, Mel emerged. She was holding the gun. After a second, Simeon stood too – and Mel smacked him on the side of the head with the gun. He went back down, falling back and disappearing.

Mel came wading towards Calvin.

'We need to get Vicky out of the water,' he said.

Calvin could hear more engines. See flashing blue lights in the distance. Imogen Evans and Steve had lowered themselves into the pool using the rusty ladder – having first turned off the hose – and they and Mel were half-carrying, half-pulling Vicky towards the steps. Above them all, Piper had collapsed to the ground and lay still. Calvin watched as Imogen untied the rope that connected the cuffs, so Vicky was able, with help, to ascend the steps. Once she was out, they would come back for him.

In the meantime, Calvin stared at the spot where Simeon had gone under. There was no movement. No sign that he would emerge.

50

Calvin fixed himself a shot of espresso and took it over to the table beside the counter, the one where he always sat when he had a spare moment. Tara continued to serve customers, a steady flow but nothing too overwhelming. It was September, the end of the season. The tourists were going back to work or school. And, finally, people had stopped coming in just to stare at him, the famous Chef Calvin. The man who had almost, along with his wife, been murdered by a pair of psychopathic siblings.

He drank his espresso and checked his phone. A text from Vicky asking if he was okay. They checked in on each other several times a day now, something he imagined would continue long into the future. She had returned to work a week after her ordeal ended. She had needed to reopen the shelter, to look after the animals that had been rounded up in the hours and, in some instances, days after Piper had let them out. Now the shelter was full again, and the last missing cat had been found a few days ago. He wasn't sure she'd given herself enough time to recover – or if there would ever be enough time – but that was his wife. The animals needed her. He didn't deserve her.

She'd also hired someone new to replace Louise/Piper. This time, the new volunteer, a retired man called Oliver, had been thoroughly vetted.

Calvin replied to Vicky's text, telling her he was fine, asking her if she was all right, and then he heard Tara saying, 'Calvin. *Calvin.*'

He looked up at her and she nodded towards the front door. He followed her gaze.

Imogen Evans had come in.

'Hi,' she said, sitting opposite him. 'I'll have a cappuccino if you're offering. And a slice of carrot cake.'

'Anything for the woman who saved my boss,' said Tara.

'I think that was actually Mel,' Imogen said. She gave Calvin a meaningful look. 'Have you heard from her?'

'No. Have you?'

Imogen shook her head. 'No. I spoke to her just before she moved out of her house and got an address in case we needed to talk to her, but because Billie is pleading guilty to conspiracy and there's not going to be a trial, we don't need to keep in touch.'

Of all the people who had been involved in the conspiracy to murder James, Calvin and Vicky, Billie was the only one still alive. Calvin almost felt sorry for her. She'd had a messed-up childhood thanks to her dad and her parents' relationship. She'd been in love with DJ, in his thrall.

But then again, she had almost helped get Vicky killed. When he reminded himself of that, he hoped they threw the book at her.

Tara came over with the cake and coffee. 'I still can't get over Calvin being saved by his stalker.'

'She wasn't a stalker!' He had heard this so many times over the last few months.

'All right, maybe not. But she was in love with you. That's why she was following you around.'

Calvin glowered at her, but was she wrong? Mel had admitted that she had been following him all day, after he had fired her, trying to gather the courage to talk to him and tell him how she really felt. After she'd seen Simeon drag his unconscious body out of James's bungalow, she had followed Simeon out to Elysian Fields and waited, unsure what to do. Then Imogen and Steve had turned up and, seeing that Calvin was going to drown if she didn't do something, she'd used the distraction provided by the cops to finally act.

'Well, thank God she *was* following me,' Calvin said.

'Although following someone around is basically the definition of stalking.'

'Can we change the subject?' he asked.

'Saved by his stalker,' said Tara again, with a chuckle.

'Stop it! Please.' But he laughed, which felt good. It had taken him a while, after the events of that night late in March, to laugh without feeling like he was losing his mind. He wouldn't say he felt normal – he didn't think he'd felt normal, whatever that meant, since 1995 – but he was holding it together. He was functioning. Maybe that was the best he could hope for.

The police had got him and Vicky out of the pool that night, freed them from the cuffs, got their wet clothes off them and wrapped them in blankets. An ambulance had turned up soon afterwards and Imogen had travelled in the back with them. Vicky had gone to sleep but Calvin had been wide awake, his head buzzing.

Halfway to the hospital, Imogen had taken a call on her phone, her expression solemn.

'Are they dead?' he asked her when she ended the call.

'Yes. Piper from the gunshot wound. Simeon drowned.' She paused. 'We're obviously not going to charge Mel for killing Simeon.'

'What about me? Am I going to prison? For what happened in ninety-five?'

Imogen paused for a moment. 'I'm going to say this off the record, but if anyone asks I would advise you to deny everything. Simeon and Milo got this crazy idea into their heads that you and

James killed their brother, that you deliberately let him drown. There's no evidence you were there. The only person who can contradict you is Billie Whitehead, who heard James confess, but you can say James was lying or a fantasist. Unless you come into the station and sign a full confession, this is not something you'll ever be charged for.'

'So I'm going to get away with it?'

She looked at him for a long moment, then at the prone Vicky. 'Do you really think you got away with it?'

He had repeated those words in his head many times since.

Tara went back to serve some more customers, and he and Imogen made small talk for a little while, chatting about the end of the tourist season, Imogen's plans to finally take a holiday, and Calvin's ideas for the coffee shop.

'Some bigger premises have come up at the other end of the high street,' he said.

'That's cool. And what about social media? You still on there?'

'I imagine you're expecting me to say no, but I actually quite enjoy it. It's good for business and I like sharing recipes and chatting with people.' He picked up his phone. 'Vicky says I need to make some real-life friends, though.'

'Good advice. Maybe I could introduce you to my boyfriend, Ben. He doesn't really know anyone around here. And you can talk about what it's like to narrowly escape being murdered by a psychopath.'

'Sounds like a solid basis for a friendship.'

Imogen stood up. 'Look after yourself, okay?' She remembered something. 'Hey, I'm thinking of getting a cat.'

'Vicky would love to see you at the shelter.'

Calvin saw her to the door and said goodbye. As she walked away, he saw a couple of teenagers across the street clock him and whisper to each other. *There's that guy*, he imagined them saying.

The guy who got away. At least people didn't think he was a cheat now. His near-victimhood had supplanted that slander.

He went back inside and behind the counter, catching Tara's eye and smiling. A customer, a middle-aged woman, came up and asked if she could take a selfie with him, the famous Chef Calvin. He obliged happily, posing with his arm around her shoulders.

'I'm following you on all the platforms,' she said, before going back to her friends. He watched her as she tapped at her phone, probably posting the picture on social media. It was fine. Good for business, and she seemed normal enough.

He wondered, briefly, what Mel was doing right now, then got on with serving the next customer.

EPILOGUE

Mel opened the front door of her cottage and looked out at the front garden and the fields beyond. Nothing but green stretching as far as the eye could see. No other houses.

It was bliss.

She'd got the idea after seeing the place where James had hidden away. A hermit, they'd called him in the news reports. That sounded pretty good to her, so when she decided she needed to leave the Lakes – she couldn't stand to live near Calvin, knowing he would never be hers – she had sought out somewhere remote and rural. This place in North Wales was perfect.

No roads or cars. No youths starting fires and playing loud music and yelling insults at her.

Although if she did get some troublesome neighbours now, she would know how to deal with them.

Just as she'd dealt with that little shit DJ.

She had been so furious after Calvin fired her. Consumed by rage. How could he? Okay, she'd put something in his drink that night to help him sleep, but it was only because he'd been so tired and stressed that she thought it would help him. He'd feel better if he got some rest. Okay, so she had also wanted to spend time with him, just looking at him, stroking his cheek as he snoozed on her sofa. Giving him one or two little kisses. It was heaven to talk honestly to him, tell him how much she loved him and how wonderful it would be when they were together. And if Vicky should happen to get so angry with him for staying over that she kicked him out – well, that would only accelerate their progress towards that happy day.

How was she to know that DJ and Billie and those other lunatics would abduct Vicky while Calvin slept?

Of course, she hadn't known who had kidnapped Vicky. How could she have? As far as she knew, Vicky had run away. She had hoped Calvin would never find his wife. That Vicky would never come back. Every day that passed without Vicky coming home increased the chance she and Calvin would end up together.

And then Calvin had fired her – all because that piece of shit DJ had been on social media accusing Calvin of having an affair with her.

Overwhelmed by fury, she had marched round to the caravan, intending on having it out with that horrible little scrote who called her Butters and tried to make her life a misery.

And he'd laughed at her, told her to sod off and keep her nose out, and then stuck *his* nose back into his video game as if she weren't there. This had proven to be a misstep on his part. She hadn't been intending to kill him, but found herself doing so – stabbing him while he killed zombies on screen – after spotting the knife lying on his kitchen counter.

Oh, it had felt good. *So* good.

One day, she had decided, she would tell Calvin, and he would be proud of her for standing up for herself.

Then she had returned to following Calvin around – and wasn't it lucky that she had, because if it weren't for her, he would be dead. Vicky too, which wouldn't have been such a shame. Except that Calvin, being the wonderful man he was, would only have hoisted her upon an even higher pedestal, right up there with his dead sister.

There'd been nothing for it but to admit to the police why she'd been there. That had been terrifically awkward, especially when she'd seen that celebrity cop, Imogen Evans, looking at her with sympathy she wanted absolutely no part of. That had very nearly set her off, sorely tempted to tell her about DJ. Except she wasn't stupid.

No one would ever know about that. That little scene was hers alone, to warm her hands over in the years to come.

Mel leaned against the fence, cradling a cup of coffee. It really was paradise here. The only thing that was missing was someone to share it with, but maybe – if things worked out – she would soon change that.

She'd spotted Sebastian online a couple of weeks ago. He was a potter, sculpting the most beautiful ceramics at his workshop in the little village a few miles away. He had the sexiest hands she'd ever seen. The things he made with them. The way she guessed he would touch her. And he was even better-looking than Calvin.

He'd been advertising a pottery class and was offering one-on-one tuition. She'd already signed up and exchanged a few messages with him. He seemed lovely. And she'd checked – he didn't have a wife, just a girlfriend who he'd only been with six months. Relatively easy to deal with. There was a barn here at the cottage which would make a lovely pottery studio. Soon, Sebastian – perhaps she would call him Seb – would be living out here with her and they'd spend their evenings at the potter's wheel, just like in that old movie, and when he'd finished with the clay he'd put his strong hands on her.

She sighed with pleasure. She was going to make this happen. Nothing would get in her way this time.

AUTHOR'S NOTE

This novel is set in England's Lake District. Drigg Beach is real but my version of Drigg village is fictional, as are the towns of Elderbridge and Reyton.

ACKNOWLEDGEMENTS

Firstly, huge thanks to my editors Victoria Oundjian and David Downing for once again helping me make this book much better than it would be if I were left to my own devices. That appreciation extends to everyone at Thomas & Mercer in the UK and US.

Thanks too to my agent Madeleine Milburn and everyone else at the agency.

I also want to say thank you to:

Emma Mitchell and Katrina Power at FMCM for doing such great work spreading the word and being so much fun to work with.

Sam Willis for visiting Drigg Beach on my behalf and checking my geography (any mistakes are mine!).

Milz Pixie and Shannon Moore for the baking advice.

All the loyal cheerleaders on Facebook who keep me going with your enthusiasm, and all my other loyal readers – and new readers too!

My family: Mum, Claire, Ali, Roy, Dad, Jean, Auntie Jo and the rest of the Hastings mob; my in-laws in Wolves including Julie and Martin; and of course my children Poppy, Ellie, Archie and Harry.

One of the great joys of being an author is that you get to be friends with other writers, and the crime fiction community is particularly lovely. There are too many to list here, but for all the entertainment, advice, chats and laughter, worried-I'm-forgetting-somebody thanks to Ed, Susi, Caroline, Fiona, Clare, John, Cally, Domenica, Lucie, Mark, Craig, Luca, Matthew, Jennifer, and not forgetting the infamous Colin Scott, who contains multitudes.

Finally, the biggest thank you and an uxorious amount of love to my amazing wife, Sara, the cleverest person I know.

You can contact me to let me know what you thought of this book by email – mark@markedwardsauthor.com – or via social media. I'm @markedwardsauthor on Facebook and Instagram and @mredwards on Twitter. Miraculously, writing this book hasn't put me off replying to my readers' messages.

FREE SHORT STORY COLLECTION

To download a free collection of Mark's 'Short Sharp Shockers' and join Mark's newsletter, to ensure you don't miss out on all the latest news and offers, go to:

www.markedwardsauthor.com/free

Turn the page to discover the chilling case that made Imogen Evans famous, with an extract from *THE LUCKY ONES* by MARK EDWARDS

PROLOGUE

As soon as she saw the van parked sideways, blocking the narrow lane ahead of her, Fiona knew she'd made a mistake. She shouldn't have cycled home, should have accepted the lift. But she could imagine the curtain-twitching old guy next door, the one with all the Neighbourhood Watch stickers in his window, mentioning to Trevor that a strange younger man had dropped her off. Besides, she'd wanted to ride home, the wind against her body, legs pumping in time with her heart – *her new, beautiful heart* – gliding through these quiet country lanes, sun low in the just-spring sky, empty fields stretching to the horizon in every direction.

Fiona had felt like a girl again, a teenager riding home from her first boyfriend's house to sneak inside, past her parents' closed bedroom door, to lie on her bed and replay the events of the evening. She thrummed with rediscovered pleasure. Every nerve ending, every hair on her body buzzed with life. The world seemed like it was made for her: the evensong of the birds in the trees was the soundtrack to her second act.

The faint, acrid scent of a distant bonfire signified the burning of her old, unhappy life. Earlier, in his bed, the sheets half-ripped from the mattress, his handsome face on the pillow beside her, an old song playing on the radio, she had experienced a wave of pleasure unlike any she'd ever known.

'I want to run naked out into the street and dance across the lawn, let everyone see how happy I am,' she told him.

He laughed, tracing a line across her belly with his forefinger. 'Why don't you?'

'Because,' she said, kissing and pulling him on top of her again, 'I'm kind of busy right now. Doing . . . this.'

She knew it was crazy. She was forty-nine and he was nearly half that. Twenty years younger! When they met, when she realised he was flirting with her, she had thought he was just being a tease. But back home, a few hours later, she had surprised Trevor by suggesting sex for the first time in months. She had closed her eyes while Trevor made love to her in his mechanical way and thought about that face, those strong legs, the muscles in his arms. It was a delicious fantasy, that was all. Except now it wasn't. Because he thought she was beautiful.

He told her age meant nothing. In her most lucid moments, when they weren't in bed, when he wasn't looking at her in that way, she knew it wasn't serious. Just fun. An adventure. The most wonderful, thrilling adventure. And today it seemed like that adventure would last forever. Didn't she deserve it? Good luck comes in threes, everybody said, and her beautiful young lover was the third thing.

She'd been lost in these thoughts, keen to get home to her bath, reliving the afternoon with a glass of wine among scented bubbles, when she'd turned into the lane and seen the van ahead. Fiona slowed down, suddenly aware that the birds had stopped singing. The sun was already setting, light bleeding from the sky, and the hedgerows crowding the lane had turned from bright green to dark grey. The lamp on her bicycle cast weak light on to the road ahead as she slowed down, straining to see through the dark windows of the van in front of her. There wasn't enough room to cycle around it. She would have to get off and push. Why would someone park across the middle of a country lane? Perhaps he had crashed, skidded to a halt and was stuck, needing help. The person inside could be injured or sick.

She took her phone out of her pocket, but she had no reception. She was torn. She wanted to turn the bike around, get the hell out of there. But what if the driver was hurt? There was no sign of life from within. And it was getting darker by the minute. She couldn't just leave without seeing if the driver needed her help. Somebody had helped her, hadn't they? The universe had bestowed gifts upon her. If she cycled away now, rejecting the chance to be a Good Samaritan, the karmic balance in the world might well shift, and all the good luck she'd experienced recently would drain away, sending her back to the darker days, the days *before*. She wouldn't risk that.

Gently, she laid her bike on the ground and took a few steps closer to the van. 'Hello?' she called. There was no response. Breathing deeply, her strong new heart pounding inside her chest, Fiona strode up to the van and put her nose to the glass.

She jumped back as a man's face loomed up in the window. He was shrouded by darkness, but she could see his teeth. He was smiling, an odd smile, the kind she'd seen on the faces of born-again Christians, people who knew they were bound for heaven. He didn't appear to be injured, or sick. Confused, she backed away, and he opened the door, gesturing for her to come closer.

'Hello, Fiona,' he said. She froze, peering closer. The pallid interior light inside the van had come on when the man opened the door, but his face was masked by shadows.

'Do I know you?' she asked.

With a sudden movement that startled her, he jumped down from the driver's seat and moved towards her. She took another step back.

'Don't be frightened,' he said, still smiling.

'What are you—?' Her mouth stopped working when she saw what he was holding. She tried to run, but he was too fast, overtaking her and blocking her way. The van was behind her. There was nowhere to go.

'You really mustn't be afraid, Fiona,' he said, arms stretched wide like he wanted to give her a hug – except one hand gripped a shotgun with its barrel pointed to the darkening sky. 'I'm a friend.'

'I don't know you,' she said.

'Does anyone truly know anyone else?'

The oily smile returned. And as he came towards her, lowering the gun in front of him and pointing it right at her beautiful new heart, Fiona realised that the happiest day of her life would also be her last.

ω

They always struggle, right until the end, when the needle slips through their skin and the warmth fills them up, takes away all the pain and sends them off. As Fiona slipped away I told her, just like I had told the others, 'The art of living well and the art of dying well are one.' I like to think there was some comprehension – gratitude, even – in the final look she gave me.

The high that hit me afterwards, in the seconds that followed the final beat of Fiona's new heart, was better than anything a needle can deliver. The rush, the buzz, the sheer pulsing ecstasy of it. I touched her face as gently and tenderly as her lover had stroked her just a few hours before. I kissed her cooling lips. And I can still feel her looking up at me. Smiling.

It used to be so different, before I discovered the secret. The first time I took a life I was driven by rage. Hatred. I pummelled him with my fists, smashed his face until nose and lips and eyes were nothing but pulp, indistinguishable features on that dirty, ugly face. I snapped his neck with my bare hands, expecting to feel something, some satisfaction, for the fury inside me to abate, the howling to stop. But it only made me feel worse. And then I was covered in his filthy blood, stinking of his rancid sweat. It clung to me, no matter how I scrubbed myself beneath the pathetic shower in our dark little bathroom. The second time was the same. And so was the third. But then I discovered the secret. I learned to do good.

I took one last look at Fiona's body, lying there in the spot that meant so much to her, and I wished we could enjoy the moment for a little while longer. But the world doesn't understand me. They think I'm doing wrong. So I must always be careful, and I was forced to say goodbye. Still, I consoled myself as I slipped through the darkness, there would be others. And I already knew who was next. I just wished I could tell him how lucky he was.

ABOUT THE AUTHOR

Photo © 2022 Tim Sturgess, Express and Star

Mark Edwards writes psychological thrillers in which scary things happen to ordinary people.

He has sold 4 million books since his first novel, *The Magpies*, was published in 2013, and has topped the bestseller lists numerous times. His other novels include *Follow You Home*, *The Retreat*, *In Her Shadow*, *Because She Loves Me*, *The Hollows* and *Here to Stay*. He has also co-authored six books with Louise Voss.

Originally from Hastings in East Sussex, Mark now lives in Wolverhampton with his wife, their children and two cats.

Mark loves hearing from readers and can be contacted through his website, www.markedwardsauthor.com, or you can find him on Facebook (@markedwardsauthor), Twitter (@mredwards) and Instagram (@markedwardsauthor).

Follow the Author on Amazon

If you enjoyed this book, follow Mark Edwards on Amazon to be notified when the author releases a new book!

To do this, please follow these instructions:

Desktop:

1) Search for the author's name on Amazon or in the Amazon App.
2) Click on the author's name to arrive on their Amazon page.
3) Click the 'Follow' button.

Mobile and Tablet:

1) Search for the author's name on Amazon or in the Amazon App.
2) Click on one of the author's books.
3) Click on the author's name to arrive on their Amazon page.
4) Click the 'Follow' button.

Kindle eReader and Kindle App:

If you enjoyed this book on a Kindle eReader or in the Kindle App, you will find the author 'Follow' button after the last page.